I0891528

At the start of Mark Jacob's remarkable new novel, thirty-seven-year-old Smith wins a "stash" of diamonds in a poker game. The only catch: he has to find them.

A Louisiana native, Smith is employed on an oil platform off the west coast of Africa, while the diamonds are somewhere in the immense, war-torn Democratic Republic of the Congo. But Smith's grown tired of the platform—one last adventure, he tells himself, and then, diamonds or no diamonds, he's heading home.

Shortly thereafter, Smith meets a girl named Béatrice, who hails from a village on the other side of the country. This village, she tells Smith, is where his diamonds are—more than a thousand miles away on the patchwork of guerilla-patrolled roads that traverse the country. If he helps her get home, she'll show him where the stones are.

What follows is a harrowing tour of hell in which a not-so-innocent American abroad comes face-to-face with the legacy of European imperialism in the heart of the African continent. In stark prose, Jacobs reveals the limits of the western gaze to give us the story of a man who discovers you don't have to travel to another country to get lost, and you don't have to go home to be found.

ADVANCE PRAISE FOR *SILENT LIGHT*

"In the timeless rainforests of *Silent Light*, the past is never past. This paradox of the Congo is the conflicting wind that steers this seductive book. Mark Jacobs sculpts his twinned heroes with a steady eye and chiseled prose—his writing dazzles in sustained bursts, evincing an airy humor in lockstep with grounded insight. His careening tale about a quest for mythic diamonds and lost families will transport you into the volcanic lungs of the earth, where the infernal past still bleeds into the turbulent present, smearing everything with European lava and American ash. In Mark Jacobs's fire-juggling hands, you'll come back bearing memories from Congolese lives. Haunting, subtly imagined . . . a feat of bravura storytelling from a dauntless writer at the peak of his powers."

—A. Igoni Barrett, author of *Blackass*

"Every now and then a novel comes along that not only reinvigorates your faith in what a novel can accomplish but reimagines for you how a novel can be made, the fluency of its movements and the potency of its meanings. Mark Jacobs's *Silent Light* steadfastly resists the blurbist's cliches (inspiring, fascinating, brilliant, and other easy lies) and instead demands to be dubbed precisely what it is: Art. Here is a novel of consequence, an intrepid foray into dark hearts seeking light, its storytelling sensibility so assured, so dignified, it makes you marvel. It also makes you grateful Mark Jacobs is here to remind us all how it's done."

—William Giraldi, author of *Hold the Dark*

"I have admired the elegance and bravery of Mark Jacobs's writing for many years. He has created a masterful canon of work in short stories and novels. In *Silent Light* he imagines even more deeply and writes even more superbly. Jacobs is surgical in capturing the heartbeat, the terror and the often-derailed promise of the American Dream. Here the American Dream of one man collides with the forces that create a seemingly permanent African nightmare. This is a sophisticated, taut character study and a revelation about the geography and geopolitics of war and greed and the enduring possibility of redemption. Smart but never cynical, humane and utterly human, this is an ode to the wretched of the earth and the angels that walk among them. Welcome a great American writer."

—Marita Golden, author of *The Wide Circumference of Love*

"Mark Jacobs is our greatest living writer of short stories, it could well be said. With *Silent Light*, after hundreds of splendid stories, it is time to examine his greatness as a novelist as well. Jacobs take us on a journey to the heart of Africa, but his journey with an orphan of war is as American as Huck Finn's journey with Jim down the Mississippi. We all need the hope—the hope given, and received—with of the last notes of this very great book."

—Evans Hopkins, author of *Life After Life*

"With *Silent Light*, Mark Jacobs, one of America's great short story writers, establishes himself as a novelistic scion of Joseph Conrad, in that he ventures into many hearts of darkness, into the jungles of Africa, yes, but also in those that reside within the human heart. The novel is harrowing, humorous, youthful, and, in the end, wise."

—Richard Wiley, author of *Soldiers in Hiding* and *The Grievers' Group*

SILENT LIGHT

SILENT LIGHT

A Novel

MARK JACOBS

Evergreen Review Books

Published by Evergreen Review Books, an imprint of OR Books
Visit our website at www.evergreenreview.com

All rights information: rights@orbooks.com

First printing 2024

Library of Congress Cataloging-in-Publication Data:
A catalog record for this book is available from the Library of Congress.
British Library Cataloging in Publication Data:
A catalog record for this book is available from the British Library.

Typeset by Lapiz Digital. Printed by BookMobile, USA, and CPI, UK.

Cover image: Senon Williams, *Untitled*, 2022. Artwork © 2023 Senon Williams.
Front cover design by Pocomeloso. Cover design by Antara Ghosh.

paperback ISBN 978-1-68219-443-0 • ebook ISBN 978-1-68219-444-7

I came into a place where all light is silent, that groans like the sea in a storm, when it is lashed by conflicting winds.

Inferno, Canto 5
Dante

For Robert Ready

PART ONE

Nkoyi

It was the diamond that woke Smith. Even asleep, you could not say Congo without thinking diamond. Coming to consciousness he found himself jammed, flat on his back at the bottom of an unlit pit. He panicked, struggling to get up, but could not move. The knees of a demon kept him pinned to the black ground. Thanks to the rye, everything hurt. Then the diamond flashed, the demon let him go, and the stone's clean light drew him to the surface. He grinned.

There was nothing wrong with getting rich. Fast or slow, it didn't matter how you got there. Given the choice, Smith would pick fast. Diamonds, for example. Diamonds were fast. He had read up on the subject. The first thing you did if you acquired a bunch of diamonds was quit your shitty job. He was halfway there; he had the shitty job, ready and waiting for him to quit.

Lying on his back in bed he sang the first verse of "Jambalaya" because it made him think of home and because the hallowed image of first responders pulling Hank Williams' misused body from a wrecked Cadillac Coupe de Ville, sad as it was, had a storybook quality about it that never failed to lift Smith's spirits. You could ruin yourself and achieve greatness.

He stopped singing after the first verse. He had been told by people whose judgment he trusted that he could not carry a tune. Any time he picked one up, it dropped and broke.

It was September, before the rainy season began but not much before. The hotel room in which he lay was in Brazzaville. Colonialism left Africa with two Congos of vastly unequal size. Brazzaville is the capital of the smaller one. It stares out of the corner of its eye across the legendary river that separates it from Kinshasa, capital of the enormous Congo. Smith did not know much about colonialism, or the two Congos, or why Central Africa was the violent impoverished place it appeared to be. His mind had a practical cast. He was good with machinery. He understood hydraulics and could fix just about anything that broke on an offshore oil rig. There had been little occasion in his life to think about broken countries or the people who lived in them.

Smith was thirty-seven. A leopard was tattooed on the inside of his left forearm. He liked to say he was in Africa because his mother had sung French lullabies to him way back when, before exiting his life in search of a new one for herself. But that was a lie, intended to entertain anybody who would listen. The truth was one-word simple: *escape*. He had jumped at the chance to escape the trap of deadend mechanic jobs he was stuck in back at home. He couldn't get any broker than broke.

It had seemed like holy luck, falling into the job with Dauphin Petroleum. But now he was tired of oil. Life at sea on an anchored platform held no charms. The confinement bored him. So did the engineers, whose high opinion of themselves he did not share. Anyway it was time to start living a normal life. Normal meant going home to Louisiana. It meant a wife and kids and the sweet complications of family. He had no fixed theory of good or evil and put his faith in taking things as they came.

"Jambalaya" hanging on in his ear's memory, he lifted the edge of the net around the bed and reached for a small ring on the bedside table. The instant his arm was exposed, mosquitos went for his flesh. The night before, coming back to the Maison des Rêves in a liquored lather, he had failed to notice that the window was open. The woman who cleaned the room must have wanted air while she worked. He heaved himself out of bed and snapped at the mosquitos with a twisted towel. He closed the window.

Then he swallowed a Malarone tablet. One of the maintenance guys on the Dauphin rig had been gassing on about a strain of malaria moving through central Africa so virulent you were dead inside three days. *Here's what happens, mon frère. You get bit, you suffer, you die.* The company doctor who prescribed the pills had told Smith not to take them on an empty stomach, they made you queasy. But Smith could not feel any worse than he already did, rye residue percolating around and through his body's interior creases.

He pulled on a T-shirt and reached for the ring, turning it over in the palm of his hand. It was not much of a diamond. Not much of a ring, for that matter, just a plain gold band to which a chip of light was affixed. *L'acompte,* the Belgian had said, throwing the ring into the pot. The down payment on serious diamonds.

Smith tried to slip on the ring. It wouldn't go. His fingers were too big. The Belgian it belonged to was a small man. Smith set the ring back on the table. As he showered and dressed, the events of the night before came back to him randomly, dots of color connecting to form a picture that remained out of focus.

A poker game at the apartment of a French diplomat, some sort of attaché in their Brazzaville embassy. That much he was sure about. Also the masks. Central African masks covered the white walls of the apartment, no two alike except in their serious aspect. They were real, meaning if the right person put one on he gained the mask's totemic power for as long as it covered his face. The diplomat claimed to know about such things. He also claimed to have been in the Mississippi Delta where he heard the guitarist in a blues band bend his strings in such a way as to condense three hundred years of struggle against racist oppression into seven notes in a minor scale. He had provocative things to say about American music. He also had a reservoir of Jim Beam he did not care to drink alone.

Once a certain amount of the liquor got into his system, Smith became aware that he was being watched. It was the masks, which gave off a faint but distinct odor redolent of nothing he had ever smelled. Their blank eyes fixed on him and stayed there, refusing to shift their gaze to anyone else sitting around the table. The unrelenting scrutiny made him feel guilty, as though he had done something wrong that had not yet seen the light of day. Smith did not spend much time, as a rule, feeling guilty.

Nothing wrong with getting rich, fast or slow.

Now, with sticky slow cognition, he recalled the other players. An African American pilot who had flown for a Christian missionary outfit until a crisis of faith grounded him; he was looking into other aerial options. A Spanish nurse volunteering at a Brazzaville clinic during his vacation from a Burgos hospital. And the Belgian. All Smith knew about Alain Lajeune was that he had small fingers and could not be trusted.

Two in the morning. *Last hand*, the diplomat announced. He had to be at the embassy by nine for a meeting with a delegation from Lyons. Smith's French had shot up, working for Dauphin Petroleum, but he heard "delegation of lions" and wondered what the noble beasts might possibly require of a diplomatic establishment. Nobody could give him a satisfactory answer, which was strange given the diverse range of international experience represented around the table.

He was down a couple hundred dollars, or up a couple hundred. Maybe it was closer to three fifty, he could not remember. That was typical of how he played cards. The higher the stakes, the less seriously he took the game. They were playing five-card draw, nothing wild. Real poker, and the pilot dealt him three kings. *One more drink*, Lajeune pleaded, making it sound like a medical emergency. *One more shot of those death-defying blues*, Smith sang out in response. That time of night, it came out sounding like insight.

But he had been alive long enough now to recognize the tinge of melancholy that colored euphoria, tugging at you, pulling you down even as alcohol lifted your spirits. He drank the night's last whiskey neat, savoring the aroma. There was something flowery in it, a bayou summer smell, that made him feel lucky. He bet high.

Everybody else folded, but Lajeune had lost in consistent dribbles all night and lacked the cash to call. Impulsively he worked the ring off his finger and tossed it into the pot. He told the table a story about diamonds. *L'acompte*. The chip in his ring was the down payment on a stash.

Smith did not believe the story. Neither did the pilot or the nurse, although the diplomat seemed to take it seriously. But alcohol transmogrified the mounded nest of dollars and Central African francs at the center of the table. In Smith's eyes it became play money whose only value was its capacity to make people laugh. Also, he didn't mind provoking the Belgian, who surrendered the little ring as though doing them a humongous favor.

I want that ring, Smith told him. There was no need to pretend to be enthusiastic. He was. His voice was louder than it needed to be. *I can't live without the ring, I need those freaking diamonds. I can't live anymore without being rich.*

"You're a greedy son of a bitch," the Spaniard said.

"In the proper sunlight," Smith told him, "greed can be a beautiful thing."

A little too sensitive for a man so far down on his luck, Lajeune was stung by what he perceived as Smith's lack of respect. Fastidiously he turned over his cards one by one to show off a flush, saving the queen for last. *Hell of a hand*, the pilot said. It was, but Smith had drawn a pair of fours on the trade. His full goddamn house bent the Belgian's flush over and took carnal satisfaction. .

Now, waiting for the hangover to lift, Smith ate a slow breakfast at the hotel's restaurant in a pleasant corner nook on the first floor. There were windows on two sides of the room, and the sun came at him from both. The light burned his eyes, which were tender as though from too much seeing. Well, if he'd been looking he hadn't seen a thing.

Buttering his toast he thought about the Belgian's reaction when he lost. Lajeune was disgusted. That was natural. He had wasted a queen-high flush. He was also dismayed. He slumped in his chair staring with painful longing at the ring he had surrendered to chance. One of the things an untrustworthy person did was act. At the diplomat's table Lajeune had put on a show.

Smith had laid his full house down on the table with no flourish, allowing the cards to speak for themselves. A groan escaped Lajeune as Smith scooped up the money and the ring. After that, his memory of sequence blurred. The diplomat, eager to sleep, was shooing people out of the apartment. Out in the street, Lajeune was talking with great heat about his dead grandfather, crying tears that were possibly real. Listening to him go on, Smith let a gratifying little fantasy play itself out. At the heart of it there were genuine gems. By the time he climbed into his taxi he had forgotten where he was supposed to meet the Belgian, and when.

It was not the fantasy that made him decide to track down Lajeune, it was resentment, and what an unkind observer would call greed. The Belgian had played him. Never mind that both of them were drinking. In place of the five hundred bucks Lajeune owed the pot, Smith had a worthless ring that did not even fit his finger. That was sort of funny, if you were the kind of person who could appreciate a joke on yourself. He believed he was.

After breakfast he stopped at the reception desk, where a thin man wearing a green vest over a yellow T-shirt sat up straight and said, "*Bon jour, Monsieur Smith.*"

"You're from the other Congo, right?"

The man nodded.

"Why did you leave?"

The man licked his lips, about to give a delicious answer. "No one can live in such a country."

"What about all the millions of people who do?"

The man frowned. "Will you be checking out this morning?"

"No."

Back in his room, Smith checked his phone for messages from his boss, who might summon him back to the rig just because he could. Kluge, the maintenance foreman, had twenty years in with Dauphin Petroleum and considered himself entitled. But there was nothing on the phone. Nothing was good.

Smith took a taxi to the French embassy, where Armand Forquer's eyes were bloodshot and he struggled to be civil. And succeeded. Forquer's curly hair was graying. He had reached his middle forties without conspicuous success. The luxury of an assignment to Berlin, Madrid, London—cafés and comforts, theaters and walkable streets. None of that was going to happen. Under the circumstances, it seemed to Smith that Forquer's being civil—inviting him into his office, making polite noises, offering him an espresso—was an achievement. Somebody somewhere ought to give him credit for it.

Sitting in a diplomatic leather chair facing Smith, the Frenchman dumped excessive sugar into his own coffee and told him in English, "You have to understand, Alain Lajeune has problems."

"What kind of problems?"

"He has a taste for hashish and—what shall I call it?—the lower life of the night. At the same time he lacks an appetite for work. This presents a dilemma. How does he pay for his pleasures? I have heard he owes money to an impatient Lebanese."

"Where does Lajeune stay?"

"So you believe that story of his about family diamonds."

Smith shrugged. "Last night, I was convinced he only wanted to see my cards, and the story was all he had to offer up. This morning my head aches, and my body tells me it has been mistreated. The pain I am undergoing makes me humble. A humble person is more capable of belief than proud people are. We are Creole Catholics in Louisiana, we understand how God wishes us to think, and we go along."

Forquer tried to smile, but his own headache made that a challenge. Eventually his lips assumed the conventional shape, and the smile gave him dignity. For the second time that morning Smith admired the man.

Forquer told him, "Lajeune's family lived in the other Congo in the old days. They were in deep. I don't mean they were powerful people, just that they were part of the colonial establishment at a time when that meant something."

Smith wasn't an expert on colonialism but he wasn't an idiot either. "Money? Power?"

"The Belgians used to cut off the hands of the Congolese. This was punishment, you see, for failing to deliver one's quota of rubber to the overseer. To this day you can walk into a *chocolatier* in Brussels and order five hundred grams of little chocolate hands. They serve them to you in a shiny foil sack. Ask the woman behind the counter why she sells them and you will get a shrug. She has no idea what the hands signify."

"Maybe she just doesn't want to discuss it with you."

"Anything is possible in the other Congo. At the same time, nothing is possible."

"Last night I did not look into Lajeune's eyes, where perhaps the truth would have been obvious. It was an oversight."

"That is understandable, with all the alcohol your system had absorbed by then."

"Maybe, but I need to correct the oversight."

"Our Spanish friend was right. You are a greedy bastard."

"Are you going to help me out or not?"

"Alain rents a room, but just now he is hiding from the Lebanese and cannot go there."

"He owes me. A full house beats a flush. It was your table he was sitting at."

Forquer considered the justice of Smith's argument and found it reasonable. He nodded.

Smith said, "So how do I find him?"

The diplomat was already writing on a piece of embassy letterhead an address in a poor neighborhood on the fringe of the city center.

The dirt street to which the taxi driver delivered Smith was cratered. It would be a mess when the rains came. The little blue house with a roof of orange tiles had a cozy look, and Smith was the last person Lajeune expected to find on the doorstep when he answered his knock.

"*Merde*. You."

"Me."

The Belgian pulled Smith inside and shut the door. He was a fine-featured miniature man, like an artist's model for a version to be built on a grander scale. He was buff and sculpted, as conscious of his good looks as he was of his stature. His eyes were ice blue, European blue, an asset to be flaunted under the right circumstances. In the background, Smith heard the weepy soliloquy of a troubled woman. The sound was coming from the kitchen.

"That's his wife."

"Whose wife?"

"Ralph Lauren's."

"Don't bust my balls."

"I'm not. That's the name her husband goes by. She's talking in Lingala, you understand. I speak the language perfectly."

Lajeune lit a Gitanes and used it to illustrate the translation he gave Smith. The subtlety of the argument was in the smoke trails the weaving cigarette left in the air.

"Her name is Angelique. Ralph, her husband, is my closest friend. Angelique is sad. In fact she is deeply sad, because her husband is such a poor provider. Ralph is worthless when it comes to putting food on the table. Of course he is a *sapeur*, so I don't know what she expected."

Sapeurs were Brazzaville dandies. They loved and were inspired by French style, French culture, a specific French way of being in the world that existed in their imagination more than in Europe. They modeled their fashion on the

French, but the colors they chose were more extravagant. So were the lapels, the ascots, the shoes, the gold knobs of their walking sticks. In town on R&R trips Smith had seen them strutting the streets of the capital, defiant and self-assured. They did not need the Champs Élysées to look good, to feel the way a man in a fine suit ought to feel. They were performance artists, and the raw material of their art was themselves.

Angelique's voice rose in regulated misery. A bill of particulars was attached to her lamentation; she felt the need to itemize her grievances. Smith wondered whether she knew that another strange white man was in her house. Did that make her sadder still?

"What is she saying now?"

"It's a story. She has a brother, a wonderful man. I have met him on two occasions, neither of them happy since he considers me a negative influence on Ralph. This brother of Angelique's works hard, and he is good with money. Last week he slipped her some cash to help her get by. Marvelous. She hid the money in a secret place. All very fine, very proper. The love of a brother and sister, no? It is what one longs for in his own family relations. Sadly, Ralph found the money, don't ask me how. With his attitude toward these things, he considered it a legitimate find. A windfall. He spent the cash on a suit. Come, I want to show you something."

Smith doubted Lajeune's translation. More than likely he did not speak a word of Lingala. But he followed the Belgian to a room in which the *sapeur* kept his clothes. Twenty suits in bright colors hung on homemade wooden racks that were suspended from the ceiling. On the floor in impeccable rows, twenty pairs of shoes stood with martial precision.

"Here, this one is special."

Lajeune took a pale blue blazer and a pair of orange pants from the rack. He held them out for Smith to appreciate, displaying the fabric like a salesman who knew his customer's weaknesses. The colors reminded Smith of a bird he used to see in the bayou as a kid, a blur of assertive color against the swamp's dark dominion.

"Ralph Lauren—the real one, the designer—he heard about our Ralph. How would you feel if a *sapeur* in Africa adopted you as his spiritual fashion father? He had this outfit made for our Ralph. They flew it in on Air France. The story made the papers, and Ralph was on television."

"What about the diamonds?"

"What diamonds?"

"Come on, Alain. A full house beats a flush, even in the Congo. You lost, brother. You played the game and you lost. Consult your rulebook. When a man loses, he pays up."

Lajeune smiled benignly. He tried to look conspiratorial, and sympathetic. He was not successful. "Remember, I was drunk. Don't tell me you bought that drivel I was spouting."

"Bought it? I'm putting it in my memoirs."

"I'm sorry, Smith. The only diamond I know about is the little one in that ring you took off me."

Lajeune was a dramatic person, and his voice rose with every sentence. They heard a door slam. Angelique was taking her unhappiness elsewhere. The coast clear, they went into the living room where Lajeune offered Smith a seat on a sofa the same shade of blue as the Ralph Lauren blazer. On the wall above the sofa someone had tacked a newspaper article featuring a photo of the *sapeur* in his famous outfit. He was a handsome man with a raffish smile. It made sense that he and Lajeune were friends.

"I like you, Alain," Smith told him. "I really do. But you need to tell me the truth."

There was a trick in the way he said the words, a way of half hiding the threat in them while making sure the sharp edge was visible. The trick had served him well in other problematic situations. There were people—on the rig, back in Louisiana, other places he had been—who had felt that edge.

"Tell you the truth," Lajeune repeated, nodding soberly as if it took real effort to order the words correctly, never mind catch their drift.

"Here's the deal I'm offering," Smith explained. "You tell me what I came to hear, or I sic your Lebanese friend on you."

Lejeune was surprised. Not an act. He was wounded. Totally an act.

"You don't even know his name."

"I found you, didn't I?"

Lajeune sat forward on his chair, looking at the newspaper photo of his friend the *sapeur* on the wall behind Smith. He folded his hands in his lap and spoke as if it were someone else's story, which he had done his best to memorize.

"My grandfather was an accountant. He worked for one of the copper mines. This was in Lubumbashi, where the big copper was to be found. In nineteen sixty, the locals got what they wanted." He sneered the word: "*Independence*. A Congolese who had no mathematics, a man who never heard of the multiplication table, that was who took Grandpa's job.

"That was the beginning of the end of our way of life. My parents could not tolerate things as they were in the new country. It was dangerous to have a white face, even more dangerous if they knew you were Belgian. Many friends were killed, many acquaintances, business associates." He began tallying the losses on the fingers of one hand but quickly gave up. "Everything you worked a lifetime to acquire, it could be gone in twenty-four hours. Mother and Father went to Antwerp. They started over. The old folks stayed behind, I can't tell you why."

The story interested Smith. It interested him quite a bit. He pretended it did not. He said, "I don't give a shit about your family."

"Grandmother died ten years ago. She got sick but wouldn't go to Belgium to be treated. Stubborn stubborn stubborn. Grandpa was just as bad. He stayed in Kinshasa. They had moved there from Lubumbashi in the eighties. Last year, when his time came, my mother flew in and marched him onto an airplane. She would not take no for an answer. Mother has a forceful character. So anyway when I went to say goodbye to the old guy in the hospital in Antwerp—his last day on earth, as it turned out—he told me his secret. 'This is your inheritance, my dear young man.' He caressed my hand, like this. I cried. You would have cried, too."

"If you believe him, why don't you go get the diamonds yourself?"

Lajeune threw up his hands, convincingly self-critical.

"I have been trying, Smith. I have thought of little else. It's that I have problems. Not a drug problem. I consume only hashish, which produces pretty pictures but no addiction. My real problem is money. Well, and I get distracted easily. I'm told I lack discipline. I was born missing all the hard virtues that are supposed to be good for a person. Not my fault. It's genetic."

Something about the man's regret made Smith understand that he did in fact believe his grandfather had left him a legacy across the river in the impossible Congo. One man's legacy was another man's stake, or could be. Smith did not consider himself all that good when it came to reading people, but this time he trusted his gut.

Of course Lajeune's believing it did not make the story true.

"Give me half," the Belgian said. "That's fair."

"Half of how much?"

"I don't know. I can tell you this, it's not a mine. It's only a package." He searched for a word. "It is . . . a certain quantity of stones. They are uncut. The great thing about diamonds is how portable they are. That's why the old guy put his money into them."

The absurdity struck Smith, and he laughed.

"What's so funny?"

"We're haggling over treasure neither one of us ever saw."

Lejeune got up and left the room, flouncing. He came back with an envelope, which he put in Smith's hand. The envelope was embossed with the official emblem of the Ministry of the Interior in Kinshasa and was not sealed.

"Go ahead," said Lejeune. "Read it."

It was an open letter in bureaucratic French advising whoever read it that the bearer was under the protection of the minister and should be extended every courtesy during his stay in the Democratic Republic of Congo.

"If you go across the river," Lajeune told Smith, "take it with you. It might get you past a guard. Even if he can't read, he'll recognize where the letter comes from. I have a cousin in Brussels. Somebody in the DRC government owed him a favor, and he had the letter done up for me."

"There's just one problem."

"What's that?"

"It says I'm you."

"Are you dense, man? No one will care. All they'll see is the signature. The man who signed that letter is a big shot in an important ministry. Two things, and only two things, are effective across the way: influence and guns. If you find the stones you'll give me half, I know you will. So, do you want the rest of the story or not?"

No harm could come from listening to a story.

That afternoon Smith's hangover lifted and he made his way to the port. He stood above the riverbank in the shade of a roof overhang watching the Kinshasa ferry being loaded. The ferry sat moored to the dock on the surface of the river, which the afternoon sun hardened to impervious blue. The river looked placid until you noticed how quickly the floating islands of water hyacinths were moving downstream toward the Atlantic, ragged chunks of the country's guts disgorged and carried into the ocean, where they unbecame.

A word came to Smith in French that would never come in English. *Inexorable.* He was not the same person in Africa he had been in Louisiana. He thought differently. He reacted differently to things. Felt differently. That bugged him. Maybe, if he thought about it, the change also intrigued him.

He was taken by the confusion of people and merchandise moving from dock to boat. There were three or four times as many people milling around the dock as would fit on the ferry, but all of them seemed to have a stake in the operation. He understood nothing of what they were saying; only the numbers they shouted were French. But he felt the urge to dive in, to figure out what was going on and be a part of it.

Too much time on the rig, probably. Oil rigs were busy, noisy places, but machines had pride of place. The people who ran the machines, they were incidental, even the engineers who thought they were God's gift to the planet, peak oil and price swings be damned.

He watched skinny, strong, bare-chested men push impossible tons on precarious wheeled carts up a plank onto the deck where other men took over and stowed the load. Men and women and children carrying bags and boxes and strapped suitcases crowded each other to get on. A wide-bodied woman with two large woven baskets used them expertly as weapons to reach the place she had picked out for herself on deck. Smith silently cheered her on. She knew what she wanted, and how to get it.

When he interviewed for the Dauphin Petroleum job, they had made him take a psychological test. They had to decide whether he had the temperament to work and live in the peopled isolation of a rig at sea. The test generated a profile, and some of what the profile alleged about him was true. He was gregarious. He was hot-tempered, and quick to come to a judgment. Lots of things made him laugh; some of those things other people did not find funny. He was bullheaded. When pushed, he shoved.

One other feature of the Dauphin personality profile came into play as he stood on the bank of the Congo River. Taking a risk. Nothing jazzed him more.

It would cost him two days to check out Lajeune's story. Big deal, two days out of his whole life. The odds of finding stones that glittered were low, not to say ridiculous. But he had not put aside any money working on the rig. The habit of saving was foreign to Smith. Every time he built up a little pile of cash he blew it on shore leave, or surfed the internet to find something extravagant to send to the last woman who had said something tender to him. That didn't make him greedy, only somewhat desperate.

He needed a stake to quit Dauphin on, start living a different kind of life. Free and comfortable, that was what he wanted. It was worth two days. He felt horny, suddenly, then realized what he was lusting for was not a woman, it was money.

Once he made the decision, all the rest was logistics. He was good at logistics. He would spend one more night at the Maison des Rêves. In the morning, pick up his go bag, along with the four thousand dollars he had deposited in the hotel safe, and take the first ferry to Kinshasa. Being ready was company policy. If you worked in Central Africa, you were obliged to plan for disaster.

His passport had a visa for the other Congo. That also was company policy. You had to have more than one escape route in case things went bad in your neck of the African woods. Dauphin shareholders did not want you to wind up as a hostage. Hostages were costly, and the French had the praiseworthy custom of paying the abductors to get their people back.

Watching the commotion of the ferry being loaded, Smith let the idea of Louisiana slosh around in his mind for a few minutes. There was a woman who might—*might*—come back into his life. She lived in a bungalow in the country outside Baton Rouge in Flannery Parish with a bunch of half-feral cats in sunshine on the back porch. Her daddy had christened her with the name of his favorite Chuck Berry song.

For the eighteen months they lived together, Maybelline Beaudry used to rub Smith's back when he came home from work. At the time he was working construction under a foreman who had been voted Asshole of the Year in Louisiana. Every muscle in Smith's body ached, and his temper was set to go off the minute somebody looked crossways at him. Maybelline had red hair and a keen sense of smell and was better than Smith at telling jokes, which took some doing. And now she was divorced. She'd emailed him half a dozen times, and he always responded even though he hated being on the computer, it made him feel he was being cheated out of his real life. What they gave you in pixels they took away in beads of soul.

Once, Maybelline attached her picture to the message. Simple temptation, complicated dare. The day it arrived, if he could have jumped off the rig and swum west to the Gulf of Mexico and then up the Mississippi River to get to her he would have done it. If the picture was anything like the current Maybelline Beaudry she still looked plenty good.

He pictured what it would be like, buying Maybelline a Camaro with diamond money. She could pick the color. Odds were good she would choose red, which was a highly sexual color. Smith was fine with red.

A fight was breaking out on the deck of the ferry in a small space not designed for combat. Daydreaming about Maybelline and her bungalow and her sun-crazy cats, Smith had not seen it coming. The loading came to a halt. Everything stopped as people stood transfixed watching two bare-chested men square off against each other. The tall one was loud and upright. The short one was quiet and carried himself like a man who sometimes found himself in these situations.

From the dock, animated teenaged soldiers pointed their rifles toward the squared-off men. They were not taking aim, just using the guns to draw each other's attention to the fighters. A rumble of human noise rose across the low expanse of the port. It did not sound like cheering. It seemed to Smith that no one was taking sides, they were only in favor of the fight because it was a fight. There was agitation in the sound, the anticipation of an event ordained to end badly.

On board, the wide woman, who was now seated, opened one of her baskets. She drew out a red rooster with feathers the color of bright rust. She held the bird above her head as though to give it a clear view of the fight.

The loud upright man went down with the first punch. As he hit the deck and the crowd of watchers expressed their disappointment, the rooster flew free of the big woman and lit on the dock-side gunwale of the ferry. It understood more of what was happening than Smith did. He did not like being dumber than a bird.

Two days. Maybelline. Red Camaro, a.k.a. Son of Muscle Car. *Here, honey, it's for you.* Sex like fireworks on the Fourth of July. The thought occurred to him that maybe he was not so much greedy for money as for a certain taste on his tongue.

He took the phone from his pocket and dialed the foreman's number.

Next morning, when a man in a mismatched blue uniform and laceless boots with loud flapping tongues came at him with a gun hollering *Infraction! Infraction!*, Smith understood he had made a mistake. He had known it on the ferry, standing on deck feeling the boat's old engines straining against the river's superior power, watching the straggling jerry-built city grow in his imagination as they approached the dock. Forget two days. Forget taking a risk. Every last Congo story he had heard since coming to Africa ended badly.

The man with the gun blocked Smith's way out of the confusion of the port, where everybody understood an unstated system for getting along. People knew where to stop, when to keep going, whom they could ignore and whom not. Seeing what Smith did not, they were able slowly to keep moving in the morning's numbing heat, pushing against and then through an invisible barrier. No one paid any attention to the man with the gun, who kept screaming *Infraction!* the way people screamed *Goal!* at a soccer match, or to Smith, who felt sweat running on his body and a sense of dislocation as though he had landed on Congolese soil in somebody else's body.

The man with the gun wanted Smith to be afraid of him. He put his face up close to Smith's and said, "Document. Now."

He was young and pumped, playing a hard-ass part he had not fully mastered although he was on his way, give him a few more opportunities to kick innocent ass and he'd be there. It was impossible to know how real the fierceness in his brown eyes was. He might or might not work for some agency of the Congolese government. If he did, he would not have collected his pay for the last six months, maybe more. He might or might not be willing to shoot a stranger in broad daylight to make a buck or a point. In any case he wanted a piece of the foreigner coming off the ferry. Smith thought about the ministry letter Lajeune had given him. It was too soon to use it. *Turn it around,* he said to himself. A moment later, he understood what he meant.

He leaned in still closer to the man's face. He did not wish to smile—smiling would ruin the effect—but the muscles of his face had their own idea of how to behave in a situation like this one.

"Customs," he barked.

The man stepped back. When he hesitated, Smith said it again, louder this time. "Did you hear me? I said Customs. Now."

It worked. The man pivoted like a soldier executing an order and delivered Smith to a booth on the sandy bare ground inside which officials with stamps and ink pads in multiple colors sat on high stools checking documents. A balding official with a belly in the shape of a swollen almond glared at the man who had brought Smith to the booth. Then he summoned Smith, parting the throng of Congolese citizens standing stoically to present the papers that would allow them back into their own country. If any of them were offended, being displaced by a foreign white man, they hid it.

The man with the belly took Smith's passport. He placed it on the counter, face down so that the seal of the United States was not visible, and asked Smith why he wanted to come to the Congo. It was a question to which Smith found no plausible answer.

"I am a tourist."

The customs official shook his head. "We have no tourism in this country."

He made it sound like a feature of the landscape, like snow-capped mountains or palm trees. Maybe he was bored and longed to be entertained, and here was his chance.

Smith told him, "I have been hearing for many years about the warmth of Congolese hospitality."

That didn't work. It was not funny in a way the official valued. He grimaced and picked up Smith's passport. With simulated dudgeon he thumbed through the pages. When he finished he tossed it back onto the counter, face down again.

"Your visa has expired. This is a violation of international law. You must take the next ferry back to Brazzaville."

"Perhaps, in your understandable desire to serve the public promptly, you misread the date."

The man shook his head ponderously, as though it hurt him to acknowledge the American's stupidity.

"You will be kept under guard as you wait for the return ferry."

He rose from his chair and called something in one of the many languages spoken in the Congo that Smith did not know. He gestured for Smith to stand aside and went back to scrutinizing the travel documents of the Congolese ferry passengers, whose patience was like the patience of those ancient turtles that used to hold up the world.

Five minutes later, a man with a double chevron on the sleeve of his shirt and a businesslike air escorted the American to a hut inside which the morning air was stifling. A thin beautiful woman wearing pants with a leopard-skin pattern was sitting on a folding chair. She held a baby in the air as if she did not quite know what to do with it. Her eyebrows were fake, twin arching mountain peaks that gave her a look of constant astonishment. When she saw Smith she shook her head, which he took as a sign that he had gotten something wrong. Five minutes ashore and he had messed up, maybe messed up big time.

The man with the stripes on his sleeve asked brusque questions of the woman with the baby. He did not look at her or listen to her answers. His mind was on something more interesting taking place someplace else. Fifteen minutes later he was folding two twenties from Smith into his lapel pocket, in exchange for which courtesy he stamped the American's passport and let him into the Democratic Republic of Congo. As Smith left the hut, the woman held the baby's hand and waved it goodbye.

Smith walked away from the port, go bag in hand, his sense of dislocation increasing. He moved steadily and with purpose although he had no idea where Grand-Père Lajeune's nightclub was located, not even which neighborhood.

The city did not so much sprawl as materialize block by block, street by improvised street, like a string of slow impetuous ideas. He passed men carrying bags of ice on their heads. Flaps of cold plastic hanging down to their ears made strange hats of the bags. Two thin-hipped women who might have been sisters balanced trays of eggs as they walked in sync down the street past a row of parked cars. A boy in flip-flops went past Smith swinging a wire cage of yellow songbirds that were not singing.

Two blocks higher up, a beat-up Renault sedan extracted itself from the slow snarl of traffic and parked on the side of the street alongside a deep, open storm drain into which a wooden cart with a broken axle had fallen and been abandoned. The driver leaped from the car and came at Smith waving his arms.

"Taxi," he said. "You want a taxi, don't pretend you don't."

He was a squat man with skin the color of dark chocolate. He wore a New York Yankees batting helmet and gave the impression of escaping a calamity. When Smith shook his head, the man drew a plastic document case from his shirt pocket and opened it to show him.

"This will confirm that I am an authorized driver of the public sector," he said.

His authorization was an identification card from the Buffalo New York police department. A picture that may or may not have been his was pasted over the spot where a cop's ID photo was meant to go.

"I can't talk to a man in a helmet," Smith pointed out.

The man removed the batting helmet. The horns of forty vehicles sounded in syncopation around them as though the street had a rhythm they were trying to catch, and a street vendor swinging dog collars of several sizes came at Smith across the broken sidewalk. The taxi driver shouted him off.

"You don't have a dog," he said to Smith. "That's one thing I know about you, you do not own a dog."

"In Brazzaville," Smith told him, "people say that the taxi drivers of Kinshasa are thieves and murderers. They abduct their passengers and beat them up. If the passenger does not have enough money on him, they kill him."

The driver nodded. "Of course. However, it is only the evil drivers who commit such criminal acts. Fortunately for you, I am one of the good ones. The good drivers deliver their passengers to the destination of their choice."

He handed Smith the helmet. "This will protect your head in the improbable event of a collision."

Smith handed it back. "How do I know you really are one of the good drivers?"

"Ask my mother, my wife. Ask my girlfriend. They will allay your fears."

"How much to take me to Le Mistral?"

"Fifty dollars."

"That's what the evil drivers charge."

"I am Christophe. Remember the name. Come, we will reach an agreement that satisfies both of us."

Behind the wheel of the Renault, Christophe put the batting helmet on. The French for "peripheral vision" did not come to Smith, but he told him he would get out of the car unless he took off the helmet. He took it off.

"Le Mistral," Smith reminded him.

"Got it."

Christophe drove Smith in thirty complicated minutes to a hotel on a side street of hard dirt in a neighborhood in which all the businesses had to do with female beauty. There were one-room salons for hair and nails, and two-room stores selling women's clothing. Street sellers went up and down the streets holding up plastic hangers on which colorful underwear and yards of equally colorful fabric for dresses were displayed. On one storefront wall someone had written *Dieu est Grand* in red block letters that dripped, leaving an impression of sloppy theology.

The hotel to which the driver delivered Smith lacked a sign with a name. It lacked an atmosphere of welcome, and a front step up to its elevated doorway, which was a rough rectangle punched in the wall three feet above the pavement. As the Renault came to a stop in front of the hotel, a man built like Christophe but twenty years older jumped down from the open door into the street. He yanked Smith's door open.

"Through the mercy of God, you have arrived at last. Monsieur, I am pleased to announce that your room is ready. The sheets are clean. Allow me to take your bag."

"This isn't Le Mistral," Smith said to Christophe.

"Not yet." After thinking for a moment, Christophe realized he had to acknowledge what was obvious. "Yes," he told Smith confidently, "I can say with certainty that this is not the destination of which you spoke. But you will want to rest after your journey. This is a safe hotel, for a man like you. Not only is it safe, it is comfortable. Andre is my cousin. We are Hutu. The Hutu are good people. Their suffering at the hands of bad people has cleansed them of sin."

"You don't have any idea where Le Mistral is, do you?"

Christophe did not answer. He got out of the car and consulted his cousin. They talked for a long time, and Smith cursed Lajeune for failing to remember the location of his grandfather's establishment.

He felt the way he'd felt one time, years ago, in a Baton Rouge bar. A woman drinking what she called moonshine cocktails came on to him. She was dressed in crinkly leather and smelled like death lilies, if you took a whiff you'd be comatose at least. He surrendered to her inside five minutes and watched her back off in less than that. She was only practicing, warming up for her main event. She leered at him and went away, leaving him with a hard-on that didn't.

Eventually Christophe stuck his head through the open window of the Renault and told him, "Le Mistral must be in Matonge."

"Must be or is?"

"Matonge is a famous neighborhood of the city. It contains many restaurants, many bars. Stupendous Congolese musicians have come out of Matonge."

"Take me there."

"*Directemente*. It is not far. It is a matter of minutes."

It may have been a matter of minutes, but the route Christophe took put them behind a funeral procession going nowhere. When the Renault stalled behind a flatbed truck, Christophe cursed, slamming the palm of his hand against the steering wheel and muttering mysteries. His rage was instantaneous. It was real.

"Relax, my friend," said Smith. "Why don't you just back up and turn around?"

But it was too late for that. Behind them the street was quickly blocked by cars driven by people no happier than they were to be tangled in traffic behind a truckload of mourners. Christophe switched off the engine. They sat.

In the center of the truck bed a black casket shone somber and holy in the day's brutal sun, an etched object not soon forgotten. Elaborate wreaths of twined white flowers on wire tripods leaned against the back of the cab. The rest of the bed was taken up by grieving people in church clothes. In the hot unmoving air the women fanned themselves, the men mopped their brows with white handkerchiefs, the children sat quietly rigid. One man lacking a leg sat on an upturned crate holding his body as if to keep the missing limb out of people's way.

"The one they are taking away," said Christophe, "the dead one."

"What about him?"

"If there is justice in the afterlife, he will rot in hell. Flames will torment him every moment of forever."

"Why should that happen?"

"Look at them."

"I'm looking."

"Don't you see?"

"I see people who have lost someone they loved."

"See how thin the bodies are, how tall the men are. Look at the noses, and the cast of their skin. They are Tutsi. The Tutsi have terrorized my people for many years. They have stolen our land. They have raped our women and slaughtered our families. This has happened more years than I can count. My uncle . . . " He stopped and put his head down. When he turned around to look at Smith he was crying and told him, "The Tutsi are evil people."

"I thought the genocide was the other way around, Hutus killing Tutsis in Rwanda."

Christophe looked at Smith with contempt. "The Americans, the Europeans. Rich white people. They understand nothing about us. You understand nothing."

In his prodigious ignorance, it was not a conversation Smith wanted to have. He remembered the September 11th attacks, of course. He had been twenty or so when the towers came down, and it never made any sense to him. Before that, he had paid no attention when jihadists blew up a couple of American embassies in Africa. He watched it on the news. Dead bodies. He didn't quite forget about what happened, but he didn't know what to do with any of it. Now, in 2017, he did not know who the good guys in Central Africa were, so how could he know which ones were the bad guys?

A little breeze blew. It came in through the windows of Christophe's Renault and passed out again. Feeling it on his bare skin, Smith could also see the relief it brought to the mourners on the back of the truck, stuck on their slow way to a cemetery where the earth would surely be baked hard as cement, resistant to the blade of the shovel wanting to dig a hole in it.

Already, two hours into the harder Congo, there were things Smith wanted to tell Maybelline. Already he understood that, if he ever got the chance, the hard part would be finding words.

The sign identifying Le Mistral had survived the death of Lajeune's grandparents, the closure of the club, the weather of Kinshasa. Something airy in the blue lettering suggested the cold French wind that had lent the place its name. Standing across the street, Smith had a hard time imagining Le Mistral as a place for late-night carousing. The two-story building looked strangely like a farmhouse. The worn white shingles and flower boxes in the windows suggested rural virtue, although the boxes were empty. Surrounding the house was a fenced yard across which the carcasses of tables and chairs lay scattered as by a storm. Everything was coated with city grime.

He approached the building not knowing what to expect and was met in the yard by a wizened woman with a bent back carrying a broom of flyaway sticks. She wore a long black skirt, and her baggy T-shirt read *Funkadelic World Tour*. Her feet were bare, the toes curled up like decorations. Her expression was territorial.

"There's nothing left to steal," she warned Smith, holding up the broom to ward him off.

"I can see that."

"Nothing left to guard, that's how I see it. Bit by bit, thieves—men and women both, you hardly knew the difference by their actions—they took everything. I did my best, but you see how old I am. I remember gardens, green plants growing in gardens. Vegetables. Things have only ever gotten worse than they used to be. That makes me a witness. Every place needs its witness. Did you bring my money?"

"No."

The woman slumped. She grumbled.

"They owe me. Ever since they went back to Antwerp, they forget I exist. They have no loyalty, not even to their own ideas."

Lajeune had told Smith nothing about a caretaker, but Le Mistral had a roof. In Kinshasa, people needed roofs.

The woman could be squatting, and telling a tale. It didn't matter. She deserved a roof.

"What's your name?" he asked her.

"Anaya. I am not like the others."

"Which others?"

She shook her head. The rheumy eyes staring him down were full of the detritus of disappointment. "After all they did to us, all they took from us, I do not hate the Belgians. Christ teaches us to forgive our enemies, does He not?"

"The family want me to go in and have a look around."

"And my money?"

"We'll talk about that later, after I've had my look."

She gave way, and he went into the house through the front door, once red, on which hung a framed announcement of the club's hours of operation. The glass covering the announcement had a crack that made it hard to read, but Smith saw that no closing time on Friday or Saturday nights was posted. He thought about the elderly couple up 'til all hours serving a rowdy party crowd. What did their old-fashioned Belgian minds think as they scuttled to deliver trays of Primus beers to men they were accustomed to looking down on?

Inside, the house had the closed-up smell that buildings in the tropics acquired when no one went regularly in and out of them, and Anaya would not leave him alone. It was her duty to stay with this unexpected envoy from the Lajeunes, and duty included opportunity. But he needed to get to the kitchen. Alone. He handed her a twenty.

'Why don't you go get us something to eat?"

"You don't eat grubs, do you?"

"Do you?"

"Just curious. I never yet met a white man who ate grubs unless he had to."

"Chicken," said Smith. "Bring us some chicken, and a cold beer."

As soon as she was gone he went into the kitchen, which was pretty much bare except for an aluminum basin heaped with peeled white sticks of cassava. It stood on a table that wobbled when he touched it; one of the legs had a crippled foot. But the old freestanding cabinet stood where it was supposed to stand in the corner, a ruddy rooster painted on the enamel door expressing limitless self-confidence. On the wall next to the cabinet he could just make out the ghost of the green garland that had once graced the stucco wall. For the first time since he had come ashore, Smith felt optimistic.

On the floor beneath the garland, one of the boards was supposed to lift. Hurriedly he bent over and drove the blade of his pocketknife into the seam between two of them. He applied pressure and lifted with the blade until he could get a finger's purchase. Then he began working the loose board up and out. A sudden sense of being watched stopped him, and he turned around expecting to see Anaya. *Just checking out these old boards, ma'am, see how they're holding up.* But instead of the old woman there stood a girl, tall and thin and athletic looking. Smith could not guess her age. He was no good at that, no good with kids, period. Twelve, maybe she was twelve.

She did not seem interested in the floorboards. In a high voice that came from a long way off she said to him, "You're here."

"I'm here."

She came across the room. She took his forearm and ran a thumb over the leopard. When she dropped his arm, she said, "Nkoyi."

"Well Merry Christmas to you, too," he told her in English, which startled her and made her glower. Galveston. That was where he had made the impulsive decision to brand his flesh with the image of a leopard. He had no memory why he had chosen a wild cat from Africa for the only tattoo he would ever have. At this point he could not even remember why he had wanted a tattoo in the first place. Alcohol was involved. So was a woman with inked arms and the aggravating habit of saying *All y'all* every other half-sentence that came out of her mouth. Nadine something. She claimed to come from a family of snake-worshipping Christian literalists. That was intended to impress him and was not believable biography. He hadn't thought about Nadine in a long time.

The girl told him, "I was waiting so long."

"Waiting for what?"

"You talk funny."

He noticed her bony ankles, her purple flip-flops, and a lightning bolt scar that ran the length of her lower leg. Her hair was shaved short, emphasizing the shape of her skull. It gave her a vulnerable look that caused Smith to remember a Black girl in grade school he used to like. One time he had picked flowers and woven them into a crown he placed on her head in a patch of surreptitious woods out behind the school. She wore the crown back to class but took it off and threw it in the trash can when the other kids jeered. Because Smith was a kid himself, it hurt.

He had forgotten more of his life than he remembered. A sense of all he had lost and would not get back hit him like revelation. There was something wrong with the way he was put together.

There was something wrong about the girl, too. She was slightly off. It was as though, suspicious of the space around her and all its ghosts, she managed to do a stutter step standing still. Some malevolent thing could come crashing down on her any moment, and she was ready to bolt.

"This is the only way I know how to talk," he told her.

"It doesn't matter," she said. "You will take me."

"Not that I'm taking you anywhere, but just out of curiosity, where is it you want to go?"

"Nyogokuru."

"Where is that?"

She stamped her foot. His obtuseness, or his cruelty, frustrated her. Smith was relieved when Anaya came back with a package of chicken and two bottles of Primus. The old woman hollered at the girl and shooed her outside before spreading the meal on the wobbly table with painstaking reverence. A meal, a genuine meal. It made Smith feel good, not good enough to justify coming to Kinshasa, but pretty decent considering the inconvenience of being there. She did not offer to give him change for the twenty, and he didn't ask. They drank their beer from the bottle. Smith's tasted like Africa, like his present circumstances.

"Who's the girl?"

"They say she's a witch."

"What do you mean, a witch?"

"Don't they have witches in Belgium?"

"I'm not Belgian, I'm American. We haven't had witches in my country for a long time."

"The girl's family threw her out. First she made her mother sicken and die, and then one of her brothers went. Woke up howling and was gone before the sun went down. After a while the father took another woman as was his right. When this new woman began to feel terrible pains in her stomach and in her back, she tried to beat the evil out of the girl. Tried hard, from what I heard. It didn't work. The father had a heavy heart, but he agreed to put the girl out."

"That's insane."

"No, it's witchcraft. She stayed for a time at a place they keep children like her, but she bolted."

"That scar on her leg . . . "

"It's not that you have no witches in America, it's that they must be very good at disguising themselves. In this place we are not so easily taken in."

"What's her name?"

"Why do you care? She's gone."

"I want to know."

"Béatrice."

"Where does she live?"

"Nowhere."

A loose floorboard beneath a garland painted on the wall next to a cabinet. That much, Lajeune had gotten right. Smith required a few more minutes of privacy in the kitchen. When they finished eating, he told Anaya, "I want to give the girl a little money."

"Not out of mine you won't."

"Not out of yours, no." He peeled off another twenty from the thin roll he kept in the pocket of his jeans. The rest of the four grand he had brought with him was in a money belt around his waist, out of harm's way. "Here, go find her and give her this. Then you and I will settle up."

The promise of back pay was enough to purchase her cooperation. She took the money and went to look for the girl. The instant she left, Smith pried loose the floorboard. He lifted it up and out. He explored the cool dark cavity with his hand methodically, reaching as far as he could in every direction while fearing spiders, anything that might sting or bite. In the emptiness under the floor, he found . . . nothing. If there had ever been a sack of diamonds stashed there—with painful clarity he understood how preposterous Lajeune's story had been—somebody else got to them first.

He was on his knees. He stood up with a sense of being observed. Turning, he saw the young girl staring at him. She pointed at the hole under the floorboard. She opened her mouth, closed it. Then she shook her head and ran away.

The day was gone. It went fast, the way it did in the Atlantic on the rig. Had to do with the latitude. Late afternoons, along this belt of the earth, the sun was in a hurry to put the spent day behind it. As the sweat dried on Smith's skin it left grit; testament to another one down the tubes and nothing worth writing home about. He was walking, wishing he had made an arrangement with Christophe to come back and pick him up. In a fever to get to Le Mistral, he had not been thinking clearly. Diamonds were supposed to radiate light, but in his case all they did was cloud his judgment. An idiot. He was. His expedition to Kinshasa turned out to be a way to hand a hundred bucks of guilt money over to a caretaker woman whose only claim on him was based on false pretenses. Both of them lied to each other from start to finish. Now that was funny.

Less funny was walking down streets on which everyone who passed by looked at him with more pity than curiosity, as if they knew he was in for something he himself did not see coming. He passed bars with doors opening onto dark interiors, heard laughter that did not come out in French. He smelled hot cooking oil. For a long minute the air was fat with the sound of a saxophone, greasy blown notes popping like bubbles.

The music died as he went around a corner, on the lookout for a place he could spend the night. Also as he went around the corner, a gang of street kids swarmed him. They came at him from every direction, screaming and pushing. The idea was to confuse him, and it worked. The other idea was to get his go bag. Not going to happen. He held onto it hard, shoving just as hard against a kid who was missing his front teeth and grinned like a Halloween skeleton.

"Get lost, you little fucker."

The kid stumbled and fell but came up still grinning as three of his business partners mobbed Smith, approaching along parallel vectors. The rest of them hung back waiting for the right moment to knock down their quarry and take whatever he had that might be worth taking. They were ecstatic, a bunch of happy kids eating ice cream at a picnic. The one who grabbed his phone was happiest of all.

There was a sound, brief and terrible. It stopped, and the gang moved away from Smith, every one of them taking off in a different direction as though they had rehearsed their escape. They disappeared faster than they had appeared. It was the unearthly sound that drove them away. Smith would not have thought it could be produced by human vocal cords except that when he turned he saw the girl from Le Mistral. Her thin chest was heaving—probably she had been running—but the expression on her face was serene.

When she did not approach him, he went to her.

"How did you do that?"

"The *shegues* know me."

"And they're afraid of you. Is that because you're a witch?"

She squinted, looking away. "They stole your phone."

"That they did."

"How will you talk to your mother?"

"Who said anything about my mother?"

The girl stopped. She frowned. She gave him a searching look, continuing until she had his full attention.

"The hole," she said.

"What hole?"

"In the kitchen. The floor."

"What about it?"

"You were looking for something."

"No, I wasn't, I just like holes. Holes are interesting to me."

She shook her head. "Liar. You were looking. It wasn't there. I know where it is, what you were looking for."

She was working him; she was working him hard.

"All right," he said. "Where is it?"

"Far away."

A screw tightened inside Smith. A half turn.

"Let's pretend I believe you. Let's pretend I want to believe you. First, you have to tell me what it is. What is the thing I was looking for?"

She shook her head, although she did not seem exactly to be saying no. "They took it. They picked it up out of the hole and took it far away."

"Who took it?"

"They took it to Nyogokuru."

"Tell me who Nyogokuru is."

"The mother of my mother."

"Your grandmother. Where does she live?"

She looked at him as though he could not have come up with a dumber question if he had practiced all day. Maybe it was. He was not in a position to judge.

She said, "Some of the *shegues* are bad."

"I guess the ones who went after me just now were little saints."

"Come."

She took his arm, and he allowed himself to be led. After a couple of blocks he realized she was taking him back to Le Mistral. The dead club was the last place he wanted to be, but the *shegues* had shaken him up, and it was foolish to stay on the street in the gathering dark.

She went into the club as if she owned the place. He went with her. There was no sign of Anaya. Maybe, after all, the old woman had another roof to shelter her. Maybe everything Smith thought, every working hypothesis about the Congo that came to him, was wrong and meant to be wrong, and he was supposed to figure out why.

He followed Béatrice up the stairs by the light of a flash she took from a hiding place behind the rickety table in the kitchen. In the room at the head of the stairs she had stacked cardboard into something like a bed. A blue sheet lay folded on the cardboard. There was no pillow. Next to the stack was a small heap of T-shirts and shorts.

This was where the kid lived.

Where did she get her clothes? She didn't walk into a Walmart and swipe a debit card. Did people give them to her? Did she rip stuff off when nobody was looking? From where? How did she wash them? Did she have a toothbrush? Who shaved her head, and how come? Did she know how to read? Was there a woman somewhere in the Congo who taught her the important things a girl needed to know? This was a new kind of ignorance for Smith. A hole was being torn in a curtain he had not known existed. Peering through it, he glimpsed a lot and understood none of it.

Béatrice pointed to her pallet. "You sleep there. In the morning we will go find the thing you want."

Smith asked her where she planned to sleep, but she did not answer. The girl did not much like answering his questions, he had noticed. He had the sense she was listening, and she understood his French even if she did not think much of his accent. But her mind took in the words and turned them into something of her own that no doubt served a purpose but did not require a response.

"I'm hungry," she told him.

He peeled another bill from his minimal roll and told her to go scare up whatever she liked. He was shedding twenties left and right. This was not what Dauphin Petroleum had in mind when they obliged their employees to move about the badlands with cash in their pockets.

He thought about Maybelline. The Camaro he bought her would be a convertible. Stick. It had to be stick, had to be a thing she could really drive. Him, Smith: he would be the other thing she drove. Together they'd be four on the floor.

If he ever found diamonds he would not be the kind of person who hoarded his wealth. Money was like sex, meant for pleasure.

He lay on the cardboard recreating in his mind the picture Maybelline had emailed him until Béatrice came back with a sack and he realized she was trying to placate as much as trick him. She had the bent aspect of a child who went without meals. She had spent the money on more chicken and beer. That was what the old woman had bought for the foreign man. It must be what people like him—white men who talked funny and did not know when it was dangerous to be out on the street—preferred.

Sitting on the pallet, he offered her half the chicken, which was rich with oil and spice and smelled like rescue. She ate her half in a ravenous hurry. When she finished, he held out the beer bottle.

"Here, wash down that bird. Tasty little creature, wasn't he? But don't go crazy on the beer. You're too young to get drunk."

She took the bottle and put it to her lips, testing. She was a street kid, she knew what beer was. Maybe she'd had a bad experience. Something made her sip, not guzzle, and as she drank he looked at her more carefully.

The lightning bolt on her leg was not the only scar. Her brown skin had tones of gold, like extra color stirred in with infinite patience so the blending was perfect, the end result being something new and fine. But irregular dark patches were visible up and down her arms and legs. Bruises, thought Smith; the kind that didn't go away.

It was her face that interested him. It was open and unprotected, a face guaranteed to attract trouble to its owner. Her mouth, her lips, had a self-possessed quality, a stillness, even when she ate or drank or spoke. Some of the girl's strength resided there. Her nose was sharp and a little long. Above the placid mouth, the strong jaw, it was a contradiction that complicated the face. Her dark eyes, just perceptibly oval, had the hardest job. They were on guard duty, no time off. Keep moving, stay alert, stay vigilant and nervous and aware. They were her early warning system.

It was impossible to guess, at least for Smith, what she would look like as a woman of twenty. Despite having been beaten for a witch, despite the wild way she lived on her own in one of the most dangerous cities on the continent, there was still plenty of kid in her.

"So," he said. "Where you going to sleep?"

No answer.

"It doesn't seem fair," he told her.

She frowned, looking away.

"I'm the one putting all the work into this conversation," he pointed out. "You, you're eating my chicken, you're drinking my beer, you're enjoying every word that comes out of my mouth, I can tell you are. You're just not contributing your fair share. Answer me one question."

She was still looking away.

"What was it you saw, down there in the kitchen, in the hole in the floor?"

Rather than answer, she got up and left the room. It was early for Smith to sleep, but there was no electricity in the abandoned club. The room was dark and his belly was full. Nothing else to do so he went to sleep. With any luck he would dream about diamonds again.

Likely it was a noise on the street that woke him in the lively late hours of Matonge. He lay on the stacked cardboard for a moment listening to traffic noise undergirding the sound of music from a club with more sound system than any three clubs needed. It was dance music, and the bassline ruled. Darkness doubled the feeling of dislocation he had experienced, leaving the port before meeting Christophe. Mixed with it now was a child's sense of foreboding, as if some sinister thing too terrible to be imagined were blocking his escape.

It was that sense of faceless danger that goaded him to get up and go look for Béatrice. With no flashlight and no idea where she had gone to sleep, he went slowly down the stairs, one hand on the plastered wall, which was night-cool and rough to the touch. He found the girl outside in a pool of blackness sitting in a plastic chair, drawn by the nightlife that also scared her. He could just make out her still figure, hands clasping her flashlight in her lap. Quietly she told him to stay quiet.

"If they hear us, they will come into the yard. They will hurt us."

She meant the men who were going up and down the street, drifting from club to club, loud and exuberant, in search of additional stimulation. Smith heard an angry voice curse.

"Is that Lingala?"

"Swahili," she told him.

"Which one do you speak?"

No answer. Why should he expect one? But he came up with a way to engage her.

"Tell me about Nyogokuru."

This time there was no hesitation. She sat up in her chair.

"My grandmother is old. Her hair is white, and she has a beautiful face. Her face is full of smiles, on her mouth and on the skin."—It took Smith a moment to understand she meant wrinkles.—"Nyogokuru is good, she is so very good. She is warm, and she smells of butter. She hurts no person, she hates none of them, not even the wicked ones. Everyone loves my Nyogokuru. If you stand close to her you can feel how warm she is."

He told her, "I never knew my grandma."

She thought about his bad luck for a moment. In her mind, his might be the equal of hers. Both of them were grandmother-deprived, the destitution tearing a hole in their innermost heart, hurting every day. Out on the street they heard the staggering sound of a drunk, who stopped and retched and then moved on.

"I'm sorry," Béatrice told Smith. Her voice suggested she had thought it through and understood what had gone wrong for him. "It was the fault of your mother. She kept you from your grandmother. She was bad."

"No. My mother was not bad." He searched for the word for "restless." "Momma was *agitée*, that's all. She was always climbing a hill just to see what was on the other side. Didn't come back, one day. But she was not unkind."

Béatrice said something in a language that meant nothing to the American. She realized her mistake and seemed to want to take it back but did not quite know how. A good kid. Smart, too. If he found any diamonds—hypothetically speaking—he would give her one.

He did not belong in the Congo. It was a problem, being touched by the plight of this hard-luck witch kid. In the dark, sitting across from her, he felt a sense of shame for pushing her to tell him what she had seen under the floorboards. That didn't mean he would stop pushing. He had come this far. He had to see the thing through. If he went back to the rig without knowing for sure, it would eat at him forever. In moments of weakness he would berate himself. *You were an inch, a day away from being rich. You lost your nerve, you spineless piece a shit.*

The girl said, "What is your name?"

"Smith."

"Nkoyi."

"I don't know what that means."

"On your arm. The animal."

"Okay, I get it. Nkoyi is how you say leopard."

"You will see, Nkoyi. You will see."

"What will I see?"

"My Nyogokuru lives in a beautiful place, a place of peace."

"What did you see, under the floor?"

"Grandmother has many cows, so many she gives away milk to people who need it. Where she lives is high up. At night, one feels cold and wants to sleep by the fire. The fire is good. And it is green everywhere. The leaves shine, the grass is clean." She stopped for a moment, straining to come up with just the right example of her grandmother's bounty. She found it. "The animals, all of the animals, they are healthy."

Smith was wrapped up wondering whether there was a gazillionth of a chance somebody had found the Lajeune diamonds and taken them to the far place where this legendary grandmother lived, wherever that was. For safekeeping, right?

Get them away from the dangerous capital city. That would be logical behavior. But Béatrice's situational awareness was more developed than his. She knew, suddenly, that they had to shut up.

On the street, rowdy men walking past Le Mistral had stopped and were listening to see if there was something worth checking out at the abandoned nightclub, which nobody remembered used to belong to a couple of Belgian oldsters, white people hanging on from the bad old days because the dispensations of the colonial era were all they knew, all they could imagine.

Béatrice and Smith sat without moving, almost without breathing. They were completely vulnerable. Smith's go bag was upstairs in the girl's room. The money belt was around his waist, but in a fight he would lose it. They would get his passport, too. It must be worth something on the black market, or people would think it was. And Béatrice was young, maybe not yet a teenager. Smith had heard stories about rape, even the gang rape, of little girls in the Congo. It was the kind of thing he read about idly, surfing the internet during a break at work on the rig, sometimes following a link to one of the grim official reports put out by organizations that were supposed to do something about the African war that never ended.

You could read those reports all day long, but nothing ever changed. Some monstrous event happened, something you thought set the standard for how low the human race could sink, although it never did, the next day somebody else sank still lower. People with good intentions heard about the rape, the torture, the dispossession, the murder. They lodged complaints where complaints could be lodged, they wrote their reports. Sometimes they established a commission to investigate the monstrous event. Sometimes they brought charges, and once in a while a bloody-handed man with red teeth, red urges, a head hot with red memories went to prison. But everything the good people did concerned itself with ugly things that had already gone down. As far as Smith could tell, they never saved a single girl from the savagery that happened next.

Béatrice and Smith waited a minute, then two or three more, before the listening men moved on. One of them belched as he went.

"Come on," whispered Smith, "we'd better go inside."

But the memory, or the story, or whatever it was that had gotten hold of Béatrice, would not let her go.

"Big wheels," she said in a monotone, ignoring him. "I remember it was very quiet on the road, you could hear the big wheels of the oxcarts turning in the dirt, that soft squeak they make. The dirt is red. Did you know that? It is beautiful dirt. And the bells on the cows in the grass, we heard those, too, it was so quiet. At night we sat at the fire and watched stars fall from the sky, fast, very fast. Nyogokuru ran and caught them in her hands, like this."

She stood, she made the swooshing sound of a meteorite entering the atmosphere. She ran across the dark yard and caught it. She brought it back to him.

"Hah! You will see, Nkoyi, you will see. You will be happy there. My grandmother's food tastes better than anything you find here, and there is so much it never runs out. There are yellow birds in the trees, and blue ones, and monkeys in the woods. The monkeys speak their own language, did you know that? They taste very good when Grandmother cooks them. There are fish in the river. It is a fine thing to see a fish leap from the water, which is clean and clear. Anywhere you stick your hand into the bark of a tree, you will find grubs."

She was hypnotizing both of them, and he did not try to put a clamp on it. When she wore down they went back inside. She pointed his way up the stairs with her flash.

"A box," she told him.

"What about a box?"

"I saw them. They bent down, they lifted the wood, just as you did. They pulled out a box."

"How big was this box?"

She showed him with her hands, suggesting a box the size of one in which a practical person would stash diamonds.

"Did they open the box?"

She nodded. "*Oui, monsieur*, they opened it."

"What was inside?"

"*Trésor*," she told him.

Her voice thrilled, but it was not convincing. Smith did his best to believe her anyway. "What kind of treasure?"

"I am tired, Smith."

It was time, from a tactical point of view, to stop pushing.

"Go to sleep," he told her. "In the morning, you will tell me about the treasure you saw."

In the morning, however, the girl was gone. He scratched the stubble on his chin and wished he could shave, but there was no water at Le Mistral. The reason to shave was vanity. Smith's hair was as black as the wing of a teenaged crow, but some quirk of genetics had flecked his beard with early gray. He took it as a cosmic insult. The god of time, who had plenty to play with, was dissing him at age thirty-seven.

Without the girl, the only option was get back to the port. He had a sense that, if there was a schedule, the ferry captain paid no attention to it. When the boat was loaded, they shoved off. Unless of course they had engine trouble, in which case the ferry didn't go anywhere at all. Smith grabbed his bag, left the club, and headed in the direction he believed the port lay, north of Le Mistral.

If Matonge had a hangover, the neighborhood had already shaken off the pain and was going about its business in disciplined chaos. The streets were busy with people selling things, moving things on carts and wagons and trucks, buying things or wanting to buy them, selling and trying to sell. It was all small stuff: men's pants and kids' flip-flops, plastic buckets from China and tins of cooking oil, pallets of bricks and twelve-foot lengths of pipe that sagged at either end, mounds of cassava stalks and a clutch of trussed bawling pigs. A boy at an intersection poked at the windshields of parked cars with a selfie stick he was trying to unload. People were getting by. They moved in a loud frenzy, but mainly they were getting by. Nobody wanted a selfie stick.

After ten minutes' walking, a Toyota pickup slowed near Smith. The driver brought the window down and asked him where he wanted to go. He spoke good French in a cheerful voice, inviting confidence, but Smith shook his head and kept walking. There was no reasonable reason why, but he did not trust the guy. *Go with your gut.*

Kluge had told him a story about a taxi driver. In the foreman's story, a French engineer who used to work for Total went with a group of wildlife enthusiasts to a bonobo sanctuary southwest of Kinshasa, a pleasant hilly spot along a small river. Scenic, and after you had looked your fill at the critters you could sit by the river and drink a Congolese beer and feel your foreignness as the fine thing it was. Consolations of the expat life. You took advantage when you could, you savored.

Bonobos were endangered apes that lived only in the Democratic Republic of Congo. The engineer had an idea for a book of photographs capturing threatened African animals, and when the group left the sanctuary he stayed behind wanting better pictures.

Bad decision. Leaving the sanctuary, he made a deal with a driver to take him back to the city. Nobody ever saw the engineer again, although a week later someone with half a heart threw his bloodstained passport over the fence around the French embassy in Kinshasa. It landed in the grass, and a gardener delivered it to the consul. It was the consul who had to call the engineer's family in France.

Thinking about rare apes and bloody passports, Smith kept his eye out for *shegues*. He was not sure whether they would come after him in the middle of what was already a brilliant morning, but one assault was enough. Ten minutes after he said no to the guy in the pickup, he approached a small iron bridge over a dry creekbed. Reaching it, he stopped and looked down.

At some point in the history of the city, the bed had become a dumping ground. For as far as Smith could see in both directions, Kinshasa's trash defaced the stones of the bed and the scrabbly ground on either side of the bed over which, at this season, no water ran. Bottles, cans, and mangled plastic shapes. Chicken bones, perforated barrels with bent lids, the whitening skulls of butchered goats. The rusted carcass of a dump truck, a lone egret perched on the cab wondering where the fish went. Broken wheels, broken chairs, broken anything that could not be resuscitated and put to improvised use. In the distance, in the middle of the bed, a tiny mother and four barefoot children picked through the litter for something worth salvaging, dragging dirty sacks behind them like vestigial organs.

As Smith straightened up, something hit him in the small of the back. It hurt like fire. There was nowhere to run, so he turned to face the attacker coming up behind him and took a stone in the neck. He swallowed. It hurt, and he bled a little. For a moment anger owned him as he saw that the hand that was throwing stones at him was attached to the arm of

Béatrice. Then he laughed, because what the hell else was he supposed to do?

"Okay," he shouted. "You've got my attention. Was there something you wanted to say?"

She came at him with a confidence anybody could admire, unrepentant and full of purpose.

When she was standing in front of him, he asked her, "Who taught you how to throw like that?"

"My grandmother."

Not only was the amazing Nyogokuru full of warmth and goodness, she was handy with projectiles. Not only was Béatrice obsessed with finding the old woman, the kid had a sense of humor.

He asked her a straight-on question. Should have known that was the wrong tack to take. "Why did you leave the house in Matonge?"

She glared sideways.

"I don't understand you, kid."

"I know where the treasure is."

It was desperation that made him take her seriously, or try. He had gone bankrupt twice back home. His problems were the consequence of bad habits, especially but not exclusively when it came to money. His fondness for weed and sleeping late had come into it. His temper was a factor, along with his predisposition to believe his situation was improving when in fact it was tanking at a pretty good clip. Apart from his time with Maybelline, he had not managed to have a relationship with a woman that went beyond a two-night stand. The job with Dauphin had been like a gift falling from the sky. But he still hadn't saved any money. His habits were always getting the better of him.

"I don't believe you," he told her, trying to get her goat.

It worked. She stamped her foot in frustration, shook her head, muttered something that did not come out in French. His skepticism really got to her. Good.

He had an idea. "The orphanage where you used to stay, where is it?"

She shook her head. There was an implication in the question she did not care for. "I am not an orphan. The orphans have no one. I have my grandmother."

"Sure you do, Béatrice."

It was the first time he had used her name, and it took both of them by surprise as though he had inadvertently touched her, she had inadvertently touched him.

A low-slung Mercedes with tinted windows rolled up alongside them and stopped. The rear window came opulently down to reveal an elegant heavy woman in a bright *pagne* and headgear enthroned on the back seat holding a cell phone to her ear. She was multitasking, talking on the phone and sizing Smith up.

When she had seen as much as she wanted to see, she told him in raw French, "Leave the child alone. Go back to where you came from."

This was what the woman considered doing her civic duty. If there was a threat attached to the words, she was saving it. The window went up, the car rolled over the bridge raising dust, and Smith's face burned. It was the first time in his life that he had been accused of being a pedophile. He resolved to get Béatrice back to the orphanage. If he had to, he would buy some rope and tie her to a chair. He would administer a dose of truth serum.

First things first. He had to convince her to take him there.

"Who looked after you at the orphanage?"

"Soeur Placide."

"And who is Sister Placide?"

"She is white like you. She is very old, as old as my grandmother."

"You have forgotten something," he pointed out.

Her look was the equivalent of a growl. "What did I forget?"

"Soeur Placide is the person who knows about your Nyogokuru."

The growl intensified. In the white light of the sun her shaved head magnified the girl's vulnerability. There were too many things that would go wrong for the kid, too few that might, with luck, go right. She was looking for the lie in what Smith had said to her but found only an interesting possibility. The scowl went away, making room for a meditative expression that might, time permitting, give way to a smile.

"Bread," she said.

"Bread."

She nodded. "Every day they bake bread at the orphanage. They teach us. I was a fine baker. Soeur Placide told me I was the best baker she ever saw."

"So where is this place where they bake bread every day?"

"In Gombe."

"How do you get there?"

She shrugged. "*À pied.*"

On foot. So that was how it was. Across a war-bedeviled city, a city periodically convulsed in violence, a city that knew all there was to know about dysfunction and dysfunction's blistered children, you walked.

When Smith looked around the Maid of Orléans Shelter for the Children of the Congo, his body aching from hours of hot walking, he felt a warm rush of relief. He wanted to think that every last homeless kid in Kinshasa had found refuge here. But his relief was tempered. The nuns didn't trust him. They swooped down and snatched Béatrice from him as though he really were the pervert the Congolese woman in the Mercedes had accused him of being. Their scowls were identical; they must have practiced.

Amazingly, to Smith, Béatrice surrendered without a fight, and one of the nuns led the American across a concrete courtyard where fifty kids played soccer and wrestled and gathered in chattering clusters. Girls sat in the shade of a hot wall braiding each other's hair and singing a repetitive song, verse after lulling verse like water running on stones until you forgot there was any sound at all going on around you. They looked like kids anywhere although they were not. Kids anywhere were not homeless witches.

Smith was not much of a novelty to them. The nuns were white, and now and then visitors from the home church in

Europe must descend on the shelter, bringing money, goodies, strangely spoken French. The children glanced at him, some of the girls from behind their hands. A few of them snickered, but there was no real malevolence in it.

The orphanage was vast. It had once served as the institutional heart of a parish back in the colonial era when the parishioners were Belgians who believed they were building for the future, and for their future comfort. The buildings had gone up before air conditioning changed the world and were designed to keep air moving, keep the rooms at a tolerable temperature. The drabness of the stuccoed walls gave them a reassuring look; they would be around a long time. In the high ceilings, fan blades turned imperturbably. Kids. Everywhere. Some of them lugged big woven baskets of bread, two to a basket each holding a handle. The bread was an occasion. It excited them.

The nun, who had an aggrieved manner as though the American stank, showed Smith into a little room with bookshelves and dusty file folders in stacks. She told him to wait. He waited. He didn't mind having a little time to think through his next move. It was simple. The hard part was making it work. He had to enlist the nuns to interrogate the witch girl on what she had seen at Le Mistral. Or not seen. Interrogate was the wrong word. Find out, anyway, whether she was lying to him. If it cost him a couple hundred bucks by way of a donation to the orphanage, so be it. Some clichés were true. You had to spend money to make money.

When the head nun finally came to see him in the office, he screwed up, began like a fatuous dribbling fool.

"It's an oasis, isn't it? You're running an oasis of care."

Soeur Placide, who had to be seventy-five and would never go back to the Belgium of her birth, crossed her arms. She had the organizational scowl down.

"There is no need to romanticize us. They are an army, the little ones of the city who lack a home. Here we are able at best to care for a platoon. We are few, we are old, for the most part, and the resources the Church gives us to carry out our mission are meager. Raindrops in a desert. You understand the science of evaporation, do you not? This is not a complaint, Mister Smith, I am merely describing the conditions under which we labor."

"I'm just saying," he began but trailed off. He was not in the habit of talking to missionary nuns and felt himself to be at a disadvantage.

"We appreciate your bringing Béatrice back to us," the nun told him.

A teenaged girl who appeared to have achieved some kind of status at the shelter served them tea. Tall and thin in a blue skirt and white uniform-style blouse, she was one of the legion of Joan of Arc's unacknowledged daughters. On her forearm was a scar the equal of the one on Béatrice's leg.

"Thank you, Adelaide," Soeur Placide said.

She was reinforcing a way of speaking, a deliberate way of thinking and behaving that might, if it took, do something to protect the girl from the streets to which she would eventually return. Self-confidence, discipline, clear thinking. Good habits, good food and water, unexpired medicine. That was what the orphans and the abandoned kids at Maid of Orléans required. It was an open question whether they would get enough of any of it to change their fate.

Adelaide performed something that in a different time and place would have been a curtsy. Whatever it was the nuns were selling, she was willing to buy.

When she left the room, Soeur Placide told Smith, "Béatrice has told us a rather odd story."

She was a large woman, close to six feet tall and formidable, like a horsewoman just dismounted from a high-spirited animal she put had through its paces. After a ride like that, the horse knew who the boss was. She wore a beige flowing dress down to the ankle that might or might not be a habit, cinched at the waist with a belt of black beads. A severe silver crucifix rested on her bosom, hanging from a leather cord. Her white hair was thick and long and free. It was the hair of a contrarian. As a younger woman her bulk would have made her awkward. Age had shown her how to own the space she inhabited with ease, in full security.

Smith had to move forward with caution. "What kind of story?"

"She said you were staying, the two of you were staying, at an abandoned house in Matonge."

"I'm not staying there. I slept there last night. That's the extent of it."

Lame. Totally lame. His words made him sound like he was apologizing. If you apologized, it meant you had something to be sorry for. All he had done was try to make good on the promise of Denis Lajeune's diamond-chip ring.

Sister Placide nodded. Smith couldn't tell whether she was being sympathetic or trying to trap him.

"The girl also said you are here in Kinshasa looking for a box of treasure."

"It's complicated," Smith said.

"She said she saw some people take a box from a hole under the floorboards in the kitchen of the house in which you were staying."

"I'm telling you, I wasn't staying there."

That was the wrong thing to say. He corrected himself. Might as well be straight with this towering figure of righteousness. She was the opposite of a person like Denis Lajeune and likely to outmaneuver him.

"Do you believe her, Sister?"

"Béatrice is a highly intelligent child."

"I can see that."

"In the time she spent under our roof, she managed to acquire a decent command of Lingala. She came to us with Kinyarwanda and Swahili. Not to mention her quite passable French. But Béatrice has an obsession, and her obsession will not permit her to be still."

"Her grandmother."

"Exactly."

"The girl has an amazing memory," Smith said.

This was craven, praising the kid's mental attributes. He could be craven, if it served his purpose. He told the nun, "She remembers every last little thing about living with her Nyogokuru, somewhere up in the mountains."

The nun smiled. The smile provoked Smith.

"What?"

"The family is from the Eastern Congo. But Béatrice was never there. She was born in Kinshasa and has lived her entire short life here. She has never seen a mountain."

"So, what, she made it all up? She doesn't have a grandmother?"

"Everyone has a grandmother."

Smith said, "I don't understand."

It was a conversation in which he would always be wanting something definite, something true, and she would always withhold it, either because she did not have it or because she believed he had not earned any certainty.

"I came to the Congo more than forty years ago," she told him. "Since that time there have been few days when I could tell myself, *Ah, now I understand.*"

"Why did you come here?"

"As a young man my father lived in Kisingani, when Congo was still a colony, of course. After he died, back at home in the bed of his forefathers, I happened to learn of some . . . events that took place while he was here."

Finally, an opening to bring her down a notch, maybe not to his level, but down from the high plains of righteousness where she normally strode.

He said, "That's vague."

"Some terrible things happened under my father's supervision. It was a chance conversation with his elder sister, after the funeral. His death hit my aunt hard, and she used my presence to remember aloud what their life in this country had been. Her act of memory was a nonbeliever's act of contrition, you might say. You might also say that it changed the direction of my life."

"So what was it that your father was involved in?"

She shook her head. "Would you like more tea? Adelaide, you see, has left the pot."

"*Je vois,*" said Smith.

"All right, you get it. Tell me what."

"You're here, you're doing this really hard work, to make up for what your father did to the Congolese."

"I cannot atone for my own sins, not without the grace of God, never mind the sins of my father."

"What about Béatrice's grandmother?"

"The family were Banyamulenge. I suppose that means nothing to you."

Smith shook his head.

"It is a complicated story," the nun told him. "More complicated, I suspect, than the one you are not quite telling me. The Banyamulenge are from the east. Physically, they resemble the Tutsi. Traditionally they lived in the highlands. They were cattle herders, once upon a time."

Smith thought of Béatrice's tall, thin figure, the nose that Christophe the Hutu driver with the batting helmet would have identified as the nose of an enemy who deserved damnation.

"She told me about cows," he said, "and how cold it got at night. Her grandmother built a fire to keep them warm."

Soeur Placide said, "Surely Béatrice has the right to remember what she chooses, even if what she recalls is collective, rather than the fruit of her individual experience."

Smith let the resentment he wanted to feel blow by him. The woman was not rebuking him. Her anger was aimed elsewhere. She kept talking. He kept listening.

"After independence, politics in the Congo became tribalized. The Banyamulenge suffered when others accused them of being outsiders. They were portrayed as Rwandan interlopers, not true Congolese. They were dragged into the conflict between the Tutsi and the Hutu. You must know something about that."

He nodded, but she waited until he said it aloud.

"The genocide," he said. "Hutus massacred Tutsis. Hundreds of thousands were killed."

She said, "You will not care to be lectured."

Then she went ahead and lectured him anyway. Evidently mass murder did not happen only in Rwanda, and it did not begin in 1994. In Central Africa, the nightmare began decades earlier. Millions had died. Tutsi also murdered Hutu. Name a tribe, and you found both victims and men with blood on their hands. The butchery went on.

"Okay," Smith said. "So there are no good guys."

He was trying to figure out how he could steer the conversation back to the box that Béatrice either saw or didn't see.

Soeur Placide said, "A distinctly American way of putting it. One cannot easily make a story out of what happened in the

Congo, Monsieur Smith. There is no acceptable way to understand it. To be brief, *interahamwe*—gangs of thugs—murdered most of Béatrice's family. Her parents escaped to Kinshasa, where the mother died of dengue fever. Poor Béatrice was accused of causing her mother's death."

"I feel bad for the kid." The strange thing was, he did, he really did. "But I need to know if she saw that box or not. If she did, and if what I think what was in it is actually in it, I have a legal right to the contents."

That was idiotic. It sounded prick-like and sanctimonious even to him, something Lajeune would say. Something about this woman of God brought out the jerk in Smith. It was the contrast that did it: their lives, their choices, the people they had chosen to be.

"Unfortunately I do not believe there is anything we can do to assist you, Mr. Smith. Please follow me. You are in luck. Alphonse, our deacon, happens to be on the premises. He will drive you wherever you wish to go in the city."

"So, what, that's it? End of story?"

"Yes," she said, folding her arms. "End of story."

Well shit. The thought of going back to work bummed Smith out. Even though nobody on the rig knew he had been chasing phantom diamonds, he had a feeling his failure to find them would somehow be obvious to his workmates. He stood out anyway, as one of only three Americans on the rig. Plus, he was known as a guy who said too much at the wrong time to the wrong person. There had been a couple of fights. Nobody reported them because Dauphin canned you even if you were only standing there watching. Every time it happened, the spectators cheered for Smith's opponent.

"I'd like to talk one more time with Béatrice," he said.

The nun shook her head, not in an unkind manner.

"Whatever it is you want, Mister Smith, you might take a hard look and ask yourself what sort of damage your desire is doing to you."

What was lower on the scale of human dejection than bummed out? Whatever it was, Smith owned it. In his funk he was unable to come up with a credible reason why he ought to be allowed to interrogate the kid one last time. It was over. The nun stood.

"You will like Alphonse."

Alphonse turned out to be a genial man with the muscle-bunched shoulders of an athlete and a glass eye that never stopped staring at Smith. Who was this Catholic deacon born in the hard Congo? It was not a question Smith knew how to ask, and he trailed the man across the grounds of the shelter listening to him gas on about the social skills the boys acquired, playing soccer with a referee. Rules. Young people needed rules, and predictability.

They went through a gate in the high concrete wall at the back of the compound. Had the Belgians built the wall back when they ran the country? Whom did they intend to keep out? Or was it their religion they were keeping in?

Stepping into an alley of hard brown dirt they saw the parish Land Cruiser parked to one side, red with knobby big tires, a roof rack, a monster winch. They also saw a circle of young boys. The boys were boisterous. They were throwing stones. They took turns, throwing deliberately. In sport, they had learned, accuracy mattered. You didn't want to waste your turn. Their target kept moving in the center of the shifting circle of hollering boys, dodging stones and screaming invective in a Congolese language. Their target was Béatrice.

The deacon stopped the stoning in a hurry. He charged the circle and collared the biggest boy, a head taller than the others. The man had enough authority to snap their pack trance and shame the boys, who quickly shut up. Even the tall boy hung his head, shoulders slumped. After a compact lecture on Christian charity, Alphonse sent the boys single file through the gate back onto the compound to confess their sin, or at least admit it, to Soeur Placide.

All the time the deacon spoke, Béatrice stood trembling. She had not dodged every stone, and her face was bleeding. So was her scarred leg. When the boys who had tormented her were gone and Alphonse spoke gently to her, she looked at him as if she did not understand what he was saying. Her mouth made a precise "o," but nothing came out of it. Smith looked for tears but did not see any. She must have been terrified, but her anger was bigger than her fear.

The nuns had given her a change of clothes. The T-shirt was a size too big. It said *Packer Family Reunion, Lakeside Village 2015* on the front. On the back, it said *Staying Strong in Love*. She had bathed, but the sweat of heat and fear had undone the good of it. Alley dust stuck to the damp spots on her body, to the red glass beads in the thongs of her new Chinese flip-flops.

"Come, child," Alphonse said. "The sisters will want a look at those cuts. And you can bathe again if you like. That will make you feel better."

He did not promise to keep the boys from attacking her again. Good. It was not a promise he could keep. But the deacon's well-meaning words appeared not to register with her. She turned and walked away down the street, moving steadily upstream past passersby who did not look at her. In the bustle of the evening she was silent, she was invisible.

Smith and Alphonse watched her go, one as helpless as the other. Before she vanished Smith said, "You're not going after her?"

"We cannot force the girl to stay with us. Béatrice is deeply wounded, and I am not talking about the stones that have cut her flesh. We have learned to our cost that the remedies at our disposal are not always effective."

"So, what, you just let her fade into the night?"

Alphonse might be forty. He might be fifty. He had a carved face consisting of chisel marks and rough angles. He screwed it into an expression of neutral curiosity and said, "Me?"

"I'm not from here," Smith pointed out. "I won't be around. I can't do anything for the kid."

Alphonse nodded, registering no disapproval in his glass eye or the real one. He took a cell phone from the pocket of his loose white shirt, which was vaguely ecclesiastical, like Soeur Placide's dress. He dialed a number, asked a question, hung up.

"I am sorry, Monsieur Smith. The ferry to Brazzaville has departed. You might contract a man with a boat to take you across, but it is getting late, and they may create a problem for you on the other side. Nor, sad to say, can you depend on the boat-owners. You could be assaulted, or worse. Better to spend one more night in Kinshasa. I will drive you to a safe hotel."

As Béatrice rounded the corner at the end of the alley, Smith was having a hard time paying attention to the deacon.

"Hang on a minute."

He wasn't ready to give up on the Lajeune family diamonds. What he had told Soeur Placide was true—if they existed, he had a legal right to them. No way was Denis Lajeune getting half.

He had to run to catch up with her. As the day disintegrated, something tight in the atmosphere was loosened. The air pressure went slightly down, and Kinshasa allowed him to breathe. When he came panting up behind her, she wheeled around with a fierce expression expecting another attack. He stopped. She stopped. Smith caught his breath and asked her where she was going.

"What do you want?"

"The truth, Béatrice. Just the truth. Tell me who it was that took the box of treasure."

Her sense of grievance was palpable. She turned away again and walked.

"I'm sorry."

It was not what she expected, and a moment engraved itself on the retina of his mind's eye. Skinny buzz-cut Venus on a half-shell of broken concrete, one hand opening to reveal something of value. The noisy city cohered around her. She wore it as a jacket, with a cape of charcoal sky. The cape was studded with gulls. Another French word came to Smith. *Implacable.*

The object in her palm was her magic. She unrolled the pale, desiccated skin of a snake from around a small cat's eye marble. The marble was blue.

She told him, "My magic is strong. It drove those bad boys away. Then the big one came. I did not see his magic, but it was stronger than mine."

The sting of defeat made her eyes tear. It was not so much the stones they threw at her as the failure of her magic. Showing him the magic that had let her down might be a gesture of trust. If it was, he did not care to have it. All he wanted was the truth from a child who might not know it if it crawled up her back and bit her.

"I'll walk with you back to the sisters," he offered.

"*Non.*"

"Why not?"

"You were wrong, Nkoyi. Soeur Placide knows nothing of my grandmother."

At least she was answering him.

"What happens now? Will you go back to Le Mistral?"

She looked puzzled. Maybe she did not know the place by its old name.

"Where we were last night," he said. "Where the old woman with the chicken and beer was."

She shook her head.

"Then where?"

"Tonight the Li'l Prince drives his fast car. I wish to see him speed."

The night was coming down like rain, and Smith asked no more questions, like for example who the Li'l Prince was, or what made his car so fast. Smith was already on Kluge's shit list because he hadn't called in. If you didn't call to let them know you were going to be late getting back for work, the Dauphin security protocols kicked in. The company spent time, money, and influence ginning up a search for you. If it turned out your throat had not been slit, you got a nasty email from the human resources department threatening consequences having to do with your employment status.

When Béatrice took off walking again, Smith went with her.

The Li'l Prince was the President of the Democratic Republic of Congo, and his car was fast because it was a Maserati. Béatrice and Smith arrived in time to watch from the shadows of a blocky concrete building as efficient squads of uniformed men—cops or soldiers or the big man's palace guard—cleared a long paved street. The President needed some straight-line distance to go through the gears, and the American man and the Congolese girl were not the only people who wanted to see the show. Up and down the street the shadows and the safe places were packed with spectators who knew enough to stay out of harm's way.

Except for one drunk man.

He stood in the street, on the periphery of fuzzy light from a streetlamp, swaying in response to an earthquake only he sensed. He wore striped suit pants, shoes with neither socks nor laces, and a sleeveless T-shirt. He radiated belligerence. In a bar, he was the kind of guy you went out of your way to avoid because you knew he was going to pick a fight with you.

His timing was terrible. When three men with plug-ugly rifles approached him, he mouthed off, waving his arms in defiance of their authority, which he spat on. Sober, he would know better. Unsober, the antagonism that went along with his euphoria snuffed his judgment. He turned his head and ducked to miss the rifle stock with which one of the Li'l Prince's men went at him, but the butt of the gun caught him in the cheek and he went down limp. The instant he hit the ground, the three men began stomping on him. Three more men, and then four more, came running to take their turn kicking the drunk man.

He was soon unconscious, and Smith expected the soldiers to back off. They did not. They kept kicking, methodically striking every inch of his arms and legs, his chest, his head. In the bad light the spilling blood was black.

"*Il est mort*," said Béatrice quietly when they stopped, stepping away from their handiwork.

Smith looked at the girl, wondering how she would take the violence.

She was grinning.

"So, what, Béatrice? This is funny?

Yet another stupid thing to say. He never ran out of them. She scalded him with a look of confusion, her shoulders heaving with the stress of watching a man beaten to death. Ashamed of having failed to recognize the shock, Smith would have pulled her to him. He wanted to comfort her, but he was a man. Not just a man, he was a stranger, and an American. He had no standing to offer comfort, consolation, reassurance, or anything a kid in her situation needed. He thought about the woman in the Mercedes who had taken him for a pedophile.

He told the girl, "I'm sorry, Béatrice. I am really sorry you had to see this. Come on, let's get out of here. We'll find something good to eat. What about Coca-Cola? Do you like Coke?"

"No."

She wanted to stay. She was an immovable object, and Smith was far from an irresistible force. He stayed.

They watched a sergeant of some kind come swaggering up to the men who had stomped the drunk to death. He asked questions. They gave him the answers he required, upon which he communicated an order with the flat of his hand and the soldiers lifted the dead man. They carried him out of the street, out of the streetlamp's range. It was not acceptable for a dead body to be lying visible along a road down which the President was expected to appear at any moment, even if the President's attention were dedicated solely to driving.

A murmur of expectation went through the hidden watchers. It sounded like bees practicing a new tune. Then, at a distance, there was the sound of a high-performance engine.

Smith had been something of a gearhead when he was a kid. In high school, he spent time working in a garage for very little money and listening to the Chili Peppers. The engine sound appealed to him. His appreciation was out of place, he knew that. You did not cheer on a kleptocratic villain in a presidential sash. Then here came the Maserati. Fast and faster. It went by them like steel privilege, unstoppable. The crowd, in their surreptitious way, roared.

That night Smith learned a new word for an old idea. *Théodicée*. Coming out of Sister Placide's mouth, it sounded like an explanation. To Smith, it was anything but.

They were sitting in her office at Maid of Orléans. Some kind of night bug had gotten into the room. It was glossy black with wings like Batman's cape, and every few minutes it flew at the shaded desk lamp. The satisfying smack of the insect's body against the shade convinced Smith that the crash was fatal, every time. Every time, the bug came back strong.

Soeur Placide opened a bottle of Calvados and poured them each a shot.

"I have a cousin at home who visits faithfully. Each year she brings me two bottles. Of course getting them onto an airplane has become more difficult now that we must concern ourselves with the explosive devices of men who are both angry and clever. Do you know Calvados?"

"That stuff is out of my price range."

"Perhaps you disapprove. A nun in an orphanage indulging her taste for expensive French brandy? Perhaps you believe the proper moral response would be to insist that my cousin bring soap, or shoes; something for the children."

"Tell your cousin to bring three bottles next time. Everybody has bad days, Sister, even nuns doing God's work in a hot country. On the bad days you'll want a double shot."

She liked his answer and poured them both a little more in the bottom of kitchen tumblers, both of which were chipped on the lip. Handing him his, she told him, "I am sure you must realize by now how Béatrice trusts you. Otherwise, she would never have returned with you."

"She fell asleep. I picked her up and carried her."

"Ah, but if she did not trust you, she would not have slept."

Smith shrugged. He did not much care for the idea of being trusted by the kid. He didn't need, want, or know how to deal with that kind of complication in his life, which was pretty simple, relatively speaking. Needs, desires, dreams: satisfy as many of them as he could before punching his ticket. Maybelline was on that list, and the red Camaro he owed her. The trust of a hard-luck witch girl did not make the cut.

"I am sorry you missed the ferry, Monsieur Smith. Does that create a problem for you?"

He had borrowed Alphonse's phone to call Kluge, who was out on the rig feeling bored and sorry for himself. It had not been a light-filled conversation.

"My boss has no imagination."

"I don't understand."

"If I'm late for work, there must be a woman involved. He's too ugly and mean to find a woman himself. He takes his frustrations out on the rest of us."

"Evidently he did not consider the possibility of your spending the evening conversing with a Poor Sister of Claire."

Smith was beat. Too much sun, a Maserati and a murder, and he had wound up carrying Béatrice a long sweaty mile. The Calvados sent vapor trails curling into his susceptible brain.

"I came to Kinshasa looking for diamonds, Sister. That's what was in the box Béatrice saw. I mean, if she saw it. I won them in a poker game in Brazzaville."

"Diamonds have been the curse of this country. There is a reason they call them blood stones."

"You think I'm a heel."

"I don't know you well enough to have an opinion."

"Béatrice calls me Nkoyi."

"It is a Lingala word. It means Leopard. You should be honored. Nkoyi is a name for the mightiest of men."

"You ever gamble, Sister?"

"In the way that you must mean, no."

"I gambled. I mean after the poker game, when I came to Kinshasa. The odds of me finding the diamonds were low. I mean, absurdly low. But the reward, if I did find them, was ridiculously high."

"Are you trying to convince me that your behavior was rational, or convince yourself?"

The shelter was quiet. The Batman bug flew at the lamp shade again. It fell on the floor again. Smith sipped his brandy. It entered his system bringing with it a sense of foreboding that was not welcome. How many kids like Béatrice were out there on the streets of Kinshasa? How many were out there in the country's unreachable reaches? There was no fix for children like them, no help, no way out of the bad spot they were born into. That was a fact, not subject to interpretation. It was one of those pictures you could not unsee.

"Nothing about this country makes sense to me," he told Sister Placide. "It's like, they looked up one day and filth started raining down on their heads and it never stopped."

She looked at her empty glass. She told Smith, "One of the priests who visit us periodically likes to call the Congo the *théodicée* challenge of our time."

"I have no idea what that means."

She shook her head. "I'm afraid I don't know the English word."

"It wouldn't help."

"A *théodicée* is a theory," she said. "It seeks to explain the existence of evil in a world that was created by a God Whom we know to be all-powerful and entirely good."

"I guess you have to take it on faith."

"A curious expression. Would you like another taste?"

"Thanks. Save it for one of the bad days."

"Do you know, Monsieur Smith, I sometimes find myself thinking that our faith makes things too easy on us."

"I'm not built to talk about Catholic theology, Sister. For that, you need the deluxe model. With me, you get the basic package, no options."

"Nonsense. You have a decent mind. Exercise it."

"Okay. Then go ahead and tell me why faith makes the Congo too easy."

"Not a day goes by without a tactical surrender."

"I'm pretty sure I don't follow you."

"Imagine that something truly terrible happens. Let us suppose, for example, that a father is persuaded by his new wife that his young daughter is a witch."

"All right, go ahead and suppose it."

"In the beginning," said the nun, "the father resists his wife's unwelcome message. The child is dear to him, after all. She is flesh of his flesh. But the wife drills at him relentlessly, convincing him finally that the girl's presence under their roof must bring harm to other family members. God has cursed the child, for reasons of His own that puzzle us. They will go on puzzling us. Beatings, however severe, however regularly inflicted, do not solve the problem. The girl's new brother comes down with a fever. 'What did I tell you?' the wife cries in triumph. One fine sunny morning the girl is put out on the street bearing her scars and nothing else."

"I get the picture," said Smith. "It stinks."

"It stinks to high heaven, yes. But what can the rest of us do about it? We cannot heal the child's wounds. Nor can we bring the family back together. At best, we are able to shelter the child for a little while, perhaps impart a skill that will help her survive on her own. And we accept this miserable pittance, we say we are 'doing what we can.' We submit to that which should not be allowed to continue existing. Our faith makes fatalists of us, when really what we must do is resist, resist, resist."

"We?"

"The Congolese, of course. Along with the handful of us outsiders who know the country and care for it. Around the world, most everyone has forgotten the horrors of the African wars, if they ever knew about them. There are so many terrible things happening on our planet at any given moment. Watching a kneeling man beheaded on the internet is so much more absorbing. At any rate we lack the capacity to feel what we ought to feel for those who suffer everywhere. Or did we once have it, and now it is lost? I don't know."

"That's too much by half for me, Sister. Remember, I'm here for diamonds. It's all about *avarice*."

The old nun shook her head in distaste. She recapped the Calvados. The bug hit the lamp shade hard this time, killing itself. It lay on its back on the bare floor. Smith got up and kicked the tiny carcass with his foot. It caromed off the wall.

The office door was open, and they could hear a child crying in its sleep. Bad dreams, worse dreams, a dark trapdoor opening to the very worst of dreams.

"Béatrice is going to run away again," said Smith.

"Yes, she will. She has a queen's heart and a beggar's crown."

"I guess that's about the size of it."

"She said something to me this evening, before she went to sleep. I'm not sure whether I should tell you."

"You've gone this far, might as well go the rest of the way."

"Goma, she said."

"What is Goma?"

"A city in the east. That's where she says the people took your box of diamonds."

Smith sat up in his chair. The kid with the bad dream stopped crying. There was a faint ticking sound that had nothing to do with a clock, everything to do with time.

"Do you believe her?" he asked the nun.

"I believe she will do whatever it takes to get to the east because that is where she believes her grandmother must be."

"But do you think she's lying?"

Later, when things got worse than bad, worse than terrible, worse than the worst he could have pictured if he had tried to imagine what would happen to him in eastern Congo, Smith wondered if the nun had been working him, that quiet night in the orphanage in Kinshasa. Was this her version of resisting, or some kind of callback?

At the airport in Goma Smith lost his nerve. Every horror story he'd ever heard about exploding Westerners ran through his mind, with an American oil rig worker replacing the traditional victim. Goma was the jumping off place to the Wild East. No rules meant no place to hide.

His fear anchored him in the order, the security, that was palpable in the terminal. While bags from an incoming flight went obediently around the carousel, arriving passengers waited with good grace for theirs to show up, chatting about sensible things like food and newspapers. There were Chinese men in identical boring suits, and North Africans in robes and skullcaps. Lebanese businessmen occupied their fastidious hands with worry beads. There were self-clumping handfuls of men in uniform; the blue helmets, people called them. There were aid workers from Europe, and Congolese men in slacks and open-collared shirts enamored of their cell phones. Congolese women in *pagnes* moved across the terminal with physical dignity as if their destination were the heart of mystery and only they knew the path.

In the morning sun the place was clean and bright; an example of how things might be arranged in a different Congo. The airport was run by MONUSCO, the United Nations stabilization mission in Eastern Congo.

He had been told it was hard to get a seat on a plane coming to Goma. But Soeur Placide made a couple of phone calls and was given two seats on a UN flight.

Two.

Béatrice, in new clothes that fit her and a pair of sneakers that also fit, looked around the terminal as if it were Disneyland and she couldn't make up her mind which ride to try first.

"Nkoyi," she said. Her satisfaction was stronger than any sense of strangeness.

"What?"

"I knew we would arrive. Here. To this place." She lifted her hands high and made an airplane of them. She flew the plane in twisting circles as far as her arms reached, avoiding invisible airborne obstacles. "I saw this airport, this very place. Before."

"Where'd you see it, in one of your famous dreams?"

She shook her head, sorry for him that he was so dense. She had plenty of words in plenty of languages. All of them would be lost on him. She landed the aircraft she had launched, letting her arms hang at her sides in a resting position. She smiled up at him.

"This place, you see, I know it well."

"Bernadette," he said. "Right? The woman was Bernadette, and the man was Bogabu. You know what they look like."

He was reminding her of the names of the people who had, according to the testimony she had given Soeur Placide at the orphanage, taken the box of diamonds from Le Mistral. Of course, she had not been under oath.

No answer. She was too happy to speak, happy with everything including the laces of her sneakers, which were beautiful and white. She kept stopping and stooping to tie and retie them for the pleasure of touching, the pleasure of new having. One of the nuns at Maid of Orléans had given her a small, second-hand backpack to carry her things, which now included a toothbrush and toothpaste, a plastic container for soap, a hairbrush, and clean folded clothes. There was also a mirror, not for vanity's sake but so that the girl knew what presentable looked like and could keep herself that way. All of it made for one small good thing. The kid had her own go bag.

She skipped ahead, then quickly turned back to him and whispered, “Look over there. That old woman.”

The woman she indicated was forty. She had a composed face, a comfortable body of generous proportions, an air of complacency that had nothing to do with being self-satisfied. She was the kind of person to whom strangers were drawn, just to get close to whatever it was she had. You got the sense she knew how to share.

“That’s not your grandmother, Béatrice. She doesn’t have white hair.”

The girl seemed as unwilling to leave the airport as he was. She had flown in an airplane to a place she understood was far from the capital that had been her world. Flying was novel, it was exciting. *En haut*, she said when they were taking off. Not another word until they touched down.

The experience changed in an instant her perception of what was possible. The gears in her quick mind were turning quickly. Why should this dazzling terminal not be the end of the journey she had been making for as far back as she remembered? Nyogokuru loved her. It stood to reason she must be looking for Béatrice just as persistently as Béatrice was looking for her.

“Come on,” Smith said. “We’ll get a taxi.”

Stepping out of the cocoon of the terminal into the bright hot air, they were disoriented. Smith had the same feeling that had overtaken him on the ferry, crossing from Brazzaville, a bone-deep conviction that he had made a mistake. Again. Your mistakes made you, that was the theory. Part two of the theory was that some of them, the major fuckups, unmade you.

A man with a mechanical-pencil mustache, in a beatnik beret and shades, drew a bead on Smith, glomming onto him with an air of proprietary respect. He spoke discreetly in the cool-cat purr of a hustler selling dope on a street corner.

"Your first visit to Goma, is it not?" he said in French.

Smith disliked the feeling of having been marked out. Unprepared he was, but not a mark. He shook his head.

"I understand," the man said, "I understand completely. One must be cautious in a place like this. Unsavory characters . . . they are everywhere."

When he patted the top of Béatrice's head she pulled away from him reflexively. Good for her.

"You are looking for Mr. Eckstein, I believe," he said to Smith.

"Never heard of him."

There was disbelief in the downturn of his thin smile. "Let us be realistic. In the Congo, just now, everyone is looking for Mr. Eckstein. I will not lie to you."

"I don't give a shit if you lie to me or not."

"What I mean to say is, I do not claim that I can take you to Mr. Eckstein. But I do solemnly vow that I can drop you quite conveniently on the porch of his Goma business manager's office. After that, well, after that you are on your own. Which of course you already knew."

"How about you take a long walk off a short pier?" Smith said, pleased to be able to toss it off in French.

The man was not fazed. He pulled out his phone, punched in a number, handed the phone to Smith.

"*S'il vous plait,* speak with Monsieur Cameron. Monsieur Cameron has lived here forever. He knows who can be trusted and who cannot. Please, speak. He will tell you I am the most reliable driver in Goma. He will confirm the facts: if I tell a man I am capable of delivering him to Mr. Eckstein's business manager, if I give that man my word, the thing will be done."

Smith took Béatrice by the hand and bulled forward in the confusion of travelers jostling one another trying to get someplace else along a straight line, no swerving allowed. The man in the beret decided the American was a born skeptic, constitutionally incapable of accepting the truth when it was offered to him with a chaser and a smile. He did not try to follow them.

"You're Smith, right?"

An American woman was blocking Smith's way. Short, Black, with short hair. In her thirties. She had a face you remembered from high school, the sort-of-cute girl who got along well with everybody but kept her distance.

"Jasmine?"

"My stage name. Use it." She touched Béatrice on the shoulder and said in easy French, "You must be Béatrice."

The girl nodded.

"I like your sneakers," Jasmine said.

"We have come in an airplane to find my grandmother."

"I hope you find her, sweet one. I really hope you do."

"I didn't expect you to meet us," Smith said.

"Soeur Placide sent me a text."

"A text."

"What, nuns can't use cell phones? You some kind of atheist?"

Smith liked her voice. It was hoarse and playful, sexy without trying to be. They were switching back and forth from English to French. They wanted to keep Béatrice in the conversation, but it felt phony for two Americans to be speaking French to one another. It was like performing on a very small stage.

"You ever hear of somebody named Eckstein?" Smith asked her.

She grinned. "Everybody has heard of Eckstein."

"Who is he?"

"Long story. He's an Israeli. Big-time gold dealer. Never mind. We have a car."

With a judicious amount of tactical pushing, and the occasional pirouette to take advantage of an open space, she led the way to a Land Cruiser that was being guarded by a couple of teenaged boys. She gave them a buck apiece, said something Smith didn't understand, and they disappeared smiling.

"Social security," she told Smith in English. "Or free enterprise, if you have Republican leanings. Do you? Never mind, I don't want to know."

A logo was painted on the front doors of the vehicle: a stylized green house, a small blue family nestled securely under the roof. Under the logo, like a solid foundation, the words *Maison Kongo*. She unlocked the door and asked Béatrice where she wanted to sit. Béatrice pointed to the driver's seat.

"Did you bring your *permis de conduire*?"

She slowly nodded as though wondering which pocket she'd left it in.

"Okay," said Jasmine. "Then how about you sit in the back? Smith and I will sit up front and figure out where we're going."

Béatrice got into the back seat without complaining. She was content to be moving. Moving meant looking. Looking led to finding.

They left the airport and drove across a landscape streaked with piled black rock, like a network of hard rivers.

Jasmine pointed to a volcano rising above the city.

"That's Mount Nyiragongo. It blew in two thousand two. Pretty much wiped Goma out. The black stuff is lava. Or do I mean magma? Whatever. It's what's left when the molten mass of ooze cools off."

"So how come they built back in the same place? Do they think it won't blow again?"

"People use the rock to build with. Walls, houses, you name it. That's a good thing, right? People being resourceful?"

Smith asked her, "What is Maison Kongo, and what are you doing working there?"

She shook her head, staring out the windshield. She was driving slowly, attending, because there were so many things she could hit. Carts and vehicles, animals, people with burdens. A man pushing a bicycle laden with jugs of palm oil; a one-man trucking company with low environmental impact. And motorcycles, a hundred of them like quick small fish in an intelligent school moving around and past their natural enemies on their way to some fishy destination.

"Not now. I have a meeting with people from the provincial government. We're asking them to put some money into a shelter that we're trying to get off the ground."

"What kind of shelter?"

"It's for rape victims with kids. The DRC has been the rape capital of the world. Sorry, you probably knew that. Foreigners who spend time here do that, they adopt this superior moral tone with the newcomers. *You haven't seen what I've seen, you're nothing*. Anyway, the women. The trauma of what they went through freezes some of them up. They have a hard time functioning. They need a place of their own."

"And the government won't pony up."

"It would mean ripping off a little less from the budget than they planned. A real sacrifice. Never mind. I made a reservation for you at the Hotel Oiseau. It's on the water. I'll drop you there now."

"Sounds expensive."

"It's not. Moderately funky is what it is. You may or may not have hot water. But you will definitely have a killer view of Lake Kivu."

There was no hot water at the Oiseau, at least not in the room they gave Smith. But Jasmine was right about the view. The hotel sat on a treed bluff. Some of the trees were eucalyptus and gave off a fresh scent. They were full of birds making a joyful racket. From the terrace at the back of the building, you could sit in a wicker chair and look out at the placid, enormous lake spreading out like an advertisement for blue.

They called this part of Africa the Great Lakes region. The heart of Africa. There were a hundred hearts, Smith realized from the terrace, a thousand, ten thousand continental hearts beating away wherever a person went. The world had an infinite number of centers.

Below the terrace was a jetty to which three small boats were tied. A man with a bamboo fishing pole sat in the stern of one of them trying to make up his mind.

"It's good, right?" said Jasmine.

"Do me a favor before you go."

"I'm not into favors. I need to save the little bit of whatever it is I have."

"Stop at the desk on your way out. Tell them I'm not a child molester."

He expected a flip answer, but she understood him. "Right. I can do that."

"Will they believe you?"

Smith liked the way she nodded. There was authority in it.

She told him, "You're a lot like Béatrice, you know."

"How's that?"

"You're both looking for something that doesn't exist."

When she left, Smith ordered some food brought up to Béatrice on the terrace, where she sat rocking in one of the wicker chairs, studying a row of cormorants on a row of rocks whose tops were visible above the water line. Smith knew the long-billed black creatures from the swamps at home. *This is who we are*, they suggested in their thoughtless repose. *This is what we do. We fly, we hunt, we eat fish from the big lake. Let's see you do better.*

Smith had no idea what kinds of things the kid liked to eat. It didn't matter. He took what they had. A plateful of French fries glistening in grease. A couple of hard-boiled eggs on a plate with a little hill of salt, a pond of pepper.

"Here's the key to the room," he told her. "After you eat, don't wander too far."

"I will look for Nyogokuru."

"No, you won't."

She bristled, not liking being told what to do, what not to do. In Kinshasa she was her own boss.

"It's not safe," Smith explained.

That made no sense to her. No place was safe, everybody knew that. You took your chances. Chances were what you had.

To convince her to stay put, he lied.

"I'm going to ask around," he said. "Talk to a few people. Maybe somebody has seen your grandmother."

The logic was faulty, but the bribe was acceptable. She nodded, and he took a taxi downtown. He wound up in the Okapi Express, an internet café with decent machines, decent coffee, decent music too loud to let a person think about blood diamonds or volcanic eruptions.

Because of the time difference he was not sure Maybelline was up, but when he sent her an email she fired back a text.

Hey there. Still in bed, just layin' here thinkin'
bout you!!!!!!!!!!!!!!!!!

Best not do that, girl, you're turning me on.

Okay, I'll stop teasin'. Don't mean I'm stoppin' thinkin'. I got an active imagination. You back on the rig?

Nope, I'm in a place called Goma.

That a country? You still in Africa?

It's a city. In the Congo, way out in the east.

What in the hell you doin' there?

Long story, Maybelline

Uh oh

What?

Anytime you say my name, means you
want my full attention. What is it you want to tell me?

I met this girl.

Course you did.

No, not a woman. I'm talking about a
little girl. Her name is Beatrice. She's
an orphan.

I'm listening I guess

How did he tell Maybelline about the Congo? When they lived together, she had not been into the news.

She never even turned on the weather report. *Why should I? Goddamn news is all bad all the time. I get enough unsatisfyin' shit goin' on in my own life, I don't need the world's heartbreak too.*

The kid's family beat her up and
threw her out.
They thought she was a witch.

Is she?

Come on, Maybelline. She's been
living on the
street in Kinshasa.

That's the capital right? I looked it up when
you said you was headed there.

Right. She has it in her head that her
grandma
is still alive, her grandma will take
care of her.

And the grandma lives in Goma

Not sure about that. The real reason I'm here, it's all related, I'm looking into another possibility.

What kind of possibility?

Promise you won't fall on your ass laughin.

I promise

Diamonds

Right.

I'm serious.

She didn't believe him. That was okay, for now. It was not something he could explain across cyberspace. If he tried, he'd feel like a doofus.

Changing the subject, ok? I seen your sister the other day. She was out at that strip mall on 27, the one with the Denny's? Handing out pamflets. Hate to say it, sweetie, but she looked old. Worn out. Like a bag lady with a mouth full of Jesus.

Lu Ann Farrier, Smith's sister, was a Jehovah's Witness, or she had been when he left the U.S. Ever since her husband got himself sent to Angola, she had been experimenting with churches, trying them on and taking them off like so many sweaters that didn't quite fit. None of them filled the hole that was left when her life got dynamited.

A mud-mouthed prosecutor had charged Willard Farrier with running the biggest chop shop in Louisiana. Some kind of state record, that was how he presented the case. He was a sly son of a bitch with local charm and a good sense of timing. He made the jury feel like they were part of history. And they bought it, convicting Lu Ann's Willard after twenty minutes' deliberation. The arrest, the trial, the sentence blew Lu Ann away piece by flyaway piece. She'd had no idea Will was up to anything illegal. All she knew was he was a good provider, a quiet man who didn't talk about work when he got home, and why should he if work was work, it wasn't fun? So she had maintained throughout months of daze, and Smith believed her. She had always shown an advanced ability to pretend.

From where Smith sat now, in an internet café in Eastern Congo, the situation looked different. He had left the U.S. accusing his sister, in his mind at least and once or twice over the phone when he'd had a few drinks, of abandoning him. She had done the same number on him that their mother did on both of them. Walked out, no forwarding address.

He wanted to talk about Lu Ann with Maybelline. She could help him think it through. But not in bubbled bullets, little poems that didn't rhyme. Face to face, that was what he needed.

Listen

Told you I been listenin

I want to spend some time with you.

How you gonna make that happen, boy?

It'll happen. Don't worry by the way if you don't hear from me for a few days.

That sounds scary. I don't like it.

Think about me.

Cant hardly think about nuthin else. Got this tingling feeling down south of the border.

Keep tingling.

It cost him not to tell her he was getting her a Camaro. But a lifetime of failing to deliver had taught him that much. You didn't overpromise. You didn't even promise. What you did was show up with the goods. In this case, you drove into a woman's driveway behind the wheel of the car of her dreams. You tossed her the key. Then and only then did she take you for a ride.

He had to cut off the conversation. It was making him stupid. He could not afford to let more brain cells leach away in confusion. He had two choices: keep his wits about him, or find himself up the well-known excrement waterway without a means of propulsion. A kid in enormous sneakers was hovering behind him, smelling of lemon and cigarettes, impatient to get at the computer.

"Diamonds," Smith told him.

The kid nodded. He knew exactly what Smith meant.

"Diamants, mon frère Américain."

It occurred to Smith, as he went out the door, that maybe Béatrice had lied to him. She was more than capable of taking off on her own if she decided she could find her grandmother. If she disappeared, there went the diamonds, real or fake.

But she had stayed put. He found the girl on the terrace of the Oiseau where he had left her. Backpack strapped tight, she was acting out some sort of story for Jasmine, who was back from her meeting with government authorities. Along with her new possessions, she carried her same old magic in the pack. A marble wrapped in a snake skin: did it have enough power to conjure a theoretical grandmother?

As she moved up and down the floorboards, twisting her torso, flailing and protecting herself with her arms, she fleshed out the movement with words in what turned out to be Swahili. When Smith came out onto the terrace, she froze. Story over.

"Did you find my Nyogokuru?"

"Not yet."

Okay, it was a lie. Leading her on, he was a long way from sainthood. He felt bad for the girl, stuck in the hard east with an unqualified escort like him, clueless where it counted. But she took the news with fortitude. Her grandmother had not been at the airport. Fine. Smith hadn't turned her up when he went out looking. Fine. It only meant they had to stay on the trail.

Smith said to Jasmine in English, "You've been holding out on me."

"What's that supposed to mean?"

"You didn't say you knew Swahili."

In French, she told him, "Béatrice has just been telling me how she and her grandmother ran through the forest to get away from men chasing them. They hid behind trees."

Béatrice raised her arms to demonstrate magnitude.

"Very big trees," Jasmine explained. "So tall their branches scratched the clouds. As they stood there hiding, monkeys threw fruit down at them from the high branches. They had to be very still, or the bad men would discover them."

Béatrice threw a demonstration fruit. A banana, it looked like to Smith, although he was not an expert on invisible fruit.

"It's not a real memory," he told Jasmine in English. "Sister Placide says she never met her grandmother. Before today she never even left Kinshasa."

"It's real in one way."

"How's that?"

"It affects her."

"Ask her old she is."

"I did. She's not sure. I'd say she's twelve."

Then she told the girl that she and Smith needed to do some work. Béatrice shrugged, meaning, *So work*.

"There's a television in your room."

"*Oui*."

"Do you know how to make it work?"

She knew. She took her backpack and went.

"Soeur Placide is right," said Jasmine.

"About what?"

"The girl has some sort of power. A force of nature, my Daddy'd say."

Smith asked her, "You don't think her grandmother is alive, do you?"

She shook her head slowly. "Why don't you go hunt us up a couple of beers?"

He went. Inside, at the bar, he ordered from the woman on duty, understanding from what was not said that rustling up two beers presented a logistical challenge that might take some time. He went back outside. As they waited on the terrace for the beers to appear, he asked Jasmine how her meeting had gone.

"Inconclusive."

"That's a lame word."

"Fair enough. How about this: we heard lots of promises, all of them empty. We were treated to a display of high emotion, all of it phony. We were promised a donation that will never appear."

Eventually an old man in a long white lab coat brought two bottles of Nkoyi to them on an aluminum tray. On the breast pocket of the coat, an embroidered oval patch read Richmond Reliable Care Providers. One of the sleeves was pinned shut; the man lacked an arm. He fumbled in his pocket for an opener but did not find one. There was something substantial on his mind that had nothing to do with the people on whom he waited. Smith uncapped the bottles using his Swiss Army knife.

"That's funny," Jasmine said.

"What?"

"We don't usually get Nkoyi out here. It's a Kinshasa beer. Nkoyi means leopard."

Smith nodded. He was not about to tell this woman that was what the kid called him.

Jasmine poured a little beer into her glass. She tapped the picture of the leopard on the bottle with a thumb nail.

Smith said, "You ready to tell me why you're in the Congo?"

"I'll show you mine if you show me yours."

He carried Lajeune's ring in the watch pocket of his jeans. He pulled it out and showed her. "I won it in a poker game. In Brazzaville. It's supposed to be the down payment on some diamonds."

"Sister Placide told me you were a treasure hunter. With a good Catholic soul."

Smith shook his head. "What about you?"

"My father was a FAO."

"Is that a good thing or a bad thing?"

"Sorry. Foreign Area Officer. That's a person in the Army who specializes in a region. Daddy chose Africa. He was my hero."

She stopped. Her eyes teared. Smith waited to learn the particulars of another unhappy ending. Why did things want to go bad? Was there a secret seed in them that sprouted specifically to rot and take them down? Given the history of the Smiths from whom he sprang, it was a question he ought to have asked Lu Ann, part of the conversation they never got around to having. And now she was passing out leaflets advertising Jesus like some kind of stain remover for the blackened soul. Suddenly, for no reason he could discover, he felt naked. Coming to the Congo he had been plucked, and foul air blew on the tender spots that feathers were supposed to protect.

"Daddy died in Afghanistan," Jasmine told him. "I don't talk about it."

"I'm sorry," he said.

"When I was growing up," she said, "Daddy often had a billet at one of our embassies in Africa. Some of the assignments, we went with him. It was a good life."

"And you learned Swahili."

They both swigged a little. The beer tasted good. Then here came the guy in the lab coat with a plateful of salted nuts. He placed it on the table between them with a gesture that suggested pain in the arm that wasn't there.

When he left, they were the only people on the terrace. The dark birds kept their places on the boulders in Lake Kivu.

Jasmine said, "In nineteen ninety-three, when things were falling apart in Rwanda, they sent my father to the embassy in Kigali."

"Just before the genocide."

She nodded. "The Defense Department sent him there TDY."

"Come again?"

"Temporary duty. He was backing up the defense attaché. The attaché was Army, too. He was what they call the senior defense official."

"Meaning he called the shots."

"Correct, at least on the military stuff. He and Daddy did not see eye to eye."

The waiter was gone, wordless and wobbly. For a moment, the terrace felt like a getaway, a good place for a plucked man to catch his breath, figure out his next move. Smith wondered what Béatrice was watching on TV. How had she learned to use a remote? There were no televisions at the orphanage.

He said to Jasmine, "So what was the embassy doing?"

"You know how they say armies always fight the last war?"

"I'll take your word for it."

"The embassy kept trying to make a peace agreement work. They couldn't see that the situation had changed, peace was not going to break out. They had to evacuate the embassy in a convoy. Daddy took a Rwandan man in his truck, a young Tutsi who had done some work for the embassy. When the convoy got to the Burundi border, there was a checkpoint. The guards took the Tutsi— his name was Fabian, he wanted to teach English, he had twin baby girls and a Hutu wife—they pulled him out of the truck and dragged him off. Daddy got out and tried to stop them."

"Pretty brave."

"It was brave, yeah. But it didn't accomplish anything. The last thing Daddy saw before he went across the border was one of the soldiers hitting Fabian in the gut with the butt of his rifle, and Fabian going down."

"That's what haunted your father."

"That, and what happened afterward."

"Which was what?"

"Daddy was good at building relationships. That's what a defense attaché does. People trusted him, they told him stuff we wanted to know."

"We?"

She shook her head, impatient of the interruption.

"Because he was good at the work, the Army kept him in Central Africa for the next couple of years. After the genocide, the U.S. government sided with the Tutsis. They were the ones who had been wiped out, right? And the Americans felt guilty for letting the killing happen.

"When the Rwandan Patriotic Forces took Kigali, lots of Hutus fled to the Congo. Lots as in hundreds of thousands. Some were killers, they were the men and the boys who had murdered all those Tutsis. More of them were just people trying not to get killed themselves. One of the things we did . . . "

"There you go with that 'we' again."

"The U.S. government."

Smith swallowed more beer and said, too loudly, "Well, shit, Jasmine, don't put me on that mailing list."

"Sorry?"

"I never had a goddamn thing to do with the American government. Anyway they wouldn't want a person like me.

They sent me out on a mission, I'd mess it up. Get lost in the woods, lose my poison pill, corrupt the wrong dictator."

"Don't be a child. It's like original sin."

"What is?"

"Political guilt. What happened in Rwanda, what happened in this country. Iraq, Afghanistan, it's the same story. Of course it's your fault. It's my fault. It's our fault because of where we were born. Like it or not, it's your tax dollars at work."

"Something pushed your daddy over the edge, didn't it?"

"The biggest regret of his life was it *didn't* push him over."

"What?"

"There was a war going on here, in this country, at the time. The dictator was losing his grip. The place was a cauldron. And then all those Hutus coming across the border, running away from the Tutsis when they took power. Chaos, violence, on a scale that blows the mind."

"And?"

"We were helping the Tutsi government locate the Hutus. That made it a whole lot easier to target and kill them. We were sending military aircraft out looking for them, then giving the Tutsis in Kigali the coordinates."

"What do you expect?" Smith said. "People fight back. It's natural. Let 'em kill a few hundred thousand Americans and see how you feel."

"You don't get it, do you?"

"Make me smarter than I was when I woke up this morning."

"The Tutsis were not just killing the *génocidaires*, they were wiping out everybody. Farmers, women, children, you name it.

Everybody. They slaughtered them wherever they found them. When they could, they raped them, they robbed them, they terrorized them. And *then* they killed them."

"You're saying the United States government was helping them do this evil shit."

She nodded. "They also lobbied to put an end to the UN peacekeeping mission in Rwanda, which could have saved some lives. My daddy knew what was going on. He knew the Tutsis were killing innocent people. He made his views known."

"Good for him."

She shook her head, still angry all these years later.

"He made his case, going through channels. They take that whole chain-of-command thing seriously in the government. The higher-ups heard him out, but they said he was not being realistic. What did he expect was going to happen after a genocide? The Tutsis and the Hutus weren't going to kiss and make up. It was natural for them to sympathize with the Tutsis. But their sympathy made it harder for them to see what the new government was doing."

"Did they boot your father?"

"You want to hear the worst?"

He nodded.

"Some of the people up my father's reporting chain thought Daddy wasn't tough enough to do the job. Because he was African American. They didn't come out and say it, but they believed he couldn't be objective because his skin was the same color as the Rwandans'. They thought his judgment was clouded, he was too emotional."

"So what did he do?"

"He stayed and did the job they told him to do."

"And it haunted him."

"One of his jobs was liaison with the new Tutsi army. Daddy had to pass his contacts the coordinates they used to hunt Hutus on the run."

The cormorants on the exposed rocks out on the lake were suddenly agitated. Did they have ears? They must. What they heard coming from the terrace was enough to send them into the sky in an explosion of indignation. Jasmine and Smith watched them skim low across the lake until they were out of sight.

Smith thought about what Soeur Placide had told him under the influence of a thimbleful of Calvados. You could not work off guilt, your own or anybody else's. It was not a bank loan, with payments.

"You Catholic?" he asked Jasmine.

The question offended her. "Momma and Daddy raised us Baptist. I fell away from the church a while back, not that it's any of your business. How come you want to know?"

"Sister Placide is lucky."

"Why is that?"

"She believes God can lift the weight from people's shoulders."

"Baptists are familiar with the concept of grace."

"No offense intended. I was just kind of wondering what the rest of us are supposed to do, I mean if we're not a Belgian nun doing good work in an orphanage. But you're wrong."

"About what?"

"All this terrible stuff. The genocide. The wars in Africa. Internet trolls. It's not my fault."

One thing Jasmine had in common with Béatrice was how dense they both believed him to be. She opened her mouth to take him to task, shut it without bothering.

"I was fifteen years old when the genocide happened," he told her. "I was a dumb kid in a jerkwater town in the State of Louisiana. My mind was on girls and cars and loud music. My mother was AWOL and my old man was a construction guy who specialized in getting laid off. At our house we didn't sit around with a glass of wine talking politics. The only Congo I ever heard of was Congo Square in New Orleans. So tell me how all the murder in Africa is my fault."

She looked out at the complacent lake as if somebody had thrown the words she required there, too far out to swim after.

"My first month here, I met a nurse from Vermont. Nancy Schmidt. She was working for a clinic. I think she had what you get before they diagnose you with PTSD. We went out for drinks one night, and she told me the Congo is an equal-opportunity destroyer. It fucks with everybody's head. Africans, Europeans, Americans, makes no difference. The country does not discriminate."

"It's not my fault Béatrice's father beat her up and threw her out on the street."

No reaction, no response. After a minute he lobbed a stink bomb into the hole of silence.

"If you'd told me a couple of weeks ago I was going to admire some little orphan witch girl more than I admired Abraham Lincoln, I would have laughed in your face. But I can't fix a single goddamn thing in this country, I'm not that kind of mechanic. On top of which, the company I work for is probably going to can me. Dereliction of duty, they actually have a rule that says that. So excuse me if I don't cry in my beer over Africa."

"I know a guy, a musician. He's a Munyamulenge."

"That won't help," Smith said. "The girl's people are Banyamulenge."

Jasmine grinned. "Munyamulenge is one. Banyamulenge are more than one. The name means 'People from Mulenge.'"

"That's a place in the Congo, I guess."

"Some people claim the Banyamulenge are not really Congolese, they're Rwandans."

"So?"

"So if you can convince yourself somebody is a foreigner, maybe you also convince yourself they're taking something that belongs to you—land, cows, whatever—and they deserve to die."

"What about your musician friend?"

"He's totally wired into the community. If anybody knows the couple Béatrice says she saw taking those mythical diamonds of yours, Paul will."

"Cool. Let's go see him. I'll buy him a steak dinner."

"Paul is hard to catch. He sleeps all day and plays music all night. The band is kind of a political project. He recruited people from a bunch of different ethnic groups to play. The operating principle is, if they can play music together, they can live together."

"So what's the problem? You don't like music?"

He liked what she said, and the way she said it.

"I like music. I like Congolese music a whole lot."

Nothing happened early at Club Mirage. At nine, when Smith and Jasmine showed up, there was no sign of Paul Kanea or anybody else. Béatrice between them, daughter-like, they walked from the Boulevard Kanyamuhanga into the sandy ground of an open patio around which the club was built.

It was a still life, composed for their benefit. Low-backed chairs sat like patient patrons around fifteen tables. The tables were covered with immaculate white cloths. In the center of each, a ceramic vase displayed an extravagant bunch of fake flowers.

The tables were arranged with an eye to three connected low risers on which the band's equipment was set up. A drum kit sat on one of them, a six-inch hole gaping in the head of the bass drum as if somebody lacking rhythm had kicked it in. On another riser, microphone cords sent silent signals into the sound system. On the third, a purple bass guitar rested in a stand, the perfect picture of sound.

At the back of the patio, a thatched roof covered a long hardwood bar behind which ranged a refrigerator and a monstrous ice machine, stacks of glassware, and shelves with rows of liquor bottles. But no bartender. No waiters, either, and no patrons to be served.

"You sure you got the right place?" Smith asked Jasmine.

She gave him a dirty look. They took seats at a table near the stage, and Jasmine persuaded Béatrice to take off her backpack. The girl placed it on the chair next to hers, finding it absently with her fingers every couple of minutes, just to be sure it was still there.

When Béatrice made it clear she was coming with them, Jasmine brought along some kids' books in French. The nuns at Maid of Orléans had spent time teaching the girl to read. Once they saw her hunger, they pushed her. She picked up a book from the stack on the table as though it were the most natural thing in the world, she read bedtime stories every night of her life in stranger places than this. Everything that was happening was new, and none of it fazed her.

Smith had made the mistake of emailing Kluge the number of the phone he'd picked up that day, a reflex of responsibility he now regretted. When it rang, he knew it was the foreman and switched it off. No point giving him the satisfaction of firing him in real time. He and Jasmine heard the disembodied clatter of pots and dishes coming from the kitchen, next to the bar. Nobody appeared.

Twenty minutes later, a statuesque woman with bouffant hair straightened and dyed copper came out from the kitchen and began setting the tables. In the short green dress she wore, her legs were weapons. She paid them no attention, not even when Jasmine waved in her direction. Béatrice picked up another book. Another twenty minutes, and a waiter with a chest muscled like Superman's brought them a bottle of Scotch they hadn't ordered, along with glasses and an ice bucket. He looked at Béatrice, turned around, came back from the bar with a bottle of orange soda.

"Did you want Scotch?" Smith asked Jasmine.

"It's what's they have."

She poured them both small shots over ice, and Béatrice drank her soda.

The evening was cool, the air had the texture of peach fuzz, and Paul Kanea walked in with a guitar case. He kissed Jasmine, shook Smith's hand, and said something to Béatrice that put her on her guard. He was built like a marathon runner and had light brown skin. Would another Congolese man pick him out on the street and identify him as a friend, an enemy? What if you wanted to be a neutral party?

Smith was ready to jump into it, getting out of the man whatever he was willing to give. Jasmine knew better. They talked about nothing in particular for a few minutes. As he tuned his guitar, Paul asked Jasmine low-key questions about the new shelter for rape victims. To Smith's inexpert eye, the guitar appeared to be a Korean knock-off of a classic American rock & roll axe. In a poster that used to hang on Lu Ann's bedroom wall when they were kids, Jimi Hendrix played a white one just like it only left-handed. The expression on Hendrix's face made you think that art hurt, and the pain was worth it. For a moment, Smith saw his sister in the parking lot outside Denny's accosting people with their big full bellies, advertising her Jesus cure. He felt an urge to shield her from their indifference, their contempt. He had some making up to do, once he went home.

Taking his cue from Jasmine's patience, he poured Paul a Scotch and asked him, "What's the name of your band?"

"Synthèse."

"Making a new thing out of old ones."

"Something like that. Coming up with a name, well." He strummed a chord. Even unamped, it sounded good. "I thought for some time the problem was insurmountable."

"Why is that?"

"We speak two hundred languages in this country, if you count the dialects. A name is a political act, don't you see? The words you speak proclaim your identity. At the same time they may spit in your neighbor's eye. Here in the east many people know Swahili, but French can be a more neutral way to talk to one another."

"The Belgians' language."

Kanea nodded. "The mother tongue of the people who colonized us, yes. What is it you imagine we lack, a sense of irony, or of history?"

"I'm too new here to imagine anything at all."

"Synthèse is still in the experimental phase."

There was something professorial about Kanea. He had a story of his own, which Smith would not hear. Playing scales up and down the neck of his guitar, warming up before plugging in, the Congolese man could not help making it come out like music, strong and steady.

Smith wished Maybelline were there with him. She'd had a thing for guitar players which she convinced him was pure admiration, nothing low-down about it. It had to do with respect for strong sensitive fingers. And her fascination with guitarists never bothered Smith. He'd had his own thing for female country singers in high-heeled cowboy boots. It was the way they clutched the mic as they sang. If that was low-down, it was a good cruising altitude.

People were drifting into the club, staking out tables, greeting and embracing one another as if surprised by the greatest piece of luck in the history of the world, finding themselves together, here and now on a glorious evening at the Mirage. The Congolese men were casual, prosperous, sure of their place with their phones, their deep pockets, their bodyguards in the background. The women who accompanied them kissed one another, held each other's hands and confided something small as they checked one another other out. They laughed loudly but sat languidly, expecting the instant deference of the waiters, which they got. Not all the women were beautiful, or young, but all of them knew precisely what they were worth.

A table's worth of UN military men showed up and parked near Smith and Jasmine. They were officers, entitled to a night out on this East Congo town, and their expectations were as high as everybody else's.

The musicians showed up one at a time as if representing different constituencies, wary of the pleasures of the reconciliation table.

It took Smith a moment to figure out what had changed. In the space of an incalculable minute the club went from the still quiet of getting ready to full-on racket. Waiters were serving drinks, leaning down to put menus into the hands of patrons, distributing little plates of nuts and olives and cubes of white cheese with toothpicks. They laughed at the customers' jokes, which might or not be funny, Smith was in no position to judge.

Béatrice put down her book. She methodically scanned the face of every woman who arrived at the Mirage, believing the big world was small enough to catch her grandmother coming across the patio.

"What do you know about Congolese music?" Jasmine asked Smith.

"As much as I know about the Civil War."

"The South never gave up."

"So I hear."

"You don't have to chase the music. Just sit here, and it will come to you."

She tipped her glass in his direction, rattling the ice. She was relaxed, ready to party. After a long day working to improve the lives of rape victims, she had earned it. An alert waiter noticed the rattle and poured her another shot with the enthusiasm of a man who had no goal in life beyond pleasing the people at the tables in his station. A patch covered his left eye, and the left side of his face was a map of burn scars.

Smith caught most of the French streaming through the club, the ripples and eddies and quick currents of words in the language his mother had whispered into his baby ears before abandoning her post. It was what mothers did, they licked their children's ears with their mother tongue. Catching the words, and the feel of the words, made him feel like a different person. Suddenly he was a man with keener ears, sharper eyes, a capacity to appreciate things he had not previously thought about, known about, imagined.

Paul Kanea was the band's anchor. He was in charge, although he wielded no visible scepter. Standing in the middle of the middle riser, he played on every song. On some of them he also sang. His voice was deeper than you would expect from such a compact body. He provided the patter, too, engaging the crowd, making them feel they were getting something special in the way of entertainment that night. Smith was only amateur audience, but he believed they were.

Musicians showed up on the stage, played a few songs, made way for somebody else, came back later and played some more in a new configuration. Some of them changed instruments, moving on a signal only they perceived from a guitar to the drum kit with the hole in the head to the purple bass, and back. A massive woman of fifty with major hair extensions in a design of spikes commanded the stage for a while, singing with a skinny man half her age in a long shirt with the same design of blue and black diamonds her dress featured. At the peak, there were eleven people on stage, and all of them had more talent than they needed, they could have thrown half of it away and still shone.

The music was loud. It was driving. It was like no music Smith had ever heard. There was percussion in the rhythm section. There was virtuosity in the musicians' fingers. The arrangements were intricate, the voices and the instruments locking into one another in repeating patterns of sound that started in one place unknown to the American and moved to another place, just as full of strange light. Then they brought him home again, a changed man.

Smith got up and went looking for the rest room. Somehow he wound up at the bar standing next to a blue helmet guy, an Italian from Brindisi. Major Vinciguerra was looking into his Scotch as if he'd dropped something into the glass and couldn't get his eye on it. He looked away long enough to diagnose Smith, in English, as an American.

"How can you tell?"

Vinciguerra shook his head. He looked like a man who shaved twice a day even when he was off duty. In his dark smart eyes a sense of duty fought with a sense of lost opportunity.

"You don't want to know."

Smith told him, "I hate this fucking place."

"Of course. You are only here because of the gold."

Diamonds, actually, Smith did not say. "What gold?"

Vinciguerra said confidently, "You're looking for Eckstein. They're all looking for Eckstein."

"Eckstein can kiss my Louisiana ass."

The Italian may not have known anything about Louisiana. The way he shook his head, it was clear he had been a tragic actor before joining the military.

"I fail to understand how so many people like you believe they can deceive the man. You imagine if only you can get close to him, he will be persuaded you are the solution to his problems."

"Fuck Eckstein," Smith said. Rising from a hidden pool, his anger was real. "And fuck his problems."

"I agree," Vinciguerra said with sudden animation. "I could not agree more."

He seemed to have located whatever was in his glass of whiskey. He drained it. The conversation was over.

Smith went back to the table. He lost the distressing sense of time running away from him, the anxiety of being in a place he shouldn't be. He tasted what Scotch did to melting ice cubes in the bottom of his glass. He put extra salt on a grilled fish that Jasmine called *capitaine*. He dumped *pili pili* hot sauce on sticks of fried cassava. He surrendered to the sound.

At a certain point he and Jasmine were dancing, halfway lit and happy, while Béatrice chased a big two-toned lizard that had crept across the sand to the foot of their table. At another point, the band took a break between sets, a sound system blared Congolese rumba tunes, and Paul Kanea came to their table. He was a journeyman, confident in his ability to build sturdy things: music, bridges, relationships. Béatrice had gone to sleep, her body curled on two chairs pushed against each other. She was hugging her backpack as though it were a baby doll.

Kanea sipped from a glass of soda water the waiter brought him.

"We are looking for a Banyamulenge couple," Jasmine told him. "Their names are Bernadette and Bobagu Mavugo. They may have been in Kin, maybe recently."

Paul was doubtful. "That's all you have to go on?"

"That's all," Smith said, more offended than he needed to be. He was still angry at Eckstein, whoever he was.

His words came out too loud, falling into a gap of silence that descended on the club in thirty seconds. The waiters stopped waiting. They, and the musicians on their break, and the patrons at their tables, were all staring at a man who had just come into the patio surrounded by uniformed men with guns and active eyes deployed in a diamond of protection.

"It's Sikatenda," Paul muttered.

"Jesus," said Jasmine.

Béatrice, her sleeping self alert to the silence, sat up. She blinked. She too stared at the man. Maybe that was why the security diamond gave way and he headed for their table.

He was lean to the point of gaunt, tall, maybe forty. He wore gold-rimmed glasses that gave him a fastidious look, the look of a man who did not like dirt. The fatigues were pressed, with a crease, and his military boots gleamed black. He hovered over their table ignoring the adults, cupping Béatrice's chin in a bony hand that had a delicate aspect. The gesture was fatherly if you remembered that some fathers were killers.

In French he said, "It's a little Munyamulenge girl, is it not?"

Béatrice glared. Her instincts were sound. No way was she giving anything away to this sinister dude.

"What is your name, little one?"

She shook her head. Everyone at the club was pretending not to be bothered by Sikatenda's presence. Waiters self-consciously began moving, serving, pouring. Canned music crackled through the sound system; someone's idea of normal. People began talking again, although they kept their voices low and looked around less than before. The gaiety was gone.

"No name?" said Sikatenda. "Too bad. I wonder what fate lies ahead for a nameless child in this country of ours."

Béatrice snapped her head back, away from contact with Sikatenda's hand. Her fit of pique made him laugh. As his bodyguards scanned the club for threats, he sized up the adults at the table. Meantime there was consternation nearby at the UN officers' table. They believed they should do something but did not agree on what.

Sikatenda's eye rested finally on Jasmine. In a soft and civil voice he said, "You are an American, no? A grand nation favored of God."

When she shook her head he told her, "Do not deny it. God has reached out his hand and caressed the forehead of the Statue of Liberty, *comme ça*."

He touched Jasmine's forehead with the palm of his hand, not quite caressing. She did not flinch. He was evaluating her and approved of her steadiness.

"The divine preference for the country of your birth is a known fact, beyond dispute. We are aware, by the way, of your mission in Kivu."

Jasmine stayed calm. Smith did not know her well enough to guess what lay underneath her unflustered surface.

"Sadly," she said, "there is no lack of work."

He frowned. Was there a rebuke of some sort in her words? He said to Smith, "And you, Monsieur le Américain. What is your business in Goma?"

"Just passing through."

Sikatenda shook his head. "Hah! Yet another *chasseur de fortune*."

It took Smith a second to process the phrase.

"I'm here enjoying the music," he told the Congolese man who was doing an excellent job creeping him out.

"I myself," Sikatenda told him, "I do not believe this outlandish tale of Monsieur Eckstein."

"What tale?"

"Please do not dissemble. You have heard what we all have heard. The notorious Israeli man of business is experiencing difficulty moving a vast quantity of gold out of the country. Yet I put to you the question: why should Eckstein have difficulty? Since colonial days no plunderer of the Congo has experienced the slightest inconvenience, removing his booty beyond our national reach."

Smith debated a punk answer, decided against it.

One of the guards took a call on his cell. He turned his head, listened, cupped his hand and nodded furiously as he spoke. When he hung up, he approached Sikatenda and whispered in his ear. Sikatenda waved him away impatiently. He spoke to Paul.

"You too. You are known, Munyamulenge man. This dream of yours, this misplaced reconciliation project, I fear it may become a nightmare. Too much blood has been shed for your foolishness to succeed. You understand that, yet you persist. It is not wise."

Paul was motionless and scared and passively defiant. He knew this was how murder happened. A word, a look, a gesture. An impulse and a reaction. If Sikatenda raised his hand, he made the musician a target, and any one of the men guarding him would shoot. They would shoot him happily while the UN soldiers dithered two tables away. Did saving a single musician's life at a nightclub fall within the scope of their mission in the Congo? Before they acted they had to calculate consequences. They could not be accused of mission creep.

There was a stare-down. Neither man looked away, although a film blurred Paul's eyes and a vein in his neck stood up, pulsing a warning. Sikatenda seemed to be curious just how long the musician would tolerate the heat of his gaze. But his mood shifted abruptly, as though a plug in his brain had been pulled. He grunted in the direction of a bodyguard, and the security diamond reformed around him. They were gone in the next minute.

The instant they disappeared into the forgiving night, the noise level at the club jacked back up. People laughed like survivors. It had been a close call but the danger, *Dieu merci*, was over and gone. Life went on. Let's raise a glass and tell the story of the night one of the Congo's notorious warlords strolled into the Mirage. I was there. I was there and lived to tell you.

"Okay," said Smith. "I'm listening."

Béatrice was listening, too, her eyes hollowed by exhaustion.

"His name is Crispin Sikatenda," said Paul. "He leads a Mai Mai gang known as the Army of the Revival of the Word of God."

Jasmine told Smith, "When journalists come to the Congo, they have this idea what a warlord is supposed to be. They poke around, they ask questions. Sikatenda is what they come up with."

Smith was drenched with sweat. His knees felt rubbery even though he was sitting. "He's scary as shit."

"I'm tired," Béatrice said to none of them. "I want to sleep."

"These people you are looking for," Paul said.

"Bernadette and Bobagu Mavugo."

"Why do you want to wish to find them?"

Here was the moment. Smith had been dreading it. It fell to Jasmine to answer Kanea's question. If she said anything about diamonds, he was screwed. There was no reason not to, but she didn't.

"There is a chance they may know something of the little girl's grandmother."

"And you?" Paul wanted to know.

Smith told him, "She's an orphan. I told the nuns at the orphanage in Kinshasa I'd bring her this far."

"Out of the goodness of your heart."

"Something like that."

As lies went, this one was thin. But Paul did not push. It was time for the second set. There was no reason for optimism, but Smith felt some. The Scotch helped. So did dancing with Jasmine. She was into it, and he was into her. The music was louder this time around. The musicians on the risers were loose and steady, riding a sound wave of their own making.

The woman with the spike extensions did a blues number she said she was borrowing from Koko Taylor, but to Smith it sounded totally Congolese. She was feeding off the crowd. The UN officers were delighted that no terrible thing had come of the warlord's appearance. In the morning they would write a report. They were on their feet clapping and calling for more.

More was a brilliant idea. Why hadn't Smith thought of it?

Smith danced. He kissed Jasmine. She kissed back. They drank. They danced.

Béatrice had gone back to sleep, snuggled on the chairs.

After the second set Paul Kanea came back to their table to tell them, "I will ask around. If these people you want to see are in Goma, someone will know them."

He and Jasmine put each other's numbers in their phones. Smith scooped up Béatrice. It was kind of a cool thing that she stayed asleep in his arms.

At the hotel Smith saw a light on the back terrace. He went there to find the one-armed waiter reading a Bible and sipping red wine. He had taken off his lab coat. It hung draped on the back of the chair from which he looked up at the American who was standing over him unsteadily.

"Restaurant is closed," he said.

"I'm not hungry."

"Bar is closed, too."

"I'm not thirsty. Mind if I sit down?"

"*À votre guise.*"

Smith took the chair opposite his. The waiter closed his Bible. After a moment calculated to demonstrate his unhappiness at being interrupted, he placed it on a low wicker table.

"I know nothing that will be of the slightest use to you," he told Smith. "I would not know a bag of gold from a bag of carrots."

"Who said anything about gold?"

Everybody assuming he was after Eckstein's frigging gold— it was starting to bug Smith.

The waiter snorted. Then, in a display of one-handed dexterity, he tapped a cigarette from a pack on the table, picked up an old Zippo lighter, delivered the cigarette between his lips, and lit it. He puffed. He put the lighter back on the table. On the case was a faint image of a woman who looked like Rosie the Riveter with cleavage. He did not offer Smith a smoke.

In the night quiet, the waves of Lake Kivu lapped like contented cats. Smith felt like talking. The man's attitude put him off— it was meant to put him off— but he took it as a professional challenge to get a conversation going.

"That the Bible you're reading?"

"It is the Word of God."

"My mother used to read it out loud to me when I was a boy."

That was an exaggeration. He had one dread-infected memory of having her read something to him that might well have been the word of God in French. But the passage she happened to choose brought on tears. They fell in hot sheets as Smith sat next to her on the couch wondering how he had screwed this one up. *I need to be a beautiful woman,* she sobbed. *Not just on the outside but on the inside, too.* In his smothering sense of responsibility for her unhappiness, Smith assured her that she was *beautiful, beautiful, beautiful, Momma you really are, I love you.* He had difficulty breathing in her embrace as she pulled him to her, rocking and crying and saying loving things that he needed to hear with the same intensity that she needed to be a beautiful woman.

"How much are they paying you?" the waiter wanted to know.

"Who?"

"The American government."

Here it was again, the same bullshit story about him and the red white & blue. It ticked him off. In column A he was an adventurer. In column B he was a spy. Wasn't there any column C?

"The American government doesn't pay me a damn thing."

The waiter nodded. "I see."

"What do you see?"

"You're freelancing. It takes all sorts of operatives to satisfy the empire's great hunger. Still, you must be very careful, eh? That beast you're feeding knows how to bite."

"I'm not a spy."

The man poured himself a little more wine.

"One day," he said, "the wrath of God will fall on your head. He will smite America for its Congo sins, not to mention all the other countries it has oppressed and kept poor." He put down the glass to add a clarifying detail. "Since the end of the Second World War."

Smith was curious. If the man was going to lecture him, he might as well take the full course. He hoped it was pass/fail.

"We Congolese once had a great man among us," the waiter said.

"Tell me about him."

"Oh, this was a long time ago, before you and I passed through the birth canal into this vale of tears. His name was Lumumba. Patrice. Perhaps you know the name. After his death, the Russians named one of their universities after him. It was a tribute to his greatness."

This was quicksand for Smith. Take a step in any direction and his ignorance would sink him. He listened.

The waiter told him, "After nineteen sixty, the situation in this country was confusing."

"The year of your independence," Smith said, having picked up that factoid somewhere, he couldn't remember where.

"Independence? Is that what you call this?" The waiter gestured with his hand, palm turned up, taking in the entire country in a dismissive sweep. "Lumumba, you see, he was the one man with excellent eyesight we could boast of having. He saw how things truly were. And he had a heart. He cared for people, how they were treated, what went into their bellies. Naturally this terrified the Belgians. They had thought they would go on exploiting the wealth of the country forever. For them, independence was a word, a sham. Just think: if the

Congolese began seeing things in their true light, they might threaten Belgium's control over their God-given natural resources. So what did the Europeans do? They called the CIA. Between them, a decision was made. Lumumba also scared the Americans to death, don't you see? They believed he was a Communist and would deliver the Congo to the Soviets."

He wanted an acknowledgement from Smith. He didn't get it.

"They murdered Lumumba, the Belgians and the Americans together. They pulled out his teeth. They burned the corpse. And they thought they were getting away with it. Who were we, a bunch of illiterate Africans, to resist them? Ah, but little did they realize, God was watching all the time. He saw every molar yanked out with pliers by an assassin's hand. He saw the blood. He felt Patrice's unbearable pain. What you must realize is that Our Father in Heaven moves at His own pace. When He decides the moment is propitious, you and every other American, well, you will wish with all your heart that you were poor black Africans. As you come crashing down, we will be lifted up."

The prospect of divine retribution for America's great-power crimes stirred the man deeply. He was ready for another smoke. Smith had heard enough. But he stayed long enough to watch the waiter perform his one-handed nicotine delivery trick again. The man had every right to the pride he took in the accomplishment.

Béatrice was asleep in the room. Smith tried to be quiet, going in. But just enough drink made him clumsy, and he tripped. She sat up.

"Nkoyi! Have you found my grandmother?"

Here was the chance to be straight with her. Now was the time. He owed her that much.

"Not yet."

She lay her head down on the pillow and went back to sleep.

The street where the Mavugos lived was like the neighborhood. The neighborhood was like the city, which was, in its faithful idiosyncratic way, like the country. All of them were improvised. Rue Nouveau Roi followed a snaky line of dull gray lava, bending where the lava flow had met an obstacle the day Mount Nyiragongo had erupted. Smith, who was good with maps, saw the street's humpbacked curve mimicking the curve of the Congo River cutting through Central Africa.

The walls of the Mavugo house were brick. The bricks were hardened lava. There was no front door, just a hole covered by a yellow curtain weighted with pebbles in a cuff sewn into the base of the fabric. Next to the doorway, sprays of papery purple flowers climbed a homemade trellis, the vines reaching up from a cooking oil tin converted to a pot. In the webwork of plant shadows crisscrossing the wall, a green lizard stuck out its tongue, believing itself well hidden.

Bernadette was a small woman scrubbed by poverty to a hard essence. She might be fifty, she might be sixty-five. She wore a torn black skirt, a green T-shirt tied in a knot at the waist as if to cinch her into her clothes. Her smile lacked teeth.

Her hands were busy with a spotted brown towel. All the time she talked she kept wiping them, wiping them.

"*Nous sommes partis du mauvais pied*," she said.

She didn't just say it, she shouted it, she wailed it, she moaned it.

We got off on the wrong foot.

It was a performance, and her drama was drawing the neighbors. They were already on the alert because of the arrival of Paul Kanea's red motorbike, followed by Jasmine's Maison Kongo car. The air was hot and getting hotter, it was the thickening middle of a dull day, and here was something promising to make it memorable.

Twenty people formed a spectatorial circle around the house, talking with heat and great excitement in languages that were not French, filling up the roadway. Twenty more, in flip-flops and ragged clothes, were on their way. Five minutes later they all got what they seemed to want, which was the sight of their neighbor bursting into tears.

Bernadette threw the brown towel over her head, weeping noisily, shoulders shaking. To the extent that Smith was able to follow what was happening, the emotion that had taken hold of the woman appeared to be guilt. Also from the looks of it, Paul exercised a certain authority over her, although the American had no idea why.

"We'll talk inside," he told her when she stopped for breath.

To the neighbors' voluble disappointment, Paul led people through the yellow curtain into the little house. It had two rooms, two chairs, two mattresses, and a shriveled cross of palm leaves hanging on one wall. In one corner of the front room, a man with a boy's shoulders sat on an upturned plastic bucket, hands crossed in front of him. A beard of silver fur made him look older than probably he was. He looked up when they came into the house but said nothing. Bobagu.

For Smith, this was it. The end or the beginning. He did not feel any hope, but neither did he feel hopeless. This must be how it was for athletes just before the game began. Let the damn thing start already.

Since there were not enough chairs, they stood.

"From this very moment I will love the child," Bernadette said, addressing Paul. "It was a mistake, what happened in Kinshasa. Not a day has gone by that I have not castigated myself for abandoning her."

She was going in and out of French. Smith paid hard attention and figured out that Bernadette Mavugo was the sister of Béatrice's dead mother. Her auntie. She and Bobagu had been in Kinshasa years back when the girl's father threw the child out of the house. They had known what was happening and done nothing.

"I am a good person, a person who loves God," Bernadette insisted. "There is room in my heart for the child, there is room in this house. The old man here . . . " She waved dismissively at Bobagu in the corner. "He knows nothing." She stopped to suck in some air. "I made a mistake."

Her shame filled the room, and Smith felt bad for her. She had to bear Paul Kanea's disapproval, her neighbors' cruel curiosity, the presumed censure of the God whose crucifixion was memorialized in the crossed palm leaves she had pinned to the wall of her home. She snuffled and suffered. Bobagu on the bucket shifted his haunches and spat on the floor. The expression of indifference on his face could not be real.

"And your mother?" Paul said coldly. "Or should I say, the grandmother of the little orphan girl?"

The question kicked up another storm of guilty grief. Out of the storm there emerged a name. Joséphine Mutebusi. The name had weight. It had gravity, and Smith felt its pull. For the first time, the grandmother of Béatrice seemed like a real person, not the invention of a lonely kid with a powerful imagination.

Bernadette believed her mother must be dead. So many had died, why should her mother be exempt? If she were alive—the tiniest sliver of possibility—she was in the south, where the family had begun, before war and the machinery of war took over everybody's life. Bernadette had wanted to go south and look for her mother, really she had. But how could she? She had no money, and the south was exceedingly dangerous. And then, the odds of finding Joséphine were staggeringly small. Still—she hung her head—it had been a mistake not to try. It was the moral equivalent of her failure to rescue Béatrice from the streets of Kinshasa, which were as dangerous as the South Kivu that had swallowed up Joséphine.

The boy-shouldered man spat on the floor again. It was how he expressed his opinion, although only Bernadette knew what that opinion was.

"The girl must stay here," pleaded Bernadette. "We will make her welcome. I will cook for her. She will grow to love me as a child loves its mother. Am I not her auntie?"

During her aunt's recital, Béatrice had quietly slipped outside. Bernadette's story was too painful for her to hear.

"Of course," said Paul. "She will stay here."

Why he was the one who got to decide was murky to the American. There was some sort of hierarchy here not visible to a newcomer like him. But the relief he felt was enormous. For the first time he allowed himself to admit how irksome it had been, being responsible for a child in a place of unabating hazard. If he had any strengths, childcare was not one of them. The only question that remained had to do with a cavity under the floorboards of the Le Mistral kitchen.

How to ask the question was the tricky part. It was solved when the neighbors outside began hollering in a chorus that sounded coordinated, as though they had practiced ahead of time for just such an eventuality. Smith had no idea what started them going but was pleased when Paul and Jasmine ran through the yellow curtain and out into the yard. He hung back.

"The girl saw you in Kinshasa,' he said to Bernadette.

He did not want it to sound like an accusation, but that was how Bernadette took it. She looked puzzled, but maybe that was only Smith's outlandish French. She shrugged. He was making her seriously uncomfortable. She went toward the door. Now or never. Smith put a hand on her arm.

"Wait."

Her voice quavered. "What do you want from me?"

"A place in Kinshasa. In Matonge. A house. A club. Le Mistral. You were there. Béatrice saw you. She saw you in the kitchen."

She shook her head soberly, as though he had accused her of something far worse than failing to rescue her niece.

"No, Monsieur."

Then she nodded just perceptibly, acknowledging something that was not obvious to him. Her eyes widened. Tears formed in them and fell in slow parallel lines down her dry cheeks. From sadness her expression turned to horror, looking at him, and she ran through the door toward the commotion outside.

For the first time, Bobagu stirred from his seat. He rose with difficulty on arthritic bones and took a single limping step toward Smith. He aimed a trembling finger at him. His voice when he spoke was high-pitched and strangely sweet, what you got when you crossed a preacher and a songbird.

"God sent you," he said.

"What is that supposed to mean?"

"It's what she believes. God sent you to torment her."

"Why would I torment her?"

"We never went back to Kinshasa," said Bobagu. "All those years, the child was living on the street, we never went back, not once." Then, the sentence that sealed it. "Béatrice never saw us because we were not there to be seen."

It was over. The bubble popped. And in less than an instant Smith understood how profoundly stupid he had been, chasing a fantasy. He had wanted off the rig that bad, the wanting blinded him. It crippled his judgment, which had always been a ninety-pound weakling when confronted with bad choices. He had thought one big score would cancel out a lifetime of bad habits, poor decisions, daydreams that destroyed the soul.

The noise of the neighbors was spiking, and in his misery he went out to see what was going on. Béatrice. Of course. She had somehow made her way through the ring of spectators and was loping back down Rue Nouveau Roi like a goddamn gazelle. If gazelles loped.

"Give me your key," Smith said to Paul Kanea.

Paul shook his head. He gave him the key. Smith jumped on the bike. A hole in the crowd appeared instantaneously; people were being kind. He shifted the bike into first gear and took off after the girl.

She was moving fast. She disappeared before he began to make any headway on her. But even Béatrice could not outrun a motorcycle. He skidded to a stop beside her, and she gave him a look of hatred, or anger, or confusion, or resolve, or all of those and more, who the hell knew what was going on in the kid's mind?

They were at an intersection. Smith dismounted. He moved the bike out of the path of traffic, which went blithely on because it will, because it does and always will. Horns honked because they didn't care, it was obvious they didn't give a damn what happened to this witch kid, wouldn't care even if they knew the particulars of her sad story. He kicked the kickstand, took Béatrice by the arm firmly enough she would not escape.

"Where you going?"

She shook her head, too contemptuous of him—he was representing the species just then, and the species had done nothing to earn her respect—too angry to speak.

"I know what you did," he said.

"I did nothing."

It was an all-purpose denial covering everything that needed covering.

"You told Soeur Placide you saw those people take a box of diamonds. You knew their names. You thought that way I would take you to them."

No response. Smith had no doubt, now, that the Belgian nun was in on it, too. Together they had played him.

"Hey, I don't blame you," he told her. "It was a smart move. And it worked, didn't it? Now here you are, you're in a good place. In fact it's really good, Béatrice. Your auntie wants you to stay with her and the old man. It will be safe. You'll have a home. No more bad streets full of *shegues*. No more orphanage. I bet your auntie sends you to school."

"My grandmother is in the south. I will go south."

"Show me which way south is."

She pointed east.

"Wrong," said Smith. "Let's go back to your auntie."

Béatrice struggled to get away from him. He did not let relax his grip. What was he supposed to do, let her take off running nowhere in the wrong direction? A fresh sense of his incapacity overwhelmed him. He was a complete fucking fool. In the kingdom of stupid he was the unchallenged lord of all stupid creatures that crawled and swam and built stock cars and threw up in bushes when they got drunk.

He had lost his job. He had chased phantom treasure to the deadest of dead ends. He had pretended—he was a champeen pretender, world class. He had been pretending for as long as he could remember.

He was going to save some money. He was going back home to live a stable life. He was going to buy Maybelline a red Camaro, make up for his previous shortcomings, which called for a calculator to be added up with accuracy. He was going to patch things up with his sister. He was going to prove that a shitty beginning did not have to lead to a shitty ending.

"Don't be like me," he said to Béatrice.

She gave him a suspicious look.

"I mean don't do something stupid. That's what I always do. Do the smart thing. Go and live with your Auntie Bernadette."

"My grandmother is in the south." Then she pronounced the name as though it meant something to her, she could tell you what the place looked like, what it smelled like, where it lay on the African earth. "My grandmother is in South Kivu."

She pulled hard, and this time he let her go. Surprised, she stumbled in the roadway. But did not go down. A sense of dignity prevented her from running now. She turned away from Smith deliberately and walked, taking mincing steps. He watched her go. Once, she stopped to adjust the straps on her backpack. There was a child's grace in the shift of her shoulders. She walked again, staying clear of the hard-hearted, blind-eyed, deaf-eared traffic, which only wanted to whiz to a place not worth the cost of the gas it took to get there.

"Stop," he called.

She didn't.

"Béatrice," he called.

The sound of her name halted her, and he called out, devising another lie.

"I know how to get to South Kivu."

Well shit. If he was going to be stupid, he might as well go all the way to total fool.

PART TWO

Hard East

The girl was shivering. It was cold on Lake Kivu at night, and for the first time since they had met Smith saw fear get inside her. An unholy circle of boys throwing stones hadn't scared her. Neither did flying in an airplane. But this, yes: on the hard front seat of a wood boat, gripping the gunwales, hating the waves on the choppy lake. Above a wilderness of black water, speeding clouds covered and uncovered the stars in a wilderness of indigo sky. The wet air clung to Béatrice's skin, and the dark affronted her.

Smith did not like the ride any better than she did. On an oil rig, you knew the ocean would kill you if it could get at you, but there was a solidity to the platform that you got used to. You counted on it. You learned to sleep at night, and not all your dreams were watery graves.

"It's okay," he told her.

No answer. She did not believe him. Why should she? Her teeth chattered, and she shrank into herself.

"Here," said Rémy, "give her this."

Sitting in the stern, the boatman was piloting the craft with his right hand on the throttle of the outboard engine. With his left he tossed Smith a blanket. Smith leaned forward and wrapped it around Béatrice's shoulders. She made a sound he could not interpret.

"The lake is safe," said Rémy. "It is not like the road. Not like the forest. The lake is safe."

He was not speaking to Smith. He was not reassuring Béatrice. He was reciting an article of faith from his personal catechism.

"I used to be afraid," he said. "At first, when I ventured out on the lake at night, my knees knocked so hard I thought it was a monster fish rising from the depths to snatch me. Dear God in Heaven, I prayed, do not permit me to become a snack for a creature with such an insignificant brain."

Béatrice giggled. First time for everything.

"Sleep," Rémy advised her. "In the morning you will need strength to walk, possibly a great distance. Possibly there will be ghosts, or wild animals. Little Munyamulenge girl, who knows what awaits you in the morning?"

Always unpredictable, she curled up on the seat and closed her eyes, hugging the blanket around her.

"You will see, Monsieur Smith," said the boatman.

"What will I see?"

"When we reach Bukavu, when your feet touch solid earth again and you contemplate the dangers you avoided on the road, you will say, 'That brave Twa boatman, that good Christian Rémy, he has done right by me and the little girl under my care.'"

Rémy made his living by keeping his distance from Congolese government officials, soldiers on the make, all kinds of combatants with guns and grudges, other smugglers, any and every sort of man who wanted whatever it was he had on board.

He was a small man. Twa was the correct name for Pygmies, Jasmine had told Smith; Twa, or Batwa. At twelve or whatever she was, Béatrice was taller than Rémy, and physically elegant in a way the boatman would never be. In the dark, in the back of his little craft, he was a compact blur taking them slowly south.

Jasmine had turned up the boatman when it looked as though traveling overland from Goma to Bukavu was going to be foolhardy. A militia group had ambushed a unit of the Congolese military along the road. Mai Mai, the militia were called. Like Crispin Sikatenda's Army of the Revival of the Word of God.

After every clash, it was the civilian population that took the hit. The winning side celebrated by pillaging and raping; they called it hunting out collaborators. More often than not, so did the losers. Either way, if you were a villager you were vulnerable. You were screwed by geography, topography, proximity.

The Mai Mai were supposed to be disarmed. The Congo wars were supposed to be over. So far, peace was showing no sign of breaking out.

"You're going to do this, aren't you?" Jasmine had said.

Smith nodded. "Picture this."

"Okay."

"Five years from now. Springtime in the bayou. My African safari is over. I'm back home with a lion head on the wall. Out in the back yard grilling whitefish, sucking on a beer. Me and the wife are watching our kid play on the swing set. *You be careful now, sweetie.* The sun is going down over Louisiana, lazy and full of peaceful color. Perfect, right?"

"Sounds pretty good to me."

"It is pretty good. But all of a sudden the whole thing is spoiled."

"Why?"

"Because this headstrong Congolese girl—she's a teenager now—every time she thinks about me she says to herself, he punked out on me."

Rémy had insisted on going at night. During daylight any number of people would do their damnedest to nail them.

"Bukavu is like this," the boatman explained when he met them at the Oiseau.

He held up a hand with the fingers spread to replicate the fingers of land whose tips dipped into the water of the lake, and the narrow coves between the fingers. He pointed to an empty space between his ring and little finger.

"This is a safe place to land. I know it as well as I know my own mind. I close my eyes." He closed them to make his point. "I see such a safe place to take a distinguished visitor."

He had unusual green eyes, and an air of patient supplication that was not completely convincing. The long white shirt he wore untucked gave him a religious demeanor that fit with his story about growing up on a mission in South Kivu.

"The lake," he had told them half a dozen times, "the lake is safe."

Out on the water, Smith did not keep track of the time. Knowing the hour was not going to get them to Bukavu any quicker. In Bukavu, according to Paul Kanea, a Munyamulenge friend of his might know something about Joséphine Mutebusi. Such as, for starters, whether she was still alive.

As the boat moved south Smith rode, dozed, woke when the waves reminded him where he was. Then he dozed again.

He came awake hard, fast, and completely when Rémy killed the engine. The boatman told him quietly, "Look over there, eleven o'clock."

Off Smith's shoulder, the light of a boat was moving across the lake. They could hear the engine, but it was far enough off that Smith could not say that it was heading in their direction, or that it was not.

Rémy asked him, "Is the girl asleep?"

"Yes. What do we do?"

"Stay still. We will lose a little of the distance we've gained, but once they have passed we will make it up. We must be cautious, you understand. It's a pirate ship."

"What in the hell does that mean?"

"They are all Congo pirates."

It was not a time for questions. If they were spotted, chased, boarded, at the very least he would lose the cash he was carrying, which included three hundred extra dollars Jasmine had given him. *Money to smooth your way,* she called it. Without money, he could do nothing for Béatrice, not to mention getting himself out of the Congo. How deep could you get into a thing you did not understand? The sound of the waves against Rémy's boat was narcotic in the wrong way. Lap, slap; lap, slap.

They sat without speaking until it was obvious even to Smith that the pirate ship was not bearing down on them.

Rémy snorted, contemptuous of an enemy they would not see, an enemy he could imagine capable of any evil he chose to imagine. He yanked the starter cord on the engine, and they moved south again, doggedly regaining the distance they had ceded to the current. The boatman carried no compass. He claimed he knew his way by feel.

The danger past, Rémy was in the mood to talk.

"I know what you're thinking."

"What am I thinking?"

"You are wondering, how is it possible that a miserable Twa, the representative of a people who have been shat on, generation upon generation, by Hutu and Tutsi alike, finds himself in possession of such a magnificent boat as the one in which you are presently riding."

Magnificent was not how Smith would describe the boat. Seaworthy would do just fine.

"You're right," he said. "That's what I was wondering."

Rémy's voice sang out over the engine noise. "Hah! What you seek to know is, in fact, the story of my life. It is not, after all, the boat that matters. What truly matters is my grandfather."

"I should have known that."

"You are forgiven, my friend."

Post-pirates, Rémy was in a terrific mood. There was humor in the air. It threatened to explode him into little bits of hilarity.

"You see," said the boatman, "we Twa were the first people ever to live in this place. Did they teach you that at school?"

"I skipped some of the classes."

"Bad boy, naughty boy. You should know that before there was Hutu, before there was Tutsi, this grand and glorious Congo was given to us."

"By God."

"Hah! I now know that to be the case, thanks to Miss Florence."

"Who is Miss Florence?"

The boatman wailed. There was nothing phony in the sound.

"She died," he said. "Miss Florence was murdered. A wicked man, a Tutsi, came to the mission with a hatchet and blood in his eyes. His name was Marcel, and I curse his name, I curse his memory. He murdered so many of us. Had my grandfather lived to witness the massacre, the shock would have killed him."

Rémy's story did not come out in consecutive pieces. He was indifferent to sequence, and some of the gripping parts he told more than once. In the version that Smith put together, Miss Florence was the heart and soul and organizing principle of a mission to the Batwa run by the Christian and Missionary Alliance. They came out to Eastern Congo with the curious belief that the downtrodden, third-class people from the forests of Ituri deserved to hear the truth of God as much as anybody else.

"Can you imagine such a thing?" Rémy wanted to know. "Who would believe it? The Batwa, people like everyone else, capable of knowing the God who made them? How absurd."

His laughter scoured the night air.

Rémy's grandfather had been a man of independent outlook, an attribute not at odds with his legendary prowess as a hunter of game in the deep woods. Having been approached by the missionaries, having been drawn into the light, he took his family to the mission they were building in a clearing on the edge of the forest. There he learned to pray, to read, to grow vegetables, and to praise God.

"The father of Miss Florence was a stern man," Rémy said, "The love in his heart was ringed by steel. It was he who built the mission. But malaria took him to his Maker after two years with us, and Miss Florence picked up his burden. Truly, she carried it forward with dignity. She was young and beautiful with yellow hair, very straight and very long, who told us every day how beautiful we were in the sight of God and also in hers. She was a short woman, for an American, but still taller than we Twa."

Smith was fuzzy on the dates, but there seemed to have been a golden age of peace at the mission. The houses had tiled roofs and did not leak. There were vegetables and medicine and nanny goats with full, swinging teats. Hymns of praise morning and evening, laughter and recitations. Shoes and useful crafts. The divine grace of God, the humane grace of Miss Florence, an ease of mind unlike anything the Twa had experienced in the forest where they were constantly on the look-out for Muntu, their oppressors.

"The day of the massacre—I remember it as though it were yesterday—I was being naughty. I ran from the garden, I escaped to the forest, because I did not care to pull weeds as Miss Florence had enjoined me to do. How fierce I was, how terrible and childish. 'I am not a garden man,' I told her, 'I am a hunter.'"

He stopped. He had to stop. He could not tell the story and laugh at the same time.

"Can you imagine, Monsieur Smith? I, a mere boy, declaiming such nonsense to Miss Florence? No vegetables for me, no ma'am. Only the flesh of a wild beast will satisfy my manly hunger."

Then, instantly, as quickly as the laughter had spun him up, he tanked. In the Congo night, in the Lake Kivu black, he was seeing details of the massacre of his people he would not bring himself to tell his American passenger.

"I began to hear people screaming. Out in the forest, my mother among them. Was this the voice of my mother, I asked myself, the woman who carried me inside her, who gave me my face, my arms, my hands? Fear made me dumb, but I kept myself hidden. I crept back to the mission. We Twa have great skill in the forest. From behind a tree I saw the Tutsi man Marcel kill them all. Miss Florence went down on her knees. She was not begging to save herself, she only wanted him to spare the children. Of course he did not."

"Of course?"

"Have I not said that he was a Tutsi? Have I not said that for the Tutsi, we Twa are less than dirt? Well, you have seen all the unhappy Twa selling their pottery on the street in Goma."

"Yes," lied Smith. "I saw them."

"So many people making pots, so few people buying any. What did you want me to do?"

His indignation was as genuine as his laughter, his grief, his pride. It was not a question Smith could answer.

"Did you want me to stay on the streets, a beggar like all the other beggars, until the day God called me home?"

"No."

"Well, then. A moment of opportunity presented itself. There was a certain Tutsi man in Goma. He owned a car, which he operated as a taxi. A good car, solid. When I was able to, I killed him. I traded the car for this boat. I call her Miss Florence, only I do not paint her name on the side because every single letter of that God-given name is engraved on my heart. Writing it would be sacrilege."

"Who was this Tutsi man you killed?"

"I understand your question. You think I don't, but I do."

"What am I asking?"

"What gave me the right to kill this man? Very well, here is my answer. A price was owing for the massacre of the mission with all its Christian Batwa living their peaceful life. It had to be paid. Vengeance is mine, saith the Lord, and truly it is. I in my humility was chosen by God to be the instrument of His vengeance."

He stopped speaking. The engine ran a little more quietly as if it too were chastened by the story of the massacre at the mission, or by Rémy's revenge. Béatrice stirred on her seat and sat up. Most kids would say, "Where are we?" Béatrice didn't. She knew. They were in yet another strange place.

Smith passed her a water bottle. She uncapped it and drank. She pulled the blanket around her. Overhead, the stars defined elsewhere.

Here was something new to think about: if Rémy could kill a man and take his car with a tranquil conscience in the conviction that God had tapped him to be an instrument of justice, what would it take for him to sell out Smith? After all, Béatrice was a Munyamulenge. Smith had no idea how the Banyamulenge and the Batwa got along. Assume they didn't.

Béatrice turned around. She tapped his knee.

"Nkoyi."

"What?"

"Are we almost there?"

The sun had not come up when Rémy shut off the engine and Miss Florence made the final fifty yards of the trip on momentum. But the east sky was pale; a theory of light. And even after cramped hours in the boat, Smith could not help feeling a little optimism. That was the whole idea of night and day, he thought as Miss Florence scraped the shore with her keel, and her prow shuddered daintily. You started over every morning, you tried again.

Béatrice was out of the boat before it stopped moving. She went over the side into shallow water and waded to hard ground. Turning around with her arms crossed on her chest, she waited for Smith.

The cove to which Rémy delivered them was long and narrow. It was north of the city, although he would not or could not say how far north. His vagueness was tactical. The land was treed, which gave the place a sense of seclusion. That was not the same as security. The shore was quiet. So was the lake. Insects hummed in the ripe air, bumping against the wall of quiet.

"Stay here," the boatman told them. "Under no circumstances should you move. You must not be seen. I will come back."

He went up through the trees toward the road. Before he disappeared, Smith was convinced the Twa was about to betray them. The American had handed over half the cash up front. If Rémy found the right interested party he would double his money.

"Where do you think he went?" he asked Béatrice.

She looked at him blankly. He wished she would shrug, laugh at him, say something to acknowledge the question, say anything. He tried again.

"Is he a good man or a bad man?"

"I'm hungry."

They went just far enough up from the shoreline to shelter behind a tree. Béatrice removed her backpack carefully before taking a seat on the ground, which was damp and dark. Squatting next to her, he handed her an orange and then a chocolate bar. She ate the candy first. At that moment he badly wanted a cup of coffee. Give it a while, and the urge would pass. They sat there watching a bird with a rapier bill feint three times and then dive. It smacked the water, went under, came back up with a fish.

"If you were that fish," Smith said.

She looked at him doubtfully.

He told her, "You would not be having a good day."

"Fish," she told him categorically, "are unable to dream."

"Tell me something, Béatrice."

"What?"

"What is Rémy going to do?"

She told him, "He will bring a friend."

As they waited, Smith ran though in his mind the quickie course on Congolese officialdom that Jasmine had given him. Soon, often, and inevitably he would have to deal with local representatives of the government. He would also find himself face to face with military men, and people claiming to be—and sometimes actually being —intelligence agents from the Agence Nationale de Renseignements. The ANR was everywhere. To a person they would want something from him. If he was lucky, it would only be money. That was why she had given him all the cash she could spare. It was important for him to find exactly the right amount to dole out. Too little, and he would provoke anger. Too much, and they would see him as a dolt and pounce.

Smith had shown Jasmine the bearer letter Denis Lajeune gave him in Kinshasa. *This isn't even your name*, she pointed out. It's better than nothing, right? *No. It might be worse than nothing*. He had considered throwing away the letter, but the impressive letterhead, the authoritative sentences, the minister's bold signature, gave him some comfort. He needed written permission to go from point A, where he would be hassled, to point B, where he would be hassled again. So stipulated. He didn't have said permission. Also stipulated. But it seemed to him that even if he had proper papers, men would still be standing in line to take advantage of him in ways he could not yet envision.

A long hour later, it was not a friend the boatman brought, it was a man in a green uniform. The uniform looked real, but the man wore Adidas running shoes, and his hair was unmilitarily long. His face was in constant motion, exaggerated expressions of friendship and hostility, suspicion and perplexity crossing over it, leaving him no facial peace. A rifle was slung on a strap over his shoulder. Smith did not know guns. This one looked pretty beat up, but for all he knew it was standard issue.

Rémy introduced them. "This is Laurent. He will take you where you wish to go. You will give him twenty dollars to do so."

Smith asked Laurent, "Is that true?"

He offered the American a sloppy salute, which convinced Smith he was an imposter. Two days in the army, any army, and a person would salute better than that.

"This is Béatrice."

Laurent nodded but did not bother to look at the girl. She was fascinated by the rifle, contemptuous of his style. Rémy tugged on Smith's arm, nudging him back toward the boat. As they walked he made it clear he was going to respect the deal they had made. There would be no extortion under duress. He wanted Smith to acknowledge his magnanimity. Getting some moral credit was important to him.

In fact Smith was grateful. If the boatman had held him up, borrowing Laurent's phony authority, or his rifle, Smith would have had to pony up. But he could not bring himself to say what the boatman wanted to hear. When he didn't, Rémy turned abruptly away and boarded his boat. The cord snapped angrily as he started the engine.

As Miss Florence headed back onto the lake, Smith and Béatrice followed Laurent up through the trees. Partway up they caught the smell of a wood fire, although there was no visible smoke. It made Smith think about camping out, fried eggs and bacon, jokes you could tell every time you went out to the woods and still get a laugh.

There was a road of dusty dirt, peaceful looking, like a highway on which you sent eggs to market. Before they stepped onto it, Laurent stopped to complain. His voice was nasal and aggrieved and came out of the left side of his mouth like steam.

"This job is complicated."

"What's complicated about taking a stroll in the morning sun?" Smith said.

"You know so little about this place."

"Everybody keeps telling me that."

"We have reason to fear. I have reason to fear."

"How come?"

"My boss; my bosses. I have many. If they knew what I was up to, there would be hell to pay."

"Hell or somebody with sticky fingers."

"Say what?"

"Never mind."

"It is the ANR we must worry about. They have their spies everywhere." Laurent pointed to a tree, and then to another tree, as if there might be intelligence agents behind both of them. "This thing we are doing . . . there are costs."

"I'm paying you the price we agreed. Twenty bucks."

Laurent shook his head, offended at the sum, and Smith called his bluff.

"All right, forget it."

"What do you mean?"

"We'll go by ourselves."

The bluff worked. Laurent hesitated. Then he leaned confidentially into Smith and grinned. "I have a sister, Monsieur. You understand."

Béatrice frowned.

"Last week," Laurent told him, "my sister had a terrible dream. The dream woke her. She ran in the dark and broke her arm. We are poor people, you see. Poor people are always experiencing these sorts of problems."

Smith refused to humor him. "So how do we do this? Do we take off down the road like Sunday morning going to church?"

"It will look best if I seem to be detaining you. I will tie your hands behind your back."

"No, you won't."

Laurent shrugged and gave in again.

"As you wish. There is a village a kilometer in front of us. After the village, there will be more people, and then the city, which of course is highly populated."

"When we come across people," Smith told him, "Béatrice and I will walk with our heads down. We will look as though we are your prisoners with no hope of seeing tomorrow."

Laurent may have had a sense of humor. If he did, he knew how to hide it. They went into the road walking slowly, Smith with his go bag, Béatrice with her pack, the phony soldier with his rifle, which he explained was a Kalashnikov even though it did not carry the brand name. Like a knock-off Rolex, Smith suggested, the kind you picked up for ten bucks on the street in any city anywhere knowing it might not tell time. Laurent did not care for the comparison.

They walked steadily, and Smith's leg muscles uncramped after the night in Rémy's boat. After a few minutes, a dump truck went by them going toward the city, stirring a mist of powdery dirt as it passed. A dozen bare-chested men with shovels were riding in the back. They hollered and pointed at Smith with their shovels. He thought they might jump down and swarm him. Their curiosity was ferocious, but the truck kept moving.

"You were lucky," said Laurent.

Smith told him, "We were lucky. Think what your bosses would say."

As the sun climbed, the heat began to sting. It was not yet overpowering, but you could feel it working on you. The trees on either side of the road were low growth with thin boles. The undergrowth was dense, bushy. Together they pocketed the light, giving back a blur.

They passed a mud house with a roof of fronds. Nobody home. Another bend and they came to two houses on a bare spot of uneven ground. In the space between the houses women were squatting over wooden bowls pounding something vegetable, something edible, into a paste. As they raised their pestles, their shoulders showed the bony nubs where wings used to be. Kids ran streaming figure-eights around the houses, arms out, happy as peach pie on your birthday. They all stopped moving and gaped when they saw a nondescript white man being led by a local man with a rifle, a tall girl tagging along with her backpack strapped tight. Laurent spoke to them loudly, harshly, berating them as though he had a right. They ignored him but made no move to come into the road.

Progress. Slow. Another ten minutes and they overtook a man pushing a bicycle overloaded with bananas. He was working too hard to pay attention to them. Fruit flies traveled with him in a cloud.

"*Bon jour, Monsieur,*" said Béatrice as they went by him.

She spoke as clearly, as courteously, as Soeur Placide would have wanted her to. Who was this kid? The man's grizzled head was down, and he did not respond. Beads of sweat fell from his face into the roadway, and the muscles in his arms were tight cords.

"Twenty dollars," griped Laurent when they had left behind the man straining to inch his banana-laden bicycle's tires through the uncooperative dirt. "It is a miserable sum for the work involved, it is an insult to a man's dignity. Perhaps you are not really American, perhaps you were born in another country, one where people are not taught to respect their fellow man."

"From now on," said Smith.

"From now on, what?"

"Every complaint you make, I hold back a dollar from the twenty."

"That's not fair."

"If you're not careful, you'll wind up owing me money by the time we get where we're going."

Whether or not he took the threat seriously, Laurent shut up for a while. They walked, the heat of the day crinkling the African air as though it were cellophane. They came to a clearing in which three small round huts with thatched roofs sat close enough to one another that a person standing in the door of one could shake hands with a person in the door of another. Except that there were no people. In the quiet of the morning the silence of the place was viscous. Béatrice pointed to a dead snake hanging on a length of yellow plastic rope strung between two trees. As they stared, a stick-thin woman in a green skirt emerged from the thicket of trees behind the huts. She waved a long-handled wooden spoon at them but did not speak.

"What does she want?" Smith said.

"They are sick," Laurent explained. "The illness is contagious. She warns us to stay away."

Béatrice told them matter-of-factly, "It is the snake that has made them sick. They have killed it too late."

The woman began pantomiming a message. She spoke silently with her hands, her arms, heaving her whole body into motion as she made a plea. For what? Laurent grinned harder than ever although it was clear he found nothing funny in the unhappy woman's situation.

"You must shoot the snake," Béatrice told him.

"It's already dead."

She shook her head. Obviously Laurent did not understand sickness or snakes or the nature of evil. But there was nothing any of them could do. As they moved down the road out of the woman's line of sight, Smith expected her to call out, to send some sort of human sound after them to touch them, move them to do something for her. No such sound came.

The warehouse toward which they were walking turned out to be located on the north end of Bukavu. That meant they did not have to parade through town like some kind of freak show. Laurent appeared to know where he was going. As they passed more people, getting close, he ignored everyone who came his way and walked faster. He was a man on a mission, which he completed with a flourish, guiding them down a series of side streets to a large two-story building with pale blue adobe walls that filled a dead-end lot. With satisfaction he pointed.

"*Voilà*."

It took Smith half an hour to shed the man. The soldier of sorts had nowhere else to go and nothing to do. He had earned twenty bucks that morning. That was twenty more than he thought he would make when he got out of bed. A decent start to the day. It made sense to hang around and see if he could double his money.

When Laurent was finally ready to accept defeat, he made a cockeyed salute and left them in the street, which was deserted in the noon sun. He moved jauntily. It was no longer worth his while to fake being pissed off.

The double loading doors of the warehouse were big enough to back a truck through, but they were padlocked.

The lock was Chinese, with a dragon embossed on its ceramic face. The dragon had a tongue of fire. Here was something else Smith had not been able to imagine existed in the world, which kept getting bigger.

"My grandmother is not here," said Béatrice.

There was dismay in her voice. There was also resolve.

Smith told her, "We're looking for a man who might know something about your family. He works here. He is a watchman."

"But no one is here."

"Right," said Smith. "No one is here."

She had the ability to make him lose his patience instantly. A gift of sorts.

"Smith."

It was a command to do something, but he was not sure what. Suddenly he was tired. He was dirty. Sweat had soaked and dried on his skin, his clothes, half a dozen times since they climbed out of Rémy's boat. He felt a blister coming on the big toe of his left foot.

"You decide," he said.

"Decide what?"

"Either we wait, or we come back later."

"Why are you sad?" she wanted to know.

He had good intentions. Not to save the girl, just to get her moving in a safer direction. Maybe that was his mistake, assuming there was a better place for her to be. Good intentions counted for something, never mind the hard history of empire, great-power politics, the inhumane in humanity, white against black.

"Who said I'm sad?"

"You are too hot. It is the heat that saddens you. What is the name of the man who knows my family?"

He was too discouraged to shoot down her optimism. She expected to hit the jackpot. Every time.

"Maurice," he told her. "His surname is Ruberwa. He is Munyamulenge, like you."

She considered his answer a moment. The idea was novel. "Like me."

He nodded. She pointed to a patch of shade along the warehouse wall where a black pig lay sleeping. She roused it with a stick and drove it away. It moved reluctantly, and she told Smith, "Rest here."

By the time Béatrice came back to the warehouse in the company of a tall man with an illegible expression on his face, Smith had made a deal with himself. One more setback, and he was giving up. You didn't have to hit him on the head with a hammer. Everything that had gone on since the kid walked into the kitchen at Le Mistral was a message from the minor gods, the humble mechanics who worked the gears and pulleys of human existence. They were sympathetic—he was a mechanic himself—and tried to be helpful. If only he would pay attention. The message was simple: give it up, pal. You don't have a clue. He was not the Nkoyi of Béatrice's expectations, he was whatever the opposite of a leopard was. He thought for a moment. Had it: the Taco Bell Chihuahua.

Maurice Ruberwa fished in his pocket for a key and opened the warehouse door. They followed him in. It was almost cool inside and smelled of flour, although the pallets of goods stacked four and five high contained consumer goods, not comestibles: boxes of pots and pans, crates of machetes, piles of plastic plates. The labels on the boxes were mostly in Chinese. Maurice led them to a room that could have been an office but turned out to be his home. A pallet on the floor. Kitchen paraphernalia, a gas ring to cook on. A pair of pristine blue Adidas, resting on their box as on a throne. They had never been worn.

No chairs. They sat on the floor. Maurice held up his phone.

"My friend Paul Kanea sent me a text."

He was a Zen master: a placid man with creamy brown skin and long hair like a quiet exclamation.

"Where is my grandmother?" Béatrice asked him.

Maurice spoke to her in what Smith figured had to be Kinyarwanda. Smith had no idea what he said, but the language brought back memories to Béatrice. Her eyes blazed, then teared, and she shook her head furiously. Maybe he sounded like her father, who had thrown her into the street to propitiate a woman who was not her mother.

Smith said, "French, please."

"Do you know her grandmother?"

"In the face of great persecution, we Banyamulenge have always stuck together."

"You didn't answer my question."

"Where were you when we were being slaughtered?"

"In a state of ignorance."

A pause, then, "Joséphine."

"Take me to her," Béatrice demanded.

Her dream was on the verge of coming true because it had to.

Maurice spoke sternly to her. She blazed, ready to fight. But she had discipline and used it. Better not flare; be patient. She had come this far. A little while longer. Her eyes fixed on his lips.

Maurice dug around in a crate and produced a liter of sugary orange drink. He poured a glass and gave it to Béatrice. The smiling woman on the label of the container was blonde. Heidi of the Unclimbed Alps.

Maurice told Smith, "Some years ago I met a man from the south. This was in a camp for displaced persons. It happened we both knew something about bricks, and the director of the camp contracted us to work on an infirmary they were constructing."

Smith said nothing. The Congo stories he heard usually began in an improbable place. Their tellers approached them sideways, sneaking up to capture what they needed to say.

Béatrice sipped her juice, eyes on the man who had given it to her.

"This man," said Maurice, shaking his head. "He was a fine bricklayer, a craftsman. He taught me a great deal about the work."

The black pig that Béatrice had driven from its patch of shade wandered into the warehouse and stretched itself flat on the floor. It grunted, going prone on the cement.

Maurice said, “The bricklayer also taught me things having nothing to do with our work.”

“Such as?”

“His people believe God created the world by vomiting it out through his mouth. Does that seem likely to you?”

Béatrice wrinkled her face in disgust. She was not vomit.

Smith told Maurice, “I don’t have a better explanation.”

“At the camp, we were not permitted to erect a building that would last.”

“Why not?”

“It was necessary to pretend the camp was temporary.”

“Why?”

Maurice shrugged. “To secure permission from the government. To maintain the goodwill of the donors so the money continued flowing in.”

“I don’t understand.”

Smith saw yellow spots in the whites of his eyes, left over from a disease. The Munyamulenge man decided it would cause no one harm to educate a transient American.

“The system depended upon a delusion. People would leave the camps, go home and live a regular life. What I saw there proved another thing the bricklayer told me. After vomiting out the world and all the creatures of the world, God grew tired of what he had made and walked away.”

Béatrice had been following the conversation with care, listening for clues to her grandmother’s whereabouts. Hearing that God had abandoned His creation, she frowned.

“What about Joséphine Mutebusi?”

"I was told she went to Minembwe after losing her family."

"How do I get to Minembwe?"

"Go to Uvira and turn right."

"I can do that."

Maurice shook his head. "It is not that easy."

"Of course not."

"The distance from Bukavu to Uvira is not great, and there are those who say the road is safe. The ones who say so were lucky. Were you to reach Uvira, the distance from there to Minembwe is much greater. Also, the road is very poor. It is dangerous. And the rains will begin soon. When the rains come, the road deteriorates. After that, naturally, there is the obvious dilemma."

"Not everything obvious to you is obvious to me."

"If one arrived without experiencing catastrophe, there is the last thing from a certainty that the child's grandmother is alive and living there."

"She is alive," Béatrice said calmly.

"Of course, little one. Nevertheless."

"Nevertheless what?" Smith asked him.

"Give me one thousand dollars, and I will take the child to Minembwe."

When Smith hesitated, Maurice said, "It is a lot of money, I do not deny it. And I freely admit the entire sum will not be spent in the attempt. I require money for one of those new cameras. I am saving up."

"Which new cameras?"

"They are digital. The technology is highly advanced. They allow the photographer to take pictures of the past."

"Right."

"If I am able to purchase such a camera, I intend to take photographs of the slaughter of my people. History must not be allowed to forget them. There must be testimony. Without testimony there can be no justice."

"I see."

"These photographs, it will not be easy to take them. It will be even more difficult to contemplate them. Still, if we are to see justice, the work must be done."

Béatrice stood as if the conversation were over. Said nothing. Shouldered her pack. Walked out through the double doors into the tunnel of afternoon light. Disappeared.

Smith had no idea what had moved her to leave. If she was transmitting signals, his receiver was no good. It had to be easier if you were a parent. You learned what you had to take seriously, what you could blow off.

"Don't worry," Maurice told him. "She will come back when she is ready. Congolese children are not like American children. They are not pets on a leash. They have a certain . . . " He searched for a word and settled on "independence."

Smith thought about his childhood, and Lu Ann's. The last thing they had been was pets on a leash. Whatever Maurice had paid for his idea about American kids, he got taken.

"Let's say I gave you the thousand dollars. Who owns this warehouse?"

"An Arab. Tawfeek. In the evening when he drinks his *arak*, he curses the ancestors who brought the family to Africa. He does not pretend to be a pious man and is as bald as a baby's ass. Nevertheless each month he pays me on time."

"Would Tawfeek give you time off work to go to Minembwe?"

Maurice looked around the warehouse as if only now realizing where he was. "This is not a job, it is mortal penance for a man whose sins are venial."

"How would you make the trip? Is there a bus?"

"A bus on these roads is like a crab. Craving a feast, hungry men will stick their hands inside and scoop out the tender flesh. To make the trip to Minembwe, I would look for a trucker. A trucker must be intelligent. If he is foolish, he does not last."

"One more question."

"Of course. As the principal investor in this project, you will want to know the details."

"What happens if you get all the way to Minembwe and there is no Joséphine Mutebusi?"

"A shrewd question. I have given it thought."

"And?"

"With a certain amount of money, a family can be persuaded to take the child in. If such a situation were to transpire, you would be relying on my honesty, my honor, to part with the correct sum."

"At the cost of your magic camera."

"It's not magic, it's technology."

"What would happen to Béatrice when the money you gave the family ran out?"

Smith waited, expecting a lie, or an evasion. But Maurice was blunt.

"The family may tolerate her. They may learn to love her. Equally they may feel obliged to lighten their load."

Smith nodded. He had been impulsive, back in Goma, telling the girl he would go south with her. Now, what Maurice was offering was the best he could hope for. A grand was a grand. He had wasted more than that, more times than he could count. Back when he was living with Maybelline, he gave five thousand bucks for a Harley Sportster that had been neglected by a lawyer who wasn't into maintenance. Smith did a valve job, but the bike never did run right. "Californication," that was the song that came to mind when he thought about the bike. A mini-soundtrack.

In his mind the deal with Maurice was done.

He wondered if he should try the road back to Goma. Maybe he could get a plane out of the country there, avoiding Kinshasa. Another boat ride across the dark lake sounded like a bad idea. But there were only two choices: on the road chancing Mai Mai, or on Lake Kivu chancing what Rémy called the Congo pirates.

"I'll give you the thousand," he told Maurice.

Maurice frowned, as if he did not much like the thought of what lay ahead. If he felt any satisfaction, better not to let it show. Smith wondered what he would do with the blue Adidas. He would not ruin them on a road trip to Minembwe.

Maurice put out a hand to shake on the deal. Smith took it. Maurice told him, "I have been in touch with The Hague."

Smith had no idea what he was talking about.

"The capital of the Netherlands," Maurice said, amazed at the American's ignorance. "It is the home of the war crimes tribunal. That is where I must send my photographs. How can the tribunal prosecute the men who murdered our people if they do not have evidence?"

Smith must have slept. He had no memory of lying down on Maurice's pallet, but that was where he came to, with a fuzzy head and a sense of having just missed something. The air inside the warehouse was stifling. Maurice was sitting on a three-legged stool frowning at his telephone. The black pig was gone.

"The girl?"

"Not back yet."

Smith sat up. "I'm going to look for her."

A long, appraising look from Maurice. A slow nod.

How did you find a kid on the streets of a city neither of you knew?

The afternoon was late, the west sky beginning to glow. One more day down the cosmic tube. He walked randomly for half an hour, which turned into an hour. The warehouse was located on the margin of what had once been a prosperous neighborhood back in the days when the Belgians still thought they had discovered a continent. The winding streets he followed took him past big, rundown houses, unkept gardens, impressive fences in bad repair, no longer as good as they had once been at keeping people out.

At the head of a circular drive leading to a house with fluted pillars, two men were taking turns with a machete. One of them wore a red do-rag. The other one had a cigarette. Both of them were shirtless. They were hacking with the machete at a tree for a purpose Smith did not grasp. The tree did not look dead but soon would be. One of the small-time mechanic gods tugged at his arm. Socket Head Billy, Smith called him.

This is hopeless, you know.

Smith knew.

There are seven hundred things going on in Bukavu at this very moment. You? You're lucky if you understand three of them.

Smith wanted to tell him to fuck off, but he was not the kind of god you could have a conversation with.

He came to a corner with an open view and saw that as the city rose, away from the water, there was less of the colonial past and more of the ramshackle life of a Congolese city that he had grown to expect. Béatrice would have gone that way, drawn by the bustle of people one of whom might be her grandmother. Smith did not need Socket Head Billy to tell him that finding Béatrice in the sprawl of city was hopeless.

He retraced his way to the warehouse, where Maurice sat in the office staring at the new Adidas, which were now on his feet. Seeing the American, he unlaced them, took them off, and put them away in their box.

"No luck?"

"No luck."

"What will you do?"

"I'll come back tomorrow," Smith said. "If she returns, keep her here."

"She gives no indication of being an obedient child. My new friend, I have been sitting here wondering."

"About what?"

"Whether you will give me an advance on the thousand dollars."

"Without Béatrice?"

"I didn't think so."

What was it about screens? The image you stared at created a picture in your mind that was confusingly unfaithful to the person you were supposed to be seeing. How that worked Smith had no idea, but the Skypified Maybelline he was talking to as though she were real was not.

Which was not to say she looked bad. In fact she looked better than a woman in her late thirties with her hard history had a right to look.

"You're looking pretty sexy there, girl."

She was wearing a ribbed red tank top with skinny straps while stroking a white cat that had climbed into her lap. It was noisy in the Happy Meal Café where he had rented a machine, but Smith thought he heard the cat purr as Maybelline's fingers ruffled the fur on its back. Much as he mistrusted the pixelated glow of the computer screen, the internet agreed with Maybelline. She lowered a red strap so he could admire her bare shoulder, which he did. Mixed in with the admiration was remembering.

"This guy I used to be involved with," she told him, "he came by the other night."

"Who?"

"You don't know him. He's a guy went to HVAC school and flunked out and is pissed off at the world."

"Give me a name."

"Danny Blanchard. But the only reason I'm telling you is, ten minutes of talking with that dickwad was all it took me to learn my lesson."

The red strap went back up. It was a modest gesture, unself-conscious, and it moved Smith.

"What lesson is that?" he asked her.

"That you are the only man I've got any interest in spending time with, any more."

"It will happen."

"When?"

"Soon."

"Soon like next week?"

"The minute I get things sorted out, I'm getting on an airplane."

That was vague. He couldn't help it. He wanted to talk about Béatrice with Maybelline. But it had to be the real Maybelline Beaudry, not the electronically generated counterfeit watching his face for clues. He longed to be sitting in a room with her, close enough to reach out and touch her actual skin, smell her personal smell. Trying to explain Bukavu, he risked lying. It would be a lie born of his ignorance. Here was a strange but true thing. If they were going to have any kind of future together, Maybelline would have to understand what happened to him in the Congo, not the version he told his buddies in a bar but the real deal. Not the slick, the grit.

She quit pushing him for a definite date.

"Can I ask a favor, Maybelline?"

"You want me to take off my top? My tits still stand up, you know."

"I can see that. No, don't take it off."

She nodded thoughtfully. "I'm glad. I kind of thought I wanted to show you my body, but I guess I don't, not over the freakin' internet."

"Will you call my sister for me?"

"Sure. What do I say?"

"Tell her I messed up."

Maybelline's face twisted.

"Never mind," he said. "Just tell her I'm coming home, and we'll go out to eat at Daddy Phats."

Daddy Phats was a barbecue joint. Smith finally noticed the thing that had been bothering him. Bug bites. His body was covered with them. He had no idea what sort of creature had bitten him, or when, only that they had come out in force. He scratched his ankle but did not break eye contact with Maybelline.

"Okay," she said.

"You're coming, too. Me and you, we're taking Lu Ann to Daddy Phats."

She nodded. She smiled. There was something in the way she agreed to make the call that comforted Smith. Generosity, that was what it was. While he was wasting his time on an oil rig in the Atlantic, she had used hers wisely, figuring out how to become a generous adult.

He felt pretty good, killing the Skype connection and standing in the café to pay his bill. He was not paying attention to his surroundings the way he ought to, so the ANR man took him by surprise, clamping a hand on his wrist.

Leaving the warehouse that evening, Smith had been drawn uphill. Pushing against the specific gravity of the Eastern Congo he moved away from the remains of colonial Bukavu toward the confusion of today. As the day declined and dust percolated through the hot air, today was crowded. It was noisy, wrapped up in getting by. The flow of foot traffic on the narrow streets went simultaneously in many directions, and more people were laughing than you might expect. Some of them were laughing with great enthusiasm, and their warmth reassured Smith.

It was the sign on the wall of the brick storefront that drew him into the Happy Meal Café on a sandy street that was half again as wide as the streets that emptied into it. The sign was tin and had been painted by hand. The logo consisted of a hamburger in a bun. The bun was a snappy three-piece suit. The burger had astonished eyes and an expression of glee. In its hand, which was formed by what looked like a piece of leafy celery, it held out a computer keyboard, promising access to the unreal world.

Smith knew the man holding him by the wrist was a government agent, although there was nothing in the way he dressed that gave him away. He wore khaki pants with a crease. The sleeves of his blue shirt were neatly folded up at the cuffs. A bracelet of gold links hung loose on one wrist. His belly was a reservoir against the seven lean years coming his way. He was not quite short. His skin was not quite black.

Once he had Smith's attention he dropped his wrist. He touched his own chest with his fist the way people used to do at Mass, acknowledging the sin that happened *through my fault, through my fault, through my most grievous fault.*

"You did not check in with us," he said.

It was a serious charge seriously expressed, although his voice was quiet and courteous. *Shit,* thought Smith. He had known somebody like this man was going to turn up and threaten him, shake him down, arrest him. Maybe the same individual would do all three. But until it happened, the idea was abstract the way the weather forecast was abstract. Sure, there was a seventy percent chance of rain, but you didn't really give a damn until your head got wet.

"How was I supposed to check in with you if I didn't know who you were?"

The clenched fist touched the chest again, but the fault lay with Smith.

"Come with me."

"Where?"

"You must see the Director."

"The director of what?"

"Your presence in Bukavu is irregular."

Every one of the dozen or so customers in the Happy Meal was looking at them. Conversation had ceased the instant the agent grabbed Smith's wrist. On the computer keyboards, no fingers moved. The man behind the counter wore a T-shirt that said something in an Asian language whose characters framed the picture of a lascivious cat. He made a subtle gesture intended to be helpful. *Don't mess with this one*, he was telling Smith.

Smith tried one more time to resist. He was not being brave. It was the contrary streak that ran through him like fat marbling meat. The streak often got him into trouble. If he happened already to be in trouble, he could not help making it worse.

"Who are you?" he said.

For a moment the question seemed to relax the agent. They were on the cusp of a normal conversation. Nobody was going for a gun, although he had a pistol in a holster on his belt. The crow's feet around his eyes crinkled when he smiled. He was older than Smith had first thought. An older man would value his job. If it included sniffing out unauthorized foreigners and delivering them to the Director, he would do so with diligence. He opened his wallet and showed Smith an ID card that looked real. He put the wallet away before the American caught the name on card.

"How do I know you are who you say you are?" he asked the man.

Smith did not expect to be assaulted, and his knees buckled when the agent suddenly put his head down and drove at him. An oof of pain escaped Smith, but before he went down the agent hugged him hard, holding him up. He muttered something not French into the American's ear, and an objective self inside Smith recognized how impossibly out of his depth he was.

The ANR man told him, "I will let go of you. When I do, you will stand still."

Half a dozen patrons, along with the manager, had followed them out of the café into the street. It was almost dark, and the air had cooled. Passersby stopped and clumped in the shadows. There was a murmur of sound, a little river of strange words flowing past and around the unlucky American.

"Let me go," Smith said.

The agent stepped back, breathing hard. Smith smelled the man's sweat. It was not the sweat of exertion, it was the lather of high emotion. In his work, weeks went by without the appearance of an illegal foreigner. Smith's goal was making sure the agent's pistol stayed in its holster.

"I'm going to show you a letter," he said.

"What letter?"

"It's in my bag. When I open the bag, the letter is the only thing I will remove. Is that clear?"

"*Il est clair.*"

Smith opened the bag, took out Lajeune's letter, and handed the envelope to the agent, who stepped into a bright square cast by a streetlight fixed to the storefront. He opened the envelope, unfolded the letter, and read. He read slowly, then read it again.

"You should have come to us," he said when he finished.

Smith watched him fold the letter back into its ministry envelope with care that expressed the respect he felt for official communications. A man who carried a letter like this one automatically earned a share of the respect owing to the minister of the government in Kinshasa who had signed the letter.

Smith put out a hand for the envelope. The agent hesitated. He did not want to surrender it, now that it was in his possession. The letter was a trophy. But there might also be a risk in hanging onto it, and slowly, with visible reluctance, he handed it back to Smith.

"You should have come to us," he said again. "The moment you arrived in Bukavu you should have come to see us. We are here to serve, you see, we are here to protect you."

He was still angling, still wanted Smith to go with him to see the Director in the uncontested safe space of his office. He could insist, and Smith would have no choice. And the Director would be more thorough than his agent. He would compare the name in the letter to the name in the American's passport. Smith had no acceptable explanation for the discrepancy. He began putting together a story in case he needed one. He stopped because everything that occurred to him was absurd.

"I leave in the morning," he told the agent. He was brusque. "There is no time."

The agent considered his options. He weighed the professional pleasure to be had from delivering Smith to the Director against the potential of angering someone in the ministry for hassling a foreigner traveling under the minister's protection. Because he was a mature man—he must be in his middle forties—he knew about impulse control.

"Next time you visit, you must remember we are here to help."

For Smith it was important not to be impressed by the threat implicit in the words.

"Next time," he said, leaving the unspoken rest of the sentence to the agent's imagination.

Monsieur!"

Smith kept walking, moving downhill in the dark without a destination. He had done Béatrice a favor, getting her out of Kinshasa, catapulting her toward a new life. She was resourceful and strong.

Bullshit. He had lost her.

The doors and windows of the small houses he passed as he moved away from the Happy Meal were thrown open. People sat on thresholds, on low chairs, on bare floors in sparse rooms, on the ground outside. The insubstantial thing he was did not interest them. This was as close to invisible as he had come to being in the Congo. A sweet smell hung in the air.

The lights on the ground, in the houses, were smoky orange, powered by kerosene. Smith got it now. It was a saint's day. They were celebrating the feast of Saint Calamitus, patron saint of perpetual catastrophe. It was a movable feast. Came around every day you beat the odds and survived.

"Monsieur, one moment. A word is all."

Smith did not stop walking.

"Monsieur, the street, this street, three blocks down it ends in a cul-de-sac."

Smith stopped. He let the man catch up.

"Where are you going?" the man demanded to know.

Smith was unable to make out the man's face. He was half a head taller than Smith and thin. His breath, close to Smith's face, smelled of clove. Not enough relevant information.

When he did not answer the question, the man told him, "You were lucky, back there at the internet place."

"I'm listening."

"The man who accosted you is an intelligence agent."

"I knew that."

"Maboso is his name. Among his duties, he is responsible for monitoring NGO activity in our area."

The reasonable thing, the logical thing, would be to ask the man which non-governmental organization he worked for. Maboso must also have hassled him. Smith did not. He turned away, moving off as though he had someplace to go. The tall man kept pace with Smith as he went.

"This Maboso," he confided, "he is not as bright as his superiors would wish him to be. They would advise him, for example, not to be put off by an official letter from the government. Such a letter carries a certain weight, there is no denying it. But, they would insist, you must ask to see a foreigner's passport. You must ask a series of questions designed to trip up a *menteur*, a *méchant*."

"So which one am I, a liar or a bad guy?"

"I was merely observing that you were lucky."

"Okay, I was lucky."

"Where are you going? The question is impertinent, but you may happen into a place that is unsafe for a foreigner."

"People in this country are always telling me where I shouldn't go."

"You will forgive me. I should have begun with my name. I am Roger Dzba. I am the regional director of Notre Pain de Ce Jour."

As he stood there in the dark, bug bites on his legs itching, pissed off at himself for losing Béatrice, roofless and without a plan, Smith's spirits tanked. He couldn't take out his frustration on the ANR man. Roger Dzba, on the other hand, was located conveniently next to him.

He said, in loud English, "Who the fuck wants to eat bread every day?"

A moment of silence, noiseless enough for Smith to hear the man gulp. Then, within earshot, a man and a woman laughed at the same thing. That set off the yapping of available dogs, ferocious and brief.

"We are a Catholic organization," Dzba said.

"Go to the devil."

Smith walked away. He was good at that. A few yards down, he kicked a stone with the toe of a sneakered foot. He stumbled, straightened up, kept walking.

"You need a place to sleep," Dzba said to his retreating back.

"Who owns the hotel?" he called back. "Your cousin or your uncle?"

"There is a spare room in our building."

Smith wondered where the trap lay to which Dzba was leading him. Think, man; think. He thought. There was just enough objectivity in him to register that he was doing something wrong. When had he begun distrusting everybody who spoke a civil word to him? He came to a halt again. This time he really stopped.

Smith had the impression that Roger Dzba was equipped with special-order eyes. They worked like night-vision goggles, allowing him to speed through the dark. He could easily have run downhill. But he kept Smith's slower pace heading for a street he called the Corniche that ran above Nyofu Bay.

"Costermansville," he said once.

He had the knack of making single words come out as sentences. It was not an urge to be mysterious, just his instinctive shorthand, and it didn't bother Smith.

"Costermansville," the American agreed.

"It is what the Belgians called the city when they colonized it."

Smith pictured an assembly of politicians with shining faces voting enthusiastically on a new name, the African name their constituents deserved, those same constituents applauding the sound of it in their mouths. *Bukavu in the Democratic*

Republic of Congo, Bukavu. He knew it had not been like that. If you wanted a civics lesson here you looked for a different sort of teacher.

They walked downhill in the dark, talking as if they knew each other. Eventually Roger pointed to a long, high wall looming darkly.

"There."

Notre Pain de Ce Jour was funded by Belgian Catholics. According to Roger, some but not all of them had family connections to Costermansville from back in the colonial day. One of the things their money bought was half a hectare of ground in the city above Nyofu Bay. Inside the compound were an office, a storehouse, a garage containing a small fleet of problematic vehicles, and a three-room house for the director with a roof that almost never leaked.

The walls around the compound were substantial, built of whitewashed bricks with shards of glass embedded in a cap of concrete on the top. There were three locks on the gate, two padlocks and a combination lock. Roger opened each of them in turn. It was his routine, and he went about it patiently. He accepted the need to shield the NGO's resources from the public, who would distribute those resources according to their own existential plan if they got their hands on them.

When he pushed open the gate and they went through it into the yard, a floodlight on a sensor clicked on. The sudden light disoriented Smith, and a woman screamed. It was a scream not of fear but of terror. For the instant it lasted, it got inside Smith and dug a new hole.

Roger cursed and ran toward the house. Smith went after him. Here, finally, was something he knew how to handle. Accost the man who was terrorizing a woman and stomp him until he quit. As Roger threw open the door and flipped a light switch on the wall, Smith was ready to take on the son of a bitch no matter how ugly mean he was. He flinched when a spray of machine gun fire raked the room.

"Gris," barked Roger.

It was enough to shut up the parrot in a bamboo cage on a pole in a corner of the room. In response, the bird hollered words of outrage at him in a Congo language.

Roger turned to Smith. "Meet Gris. An African grey, and she has been through a lot. Knows what abuse is, animal and human. She'll shut up if I cover the cage, but I don't want to do that. The frustration builds up, and the next day is miserable for both of us."

"I understand," said Smith, who didn't.

"Have you eaten?"

Smith told him he hadn't.

"Talk to Gris. Ask her questions about her time in a camp across the border in Rwanda. Ask her about the woman whose voice she was mimicking just now. Meantime I will fix something to put in our bellies. Do you consume meat?"

"Yeah, sure."

"Then it's a pity we have none."

Smith took a seat but did not ask questions of the parrot. He watched Roger make some soup, slice a loaf of bread, uncork a bottle of red wine. As Roger worked on dinner, Gris rehearsed her amazing repertoire of sounds. There was gunfire of several calibers, in single shots and sustained bursts. There were altercations, a chorus of angry voices, scared voices, put-upon voices. There was a faithful imitation of a helicopter, the pockita-pockita of its whirring blades varying in volume as the aircraft landed and then took off again. Mission accomplished.

"You have a pretty smart bird there."

Head down, stirring the soup pot, Roger told him, "The African grey is intelligent, as a species. And of course all these years of war have expanded her natural scope for expression. She is a bird, par excellence, of unhappy experience. Here."

He handed Roger a glass of wine. The wine was tart. It sought the taste buds under Smith's tongue of its own volition, making a muddy statement. They sat across from each other at a folding table on folding chairs that served as Roger's field office when he was out distributing rations.

He told Smith, "The board of Notre Pain would very much like to get out of the business of delivering food to people. As an organization we make plans, quite good plans. They are detailed, they work toward worthy ends. The board envisions green and peaceful fields, fat with sustainable crops, the people working them smiling. So we make our plans afresh every year. Then a catastrophe happens. War. The catastrophe has repercussions."

"People don't have anything to eat."

Roger sat up in his chair. He put his wine glass down and smacked the table with the flat of his hand. "We are reduced to a minimal outcome. We give food to those who lack it."

"It's an honorable calling."

Roger shook his head. "Honor does not enter into it." Then, as though one thing led to another, he asked Smith to tell him what he was doing in Bukavu. Smith told him.

"It's too bad," Roger said.

His sympathy for the missing Béatrice was limited. In the work he did, there was a heavy call on his sympathy, his empathy, his fellow feeling. He could not afford to spray those things around the way his parrot sprayed the sounds of war.

"Since the child has disappeared," he said, "you will no doubt leave the Congo."

"First I have to get back to Goma."

"Maybe I can help."

Notre Pain relied on an unstable network of unreliable shippers. Moving supplies in, sending them out, Roger consulted people who knew the situation on the roads. Sometimes the situation was good, and he hired a truck, or he hired a driver to chance it with one of the two Chinese flatbeds in his fleet, if one of them happened to be roadworthy. When the situation on the roads was bad, he knew the captains of a handful of small-time cargo ships. If one of them was headed for Bukavu, he worked something out with the captain.

A light bulb crackled, fizzed, and went out. The parrot berated it. The soup was tasty, and they emptied the pot. Roger poured them more tart wine.

"You're saying you can offer me a ride, possibly back to Goma, possibly to another city. But you're not sure when or how."

"A perfect encapsulation. With luck, you might be on your way in a couple of days. Do you have a wife, Smith?"

"I'm not married."

"I'm sorry. Myself, I do have a wife. I was speaking with her, over the internet, when the ANR man began hassling you."

"What is your wife's name?"

"Giselle."

"And where is she?"

"Spain. Barcelona. She went there legally. She has quite an organized mind and landed herself a significant computer job."

"From the sound of your voice, I'd say you want her to quit the job and come home."

"How shall I put this? Self-pity is a sin in any religion. The length of my wife's stay in Europe is a topic of conversation between us. For a woman of Giselle's abilities, Bukavu offers little. She requires mental stimulation, and the companionship of colleagues."

The parrot sighed dramatically. Smith wondered if it was capable of picking up on its master's mood.

"What about you?"

He shrugged. "Me? I also have my dreams."

It was a private comment, and Smith let it go.

"Giselle will come home," he told Roger.

"You sound certain."

"I'm only certain of one thing."

"What's that?"

"While I'm here in this Congo, my boss in the other Congo fired me."

Roger nodded. Such an outcome was hardly surprising. Actions had consequences. "The morning of the day you are to leave Bukavu, you must eat heartily. You will rely on me to make sure that happens."

Roger cleaned up the kitchen space. He covered the parrot's cage. When he spoke it was to Giselle, who was still in Barcelona. Smith did his damnedest not to hear. What he could not help hearing, he tried not to understand. Roger set up a cot for him in the corner opposite Gris, and he fell asleep.

In the morning Smith woke knowing Béatrice was no longer in Bukavu. While he slept, his undermine had figured it out.

"She was there when I was talking with a Munyamulenge man," he told Roger. "She was listening hard."

Roger had been up a while. He had heated water and was steeping a pot of oolong tea. When it was ready he handed Smith an enamel mug, pouring in a shot of long-life milk from a cardboard carton.

"And what was it the young girl overheard?"

He had cleaned up, shaved, and put on a white shirt with short sleeves. Pushed up on his head were wraparound sunglasses that gave him the look of an aviator on dawn patrol. He was a nervous man, intense, who had learned to moderate his gestures.

"The guy told me her grandmother might be in Minembwe."

Roger nodded. "Minembwe has become, these years, a town of the Banyamulenge."

"He said you have to go through Uvira to get there."

"So she is on the road to Uvira."

Smith nodded. "Walking."

Roger sipped his tea. He got up to lift the fabric cover from the parrot's cage. The bird stirred on its perch and muttered. It shifted on its haunches and shat a tiny black pellet.

"Regular as clockwork, this one," Roger said. "You are not going back to Goma,"

"It's hard to explain."

"You feel responsible for the child." A pause, then, "You expect me to be critical. It is not quite the thing, is it, for an American man who is white and at the same time green. In Africa we have had more than our fill of white saviors. Look what it has done for us. Yet it is not merely a question of your intentions, or your capacity."

"What else is there?"

"Last night, what Maboso told you about the authorities' permission. He was correct."

"I know that."

"You need permission not just to be here, but to go to another place."

Smith thought of duck-duck-goose, squatting in a circle of ruthless competitors waiting for the music to stop, hoping you didn't become the designated goose.

"I have a letter. The minister of the interior signed it."

He did not add that the letter was intended for a specific Belgian national, not an American oil rig mechanic.

"Your letter," Roger began. He spoke slowly as though negotiating a treacherous curve in a road known for them. "It counts for something, yes. But not for everything. Each official who becomes aware of your presence will demand a piece of you."

"There's not that much to go around."

"They will be happy to supply you with a *feuille de route*. But their blessing comes at a cost. Because you are an American, the cost will be notably higher. I apologize."

"Why? It's not your fault."

"Nevertheless." He looked away as though the subject he was about to bring up embarrassed him. "You wish to clean up."

"I do."

"Out back. It's not . . . "

"Not what?"

"What you're used to."

Smith did not answer. It was already old, being told every day in a different way that he did not belong to this hard country. He picked up his go bag. Not that he distrusted Roger. But his own personal Congo policy was still evolving. At the top of the list of things not to do was let the go bag out of his sight.

At the back of the compound stood two large buildings of brick coated with grainy, whitewashed adobe. Both had metal roofs. One of them was the garage, the other a warehouse. Behind the warehouse Smith found a cubicle.

He stepped inside onto a broad board that ran the length of the concrete floor. The purpose of the board was to avoid the skin of scummy water on the floor, which had backed up through a clogged drain hole. The drain bubbled lazily. Black splotches covered the walls, their outer edges green as the mold spread, taking the room slowly down. He took another step in.

On a small, high metal table sat a wash basin. Next to the basin was a bar of gritty orange soap. No towel, but he had one in the bag. Overhead, a shower head dripped. Also overhead, fixed to the ceiling tile, a bat slept in a corner. Bat disease. It gave you radar, which was cool, but it also made you blind. He disliked the complacent look of the thing hanging there.

Smith went outside. In the garage he found a broom. He went back and poked the bat from the doorway until it got riled. The instant it moved, Smith did, too. There was only one way out, and the creature found it. It flapped out, made a dizzy swooping circle, and headed for a tree on the perimeter of the property. Smith went inside again and took a shower. The gritty soap rubbed his flesh raw. The scum had coated the board where the water rose over it, and his feet felt dirty no matter how many times he scrubbed them. Still, it felt good to wash off the road.

Back in the office, Roger was waiting as if he expected a complaint about the facilities. Smith told him, "Here's my problem."

"Yes?"

"I don't have a lot of money. I can spend half of it, but I have to save the other half to get myself out of the country."

"And you will not know when you have reached the halfway point."

"Exactly. Let's say I spent whatever it took to get the permission. Would that solve the problem?"

Roger shook his head. Gris laughed derisively.

Smith said, "They would still want a piece of me."

"*Il est inévitable.*"

"Fuck it, then. I'll rent a car. Béatrice is on foot. In a vehicle I can catch up."

"Must the vehicle have four wheels?"

Smith assumed he was offering him a motorcycle. It was better than that. He was offering to go along with him on the road to Uvira. The Notre Pain fleet included a couple of two-stroke Kawasaki bikes.

When they went out to the garage, neither would start.

"We used to have a man working here. He was a wonder with the engines."

"What happened to him?"

"He disappeared. So did our best motorcycle."

Smith wondered what it took to steal from a place dedicated to feeding the hungry. A different kind of hunger.

Roger said, "Last week."

"Last week what?"

"One of them started."

"Which one?"

The bikes were identical, both of them red, and Roger was not sure which one of them had recently turned over.

Smith asked him, "Do you believe in cannibalism?"

"That's what they told you before you came here. The Congolese eat one another. In the absence of a protein source, they turn to their neighbor."

"That's not what I had in mind."

A white cat with tawny feet chased a rat across the garage floor. The rat escaped. The cat returned and sat at Roger's feet expecting praise for a job well done.

"Give me an hour," Smith told him.

But an hour turned out short. Roger went to the port to track down two hundred and fifty missing hoes, part of a shipment consigned to several NGOs none of which had received what they were promised. Smith lined up the two Kawasakis side by side on the garage floor, whose pebbly cement was marked with oil stains. He studied the bikes for a moment, then squatted to study them some more. As he did, he became aware of a small boy squatting ten feet behind him and off to one side.

He looked over at the boy. His chest was bare. He wore crimson gym shorts and yellow flip-flops. The flip-flops were twice the size of his feet, which gave them a ceremonial look as if they were meant for a ritual.

"Cigarette," the boy said.

Smith didn't know whether he wanted one or was offering to go run for some.

"What's your name?"

The boy shook his head. He frowned.

"Looks like we're going to get some rain," he said.

The sky was cloudless, the air dry as old bones. No response from the boy.

"This morning," Smith told him, "I saw a herd of elephants coming across the lake waving their trunks and hollering."

No response. Smith would have been satisfied with a grin. He kept at the boy for a good five minutes at the end of which he was convinced he was not playing him; the boy did not know French.

But he did know tools. When Smith put a hand on the throttle of one of the bikes and twisted, the boy disappeared and came back with a small toolbox. By the time Smith was ready to inspect the carburetor, the boy had anticipated him with a wrench and a screwdriver. He handed them to the American the way a nurse in an operating room handed the tools of his trade to a surgeon.

Smith worked methodically because that was how you fixed things. That much he inherited from his old man. As a kid, he had worked with his father when Baylee Smith built a deck on the back of their trailer, replaced the transmission in his Ford 150, tore down a tobacco barn and salvaged the boards to sell to people with money who suffered from *nostalgie de la boue*. Hurry did not enter into Baylee's calculations. Anyway catching up to Béatrice would be easy on a bike. Unless somebody offered her a ride, and she took it. Smith had no clue how likely that was, but his ignorance of Congolese likelihoods would not drive him to be sloppy in matters of engine repair.

He wound up cannibalizing the bike whose engine was in terrible condition to make the other one healthy. He took the carburetor from the tired bike and put it on the hopeful one, tuned it and gapped the plug. The fuel lines from both machines were in bad shape. He drained one of them, and then the tank on the bike with a future, which was seriously gunked. Somebody had been filling up on some pretty shitty gas. He found rust in the accelerator cable and cleaned it. He adjusted the clutch plate.

Returning hoeless at noon, Roger approved.

"When I left, we had no functioning bike. Now we have one. This is a success."

"There was a kid hanging around all morning."

"Ah, yes. Gaylord."

"He's a born mechanic."

"I once caught him stealing rice, hauling away a fifty-kilo sack in a wheelbarrow he stole for the purpose. Now, when he hears me coming, he expects retribution and takes off in a hurry."

"And would you?"

"Would I what?"

"Visit some retribution on him?"

"Gaylord has no parents. He lives in cardboard."

"You don't get used to this, do you?"

Roger knew exactly what he was talking about, which was why his answer was a deflection. "You are not so huge as the Americans in the movies. You are, like me, of medium size."

"So?"

"We will ride together."

Smith must have given him a funny look because Roger said, "You don't know the right questions to ask, or how to ask them. The girl can make herself invisible."

"Magic," Smith said.

"Something like that."

"We need to put some clean fuel in the tank."

The Kawasaki two-stroke ran well. Roger piloted the bike through a flow of non-linear traffic heading for the road to Uvira, Smith behind him holding his go bag. The street they took out of the city was wide, as if it had been built to accommodate the gigantic yellow earth mover they came to, parked crossways at an intersection. There was no driver, no indication why it was there. Kids were using the bed of the half-raised dumper as a slide. Coming down, they scrambled to break their fall at the lip of the open metal maw. Some of them fell out, pushed by the weight of the kid behind them. The ones who fell picked themselves up from the ground, laughing and limping, and climbed back into the truck. They slid again.

As cars and motorbikes approached the intersection, they created a new traffic pattern around the earth mover, but trucks could not get past it. A man in a Zorro cape had taken it upon himself to reroute the trucks, waving a gnarled shepherd's crook at the driver of every big vehicle that rolled into view. He lacked authority, and the truckers went their own way. The man in the cape harangued them until they disappeared from sight. The cape was long. It trailed on the ground. The ends of the black fabric were ragged and dirty, and the whole thing had a dull patina of dust.

Roger followed the flow. Over the whine of the engine Smith heard the caped man shouting at them. As they left the city the landscape opened up. Smith took in red dirt and green growth over low hills separated by sheer drops. The drops had been scalloped by titanic forces that predated the Belgians, the Congolese, the whole idea of time as something you could slice into edible epochs. The green was brilliant but had the cropped look of deforestation.

On the outskirts of the city they went by a market where the vendors had spread their merchandise on the ground, sitting alongside piles of manioc and melons, kids clothes and batteries and cell phone gear. Everyone was talking. It was not clear if anyone was buying.

They went past an open courtyard where the sun had cracked the hard dirt into a pattern of lines separating irregular oblongs, like a tile floor preserved for centuries until archaeologists uncovered it.

Once, where the road flexed an elbow, the ground on the left fell steeply away and they saw the lake filling up the distance. It was blue and calm and looked friendly. Men were fishing from narrow boats. The long poles they held, dipping to the water, had the nimble curve of suspension bridges.

A hundred yards on, along the west side of the road, they passed women in *pagnes* with buckets in their hands. Two of the women had dropped their buckets and faced off against each other over whose turn it was to draw water. The older one was thick in the middle. The younger one was slim and seemed to be ahead on points. She was poking the older woman in the chest, hollering things Smith would not have understood even if he could hear them. The older woman windmilled her arms as though trying to keep her balance, or else she was expressing a point of view. Around them a dozen more women milled and hollered. They had a nervous look as though they were aware of a cataclysm coming down that was hidden from the American. Even from the road, going past them fast, their intensity was overpowering.

They went by a field of tall grass that was being trampled by the feet of boys playing soccer. There were enough boys for three teams, or maybe four. When the ball hit the ground it disappeared in the grass. Running after it a tall boy kicked, sliding, and the ball popped up. Before it came down Roger had powered the bike past the field.

Then they were out of the city. It tapered off into countryside without giving much warning. Thirty minutes later Smith became aware of a black lozenge hanging over the lake, swelling to cover the sky. It came on fast. So did the rain, falling in a stinging sheet that slicked the road and blinded Roger, who was wearing his sunglasses to protect his eyes from bugs. He eased off the throttle but downshifted too fast, and the Kawasaki skated out of control. Smith rolled off as the bike went down, skidding in the wet dirt that was not quite mud, not yet, but Roger held on. When the bike fell on its side, the engine burned a hole in his pant leg and puckered the flesh of his calf. He got up refusing to curse as another man might.

He clutched the St. Christopher medal on a silver chain around his neck. "Welcome to the rainy season."

"I thought the rain wasn't supposed to start yet."

"Any day now."

As Roger gathered himself, Smith righted the bike. He wheeled it off the road into a patch of woods where Roger pointed.

Roger went first, limping. Under the canopy they did not feel the rain as intensely, but the patient roar of the sky continued. A red bird with a hooked bill moved ahead of them from tree to tree guiding them away from its nest. From the fork of a massive, double-trunked tree being strangled by murderous vines, a monkey waved its fist at them. Snakes, thought Smith. This was not the great Congolese forest, which ate colonialists, Twa hunters, heedless kids who strayed while playing. It was just a patch of woods. Still, there had to be snakes. At home, fishing with his father in a swampy lake, he had once watched a copperhead emerge from the water, climb a tree, nail a napping jay.

They were on a path. Not much of one, but if you looked carefully you saw the line it traced through the trees. Walking the bike was like walking a balky mule. After a few minutes they came to a shack. There was an abandoned feel about the place, and you could see the forest encroaching on the clearing around it, relentlessly taking back the space humans had hacked out of it.

The hut was a single round room made of poles and baked mud with densely bunched, overlapping sheaves of leaves thatching the roof. There was no door, just a hole they stooped to go through, Smith lugging the bike in with him. The first thing they noticed was that the roof did not leak.

It was good to get out of the rain. They sat on the floor, Roger preoccupied with the burn on his leg. The hike through the woods had strained him even though he was young and strong. The burn had sapped him. He poked at it as if wanting to prove it was real.

Smith looked around trying to guess how long the place had been empty. He had no idea. There might be clues. If there were, he was incapable of seeing them. The only human evidence he saw was a single man's shoe lacking a sole. The brown leather of the upper was cracked and scuffed, but the lace was neatly tied. That was what bothered him, that the lace was tied.

The only other sign of life and death was a perfect spider's web hanging like a sheet from the thatch. A beetle was trapped in the web. This was why Smith was in the Congo, to watch a beetle wriggle in a web, go still, wriggle again. Every time the creature moved, the spiderweb swung as if fretted by breeze.

"This morning I told Gaylord it was going to rain," Smith said. "He didn't believe me."

Head down, Roger prodded his wound.

Smith told him, "Maybe you'd better go back to Bukavu, have somebody take a look at that."

"There are plants out here," Roger said, not lifting his head. "They have powers. You apply them to the burn, and the flesh quickly heals."

"So go get some."

"I don't know what they look like."

He quit poking.

Smith went out into the rain, pulled some tangled ropes of viny leaves and wiped the mud from the bike engine with them. The engine was still warm, like a thing that had a certain quantity of life in it that needed protecting. He wheeled it outside and hit the starter button. The engine turned over the first time. He switched it off. It was pretty stupid, feeling pride in his competence as a mechanic. All he had.

When he went back into the hut, Roger told him, "It is unusual for a Congolese to be the director of an organization like Notre Pain."

"Why is that?"

"They don't trust us. It's the old colonial feeling." He shrugged as if he didn't much care. "They fight it, some of them. They resist their instinct to disparage us."

He took a plastic bag from his pants pocket. Inside the bag there were two colossal joints rolled in blue papers, along with a book of matches. He lit one of the joints and inhaled, letting the smoke tantalize his lungs. He exhaled and passed it to Smith. Smith took it. He did not get high often. His attitude toward marijuana was mixed. The ambivalence went back to Foulard's Garage.

His last year of high school Smith cut as many classes as he went to. Mostly he hung around Foulard's, where he thought the owner might give him a real job. He was close-to-free labor for Guy Foulard, who was a first-class mechanic. Now and then, needing cash, he sold weed to people he trusted. Now and then, needing companionship, he offered Smith a hit. Guy didn't mind when he blasted Usher from the sound system, which showed he had an open mind.

One morning they were replacing the head gasket on the engine of a Chevy Impala. Guy had the gift of feel and could make metal cooperate. As they worked they toked on some prime Northern California buds. They had climbed to cruising altitude by the time three sheriff's deputies blew into the garage with their guns drawn.

It was not a positive experience. In Smith's condition of stimulated awareness they looked like aliens. Their two-tone uniforms and bristling gear made them into metal-munching cop-bots from a planet where darkness held sway. And they had a plan. One of them hauled Smith out behind the garage and bent him back over a fifty-five-gallon oil drum. He shoved his pistol into Smith's mouth and muttered muzzy things Smith was too high to translate into words. The gold tooth in his evil grin complicated everything. Somehow he made Smith understand that he was supposed to open his wallet. Open it he did, not that there was much inside.

By the time the deputy let him stand up, the other two had cleaned out Guy's stash. The three of them drove off with their lights flashing, siren wailing, hauling ass to the scene of another crime. Guy was a decent human being and pretended not to notice his junior helper throwing up in a tin basin in a corner of the garage. The deputies had left laughing. It wasn't a serious raid, all they wanted to do was punk a couple of gear-heads.

"There was never no goddamn chance those boys was going to arrest us," he told Smith.

Now, the smoke from Roger's big blunt was acrid and tasted like jungle. Smith felt himself letting go. With great absorption he watched a mosquito approach the halo of blue smoke around the Congolese man, turn tail, and fly away in disgust. It was like watching a nature program on TV, but cooler.

"There are seven of them," Roger said.

"Mosquitoes?"

"Members of the board. Last year four of them experienced a fit of collective remorse and voted me director. Me, a Black man, responsible for their mission, their budget, their public image."

The marijuana was affecting both of them at the same fast rate. The smoky blue cloud of dope smoke inside the hut protected them from the mosquitoes, but Smith began worrying in a big way about the spider. When he put his mind to the subject, an iron chain of reasoning made itself apparent. He followed it link by link. If there was a cobweb—there was—and it snared a breakfast bug—it did—the spider who spun the web would show up hungry. It stood to reason. Making its predetermined appearance, the spider at the end of the reasoning chain would stun the bug, kill it, eat it. Then it would shit little beetle bits on the floor of the shack. The waste would biodegrade over a period of days or months, offering up its atoms for the making of a different predator. This was what people meant when they said it was a dog-eat-dog world.

Comprehending the airtight logic of the case pleased Smith more than it ought to. It also distracted him so that he missed some of what Roger was saying. That was okay. He said it again.

"They hate us."

His breathing was suddenly labored as if he had run a mile. His chest heaved. He was wearing a T-shirt with the Notre Pain logo, a cheery yellow sun over a green field, and the image swelled as he inhaled.

"They pretend we are brothers in Christ, but they despise us."

In an instant he went from dejected to furious. In the same instant he rose to his feet and pulled a machete from between two roof sheaves.

Smith had not noticed the thing up there. So much for situational awareness. Alarmed by Roger's supersonic mood swing, he got to his feet and faced him. The weed was affecting his perception, his balance, his practical grasp of physics. Anything was possible in a universe in which time was always fucking with space. He wobbled.

Roger raised the machete. He seemed to want to use it. The complicated frown on his face was the most expressive human look Smith recalled seeing. He could have studied it all day, certain that it would explain some of the things that were troubling him. But if he stayed where he was, the machete would cut him, possibly in half. As he sidestepped, the sound of the blade slicing air filled his buzzing ears.

He hollered. The good thing was it came out in French. Roger dropped the weapon. He stooped, picked it up again, hefted it. He seemed puzzled and did not attack the American.

"They hate us," he insisted.

"I don't hate you."

Roger sat down peacefully, crossed his legs, laid the machete across his lap. Smith sat down facing him.

"You almost killed me."

Roger shook his head. Was he denying it? That was bullshit.

Smith asked him, “Who are you?”

But the question irritated Roger. “I am the director of Notre Pain de Ce Jour.”

“That’s not what I mean.”

Avoiding the machete had cleared the American’s head. Using it did the same thing for the Congolese. They were not exactly sober, but they descended at roughly the same rate to an open plain and discovered that reason existed, or could.

From that safer altitude Roger said quietly, “You want my story.”

Smith nodded.

“I am a man of Africa. Born in the Congo.”

“That’s it?”

Roger shook his head. He glared, but there was no heat in it. “There are too many stories in this country. They drag us down.”

“So you aren’t going to tell me what happened to you.”

“I tell it to God.”

“And does God listen?”

“We maintain a dialogue.” He stopped. “A monologue. I talk, He listens.”

Smith admired the man’s stand, which was based on principle and looked forward to an improved Congolese future. He would have admired it more if Roger had not just swung a rusty blade at him.

With a start he realized that he had been right all along, the spider was back. It was crossing the web with deadly purpose.

At the center of the web, the trapped bug was absolutely still. An all-powerful God could will a world that allowed an insect to lose its limited consciousness the instant before being consumed by a more complex creature with a bigger brain. A world like that would be worth inhabiting.

Roger replaced the machete in the ceiling.

"Listen," the man of Africa said, pointing up.

It took Smith a moment. He thought Roger was indicating the direction he sent his monologue, the traditional location of Heaven. But he was pointing to what was not there. Rain. The forest was momentarily quiet, as though the storm had subdued it. They heard drops of rainwater plopping on leaves. From an unspecified distance came a muted conversation among birds. Roger limped back toward the road. Smith went after him wheeling the healthy Kawasaki.

Enough rain had fallen that the road was sloppy now. Roger drove slowly. He seemed to accept the burn on his leg, throbbing pain his new normal. He didn't fight it, he adjusted. The bike's back tire lifted and dropped a continuous ribbon of wet dirt as they went. The sky cleared quickly, and the air had a fresh smell, like starting over. They passed people walking, carrying bundles and packages. People on motorbikes, also with bundles. People pushing Chinese bicycles with clunky black frames laden with things to sell. Within a kilometer they passed two cars with flat tires and no visible spare.

Once, for no reason Smith could make out, Roger stopped to talk to a scrawny man pushing a bicycle overburdened with sacks of charcoal. Wet from the rain, the hunks of charcoal that showed at the mouths of the sacks glistened like prizes. The man had a crinkled face of leathery brown skin. A rim of graying beard gave him a crafty look. He spoke emphatically, glad of a chance to stop pushing his load down an uncooperative road. Roger told Smith the man had neither seen nor heard of a Munyamulenge girl traveling alone.

They rode another twenty minutes slowly before Roger parked the Kawasaki in front of a makeshift roadside stand offering for sale coconuts and three cans of orange soda. The counter was a plank sitting on two big rocks. The rocks were not of equal size, so the plank leaned. To keep the merchandise from rolling off, the woman behind the stand wedged each coconut and pop bottle with a small stone. She had a head that looked too big for the rest of her body, but that may have been the effect of the blue turban on it.

While Roger talked to the woman, Smith stretched his legs. The woman glanced at him once, then looked away. He was not as interesting as she might have supposed. Speaking to Roger, she patted a coconut idly as though it were the head of a restless child. From where he stood, Smith did not hear a word of French. He would be incapable, on his own, of finding Béatrice.

There was something patronizing in the way Roger informed Smith that they had to turn around, they had missed the girl. Either that or Smith's abject helplessness was making him oversensitive. He was aware again just how little he liked being led by the hand from place to place as people reminded him that he did not know enough to be useful to his own cause. The coconut seller's goodbye smile was a smirk.

They retraced the route they had just traveled. When they came to the first car with a flat tire, seven adults were standing in the road watching an eighth man with a tire iron demonstrate a point of practical interest. Roger skirted the group, piloting the bike with respectful caution around them. Before they reached the second stopped car he left the road taking a narrow track through grass that rose above their heads on either side of them. Not far down the track, a boy stood in their way. In one hand he held a tether attached at the other end to a black goat. The goat had a curly goatee the color of dirt. In the other hand the boy held a sinewy stick twice his height with which he was beating the grass. Not, it seemed to Smith, for any purpose except feeling good.

The boy did not want to yield to the bike coming at him. Just before they made contact, he yanked the goat's tether and slipped into the grass, which assimilated both of them.

Roger came to a stop. He shut off the engine and called to the boy.

It was like hollering at grass.

Another third of a mile in, the path gave onto a clearing. In the clearing stood a house of mud and poles like the one in which they had sheltered from the rain. Behind the clearing was a tangle of trees, the undergrowth thick with spiky leaves and dense banks of purple flowers. Bees hovered and hummed in the banks. From the yard, half a dozen kids stared at them.

As they stepped down from the Kawasaki a short, thickly built man stepped out of the house. After him came a woman. After the woman came Béatrice.

When she saw Smith she started toward him. But before she was halfway across the clearing the man came up behind her and knocked her to the ground, clipping her in the neck with the flat of his hand. The surprise hit dazed her. After a moment of stunning pain she got to her knees and looked around trying to remember where she was. When she got to her feet the man knocked her down again. He said something that meant *Stay down*. She stayed.

The stupid thing that Smith did was not triggered by anger. He was angry all right, but ever since the roadside seller had smirked at him he knew he had to do something. He could no longer go passively through the Congo relying on strangers. A switch flipped. Suddenly he had no more patience, strategic or tactical. Do something. Doing the wrong thing was better than doing nothing at all.

He took off running until he came face to face with the man who had hit Béatrice. He stopped and fired a clip's worth of pretty decent French abuse at the guy, who was startled to find an angry white man berating him in his own front yard. Startled but not intimidated.

The man wore blue pants, a sheeny white shirt with sweat stains, a pair of boat shoes in good condition. The shoes featured those decorative rawhide laces running around the uppers. His face was flat, with scars as from a knife on both cheeks. The scars did not match. They were not deliberate but gave his face the look of a mask, past which the American could not see. There was more gray than black in the man's hair, and he looked worn out, like someone who had been carrying a heavy thing a long way.

His wife, standing behind him and off to one side, was small and short. Her face was bruised, her lips swollen to a grimace. She had the cowed look of a woman who had been knocked around and expected more of the same. Her feet splayed out in the dirt, fixing her there. Did she ever fight back?

Béatrice, on the ground but not cringing, knew enough to keep her mouth shut. She was furious, which even in that moment of maximum tension made Smith want to cheer. Do something. He shoved the short man with a hand on his chest. The man bent a little, moving backward, but did not give ground or register fear.

Smith pointed at Béatrice and said, "The girl is my daughter."

If he had thought it through, he might have come up with something better. Didn't matter. Maybe the guy did not understand him. If he did, he did not give a shit. He looked around, slowly, taking stock of the situation. He ordered his kids, his wife, and Béatrice inside. The mother put out a hand for Béatrice, who took it. Standing, the girl was as tall as the woman who led her into the house.

Something, a flutter, drew Smith's attention, and for the first time he noticed a hammock strung between two trees in a patch of speckled shade along the edge of the woods. A man was lying in the hammock. He was holding an automatic rifle. Seeing that he had Smith's attention, he put a foot on the ground for purchase and set the hammock swinging, slowly. At the top of the hammock's arc, the muzzle of the rifle pointed itself at the American. After the arc, the hammock moving in the other direction, back toward the woods, the rifle lost interest and cast its one hard eye on the ground.

For several strung-out seconds Smith could not look away. Every time the hammock approached its arc, he flinched. Meantime the father of the family stood passively facing the American. Illumination visited Smith, and it occurred to him that the guy could be a Hutu.

The man moved his jaw back and forth, coughed and spat on the ground. That broke the spell, and Smith reconsidered his approach.

It was like being a kid again. You were a witness to big things, important things, some of them terrible and some of them unspeakably sweet. All the words you heard going on around you were in a language that was foreign to you. But even if you understood what was happening, you had no way to express what you felt. Sometimes, you did not even know what you felt, all you knew was that there was a battle going on, and you could be blasted to smithereens.

Then Roger was there, speaking conciliatory words to the father while putting a hand on Smith's shoulder, backing him down. It was also prudent to bring the man with the rifle into the social circle. Alone, watching from the edge, he was more dangerous. He wore a ripped yellow T-shirt, camo pants with excessive empty pockets, no shoes.

Roger invited him in. None of the back-and-forth happened in French, but it was obvious to Smith that Roger was exercising the skills of a diplomat. The Belgian board of Notre Pain de Ce Jour knew what they were doing, naming him national director. What had happened in the shack, with the machete, already seemed like a dream. A misunderstanding between two other people.

The hammock continued to swing, causing the rifle muzzle to be trained on the American every couple of seconds. The man moving the hammock shifted the rifle casually. Smith wondered what kind of gun it was.

Talk was cheap on the Dauphin rig, and the crew had spent a lot of it one night discussing Kalashnikovs. One of the three Americans on the rig did a good job reinforcing the Europeans' ideas of gun savagery in the New World. A Texas flatlander with a lonesome cowpoke moustache, Pickerell was always thumbing through the pictures on his phone, foisting a slideshow on anybody who would stop and look. He had multiple views of every weapon in the arsenal he stored back home in his daddy's basement in Cruz City. The pictures were displayed against a black backdrop with indirect lighting, like objets d'art. There were seven pictures of his favorite, an AR-15 assault rifle, including a full frontal shot.

Gun porn, Smith called it once when he was in the mood to pick a fight with somebody like Pickerell, and Pickerell himself was handy and fit the description.

After a tedious long minute the father of the family nodded, and the man rolled out of the hammock, slung the rifle over his shoulder by its worn leather strap, and sauntered over.

"Names," Roger said in French. "We need to start with names."

The name of the man who had hit Béatrice was Aristide Kavaruganda. The man with the rifle was his cousin. The cousin's name was Roy. The name of his rifle was in fact Kalashnikov, first name Mikhail.

Roger was right. Speaking each other's names brought the tension level down a notch. But only a notch. Smith's senses were still vaguely dope-aroused, and he picked up the faint whiff of murder the rifle emitted. There was a smell of burning wood in the clearing although there was no fire. And every man gave off his own funky sweat smell, as individual as a fingerprint. Smith wished he could take a shower.

Aristide called for food. The woman brought out a pot of gloppy gray stuff and put it on the ground at his feet. No sign of Béatrice. Smith hoped that meant the mother was on her side, keeping her away from her husband and her husband's anger. Roger, Smith noticed, did not demand that the woman's name also be known.

Aristide pointed at the pot. "*Fufu.*"

Smith was not sure whether that was the name of the food or a command to eat it. When the other men sat on the ground, he sat with them. He watched them scoop out hunks of the gray stuff. He scooped a hunk for himself. It did not taste like anything he knew but was bland and not too bad. He chewed slowly. He was hungry and had not thought about food.

A few minutes of concentrated chewing. The rifle lay on the ground next to Roy. Probably he slept with it. Aristide Kavaruganda's sullen anger polluted the air in the clearing. The day was getting short.

After ten minutes Smith's patience gave out again. Roger was in no hurry. Eating his *fufu*, fingers occasionally finding the burnt flesh of his leg, he seemed ready to make peace. Compromise, wasn't that what diplomats were known for? Never mind the weak hand Smith was playing, he would accept nothing less than Béatrice walking away free.

"I will take the girl with me," he said to Aristide, doing his best to make it a confident statement of fact.

Aristide looked at him for a moment. Then he exploded. Few of the words he spat came out in French. He raved, he stopped, and then he called for beer. One of his daughters brought out a bottle. He shared it with his cousin. When they had drained it, Roger spoke slowly to them in the reasonable tone of voice Smith had been trying for.

He turned to Smith. "I will translate."

"So translate."

Roger looked at Aristide, making sure the man understood what was going to happen. Aristide ground his teeth. His voice, even while muttering, was a rich baritone. In a different social order he would be narrating soccer games on the radio.

"He says," Roger began. "He says the Banyamulenge are in league with the Tutsis. It is the Tutsis who are responsible for the misfortune that has been visited upon his people."

"He is Hutu."

Roger's nod was a concession.

Smith pointed out, "He said a lot more than that."

The snippet of French made Aristide suspicious, and Roy by extension. He snapped at Roger, who explained. Roy touched the stock of his rifle and spoke.

Roger said, "Roy wishes you to know that the rifle is a defensive weapon. Its purpose is to defend himself and his people from the aggressors. It is not a weapon of war."

"Course not."

"The Hutus are a people peaceful by nature and inclination. Since the dawn of time, the Tutsis have oppressed them. They have made servants of them, they have ground their faces in the dirt. There is, first of all, the example of Aristide's cattle. It is, he says, a typical story."

"What about the cattle?"

"He had many cows."

"How many?"

When Aristide understood the American's question, it angered him. It suggested skepticism, and skepticism implied doubt. Doubt was a form of disrespect, and he refused to answer.

"There was a Tutsi man living near Aristide," Roger went on. "This was back in Rwanda."

"Before the genocide," Smith said.

The Hutu men might not know much French, but they damn straight knew *that* word. They didn't like it. Smith saw a family likeness in the way they glared at him.

"The Tutsi man of whom he speaks," Roger said slowly, "stole Aristide's cattle. Aristide went to the police. The police chief was a Tutsi. So was the judge."

"What happened to the Tutsi?" Smith wanted to know.

"There is no good to be had in asking him to answer that question."

"Then how about this one: does beating up a little girl make up for the bad shit that went down in Rwanda?"

"I won't translate that."

He didn't have to. Aristide somehow got the gist of it. It launched another tirade. He stopped only to be sure the American knew what he was saying.

"People have the wrong idea," Roger began, sucking in his breath.

He disliked having to rehearse in French an old bad story. It was too familiar, too predictable.

"People?" said Smith.

"Everybody who is not a Hutu. The whole world thinks every Hutu is Interahamwe. Gangs of Hutu thugs from the days of . . . the mass killings."

Telling his story, however partial, however passionate, did something good for Aristide. He called for another beer, which his unnamed wife brought to the circle of men, along with an orange plastic cup. This time he poured the beer into the cup and offered it to Smith, to Roger, before helping himself. But when he heard what Smith wanted, he shook his head.

It might go on this way into the night. Time to push it where it had to go.

"So what's it going to take?"

Roger did not care for the question. It was too blunt for the moment. It contradicted his timing. It was what one expected of an American. But he passed on the question, translating in a monotone to keep the emotion at a tolerable level. A few minutes of respectful listening followed. Then he told Smith, "He wishes you to know that he is protecting the girl. Here, in the bosom of his family, she is safe. He will oblige his wife, his children, to love the child. As for him, as a father cherishes the daughter God sends him, so will he cherish Béatrice."

Aristide was studying the American to see how he took it. He put a hand on his heart. The gesture was false. He wanted Smith to know he was mocking him.

When Béatrice had come his way, Aristide knew a good thing when he saw it. Free labor for a few years, until she got too big to handle. He must know already she was the last thing from docile.

"She goes with me," said Smith.

The sentence did not require translation. There was a signal from Aristide that Smith did not see. But Roy did. He grabbed the Kalashnikov and leapt to his feet. This time there was no doubt that it was aimed at Smith. Roy threw back his head and let out a war whoop intended to intimidate the American. The rifle and the whoop: together, they did. Smith wanted to stand up. On the ground he felt more vulnerable, but his legs refused the request. At one level, in a place of semi-calm, he assumed this was part of the negotiation. That made sense. You used what you had at hand, and Aristide had quite a lot, including possession of Béatrice and a nearby relative with a gun.

Roger and Aristide were on their feet now, too. Roger put out a hand and pulled Smith up to be on their level. And he laughed. This too was a tactic, not as convincing as a rifle but reasonably effective. The director of Notre Pain had a laugh like butter melting in a pan, smoking up the kitchen as it melted. It oozed and spread out across the clearing giving him the opening he needed to go on an extended riff. The gist of the riff was this: Smith was happy—no, he was jumping-up-and-down delighted—to compensate the Hutu man for the pain and suffering associated with relinquishing the Munyamulenge child from his loving protection.

Aristide listened patiently. Roy listened impassively, the rifle still trained on Smith but less menacing at the muzzle, if that were possible. Smith felt some strength coming back into his legs.

At a certain point Aristide said, "*Deux cents dollars.*"

Smith took two hundred-dollar bills from the pocket of his jeans. Not wanting to show his stash, he had peeled the bills from his roll and stuck them there before they arrived. How he had known what it was going to cost was a mystery. As a lapsed Creole Catholic he had the right to believe in mysteries.

He made sure the money was visible but did not hand it over.

"The girl," he said.

Aristide hollered toward the hut. A fast second later Béatrice came out. She was steady. She was upright. She was not carrying her backpack. She crossed the clearing and stood behind Smith. Not too close. She waited.

Roger said nothing because shutting up was the smart thing to do. Aristide stretched his hand toward Smith, palm up. The hand was shaking, and Smith wondered if maybe he was sick. He lay the two hundreds on the palm. When Roger turned away, so did he.

Their exit required dignity, real and correctly asserted. Roger knew how to do that. He did it. They crossed the clearing at the pace he set, Béatrice walking between them. When they reached the motorcycle Roger told Smith, "Wait for me at the road."

The bike started first try. Béatrice climbed on behind Smith, and they made their way back through the high grass to the road, where Smith killed the engine and they both climbed down.

"It's over," he told her.

She forgave him the stupid comment.

"And your backpack?"

"It angered him. He opened it. Each thing he took out, he took them one by one, he gave them to his girls. The big girl, the mean one, she got the pack."

What else did he do? Smith wanted to ask but didn't. Something had gone down under the roof of Aristide Kavaruganda. You could see it in the way she carried herself, as if she were fragile and way too heavy for her feet at the same time. The intuition made Smith sick.

When Roger appeared he was singing a French hymn. *C'est un rempart que Notre Dieu.* Smith knew it. His mother was fond of the tune and had sung it around the house when she was in one of her moods. A Mighty Fortress is Our God. In Smith's recollection the English lines married the French without effort.

"We must depart," Roger told him.

"Will he come after us?"

"Not for the child. The spell, that horrible spell, has been broken. But he will be fascinated by the thought of how much money you carry on your person. His imagination will exaggerate the sum. There will be a fierce discussion of all this with Roy. Already they will be upbraiding themselves for letting the child go so cheaply."

"If they come, Roy will bring his defensive weapon."

"*Certainement.*"

The three of them rode the bike. It was slow going. A small motorcycle meant for a single rider. A poor road in poor condition. Two men, one of them with a burnt leg that did not permit him to sit properly. A girl carrying her trauma.

"This isn't going to work," Smith hollered after maybe half a mile.

"It has to," Roger said.

A little farther down the road, he tapped Smith on the shoulder where he wanted him to turn. Then it was no longer a road, it was a path, and then the idea of a path. The high grass gave way to woods. The woods seethed. Smith felt it. The overloaded bike was no protection against it. Everybody on the planet had an idea about Africa, and the wildness of Africa. How lucky was he, surrounded by the real thing? Not much farther, Roger insisted, and they would come to Mother Madeleine's.

Mother Madeleine lived halfway up a green hill covered with low grass that looked like moss. At the foot of the hill Roger dismounted and began hiking up. He went slowly because of his bad leg, and Smith gave him a head start. Béatrice stayed with him on the back of the bike, though she refused to wrap her arms around him for stability. She knew about balance.

He went up at an angle as slowly as he could and still keep the motorcycle upright, reaching the Congolese woman's place just as she fell to her knees in praise of the coming of Roger. Roger did not much care for the adulation. He shook his head and told her to get up. She refused. She grabbed his hand, pulled it to her mouth, kissed it lavishly. She looked like the picture of a saint whose name Smith did not remember in the church where he took his First Communion.

This was how a person's mind worked. He could have gone the rest of his days not remembering the Communion, and here in the hard east Congo it came rushing back thanks to a crazy woman shattered by more loss than any five mothers deserved.

Pictures: the crumpled damp Kleenex in his mother's hand as she held his, a skinny priest with pimples telling a joke beyond Smith's ken, his father blinking in the sunlight after the sacrament had been performed, the Mass concluded, the stone steps descended and pictures taken.

Baylee Smith reached into the inside pocket of his black blazer for a smoke, smiling as though he'd been caught doing something he could not explain in polite company. He had a good weather eye, born of social abuse. He understood that the Flannery Parish sun was on his side, he could draw an easy breath. He laughed. So did his son, who heard in the moment in front of St. Eustace a kind of indecipherable chirping.

By the time Smith parked the bike on the edge of the tiny clearing that surrounded her house, Mother Madeleine was on her feet holding Roger by the hand as if she would never let him go. She must be pushing fifty. Loss had blanched her hair, which she wore in disobedient cornrows. She was gaunt in a baggy blue and yellow dress. She had big knees and a way of rotating her head from one side to the other as she walked as though doing some sort of stretching exercise. Zen for the shattered parent.

She had five sons. Every last one of them disappeared, and no daughters to assuage her grief. They had joined the Mai Mai. Kind of like local militias, in Roger's explanation, although there was something in the word itself Smith found sinister. They started out believing they were protecting their home territory, they believed in the power of their magic. The magic would turn to water any bullet sent their way. Was it not God who gave them their magic? They sang, going into battle. What they ended up believing afterward—the ones who lived—that was something Smith would like to know.

The inexplicable thing was the void into which Madeleine's sons fell. *Radio trottoir* worked pretty well; it worked for everybody else, at any rate. You heard things. People were constantly on the move. The war dislocated millions, and as they migrated from one temporary refuge to the next they carried word with them. Rumors, gossip, stories, speculation. You heard, you sorted through the contradictions, you triangulated sources, even if there was never the proof you had the right to demand but could not because no one was in charge of anything. In the case of the five sons of Mother Madeleine, *radio trottoir* was silent. She had been waiting for years. She would keep on waiting. What else was she going to do?

Smith expected her to take an interest in Béatrice. She was a child, after all, and Madeleine was a mother lacking one. But the girl was not one of her missing sons, and she ignored her. It fell to Roger to say, "The child is hungry."

"Of course," said Mother Madeleine, but she did not take the hint. People were hungry. That was normal.

"Is there something you can give her?"

"*Fufu*."

Shit, thought Smith.

But he ate it when she brought out a pot. They sat together in the grass not much like a family. She also brought sticks of cassava, starchy and yet more tasteless than the *fufu*. Some salt would help, but salt cost money and Madeleine had no way to earn any cash. As a treat for Béatrice, she handed the girl a leaf, indicating she should spread it on her palm. Béatrice did as she was told, and Madeleine dumped half a dozen just-dead caterpillars onto the leaf. Béatrice ate them one by one and seemed to enjoy them. Then she bunched up the leaf and ate it, chewing slowly. Smith was grateful that the woman's maternal instinct had kicked in and she gave all the caterpillar nourishment she had on hand to a child who needed protein and love.

Madeleine spoke enough French that Smith was able to follow some of what she said to Roger. She was expecting news of one of her boys. It was imminent, any moment now and she would race away to greet them and bring them home. She recited their names like short prayers, holding up a finger for each. Isaac, Benoit, Gabriel, Luc, Olivier. She no longer cried. Tears belonged to the desperate, whom she refused to join. What glistened in her eyes was only love. It was the war. Such a war as this one was not known in human memory. Millions were displaced from the homes that knew them, claimed them, wanted them back; she did not say killed. She listened to the radio for news when she had batteries, which just now she did not.

Roger promised her batteries and told her Béatrice and the American needed a safe place to spend the night.

"Safe," said Madeleine.

The way she said the word, it might mean there was no such thing in Central Africa, but it might just as well mean there could be no doubt of her guests' being safe in her home. Smith was tired. Discouragement wore him out. He was tired of figuring out what people meant when they said a thing, and skeptical when Roger told him he was taking the Kawasaki back to Bukavu.

"I will send a driver in a truck tomorrow morning."

"Sure," Smith said.

There was a breeze, just not enough to keep the mosquitoes from climbing the hill to pester them. They slapped their arms, their faces, anywhere their skin was exposed. In the briefly purple evening air bats swooped and then swooped again. The birds whose job it was to announce the end of the day went about their work. Béatrice got up and wandered. She explored inside the hut, came back out, walked to the edge of a patch of thin woods that straggled uphill and stood there looking through the trees as though she expected a creature more interesting than dangerous to come charging out.

"In the morning," Roger said to Smith.

"In the morning."

"You must retrace your way to the road."

"To the road."

Smith's repeating his words bugged the shit out of Roger. It was meant to.

"The truck is a Volvo, a diesel."

Smith had seen it in the garage.

Roger assured him, "You can trust the driver."

"The driver."

"Getting to Uvira, that is the easy part. After that, you are on your own. Reaching Minembwe will be much more difficult, if you choose to continue. As for me, I strongly advise you against trying."

"How come?"

Roger ticked off the reasons the way Madeleine had just ticked off the names of her sons.

"The road is bad. The way is long. The rains are coming. And you must at all costs avoid the armed groups."

Smith nodded. He was having a hard time remembering with any precision what his life used to be like, working on the Dauphin rig. The old pleasures, the old enmities. He had become a person of small habits. Now they were all gone, they had been exploded by the Congo. Which suddenly struck him as funny. It was the contrast with what he was doing now, the sheer goddamned unpredictability of living from one strange moment to the next. Laughing made him feel better, and he went on for a while.

Roger lifted his head from the contemplation of his burnt leg. He looked at Smith, worried for his mental health. Mother Madeleine also looked at him, wanting in on the joke. Béatrice was back. She had something else on her mind and no interest in sharing it.

"Do me a favor," Smith said to Roger.

It was too fast for a dream, it was more like the compressed file of a dream: SexDream.zip. Maybelline featured prominently in it. They were their own cradle, and they rocked. But something was wrong, and it woke him up.

There was no Mother Madeleine. After Roger left she spoke to Smith in a jumble of French and another language explaining something he failed to understand. Nevertheless she was relieved, thinking she had conveyed all that needed conveying. Her smile was warm and sad. *You will be safe in this place.* She picked up an empty sack, folded it over her arm as though it were a purse, and went away.

Now, he was lying on his back on the floor of her hut-home. His head was pillowed on his go bag, his neck aching from the bad angle it had taken. Before falling asleep he had pulled a sheet over himself; the woman owned two. The sheet was gone, his pants were open, and he had an erection. In the dark he sensed Béatrice squatting next to him. Her hand was wrapped around his dick, stroking with methodical fury. Jesus.

He swung his arm harder than he meant to. It connected, and the force of the blow knocked the girl away. She cried out once—it was indignation, not pain—then scuttled to a corner. The hut was small, and he could hear her breathing. The sound was oddly patient, and uncomfortably intimate.

He zipped up, jumped up. Jesus.

"What the fuck do you think you're doing?"

It came out in English, and he had to say it again.

No answer. There was never any answer from this kid. But the wave of anger was already subsiding, and he wished bitterly that he had not hit her.

"Béatrice?"

She breathed.

"I'm sorry I hit you."

He wanted to ask her why she had done it. He wanted to make sure she understood he was not the kind of guy who would consent to being jerked off by a tween. He wanted her to know he was appalled—she had to know it was only his dreaming imagination that made his goddamn conscienceless dick stand up—but he was not blaming her, he would never blame her. He could not say any of that. Too complicated. It was a worm ball.

He was seven and had gone fishing with his father and a couple of layabout semi-friends of Baylee's one night. They were on the bayou. They were in a boat. They were drinking more than they ought to. But they had a system. One of the men dunked a ball of worms on the end of a line into the water. When he felt a tug he jerked it out. Every single time he hauled it up, one more stupid fish was hanging onto the writhing, wriggling mass of worms. They never let go of the ball, not until they were flopping on the boat floor and Baylee clubbed them off and tossed them into an aluminum bucket. There was a lantern in the boat, and in its spooky light the worm ball was a thing of disturbing wonder for a seven-year-old boy to behold. The men laughed, which caused the boy to giggle. Baylee raised the gaff over his head like a war lance, hollered some phony Creole nonsense, and clubbed the next fish.

"I'm sorry," Smith told Béatrice again.

The image of Soeur Placide came to him, implacable and large, standing with her arms crossed on her chest at Maid of Orléans Shelter for the Children of the Congo. The shame burned. And Maybelline. He wondered if there would ever come a time when he could tell her what had just happened to him. In his mortification he felt like reaching for the hand of a woman who was not there.

Béatrice ran out of the hut. Jesus, and again Jesus. Should he go after her? She might think he was still angry and wanted to take it out on her. Would she run away? Not even Béatrice could see in the dark, and they were on the side of a hill. She had nowhere to run, and it was counter to her nature to hide. Worm ball. A complete and total worm ball.

He felt in his bag for the flashlight. It was a good one. He had picked it up at an REI the last time he was home, back when the idea of putting together a go bag felt like a cool adventure, something he could casually brag about to his buddies back home, selling it with understatement. He put on his shoes, laced them, and went out into the yard. He called her name. The night into which he sent it was anything but silent. Some of the racket came from nocturnal birds, some of it came from animals, some from insects. He had a hard time distinguishing which was which.

He played the light of his flash across the yard. On the second circuit he made her out, standing on the verge, her hands balled into fists. She was looking somewhere else. The flashlight was intrusive, and he switched it off. What happens, Smith asked himself, when we get to Minembwe and there is no Grandmother Joséphine? Back to Kinshasa, or to Auntie Bernadette?

"The lion."

"What about the lion, Béatrice?"

"Does he live here?"

"No, he lives in a different part of the country."

"Nkoyi?"

It had been a long time since she said the word "leopard." This time she was not talking about him. "No, no leopards. We are lucky, being here."

"How?"

"All the animals in this region are friendly."

In fact he had no idea what was out in the woods, climbing the hills, slinking through the night's high grass after prey. For all he knew there were killer apes in the trees gearing up to jump down and maul them, eat them raw. But she was talking. If he was going to ask her the hard question, it had to be now.

"What happened at the Hutu family?"

The unquiet silence of the night filled his ears and made them ache.

"Did he touch you?"

"The woman."

"Aristide's wife."

"She was there. He beat her."

"Why did he beat her?"

"She was there."

Stop. Give her time. No coercion.

"What is the woman's name?"

"Calandre."

"I once had an alligator named Calandre," he told her. "I remember its vicious teeth. They were long and yellow. Well, of course, every time I tried to take the animal for a walk, it ate through the leash, and where did that leave me?"

This time the girl's silence had the quality of appreciation in it. He told her, "I saw the bruises on Calandre's face."

Her voice went up just perceptibly as she said, "On her arms, also. On her legs."

"She was protecting you, was she not?"

He was getting better at understanding her silences. This one, this time, meant yes. Aristide had attacked her, and against all odds, Calandre stepped in. In the face of her husband's wrath she performed a heroic act.

Christ on a popsicle stick, you had to be a psychologist to have this conversation. A psychologist he was not. And it was not Smith who loosed in Béatrice what needed to be loosed. It was a howl. It came from the woods and sounded close. It sounded like an animal. It was a cold and soulless noise that a human being could take to mean anything he wanted it to. It jeered, it expressed outrage, it told the other animals awake in the woods at night that it was hungry and mean and had claws. It reminded every creature that heard it that the world was dangerous and did not care whether they lived or died. It was the cry of a thing alone.

When the howl of the animal died out, Béatrice began not to cry but to keen. The sound shivered Smith, it changed him. In half a minute he was a hundred years old, listening as, in the darkness, she spoke to darkness. Some of it came out in French, some of it was Kinyarwanda. Smith was meant to be a witness, and to keep his mouth shut. She used a word he didn't know that must mean penis, and the ugliness between Aristide Kavaruganda's legs. For a while, her sound shut up the birds, and the animals moved off deeper into the woods, out of earshot, an animal gesture of respect.

When she finished speaking, she told him, *"J'ai envie de dormir."*

The turn of phrase struck him. Except when she was talking about her grandmother, she was a matter-of-fact person. She gave nothing of herself away. In her vulnerability she had figured out how to protect the feeling core of herself.

"Me, too," he told her. "I also long for sleep."

Guilt troubled Smith's sleep. His dreams called him to account, and running from judgment wiped him out. He woke before the sun came up with a feeling of narrow escape and scanned the room with his flash. Béatrice was sleeping soundly. He got up and hunted for something for their breakfast. Found nothing. He hated shaking the girl awake, but they needed to move.

She sat up alert. "I'm hungry."

"There are two chocolate bars in my bag. Eat one now. We'll save the other one for later."

"And you?"

"I had some caterpillars."

A pitcher of water stood on a fruit crate. They took turns draining it. Smith knew as the water went down his gullet that it was a mistake. It burned, scraping hot fingers in places it had no business going.

"What?" she said.

This was more responsive than she had been. That couldn't be a bad thing.

"It's going to make me sick," he told her.

"It's only water."

"Right."

They picked their way downhill using the beam of the flash. Overnight, the arms of trees and the bodies of bushes had done their best to obliterate the trail. Twice, they lost it, stepping off into undergrowth that grabbed and held them. Twice, damp cobwebs draped his face, and Smith peeled them off in disgust.

"Joséphine," Béatrice said once, trying out the sound.

"Did you know that was your grandmother's name?"

"Of course."

That was a lie, the same one Smith would tell if he were in her shoes.

As they moved downhill and the east sky lightened, Smith felt his gut clench. He held it until they reached the bulge in the road where Roger had told him to wait.

"Stay here," he told the girl.

He ran back into the trees, away from the road. He took off his pants. He squatted. Blades of stiff grass poked him in the ass, reminding him where he was. He let loose. The relief he felt was cause for embarrassment. He stayed as he was, in a compact squat, waiting for the second wave, and the third. They came, and he went. The bad water at Mother Madeleine's did its worst, which was plenty bad.

At the garage where Smith had hung out as a kid, Guy Foulard was not just a wizard mechanic, and a reliable purveyor of weed to grown-ups seeking color enhancement, he was a philosopher. He put a lot of thought into his pronouncements, working them over, polishing them until they shone. Once, looking for the fault in the fuel injector of a Charger engine, he straightened up. He wiped his hands on a rag, wiped his nose with the back of a newly clean hand. He took a drink of Gatorade and lit a smoke. Smith was the recording angel.

"There is nothing in the State of Louisiana," Guy told him, "more overrated than a good fuck, so called."

Smith knew that was only the first half of the statement.

"You follow me?"

"I follow you, Guy."

"On the other hand—and this is important, you might wanna write it down—there is nothing quite so underrated as a good dump."

Smith nodded. He wrote it down in his mental notebook.

Maybe it was true in Louisiana. Smith had admired the statement at the time, not because Guy was sort of his boss but because it turned what most people thought upside down, which was a thing Smith generally respected. In the Congo, under different circumstances, he was not able to evaluate the relative advantage of defecation or anything else. Still, when he stood, shat out, a relief that felt like sainthood overcame him, and the refrain from "Honky Tonk Blues" came to his lips like a hymn. He really liked the way Hank squeezed extra syllables out of the key words.

Possibly Smith was singing them as he made his way back toward the road. That would explain the urgency of Béatrice signaling him to be quiet. He shut up. Get down, she signaled, and he got down. She crouched low at the same time, and

Smith, late, heard the truck as it went rolling by. Not just a truck. It was a panel truck without any panels, and it was carrying government soldiers. The chassis was painted orange, the wheel wells were yellow. It had the look of a circus wagon rolling to war.

A couple hundred yards past the spot where Béatrice and Smith were hiding, the brakes squealed melodically, and the driver came to a slow stop. Was it better to sneak deeper into the woods, or stay where they were and freeze? Before Smith decided, the soldiers jumped down from the truck. Some of them lit cigarettes. All of them, or almost all of them, took a leak in the road. It was a piss break.

When Smith forced himself to look away from the urinating soldiers, he saw that Béatrice, crouched like a runner, was unwrapping her magic marble from the snakeskin she carried it in. And it worked. In the nick of time, the girl's magic made them invisible. When she noticed him watching, a look of serene authority appeared on her face. She didn't have to explain anything. He could see for himself the power of her mojo.

They watched a loud man with a bandolier on his chest aim his rifle at the woods. The woods cowered. He was a clown and wanted everybody to laugh on command. The problem was, none of the other soldiers was paying him any attention, they were too busy smokin' and jokin', pissin' and grinnin'. There was only one solution. He warned the trees. There was real menace in his voice. When the trees refused to surrender, he raked them with a burst of fire. That brought on the applause he was after. It also brought on a smack in the face from his sergeant, who shoved him up against the side of the truck and blistered him. The sergeant was a man who knew how to get in a grunt's face. Now there was something worth laughing at, and the soldiers did.

Inside another two minutes they were climbing back into the truck. When the truck moved on, Smith and Béatrice got to their feet.

"One thing I can't figure out," Smith said. "How did you manage to hide your magic from the Hutu?"

Her look gave him the logical answer: it was magic, wasn't it?

They waited an hour, both of them hungry and getting hungrier. Little traffic passed down the road except for a few bicycles, a few people on foot. None of them bothered to scan the woods. Béatrice and Smith stayed out of sight. It took no convincing on Smith's part. The girl had the kind of patience people who never heard of multitasking had, on top of which she was world-class stubborn. She understood that being seen with a white American man would slow her down.

Sitting, Smith was lightheaded. Closing his eyes, he saw a compass wobbling, and felt a powerful urge to eat bacon. He salivated. But he recognized the sound of the Volvo diesel downshifting as it hit the bulge. He stepped into the road. Béatrice, less trusting, stayed under the trees. The glint of morning sun on the windshield blocked Smith's view. He was hoping the driver spoke French.

He did. Because the man who stepped down from the cab was Roger Dzba. He looked fresh, like a person who had slept in a bed. The wrapped bulk of the bandage around the burn was visible through his pant leg.

"You," said Smith.

"*Moi*."

Seeing him, Béatrice came out into the road. Roger reached back into the cab and brought out a small backpack, purple with blue piping. He handed it to Smith. "This was your idea."

Smith gave the pack to Béatrice. She accepted it with suspicion and eagerness. Inside, Smith hoped, were things to replace the things that Aristide Kavaruganda, a generous father, had shared out among his kids. She went back into the trees to open the pack in privacy.

"What happened to the driver you were sending?"

Roger shrugged. "Ah, well."

"Well what?"

"He chose not to make the trip."

"What, he had a better offer?"

Roger looked at him, sizing him up. "There are rumors."

"What kind of rumors are we talking about, Roger?"

The Congolese man bent down. He patted the bandage on his leg. It was a reassuring gesture. It was avoidance. "Fighting."

"Around here?"

"Possibly."

"Who?"

"That's hard to say."

"Why is it hard to say?"

"It may be the government going against one of the Mai Mai groups. It may be one Mai Mai group against another. It may be all of that and more."

"Why now?"

"There is another rumor."

"Why don't you go ahead and tell me the whole story, save us some time?"

"The rumors talk about a shipment of gold, a fabulous amount of it. Supposedly this gold is in South Kivu. The thought of it is enough to set people against one another. The gold was on its way out of the country to Israel, via Rwanda. It belongs to a famous dealer in gold, Eckstein. You've heard of him."

"No, I haven't," Smith lied.

Roger shook his head. "Somehow Eckstein's shipment has been . . . mislaid. Now everyone wants it. Eckstein has dispatched a group of mercenaries to recover it."

"Is any of this real?"

Roger's hands mapped the Kivus. "Anything can be real."

"And yet here you stand."

Roger pointed to the back of the truck where blue tarps were lashed over humps of cargo.

"There is an orphanage in Uvira," he said. "The director there wishes to teach the children to plant gardens. This is admirable, no? He submitted a funding proposal. Our board approved it. These materials represent a better way to feed people."

But there was more to Roger than obligation. No one would blame him for lying low until the gold fever died down and it was semi-safe to travel the roads again. No matter how you looked at it, picking up Béatrice and Smith was an act of courage. In Smith's condition, nutrient deprived and empty bowelled, his perception was off. As he stared at the director of Notre Pain de Ce Jour, a glow appeared around the man's head and shoulders.

"Let's go," Roger said.

Béatrice, however, refused to ride between the two men in the cab. She would not get in. She stood in the road, arms crossed on her chest, saying *non* with lavish disdain. Smith knew that look. It aggravated Roger, but Smith did not let it get to him. He rode next to Roger, legs bent to avoid the shifter in the floor. Béatrice took the window seat, arms around her new pack. As they went, they ate crackers and white cheese Roger had brought for them from Bukavu. They shared a thermosful of hot sweet tea.

The food revived them, and they listened to a story Roger told about his parrot. In the story the Congolese man credited the bird with a level of emotional intelligence that went farther than the consensus view of parrotologists supported, but Smith was feeling grateful.

Roger drove steadily but not fast. Best not to catch up to the truckful of soldiers ahead of them on the road. The Volvo's suspension was shot, and the ride was rough. Inside the cab, they bounced. Smith held himself back from singing. It would be annoying to be stuck in a small space with a person who sang as badly as he did.

But that did not stop him from thinking about Hank Williams, which by corkscrew logic made him think about Maybelline. He was not entitled to the sense of loss he felt when he did. Even when they were living together, she had not been his, he had not been hers. Not in the secret deep way that suddenly seemed possible as the truck shuddered down the bad road. It was what he wanted.

They approached a wash-out where the road cratered and disappeared. To get past it, Roger dropped the transmission into low and eased the truck into the brush along one edge of the road, following the tracks left by vehicles that had made it through.

"So what do you hear from Giselle?" Smith asked Roger.

It was the wrong question at the wrong time. How could Smith know it would blow up in his face? Roger Dzba was courageous. He put everything he had into feeding hungry people. Just by showing up to work, he took a risk. Notre Pain's stock in trade was commodities. People killed for commodities: sacks of flour, tins of cooking oil, bags of salt and sugar. On a given bad day, any item in the warehouse could be a motive for murder. And yet he showed up, day after day. Angels protected Roger when he lay down to sleep. They soothed his forehead, they sang him lullabies and told stories that laminated his heroic deeds. So how come he went off on the American now?

He slammed the flat of his hand on the dashboard, and Béatrice flinched.

"Hah! I see. Yes, I see it now, I see the whole thing."

"What do you see, Roger?"

Béatrice shrank away from both of them. The men in the truck in which she happened to be riding had a disease. No way she wanted to catch it. If she did not let it touch her maybe she stayed clean.

"You're Eckstein's man," Roger said, voice rising remarkably in a short sentence.

It was strange, being the target of Roger's wrath at the same time that he seemed to be concentrating completely on getting the truck past the wash-out. Talk about compartmentalizing. The driver's side window was open, and tall grasses with heads like fuzzy buzzards came in after him. They brushed his face, he brushed them off in a cold fury.

"The Israeli is well known for using spies to do his dirty work." He spoke across Smith to Béatrice as though she were the one who had asked the question. "Eckstein is brilliant."

"My grandmother's name is Joséphine."

"What better disguise than to send a bumbling white man from America, a man so helpless he requires assistance to go from Bukavu to Uvira. He *says* he is taking the child to Minembwe. Hah! He *says* he wishes to help her find her grandmother. Hah! What do they call that in the spy novels? Cover story. Yes, that's it. Only Eckstein himself could come up with a cover story at once so perfect and so absurd. It's gold lust that makes the man clever, but since you are on his payroll you already know that, don't you? There is a rancid hunk of flesh where the man's heart ought to be. People of the Book, my ass. Tell me, Smith. How much do you get if you recover the Israeli's gold? Two percent? Three percent? Eckstein is ruthless. Only a fool would doublecross him. You'll take your three percent, and it will make you rich. You'll go someplace nice, with a beach. Dark-skinned women with glistening tits will bring you cool drinks. You like Black women, don't you?"

It went on. Mile after jouncing mile. One moment he seemed to be coming down, the worst of his temper spent. The next moment he spun himself up again. Every time he went up, he invented a still more elaborate plot against the Congolese people, who were the true owners of the gold, on the part of the Israeli dealer and his hapless American henchman.

Smith let him rave. There was no way to stop him. Besides, all the while Roger ranted, they were making progress toward Uvira. If this was the transport tax, he would pay it and keep his mouth shut. Meanwhile, Béatrice kept her distance. You couldn't blame the kid. Smith wondered how much of the rottenness Roger was slinging at him would stick in her mind. He wondered with fresh force what she thought of him.

A moment of things coming together: Roger slowed when a rider straddling a dead motorcycle sat dead center in the road, arms out like the wings of frustration blaming Heaven. Roger notified Smith that he was going to turn him in to the authorities in Uvira. He would collect a reward. The money would pay for the gas he was burning. The American would be tried in a court of law and found guilty of defrauding the nation of its rightful patrimony, the gold that God had put in the ground for the sole and exclusive use of the Congolese people. And Béatrice opened the door. As the truck slowed almost to a standstill, she jumped. She hit the ground. She stumbled and fell. She got to her feet and ran, clutching the new backpack to her chest as though it were a baby.

"God damn it," said Smith. "Stop the truck."

Roger stopped the truck. Both men jumped down into the road on dirt that was spongy under their feet. Overhead, white clouds raced, lashed by overseer sunlight. The man straddling the motorcycle watched them with fatigued curiosity. Even at a distance Smith could make out beads of sweat on the guy's forehead. His skin was the color of cocoa, and he was handsome, meant for better things that would not come to him. There was no Béatrice.

"She went into the woods," Roger said.

Smith told him, "I'm going after her."

Roger gave him a look that conveyed his hostility. But the source of his anger was different now. It infuriated him that the American would presume he was not going into the woods after the Munyamulenge orphan. Who did Smith think he was, Eckstein? The man on the motorcycle pointed in the direction the girl had gone, and they went.

But not far. A military transport vehicle came up behind the Volvo, and a dozen soldiers jumped down. They did not mill around in the road and piss the way the first group had done. They stood in formation facing the Volvo as though capturing the truck had been their objective all along. They gripped their rifles. All of them carried Kalashnikovs, which Smith recognized because it was the same article Aristide's cousin Roy had aimed at him from the hammock on the edge of the woods. A formation of quiet, disciplined men in green uniforms, armed with the same rifle. It got your attention. It tightened your sphincter. Hank Williams never sang about anything like this. Despite his many appealing qualities Hank was not, just now, part of the picture.

The leader of the squad was an officer. Smith wished he had bothered to learn the insignia of military ranks. From the bars on his shoulder he guessed the man was a lieutenant. The lieutenant was calm and projected authority. He wore Boss sunglasses. His black boots shone spotlessly the way you wanted a soldier's boots to shine, but when he moved the left foot, it dragged a little.

"Do not show him that blasted letter you carry," Roger said out of the side of his mouth. "If they search you and find it, tell them it belongs to someone else, you are delivering it to a friend."

Smith had been weighing the idea of using the letter but knew that Roger was right. One of the handful of things that were obvious about the lieutenant was that he knew how to read.

The lieutenant spoke to Roger in good French. "Hands up. Clasp them on top of your head."

Roger and Smith did as they were ordered to do.

"Come here."

They came. Smith was dimly aware that the man astride the motorcycle was gone. So was the bike. How had he managed that? Despite the French beginning, the conversation between Roger and the lieutenant took place in Swahili. Both men were polite, as though conscious of being observed by critics. Smith was asked to produce his passport. He did. Ramazani. That was the name on the pocket flap of the lieutenant's uniform blouse. Ramazani spent no longer than he had to scrutinizing the document.

He put the passport in his pocket, along with Roger's identity card. He asked to see Smith's travel permission. At that point Roger spoke up. Later, Smith learned that Roger had presented him as an American Christian, a man of conviction who had provided funds for a donation to the orphanage in Uvira because that was what Jesus would do. In fact, they were headed to the orphanage now. They had only stopped to take a leak. Roger pointed to the cargo under tarps on the back of his truck. The American, foolishly, had left his travel permission back at the hotel in Bukavu.

That was when it could have gone bad. Leaving your travel permission behind in your hotel was not just sublimely foolish, it was criminal. It opened a person to retribution. Jail, extortion, a beating. It removed the need for a pretext. Although he did not understand the words going back and forth between the two Congolese men, Smith had a good sense of the dynamic.

Ramazani said something about Eckstein. Something about stolen gold, and Rwanda, and unscrupulous businessmen.

The conversation came to an end. There was a high ticking in the woods. The local insects had decided that men standing in the road were the new normal. But a monkey hectored them from a safe spot. And the birds, unlike the bugs, had not reconciled themselves to the presence of men. Standing on the side of the road, Smith could not keep his eyes off Lieutenant Ramazani's shirt pocket, where his passport had gone.

The lieutenant gave an order. Working in practiced tandem, his soldiers removed the tie-downs that held the tarps in place, and then pulled the tarps off the cargo. When the sacks and boxes were revealed, the soldiers could not resist a guttural "ooh" of appreciation at the sight of such packaged plenty. They were looking for gold but delighted with agricultural implements.

Giving orders in a reasonable voice, Ramazani directed that an inventory be conducted. Two soldiers climbed onto the back of the Volvo and performed the inspection, calling down the results to a man with a broad, flat face who wrote words and numbers on a pad of yellow paper. Smith, standing next to Roger, heard the director of Notre Pain suck in his breath and hold it. There was no sign of Béatrice.

When the men on the truck finished tallying the load, the broad-faced man with the paper presented his report to the lieutenant.

"Tell me what twenty percent is," the lieutenant told him.

It was obviously a test, and just as obviously the soldier who had written everything down knew precisely how to calculate twenty percent of what sat on Roger's truck. The purpose of the test was to give an object lesson to the soldiers: be more like this guy, less like the ignorant fool you drank beer with last night.

He said something to his lieutenant. Ramazani nodded slowly, and twenty percent of the sacks and boxes came down.

After the soldiers had moved the stuff they were taking onto their own truck— it was going to be a tight ride— Ramazani declined to make a big deal out of returning Roger's ID card, and Smith's passport. He handed both to Roger, saying something clipped. Five minutes later the truck was gone, not toward Uvira but back in the direction of Bukavu from which they had come.

"A great man," said Roger.

"Say that again."

"You have just met a great man."

"Because he stole from orphans?"

Roger shook his head impatiently. "This one is a humanitarian. He has a heart. He took twenty percent."

"I saw that."

"Ninety-nine out of a hundred men would have confiscated everything, and roughed us up at the same time, just on principle. This one has a heart, he has a conscience. With men like this we could build the nation we deserve."

Smith was feeling hungry again, and weak. As if to remind him how vulnerable he was, a wave of pain went through his gut. He was not in an ideal position, mentally, to decide whether Roger was pulling his leg.

"And the girl?" said Roger.

"Any minute."

The center of gravity at Travail d'Amour was the church. It was a long, low structure of boards with a roof of red tiles, situated on a flat stretch of ground. A white-painted crucifix was attached to the ridge beam of the roof, the cross looming in welcome a little too large for the structure it blessed. Like the doctor of love himself.

Roger was gone. Back to Bukavu. There had been no good-bye. They did not shake hands. The ragged ending nagged at Smith.

He walked into the church and took a seat on the bench closest to the back door. He had nothing against going to church but felt he was there on false pretenses. He was not that kind of lapsed Catholic. He waited.

The church was empty, the long windows open to the evening air. Kerosene lanterns burned to mark the occasion. Doctor Ace, who ran the orphanage, believed that structure was a good thing for children who mostly knew chaos. They wanted shaping, and a discipline of boundaries. They would process into the church in orderly rows.

The children were going to make a music video. Doctor Ace believed their talent would soften the hearts of well-meaning people around the world. The idea was to post the video on YouTube along with a plea for money to support Labor of Love.

Smith did not mind the wait. He used the time to wonder if he was engaged to Maybelline Beaudry. Doctor Ace had let him check his email.

There would be people who looked for self-aggrandizement, material or spiritual, in the preacher's enterprise. They would find nothing in the way he lived to feed their skepticism. A round table with a warped top covered with a thin sheet of cracked linoleum. Two chairs, one with a split seat. A filing cabinet with a padlock. The pallet on the floor was extra-long, built to accommodate Doctor Ace's extra-long body, but the sheets were of regular length.

The computer sat on a board stretched over twin stacks of bricks. There was a string of messages from Dauphin Petroleum. The first one was lethal. Somebody named Nestor in HR regretted informing him that his ass was grass. His contract was being terminated for non-performance. It got worse. They were dunning him for money the company had fronted him for an R&R trip to Paris.

It was a problem, but not one he could take on from South Kivu.

There was a message from Jasmine in Goma with the subject line, *If You're Still In Congo Be Careful.* She had picked up on the rumor of Eckstein's gold, heard stories about the turmoil it was provoking across the Kivus. If he was still in the Congo he should go to ground.

And there was a message from Maybelline, just hi-how-ya-doin'. In response, he asked her to marry him. Simple seemed best. *Seen a lot in this country,* he wrote her. *Made me start thinking. Where I come out was you.*

Doctor Ace's belief in structure was informed by his sense of style. When the orphans were assembled, two of the bigger boys took up their stations on either side of the back door. They folded their arms on their chests like security guards at a concert, and the kids filed through the door. Going past him, Béatrice gave Smith a look he wanted to interpret as contentment. Against gigantic odds, she had found a place where she belonged.

The choir had practiced, and practiced some more. The children knew where and how to stand. One boy made a beeline for the throne behind a drum kit. A girl picked up an electric bass hooked up to an amplifier powered by batteries.

There was nothing priest-like about Doctor Ace's entrance. He needed no lanterns. The fire of God lit him up. He was a shining tower of light, a match. Lit by the sight of him, the choir flamed into song.

Doctor Ace Mambwete was tall, six-seven easy, and had the kind of goatee that conferred authority. He was a talkative Christian. You could not be around the man for five minutes without getting drenched in a spray of Godtalk. Every time he opened his mouth, hosannas popped out like bubbles. He was constantly astonished by the goodness of God, whose generosity in sacrificing his only son on behalf of derelict humanity defied adjectives. But in those same five minutes you could not help realizing he meant every word he said. There was no hypocrisy in the man, there was only *exubérance*.

Sitting in the back, Smith shivered. The music wasn't good, it was better than that. It was complex, and textured, and perfectly timed as though they had done nothing in their lives except get ready for this moment. Warm waves of cadenced sound washed across the church. The fire spread.

The preacher's project was not a pipe dream. Hearing this music, a roomful of Scrooges would be writing big checks before the second verse.

When it was over, and Doctor Ace blessed them with passionate words in several languages, the choir members processed out in the same disciplined rows in which they had entered the church. Going past Smith Béatrice waved, mouthing a single word. *Nkoyi*. It seemed like goodbye, and the relief he had been feeling since they arrived and she liked the place overpowered him. The only question was whether to say goodbye.

He was the last one out of the building. The lines had dissolved. The kids were everywhere, jubilant and loud, drinking something sweet from a vat that had been carried out from the kitchen, eating rolls, clustering and reclustering into groups the way kids did. Doctor Ace had invited Smith to spend the night at his office-home. As the American arrived some boys were making up a second pallet for the guest. The two men sat outside on the ground, and Ace opened a bottle of Primus beer.

"They brew this in Bukavu," the preacher told Smith, pouring him a glass. His speaking voice was mellow, resonant, easy on the ear.

"In our country we have forgotten how to do many things. We scarcely know how to build any more. Our schools are empty shells. Our roads are a disaster. We used to have trains, did you know that? When we insisted that the Belgians leave our country, we allowed the trains and the tracks to go to ruin. Yet throughout this project of national decline we continue to produce vast lakes of good beer."

Smith said, "Béatrice likes it here."

“You have done a worthy deed. You must feel the warmth of divine love on your face.”

“It’s the first time I’ve seen her look content.”

“You find the child to be special.”

He nodded. “Do I say goodbye?”

“Béatrice has had enough abandonment to last the rest of her life. You must say a proper goodbye. So, you wish to leave the Congo. Very well. Do you have an escape plan?”

“No.”

“Then you must go to Kalundu.”

Kalundu was a port at the southern end of Uvira. There were boat connections to Bujumbura, across Lake Tanganyika. Smith knew nothing about Bujumbura except that it was not the Congo.

“You will be hassled at the port,” Doctor Ace warned him. “I regret not being able to accompany you.”

“You’re a good man, Doctor Ace.”

“I wish I were. As a young man I was filled with hate.”

“I have a hard time imagining that.”

“Only because you see me now, after the conflagration.”

A pause. They both drank a little beer. The sounds of excited children drowned out the sounds of night in the Congo countryside.

“Mai Mai entered our village. They killed everyone. I lost my parents, my brothers and sisters, my aunts and uncles. They killed all the old people, and all the young people. You will naturally ask why.”

“Why?”

"They were offended. They believed our people were sympathetic to their enemies. We had provided them food."

"Who were their enemies?"

"Tutsis who came across the border from Rwanda, hunting Hutus."

"Why didn't they kill you?"

"Because of the transhumance, and a dispute with my mother."

"That means nothing to me."

The preacher found Smith's ignorance hilarious. His laughter was happy thunder.

"We were people who lived from our cattle. Each year we moved them from the lowlands to the high plains, and then back again, for the pasture. I was young, I was restless. There was an argument with my mother. I took four cows and left days before she wanted the family to leave. When the Mai Mai came, I was gone."

Smith waited for him to talk about God's grace, how it had saved him from slaughter, preserving him so that he could spend his life taking care of orphans. But maybe that was a step too far. God's grace had not been spread widely enough to prevent the murder of his family.

"A boy from a neighboring village brought me the news," said Doctor Ace. "He was cold in delivering it to me. Now, I understand that he had been traumatized. It required strength to inform me that my family were gone."

He was quiet. Around and below them, his assistants were putting an end to the party, sending the children to bed in twin dormitories facing one another across a grassy space in which banana trees were being cultivated in rows.

The story when it came was like something out of the Old Testament. After the murder of his people, Ace Mambwete sold his four cows. That was the same as selling his birthright, and his identity. A man with nothing, he wandered in isolation, driven by the pain of unbearable loss into perfect isolation. With no plan, no destination, he moved toward the center of the vast war-ravaged country as if there might be sanctuary at the heart. He wound up in deep forest, where the wrong mosquito bit him and he contracted malaria. He kept moving until he couldn't. Out of his head, wracked by fever, he experienced hallucinations.

"I saw my mother in a pit of fire. She was holding out a jug of milk but could not reach past the flames. I saw Mai Mai slaughtering cows and eating the flesh raw, tearing off great strips of those beautiful animals. I saw my uncle's severed head, and the bodies of my cousins in a terrible heap. I saw dogs with red eyes and long tongues."

When he could no longer walk, he fell. He was unconscious; he could not say how long. When he woke, a Batwa man was squatting on the ground a couple of meters away, a bow strapped his back.

"I was too weak to stand up. A perfect target."

But the small man with the big bow did not shoot at the very tall man. Instead he brought him water in a gourd, and some foul-tasting meat. The meat gagged Ace, and he threw it up. The Batwa caught what he spewed and put it back into his mouth. He sealed the sick man's lips closed with two fingers until he swallowed.

"His name was Matope."

Saying the name derailed the story, bringing back with fresh force what never went away. The preacher set his glass on the ground next to him. He went into himself and stayed there a while.

"I did not go into the forest looking for God," he said, coming back.

"You were in shock and had to keep moving."

Doctor Ace shook his head ponderously. "I was looking for a reason not to die, which is not the same as a reason to live."

Ace Mambwete had the same prejudices against the Batwa that everyone he knew did. They were dirty, they were stupid, they smelled bad. They were beyond the pull of civilization. When Matope disappeared after feeding him bush meat, Ace expected him to come back with more of his own kind and put an end to him. He lay on the ground going into and out of unconsciousness so effortlessly it was hard to judge which was which. He attributed his passivity to weakness.

"I was wrong, of course," he explained. "I was passive because I did not care to live."

Matope returned with half a dozen Twa. One of them was a doctor in the Batwa tradition of rough healing. Ace submitted to the cure the man inflicted on him with indifference. These foolish stinking little men, he thought. How ignorant they are, just like the Belgians thought we all were. Stuck in the muck of ourselves, incapable of evolving. He swallowed the infusion the medicine man forced down his throat, thinking about his mother. They had parted on bad terms, and now she was dead. Remorse overwhelmed him. Unconsciousness was the only place to go.

He could not stay there, of course. So he was awake and had to acknowledge, eventually, that the Twa were taking care of him. They nursed him back to something like health. They built him a low hut long enough to lie down in. They laughed at everything about him: his preposterous length, his uncouth language, his helplessness. They taught him words for the things he required: food and water, knife, fire, memory. They did not so much bring him into their world as make a temporary camp around the tall, sick stranger and go about their daily business of surviving.

For the months that Ace spent with the Batwa, Matope treated him not as a find but as a friend. He was of middle age with grown children, grandchildren, years of experience and disappointment. He had the kind of eyes that saw himself as clearly as they saw the people and things that crossed his field of vision. He was particular, almost fussy, in his habits and expectations. He looked on Ace as an improbable son, an accomplishment no one of his acquaintance could brag of.

"You are a Westerner," Ace said to Smith. "You will not wish to hear the story of how God allowed me, through the agency of Matope, to perceive His love. For you, God is an embarrassment."

"I have an open mind," Smith told him, hoping it was true.

It was quiet. In the dark dormitories the children were asleep, or ought to be. Smith was thinking about Bujumbura. He'd hop on a flight to Paris. From the Eiffel Tower you could see Louisiana.

One of Doctor Ace's assistants carried Smith to Kalundu on the back of a motorbike. He pretended not to understand the American's French, dropping him dockside where he saluted and disappeared. He was not up to defending the American from the onslaught of people wanting something from him.

Saying goodbye to Béatrice had been easier than he thought. She was working with half a dozen other girls weeding raised beds in the vegetable garden. When he told her he was leaving, she glared at him. The girl next to her whispered something, and Béatrice shrugged her shoulders. She put her head down and went back at the weeds with a vengeance. What had he expected, tears and gratitude?

Six feet. That was how far he was able to walk before ten, a dozen, fifteen people glommed onto him. They knew better than to speak Swahili, or whatever language it was that people spoke in Uvira. Their pleas came out in plaintive French, with a handful of English phrases tossed in like I *need your help so very much*, and *the murder of my husband an innocent man.*

Another hundred and fifty feet and he would reach a thirty-foot boat tied to the pier with a green plastic rope. On the deck, a hand-lettered sign on an easel advertised transportation to all destinations national and international. No reason for that not to include Bujumbura. The water of the port was placidly blue and welcoming. It gave every indication of being a body of water a person could travel on. And the boat was in decent shape, *Tres Belle* newly repainted on the gunwale in precise white letters.

A shirtless man in a blue captain's hat with crossed anchors stood with his arms on his chest looking to see whether the foreigner was coming his way. He was a neutral observer. If there was something he could do to cut away the crowd of persons hanging onto Smith, he did not do it. Only those hardy enough to run the gauntlet earned the right to be his passenger.

The noise of people screaming, supplicating, threatening him was driving Smith crazy. His temperature was rising, his aggravation making itself felt.

He was not going to make those hundred and fifty feet to the Tres Belle. Not because of the crowd hanging all over him, but because of the man in camo and high boots who came running and beat people off with a truncheon. The truncheon was black and thickly dick-like and efficient. Inside a minute there were just the two of them, the American with his bag and the Congolese with his big stick. Nobody seemed to mind being hit.

Smith told him, "Show me your papers."

There were two ways that could go. It went the right one. The man threw back his head and laughed. He was lean, with a sheen of health on his black skin. His face was marked by razor burn. He removed his sunglasses, rubbed his eyes, asked Smith what papers.

"When I met with Monsieur le Ministre in Kinshasa, he told me that citizens of the Congo must be prepared to show me their papers. It is an obligation of the constitution, *un devoir civique.*"

"Monsieur le Ministre . . . "

Smith gave him the name of the interior minister who had signed Denis Lajeune's safe-conduct pass. The man nodded.

"And for what purpose did the minister authorize you to go around the country demanding to see people's papers."

"You know who Disney is, don't you?"

"The father of Mickey Mouse."

"That's the one. Does it not seem strange to you that there is no Disney World in Africa?"

Another nod, a slow sweet smile. "I have given the matter considerable thought."

"As well you should. I'll tell you the truth. I have been authorized by the company to purchase a site suitable for the construction of Disney World Africa."

"Disney World," said the man in camo. He scratched the side of his face where his razor had scraped the flesh. "In the Congo."

"Nothing is certain at this point. This is my first visit. Your country, I understand, has had its problems. Wherever I go, people tell me sad stories. And for a company like ours, social stability is an important consideration."

"Naturally."

"I might well be forced to choose Botswana."

"That would be a shame."

"I couldn't agree with you more. And I'm not giving up on the Congo. I will be leaving the country soon, but it would be useful to have a man on the ground here."

"A man to do what?"

"Liaison."

"I see. Would this be a paid position?"

"For now, I can offer a small retainer."

It cost him a hundred bucks. Worth it. Smith followed the man into a two-room bar to hand over the cash in something like privacy.

"Mister Disney," said the man as he folded five twenties into his shirt pocket. "Do you know, I thought he was dead."

"Disney will never die."

The bar was dark, and Smith went momentarily blind as he stepped outside again. He blinked, and when his vision returned there was the captain of the Tres Belle across the way on deck. He was smoking a pipe now. Smith supposed that was something all ship captains did. Basic seamanship. He walked in the direction of the boat hoping not to draw another crowd of people wanting something from him. The well was drying up. He needed to hang onto enough money to get off the continent.

It was not the population of the port that held him up this time. It was a tall, thin girl stepping down from the back of a motorbike whose driver made a gesture of helplessness when he saw the American looking at him. He had no choice. The kid had demanded a ride.

Smith was a target. She walked him down.

"What's wrong?" he said.

"Last night I dreamed."

"You dreamed."

"About my grandmother."

"What about her?"

"She was not able to walk."

"It was only a dream, Béatrice. Go back to Doctor Ace's."

"She is sick. The sickness prevents her from walking. If she cannot walk, she will not find me."

"So what are you going to do?"

"In my dream, Grandmother was in Minembwe."

Smith wondered what "Minembwe" meant to her. The name was a myth, like the woman she was looking for. Which didn't make either of them any less real.

"How will you get there?"

She shrugged. It didn't matter how she got there, only that she went.

"It's a long way," he pointed out. "The rains are starting, and the road will be bad. And there are men with guns out there, there are men like the Hutu man who will want to hurt you."

She was still wearing a clean green shirt with the Travail d'Amour logo on it. Her hair was beginning to grow out a little, and she seemed taller than she had been in Kinshasa when they met. Was that possible? It felt like a hundred years. She looked at him and saw his dilemma, his frustration, his aggravation. Maybe other stuff.

"Roger," she said.

"What about him?"

"It is his wife who made him angry."

"Giselle."

Béatrice nodded. "*Oui.*"

"What did she do to anger him?'

"Roger has a cousin. He lives in the same city as Giselle. Over there." The girl pointed in the direction she thought Barcelona lay.

"I see."

"Roger's cousin saw Giselle come out of a dance club with a white man. This was at an hour when people must sleep. The white man had red hair, and in the darkness Roger's cousin saw him touch Giselle. He put his tongue in her ear. Therefore Roger is angry. At the same time he is very sad."

Smith nodded. "I will give you some money. You'll need some."

"I don't want money."

She turned away. He let her go. The captain of the Tres Belle was waiting for him to make up his mind. On deck, his old-salt head was wreathed in pipe smoke that gave him the look of a statue, something people bowed down and prayed to in the hope of luck. Béatrice did not look back until the last possible moment, on the verge of disappearing around a corner. Smith thought her pride would stop her from making any kind of goodbye, but he was wrong.

Now you're lookin' at a man that's getting kinda mad
I had a lot of luck but it's all been bad
No matter how I struggle and strive
I'll never get out of this world alive.

In 1952, Hank Williams released "I'll Never Get out of This World Alive." On the first day of 1953, he didn't. Smith was into the second verse before Béatrice turned and waved.

He waved back. Then he raised his arms making stiff wings of them. He took off from the dock and flew a small circle. She got it. He watched her raise her own arms, her wings acknowledging his.

PART THREE

Milk

It was taking the pilot way too long to crank up his Cessna. The cowling up, he had his head down near the engine, diagnosing the silence. In one hand he held a screwdriver, in the other a socket wrench. In the ten minutes Smith stood there watching him he had applied neither to the engine. He was the picture of diligence, but only the picture. It was ten o'clock in the morning, and Demas Papandreou had been drinking. The question was how much.

Next to him in the shade, Béatrice asked Smith, "What's wrong with the airplane?"

"Nothing. He's making an adjustment."

"Why don't you fix it for him?"

"I don't think he wants my help."

"Are you sure he knows the way to Minembwe?"

The kid was right to be skeptical. The pilot did not inspire confidence. He was fifty and frazzled, with a broad, flat face on which thirty years of Congo life were etched. He had come south from Thessaloniki as a young man in response to a job offer that evaporated before his plane touched down in Goma. He had an uncle in the city and stuck around, expecting another job to turn up, an opportunity to present itself. Maybe peace would break out, and everybody's business would prosper. Some years later the uncle died, leaving him an old Cessna 172 and a repair manual. According to the uncle, the plane had once belonged to the CIA. It had come into his hands at the end of a chain of events he never fully explained to his nephew. Because Demas believed the story, he believed his plane was invincible.

Papandreou had thick, stiff eyebrows and spoke English like a person who had picked up the language from books. His white ribbed T-shirt did a poor job covering his belly, which was a testament to just a little more than survival. He had developed the habit of expecting big things to go wrong, and then the little ones, too; so many rats following the piper of doom over the edge into oblivion.

"Eight hours bottle to throttle, that's my rule," he had sworn to Smith when the American asked him how much he'd drunk that morning.

Smith did not believe him. But Papandreou's Cessna was the only airplane at the landing strip outside of Uvira, and now was the time to go. Any day now and the rains of autumn would begin. The strip was hard-packed dirt. A yellow wind sock with a Primus Beer logo hung limp on a pole that leaned at a thirty-degree angle. Across the way, chickens hunted through the grass in the vicinity of a hut where, according to Papandreou, the airport manager lived. If there was such a person, he was away for the day.

"How's it going?" Smith hollered at the pilot.

No answer.

Smith did not much like the deal they had come to, but he recognized it was his last best shot at getting Béatrice to Minembwe. There was no air strip there, Papandreou conceded. But he didn't need one. He knew every inch of the Kivus from the air. The high plains had plenty of flat places on which a skilled pilot could bring his airplane down. He had landed near Minembwe before and would do it again.

The deal was, he would deliver Smith and Béatrice to Minembwe. If a woman named Joséphine Mutebusi could be found there, the girl would stay with her. If not, she would fly back to Uvira with Smith. Smith would leave her with Doctor Ace. Either way, it would be the end of the search.

To Smith, it was worth the fifteen hundred that Papandreou demanded. An unspecified percentage of the price was what the pilot called an uncertainty tax. A fever for Eckstein's gold was making the Kivus hot. Papandreou tried to explain it to Smith.

"Just imagine. All the labor of extracting a significant quantity of gold from the ground has been done. But there is a problem. Somewhere the treasure sits ready to be transported. Whoever gets to it first is a rich man."

"So you believe the gold is real."

"I met Eckstein once. He was in Goma on business. He travels with seven bodyguards. You can't get close to the man unless he wants you close. He knew my uncle."

Smith let it go. He still had a few thousand bucks in a bank account. Better to spend it getting out than reimbursing Dauphin Petroleum for his Paris R&R. He'd pay the company back—he had never walked away from a debt and did not intend to start now—but he was putting first things first. One final push to find Béatrice's grandmother. Then out of the Congo. Propose to Maybelline face to face, in case the email version didn't take.

Papendreou had insisted on three hundred bucks up front to buy fuel.

The airplane engine turned over. The propeller spun in the sun, flashing silver. Papendreou looked over at Smith and shouted something the American did not hear.

"Let's go," he said to Béatrice.

They ran to board the plane. There was a bad moment when the passenger-side door would not close, but Papendreou solved the problem by taking off his belt. It was a wide belt of black leather. He used it to tie the door shut.

The leather of the seats was ripped. One of them was gone. In its place was a lawn chair on which Papandreou's suitcase sat. Strapped to the suitcase was a toothbrush.

"What did I tell you?" he said to Smith. "There is no problem. This ship will outlive all of us. The CIA knows everything there is to know about airplanes."

Smith smelled liquor on his breath. Papandreou pointed to the motionless wind sock, then the cloudless sky overhead.

"A perfect day to fly."

The strip was not real long, and Smith had his doubts. But ten feet before the end of it the wheels of the Cessna lifted from the hard dirt, and they were in the air. When Béatrice felt the takeoff, she clapped. She really liked flying, the sheer sensation of it, plus you touched down in a new location. Off to the left, Lake Tanganyika sparkled like a playground.

They climbed, and the airplane banked, heading inland. Smith saw the low fuel light go on and pointed at it. The pilot shook his head.

"Relax, my friend. The gauge refuses, sometimes, to tell the truth."

They flew, and Smith relaxed. Flight felt like escape. But seven minutes into the trip, the engine coughed. It coughed again. Papandreou scowled. The plane shuddered.

"We'd better turn back," he said.

When the engine went out, they quickly lost airspeed, and then altitude. To compensate, Papandreou lifted the nose looking for and finding a glide altitude the aircraft could handle. It worked, and he aimed the airplane at the strip from which they had just taken off. It was a soft landing, and they coasted to a stop.

"I can't understand it," he told Smith.

Papandreou was right about one thing. All the big things, and then all the little ones, too. Rats off a cliff. Climbing out of the plane after Béatrice, Smith was three hundred bucks lighter and felt it.

The reporter from the *Minembwe Trompette* jammed an imaginary microphone at Smith's lips. He was a tall, sculpted Munyamulenge man with a reedy voice that managed to come out with authority, like a king calling for his pipe and his bow. And while you're at it, send in my fiddlers three.

It was an audition, and Gideon Muhamiriza knew it. He struck a dramatic pose.

"Here you stand, Monsieur Smith."

"I'm sitting down."

In fact Smith was sitting on a chair at the Bill Gates Masculine Hair Salon. It was the only chair. It was placed in front of a fence of corrugated aluminum on dirt where there should be a sidewalk, down a side street at the port. The name of the shop was painted on the fence, along with a stylized head, in profile, depicting the founder of Microsoft. On either side of the place of business he had willed into being, the barber had swept trash into neat piles. A lone white chicken picked through one of the piles with dull curiosity.

A crowd had gathered to enjoy the novelty of a white American man having his hair cut by black hands in a public space. The barber had a baby face and the arthritic demeanor of a geezer; hard to say how old he was. He was silent as he cut, concentrating but at the same time getting a kick out of working before an audience. By chance, Smith had seen his own face in a mirror and decided he could not figure out what came next until he cleaned up. When he had approached the barber, the man studied his head for a few moments before telling him he wanted one hundred dollars to do the job. But he respected Smith's *Pas question*, and told him he would take whatever the American thought was fair.

When Gideon waggled the microphone in his face again, Smith had an urge to grab it from his hand. If it hadn't been imaginary, he would have.

"You must understand," the reporter said, "the public demand to know."

He was playing to the crowd, and he huffed a little. His show of impatience made Béatrice laugh. She stood with the others, watching as if she had never seen Smith before. Her reaction was a point in the reporter's favor as Smith made up his mind whether to hire the man to guide them to Minembwe. The fiasco of flying with Papandreou had left them without options.

"What do people demand to know?"

"You appear to be lost. Do you have any idea where you are?"

It was a good question. Smith knew a little about playing to a crowd.

"Of course I know," he said, sitting up straight in the chair so that the barber had to stop cutting. "Is this not the navel of the known universe?"

That drew some applause, though not as much as Smith would have liked. A tough audience, and his delivery in French was not all that great.

Gideon kept up the questions for the duration of the haircut. Smith liked what he had seen of the man so far. He was waiting to see if he could trust him. The Greek pilot had let Smith down. It might have been a scam all along. Get a few hundred bucks for gas up front, put the plane up in the air, then fake a problem with the engine. Land, spend a perplexed hour under the cowl trying to get the damn thing to run again. Fail. Apologize. Curse colorfully while raising your hands to Heaven. Apologize again. Quote a Greek proverb on bad luck. Shrug your shoulders and wave goodbye.

Do that twice a week and you could make enough to get by while avoiding wear and tear on your airplane.

When the barber finished, Gideon stepped forward to pay him. The barber glowered, hoping for more. Another point in

Gideon's favor. People in the crowd saw that the American was under escort and drifted away.

"It was a serious question back there," Gideon told Smith as they walked up the street, Béatrice trailing behind them. "Do you know where you are?"

"I have a map. Uvira is on it, but there's no Minembwe."

At an outdoor stall selling cold drinks and sticks of fried pork with hot sauce, they split a bottle of Primus, and Gideon unfolded a map of the region. He spread it on Smith's lap.

"A journalist must know where he is at all times."

There was something absurd about him, and something credible in the absurdity.

Smith looked at the map a long time. On it, the city of Uvira where they were drinking beer was snugged into the north end of Lake Tanganyika on the west side. East of the big lake lay Burundi, whose capital was Bujumbura, which Smith now associated with escape. On the Congo side of the lake, Minembwe lay to the south, surrounded by nothing.

"There's no road," Smith pointed out.

"Not on the map." He raised a hand. "I make this solemn vow to you, here and now."

"I'm listening," said Smith.

"The vow has two parts. Part the first, you will not be taken advantage of by the owner of the motorcycles you must rent for the journey. I know the man, I know how he thinks. Part the second, I will shepherd you safely here"—He tapped Minembwe on the map with an index finger—"as surely as Jesus leads his flock to Heaven."

"You have seen my grandmother," Béatrice told him. It was not a question, it was an accusation.

Gideon said something in Kinyarwanda, but Smith had the sense she did not understand the words. She glared sideways at an iron-mouthed man minding his own business at another table, going through papers in a briefcase hunting for the document that would change his life.

Béatrice had every right to know whatever Gideon might know about her grandmother. After all, he claimed to be from the same place Nyogokuru lived, up with the cattle where the earth was radiant red. But Gideon had been away from the high plains a long time. As Smith understood it, the *Minembwe Trompette* was a newspaper published as a blog. Gideon was the paper's only reporter. He was also the editor. If they carried a picture, Gideon was the one who took it. His access to the internet was spotty. If he posted an article a month, it was a good thirty days. It happened that one of those articles had angered "certain people." Not just the Bembe who hated and resented the Banyamulenge, but many of his own Banyamulenge as well. With seven hundred and fifty hundred words, he had pissed off his own people. It was an editorial that got him in hot water. The subject was peace, and the utility of compromise in reaching that desired state. It was all in the phrasing.

To save himself, Gideon had slipped out of Minembwe in a hurry, abandoning his family to travel alone at night, descending from the austere cool air of the high plains to the muggy heat of the lowlands. He did not much care for the change that was forced on him. Now, after twenty-seven months in exile, he had made up his mind to risk going back. His wife was there, and his children. He had it on good authority—his favorite cousin, Anatole—that she had stayed faithful to him despite considerable pressures both social and financial to take another man.

"So tell me how this works," Smith said. "We get to Minembwe. You're home. Things look good, your wife is happy to see you. You decide to stay. But I have to bring two motorcycles back to Uvira."

"The girl can drive one of them, always supposing we locate the person we are seeking," Gideon suggested.

"Bad idea."

"Of course it is. My cousin will drive the second machine."

The man who had misplaced an important document looked over at them. What made him suddenly get interested in their conversation? Smith felt a twinge of paranoia. The paranoia made his decision more difficult. Could he trust Gideon Muhamiriza? He could not make up his mind.

"What do you say, Béatrice?"

She had stuck her tongue into a bottle of ginger soda, reaming out the last bit of sweetness.

"I say . . . " She placed the empty bottle on the ground and looked at Smith, squinting. "This is the man who will take us to my grandmother."

Béatrice chose to ride with Gideon. Smith considered that a good thing. Her antennae were powerful, and if she trusted the reporter, it meant Smith had done the right thing. They left early the next morning while the sun still balanced on the rim of the east sky and human hands had not yet spoiled the day. He had a sense of moving, finally, in the right direction. But ten klicks out of Uvira he felt the rear tire on his bike going flat. He signaled to Béatrice, who tapped Gideon's arm. By the time the bikes came to a stop, all the air was out of Smith's tire.

Gideon took off his helmet. The bikes had come with two blue helmets; Béatrice wore the other one. He stepped down, kicked the kickstand, and came over to inspect Smith's bad tire. Béatrice's helmet was too big for her head, but she liked it and did not take it off. She stood in the road with her covered head, the new pack on her back. It gave her an armored look.

"It's not my fault," said Gideon. He looked into the woods on both sides of the road as if to get his eye on a saboteur.

In the sudden quiet they heard thunder. It made a sullen sound, full of resentment. It began slowly and kept rolling, like the grumpy old guy down the street working himself up to holler at the neighbor kids. *You little shits, stay the hell off my grass.* Across as much of the sky as they could see, black clouds were sliding into place.

"It's not my fault," Gideon said again.

"Did I say it was?"

"This is a tragedy."

"It's not a tragedy, it's a flat."

The evening before, Smith had checked his email at an internet café. He ignored the latest dunning letter from Dauphin and opened Maybelline's message. *Hey there boy. You and me got to have us a conversation. I'm talkin bout the real deal, not this computer crap back and forth. I need to see your face, Smith. If I remember right that's where your mouth is. I need to see for myself the words coming out of it.* Okay. He had a goal of his own now. Life after Congo.

"We must keep moving," Gideon fretted. "Once the rains start, the road becomes our enemy." He paused a moment before making a partial confession. "I am no mechanic. I have never changed a tire."

"It's okay," Béatrice told him. Coming from the helmet, her voice belonged to somebody else. "Smith knows how to do it."

The man who had rented Smith the motorcycles wanted his property returned to him in serviceable condition. With the rental came a tool kit, tire patches, an extra tube, and a hand air pump of the old-fashioned kind Smith had used on bike tires when he was a kid. The gear was strapped behind him on the bike, along with a jerry can of the gas and oil mix the two-stroke engines ran on. They were Chinese motorcycles, Adventure 250s, black with a red stripe on the chassis for emphasis. The engines were straightforward and would be easy to work on, if it came to that.

When Smith picked an aluminum nail out of the tire, Gideon expressed his outrage.

"They did that on purpose!"

"Who did?"

"Whoever it was that wanted to puncture your tire."

Smith looked around. There was no one to be seen, and not much to look at except for a rabbit that came out from under the trees thinking to cross the road, changed its mind, made itself quickly scarce.

Gideon relaxed, seeing that Smith was capable of repairing the tire.

"You may speak as you work, Monsieur Smith, no?"

"What do you want me to say?"

"I should like to conduct an interview for the *Trompette*." He had his telephone out, ready to record.

Smith asked him, "About what?"

"Your point of view on the issues of concern to our readers."

"Give me an example."

The road was empty. Was it the weather ahead, or were people worried about getting trampled in the rush for Eckstein's gold?

"The war," said Gideon. "Most definitely the war. Poverty in Africa, and how we are to escape the burden of the past."

"I'm not the kind of person that does interviews."

"You do yourself an injustice."

"Listen," Smith said. For an instant he was angry, but a sense of how ridiculous the idea was pushed the anger to one side, and he laughed. "I don't know a damn thing about any of that stuff."

Gideon thought it was false modesty on the American's part. He pushed. He cajoled. He flattered. It was Béatrice, finally, who told him to give it up.

"He knows nothing," she told Gideon.

Smith looked at the girl. "Take off that helmet, will you?"

She took it off.

"Thanks for the vote of confidence."

She shook her head. She put her helmet on the ground, wriggled out of her pack and placed it next to the helmet. Then she raised her arms skyward, commanding the rain not to fall.

They rode. Smith went second. Gideon was a good rider obsessed with getting home. Smith expected problems with the bikes, but the Adventure 250s ran like metal monsters. A two-stroke buzz entered Smith's hands, his feet, his ass. It traveled through him until there was no place in him that did not vibrate.

He had been on the road for a long time now in a place that remained strange to him. He tried to add up the days since he had come across the river from Brazzaville. Couldn't. But counted or not, the days were taking their toll on him. Not to mention bad food, dicey water, troubled sleep, the constant sour smell of danger, the acquired sense of precariousness. Holding the handlebars, he felt himself being hollowed out by an augur. Pretty soon there would be more hole than wall. It was a new way of being thin.

As they made their way up the road a movie trailer was looping in his mind. The movie starred both of them, Smith with his new Africa thin, Maybelline with her lovely doubts. Why wouldn't she wonder about him? Throughout the trailer she kept asking him *How come?* No matter how many times the clip played, he never gave her the answer she deserved. How come you did that, Smith? How come you kept going all that time, all that damage, when you knew good and well there was no grandmother waiting to scoop up the kid and drown her in kisses? Answer me. You ain't no rocket scientist but you're no fool neither. You knew all the time what wasn't there, and still you kept going. How come?

The trailer got stuck every time in the same spot. He had no answer. He had to wait until he was back in Louisiana, standing in front of Maybelline, up close. Then they would see how the movie turned out. It was in the nature of trailers to leave you hanging.

Wash-out. Stop the bikes and walk them around the hole, body buzzing. The body was no rocket scientist, but it was no fool, either. The body knew what lay ahead.

Smell the difference in the air as they climbed. Maybe that was a trick of the mind, ordering your nose to pick up a difference in this cleaner place, higher up.

Friends or enemies? That was the main thing the people they passed wanted to know about them. People on bikes, in the cab of a truck. Wheeling a bicycle laden with jugs of fuel. Sitting on the bare ground in front of huts. Those strangers on the Chinese motorcycles, that *mzungu* riding with the other two, were they friends or enemies? There was no such thing as a noncombatant. The naked kids in the dirt, the birds in the bushes, the apes in the highlands, they all knew that.

Trees. Somebody ought to go around the country and tally up how many trees there were in the Congo. Even as they climbed and came to rolling hills and grasslands, there were more trees than untrees, more forest than not, more places to hide and fight and die.

A break. Crackers, a tin of sardines, a hunk of crumbly goat cheese. Béatrice was impassive, sensing she was finally on the right road. Smith's body would not stop buzzing. He had always hated the whine of a two-stroke engine. It made up in aggravation what it lacked in muscle.

Buzz. Trees. Wash-out. Friends or enemies?

The thing about being hollowed out was, after a certain point the walls of you collapsed. And then? A science project. Observe carefully, find out what came next. In high school, Smith's projects never worked out the way they should have. Once, he got a late start and tried to grow some mold. That was scientific, wasn't it? It grew too slowly. The teacher saw through the ruse and gave him a C-minus.

Motion under stress; the stress of motion. It brought back a memory of the time Smith's father got the two of them good and lost out on the bayou. That was not supposed to happen. You were supposed to know those waterways like the veins in the back of your hand. Baylee remembered a spot where his grandfather had hooked a bass the size of a pony. A struggle for the ages. Sweat and straining muscles and the merciless Louisiana sun giving unfair advantage to the fish. But finally the old man landed the enormous creature. Baylee had observed the catch with his own young eyes and wanted his son to see the site of the legendary competition between man and fish. Knowing Baylee, he probably imagined hooking his own famous bass in the same place, a story to be passed down to the next generation of heroic fishing Smiths.

Hours, they were lost. A whole day, more than likely, although Smith's memory was not to be trusted. On a branch jutting out over the water a cottonmouth stretched its full four-hundred-foot length like an advertisement for murder. Its eyes locked onto Smith, who was too young to know you could not let that happen, you could not allow yourself to be hypnotized by a venomous snake out in the wild or that was the end of you. Luckily his father saw what was happening and clipped him on the side of the head, which broke the spell.

They ran out of gas. They drifted, Baylee cursing monotonously, feeling put upon because of this particular tribulation. Why him? Eventually somebody in a johnboat rescued them. It made for a durable joke on Baylee Smith, the time he got himself and his little boy lost on the bayou like a couple of tourists with high-end fishing gear and no sense of direction.

Friends or enemies? Trees. Hills of grass. Trees again. A woman in a spectacular purple *pagne* slugging a sack of something heavy. Smith was not mistaken. The air did have a cleaner smell, a fresher taste, as they ascended. It was thinner, maybe, but easier to breathe.

Even the power of Béatrice could not hold back the rain once it made up its mind to come. There was no warning. No practice shots. It fell hard and fast in long twisting ropes that lashed the trees, the earth and everything on it. Gideon, who knew what they were up against, stopped his bike as soon as he could. He and Béatrice jumped off. Together they stretched a tarp between trees, lashing down the grommeted corners with rope. The two men pulled the motorcycles under the shelter, and the three of them sat on the ground. There was no wind. The rain fell straight down. But it hit the earth with force and splashed sideways, soaking them.

"How long will this last?" Smith asked Gideon. He had to holler to make himself heard over the uproar of rain.

"A quarter of an hour."

He was right. It stopped instantly as if a spigot had been screwed shut. As Smith stood, hunched under the tarp, Gideon took his arm.

"You see, now."

"I've seen rain before."

"This is what we face. It is the season."

"Are you asking me do I want to keep going?"

Gideon shrugged. "I will take the girl. You go back to Uvira. I will send Anatole back to Uvira with the motorcycle."

"I figured something out," Smith said.

"What is that?"

"I can trust you."

Gideon nodded. "She belongs to my people. She is one of us."

Around them, across the forest, several million raindrops that had fallen onto the leaves and branches of the trees were loud, making up their mind to fall farther, down to the ground. Birds celebrated something with clear voices: rain, or the end of rain?

Squatting on her haunches, Béatrice whispered something to neither of the men.

"What did you say?" Smith asked her.

She shook her head.

Gideon told him, "She said 'nkoyi.' It means . . . "

"I know what it means. Here, grab one end of the tarp. I'll take the other end."

The conversation was over. They shook out the tarp, folded it, strapped it onto Gideon's bike.

Ride. The going was slower now. A lot of rain had fallen in a short time, and the surface of the road was greasy.

Ride.

They spent the night in a hut that had been abandoned, along the side of the road.

"Why?" said Smith.

"Why what?"

"Whoever built this house, why did they leave it?"

Smith understood that the answer Gideon gave him was a story and had the full force of truth.

"The man of the family," Gideon told him, shaking his head. "He was something of a hothead. He used to work for a merchant in Bukavu. A flour and oil merchant. When the war began, one morning he was beaten by a gang of men as he made his way to the warehouse. He survived the beating, but it left him quite angry. He was caught up in events. He became a willing participant, and joined a militia. He saw some brutal fighting. It did something to him, inside. Then, when the militia was disbanded, there was no work for him. He came here because his wife's people lived nearby."

"What happened to him?" Béatrice wanted to know, and Smith wondered whether she knew that the story was an illustration.

"Sadly," Gideon told her, "the woman's brothers disliked the man. The war had made him unlikable. There was an altercation. When it finished, he was dead. What was the woman to do? She took the children and went to another place. She could not abide a night in the house where her brothers had slain her husband."

Béatrice was listening carefully. There was nothing new in it, nothing she had not known. She studied the dirt floor of the hut as if a dark patch close to the center were a bloodstain from the murder.

In the morning, they woke to rain. It made a conspiratorial sound as though wanting to draw them in, make them lazy, make them stay where they were, dry and protected. When the rain stopped, they started.

Trees. A slick road. Enemies or friends? A sky that rumbled continuously although you could not hear it over the sound of the bikes.

Once, on a break, eating crackers, Smith asked Gideon, "How much farther?"

Gideon was a young man. He was used to hard walking, long walking, only walking. Motorcycle travel was a luxury. The more time Smith spent in his company, the more he liked him. He had Roger Dzba's strength of character but not the bitterness that overtook Roger, not the instantaneous anger. He was an optimist. At the end of the trip his wife was waiting for him. Her name was Cadencia, which was exactly the right name for her because there was so much music in her voice. And he had a son, born after Gideon had fled Minembwe because of his inflammatory editorial in the *Trompette* on the topic of peace.

"Not much farther," Gideon told Smith.

It was the answer you gave to a child who was tired of traveling.

Béatrice picked up the theme. "Soon, Smith. We will be in Minembwe very soon now."

Going through a patch of low-canopy woods, halfway or something more than halfway to Minembwe, the road made an energetic dogleg. Gideon and Smith slowed down going into the turn. They did not see the tree lying lengthwise across the road until it was too late. It was not a big tree. It didn't have to be.

Gideon knew what was happening. He hit the brakes hard, and his bike went into a skid. Smith slowed as Gideon did, but they could not turn the bikes around in time. When they came to a stop, four men with rifles were standing in the road behind them. More armed men came out of the woods on either side.

Some of them wore camouflage fatigues designed for desert combat, the kind you saw on CNN when they showed soldiers coming home from Afghanistan to hug their family. On television, there were always people holding balloons and waving welcome-home signs, and if you believed the reporter the war was a story with a happy ending. In the forests of Central Africa, those same fatigues didn't hide the men wearing them, they made them stand out.

Some of the men—they were boys, really— wore jeans and bright T-shirts. They had gone to war with flip-flops on their feet and guns in their hands. One of them wore a necklace of rifle cartridges around his long skinny neck. It gave him a ceremonial look. He was being initiated into a brotherhood. His T-shirt said *We All Tattoos on This Town.*

Smith tried to count the men surrounding them, but fear debilitated him. He had been afraid before, in the Congo. The *shegues* who swarmed him on the street his first night in Kinshasa scared him. The ANR agent who grabbed him at the internet café in Bukavu scared him. Anytime he saw a man in a uniform, a man with a gun, a man who stared back at him with hostility or curiosity, he felt a twinge of apprehension. This was different. It went deeper, activating alarm cells he hadn't known were in him. His brain refused to count, but there had to be a dozen of them, all hollering like the crowd at a football match. The wrong team had just scored a goal. He had heard enough Swahili by now to be sort of confident that the language they were speaking was something else. As if the words coming out of their mouths made any difference to how this turned out.

A burly short man in fatigues, standing on the edge of the road in tree shadow, appeared to be in charge. Abelino, they called him. He wore an American flag bandana on his head and looked a little older than the others, or more mature. The buckle on his black leather belt featured the lone star of

Texas under crossed bull horns. He did not anticipate resistance from two men and a girl on motorbikes; his rifle was slung on his back.

He lit a cigarette and told his men to shut up. They did. He pointed at Gideon. In the incalculable lag before anything happened, Smith knew they were screwed. Above them, a cloud the size of a small country was being torn apart by wind. Between the shreds, fierce sunlight rained down on the road, and a breeze traveled past in its own narrow corridor. Then one of the young guys stepped forward. He was the kind of person who did not need to be told twice to carry out an order. He raised his rifle and knocked Gideon in the head with the butt. Several of the men cheered.

Mai Mai. The name had to do with water, and the magic of protection. On the drive to Uvira Roger Dzba had told Smith stories about them. Before going into battle, Mai Mai fighters went through a ceremony. In the ceremony, a *féticheur*—some sort of magic man—gave the fighters medicine guaranteed to turn into water any bullets sent their way. If a bullet couldn't stop them, they were invincible. Another part of the ceremony was getting high. A buzz made it easier for them to throw themselves into the fight.

There was something about the rifles these guys carried, something he ought to pay attention to, but Smith could not say what it was.

Gideon's helmet protected his head, but the force of the blow knocked him off the bike. When he fell into the road the order-follower stood over him hollering something that meant, *Take off the helmet*, or *Take off the goddamn helmet*.

Gideon slowly lifted it off. He had the demeanor of a thoughtful man coming to the realization that he was condemned. Béatrice stood next to the motorcycle, watching. For the moment, none of the Mai Mai was paying attention to her. She was fingering her magic marble. Too late for that, too. Looking at her—her beauty, her strength, her holy passion—Smith was hit by revelation. He had just delivered the girl to her enemies. The disgust he felt for himself bled into his anger at the Mai Mai.

The boss in the flag bandana identified Gideon by his features.

"Munyamulenge."

It was a bullfrog voice with the snap-back twang of a banjo string. The identification was an order, too, one that did not need spelling out. The kid standing over Gideon smashed the butt of his rifle down on his naked head. Gideon slumped and fell over in the road. His head bled.

Smith moved toward him, but three men blocked his way. They did not touch him. It was possible that, for the moment, his white skin protected him. They did not know what to make of him; he did not yet have a category. Béatrice, meanwhile, cursed in French the guy who had attacked Gideon. It only made the Mai Mai laugh. The skinny little girl screaming at them was no threat, she was entertainment.

The man with the bandana stepped into the road. He moved at a halting gait, as though one leg were shorter than the other and needed time to catch up. In his froggy voice he said to Smith, "Show me your papers."

Smith understood that the man would not be placated, or sidetracked. He would not be jollied by a joke. Here was rubber meeting road. All things considered, Smith's luck had been pretty good. Until now. He had been unrealistic, thinking it could last.

Several of the men seemed inclined to do violence to Smith. Getting the Munyamulenge out of the way had been too easy. There was no sport in it. But the sergeant was not ready to let that happen. That was the virtue of maturity, you took the long view of a situation.

All around him Smith smelled wet leather and smoke, sweat and human excitement. The whites of Abelino's eyes were yellowed as from jaundice. In his left ear lobe, a small silver cross looked like purity. He had the kind of exquisitely muscled body gym rats spent their life building.

He held out his hand. Smith gave him his passport. The sergeant held it in one hand and traced the eagle on the cover with the index finger of the other. He pointed to the arrows the bird clutched in its claw.

"What are these?"

"Those are just for target practice," Smith told him.

No response. It wasn't a bad line, but if the Mai Mai boss had a sense of humor, Smith had not located it. The man opened the passport and compared the picture to Smith's face. He held it up, showing it around the circle of men and boys who awaited his verdict.

"An American."

They clapped, they whistled, they cheered. And went silent when the man signaled for quiet. No one seemed to care that Béatrice had gone over to Gideon lying in the road. She crouched next to him, crooning in a whisper as if her secret words would bring him back to consciousness.

"And your travel pass?"

The man's French was bad, and he knew it. *Prise en grippe.* That was what Smith had felt for Kluge, the foreman on the Dauphin rig. Instant dislike. A mutual irritation of the skin. He felt the same thing now for the man who was asking for the travel pass he did not possess. Not that you would expect to feel tender regard for a man who had just ambushed you, assaulted your friend, threatened your mobility. Still, what Smith felt toward the sergeant was distinct and strong with its own vinegary smell.

"My travel pass," Smith echoed. His brain, under pressure, refused to perform.

"Give it to me."

"Yeah, well, I'm sorry. There was a little confusion about all that back in Uvira. My lawyer . . . something about the paperwork."

The Mai Mai gave a signal Smith did not see, and the boy with the bullet necklace grabbed his go bag from him. He emptied it into the road. Smith's belongings scattered. There, stuck between two rolled T-shirts, was the envelope with the Congolese interior ministry seal.

"Sergeant Abelino," the kid said, picking up the letter with the tips of his fingers as though worried it might explode. "There is this."

Who the hell made the man a sergeant anyway? The kid handed the letter to his boss, who read it slowly. He took a long time at it. The man did not read much; that was obvious. But he picked up enough of what was in the letter to note the discrepancy in the names. In the passport, the foreigner was an individual by the name of Smith. In the letter, he was Lejeune.

"Who is Denis Lejeune?" Abelino said.

Roger Dzba had been right. He was completely and devastatingly right. Carrying the letter was a bad idea. Not a bad idea, a stupendously bad idea. He wished he had burnt it.

Smith said, "Lejeune? He is a friend, that's all." A defiant impulse that was going to do him no good made him add, "We used to sing in the choir together, back when we were boys. Denis's father is quite well known. Perhaps you've heard of him. He invented the wristwatch? Did really well with it."

The sergeant spat in the road. He did not have to understand the joke to know that it was on him. *Prise en grippe.* He did not like the American he had captured any more than the American liked him.

"And the gold?"

"What gold?"

He spat again. "The Congo gold stolen by the Israeli."

"I don't know any Israelis."

"Monsieur Eckstein."

"Never heard of him."

Something prevented Abelino from smacking Smith, knocking him down, although he wanted to. He had the coiled arm strength to overpower the American easily even if he hadn't been backed up by a dozen armed men. Smith had no idea what it was that held him back but did not think, any more, that it was his white skin. He put out his hand.

"I need my passport."

They were all watching; Béatrice, too. But there was no chance the Mai Mai sergeant would hand the American his eagle passport and send him on his way with a courteous salute. An image came to Smith. Because of the fear he felt it took a moment to come into focus. It was a country-time tableau: old woman, placid cow, pitcher of milk. Great. Now he was experiencing the same hallucinations Béatrice did. *This,* he thought, his mind dull. *This is what my fuck-up will keep the kid from seeing.*

Fact: they were prisoners. Abelino gave orders. Water from a canteen revived Gideon, who sat up knowing everything. He had a bereaved look, expecting not to see Cadencia and his son, not soon or ever. At a word from Abelino, two men took the motorcycles. They really liked the blue helmets. The helmets were definitely a bonus. Whooping, they started the engines and took off down the road back toward Uvira.

The kid with the cartridge necklace collected the stuff from Smith's go bag that was spread across the road, repacked the bag, held onto it with a sense of self-importance. He was twelve or thirteen, Béatrice's age. His smile was warm. He was skinny and lithe, and his brown skin glowed with health. In the bustle as they formed a procession to lead the prisoners into the woods, the boy surreptitiously pulled something from his pocket to show Smith. He held it in his open palm for just a second. It was a gold-colored tie bar with a small American flag, a fashion artifact of the twentieth century. Another second, and the tie bar was back in the pocket of his blue pants, which were torn and dirty.

The gesture meant something, but Smith had no idea what. Another Mai Mai, a man in his twenties with a mouthful of broken teeth, brandished his rifle in the American's direction, not to threaten him but as if to show him something encouraging. What?

Gideon wobbled and bled when rough hands pulled him to his feet. Someone slapped him in the face with the flat of his hand. Another man grabbed Béatrice. She resisted, but he was twice her size, with twice her formidable strength. Anger shortcircuited Smith as the man twisted her small breast until she cried, struggling to get away from him.

"Stop it," he yelled. "For God's sake, she's a child."

The man holding onto Béatrice looked at him with respectful curiosity but did not let her go. Another man tied Smith's hands behind his back with a braided rope each strand of which was a different color. It made him remember his mother reading him the Old Testament story of Jacob in his coat of many colors being betrayed by his brothers because he was his father's pet, marked by God and a family feud. It was probably a false memory.

He understood none of the conversation going on around him. Didn't need to. If there was ever a time in the Congo when he was more or less in control of what he did, and the decisions he made, that time was over. Abelino spoke into a radio. Whatever he said, there were no French words in it. In something like single file the Mai Mai and their prisoners went into the gloomy woods.

Smith lost track of time and then could not find it again. One of the boys— his voice had not yet cracked; he sounded like grade-school recess happy out on the swings—took his watch. Strapping it onto his own wrist he thanked Smith with sincerity as though it were a gift, a token of his new American friend's regard. It was a decent timepiece, a Shinola made in Detroit. Smith was partial to it because it had been a gift from Maybelline back when things were easy between them, one of the no-occasion presents she was good at giving, making something out of a nothing day. *Here you go*, she told him. *How many times you been told you don't know shit from Shinola? Now you do.*

Losing the watch to a baby thug bothered him, but what really got to him was having no sense of how long they walked through the forest. Hours, anyway. That much he could tell from the angle of the declining sun despite having quit Boy Scouts after the first campout. The Mai Mai kept their prisoners together in an enforced file, Gideon first, Béatrice after him, Smith last. Gideon got the worst of it. Any time one of the militia men thought about him, he fell out of line and clubbed the Minembwe reporter with a rifle, or spat in his face, or cursed him in a language that was new to Smith's ignorant ears.

Every blow to Gideon was an assault on Smith's sense of himself. Along with the sympathy he felt, and the outrage, came a quiver of relief. As long as they went on hitting Gideon they were not going after him.

Abelino led the line, moving more steadily than Smith would have thought possible with his short-leg gait. He enforced silence on his men not because they were in danger of being attacked but because a fighting force required discipline, and practice helped.

Béatrice went into silent mode, which brought home to Smith for the hundredth time how little he knew the kid. She was one more Congo language he neither spoke nor comprehended. He had no idea what she was thinking. She knew better than try to defend Gideon or protest the abuse since that would only bring down more of the same on her without doing Gideon any good. No kid her age should have to know that.

I'm sending you this because I'm dead, and sorrier than I can say not to see you again. I'm dead because they attacked Béatrice and I had no choice except try to stop them even though I knew how it was going to end. If I hadn't done my best, you would not have wanted to marry me.

Would he do that, would he get himself killed because it was the right thing to do? Or would he hang back, watching it happen, telling himself she would survive, she would get through it and live, so why get himself killed for a gesture that was doomed to fail? Would he hang back because he was afraid? He had no idea.

The line of Mai Mai and their prisoners kept moving. It was not exactly a march, but under Abelino they traveled with military order, like real soldiers. Despite their silence, the moving line made noise as they went, like an alligator thrashing its tail as it slithered across the ground.

There was the time, which Smith could not keep track of. It crashed quietly like water over a falls. He was a rock at the base of the pool, the pressure of falling water wearing him away.

There was his slow burn. It got a little hotter every time one of their captors hit or humiliated Gideon.

There was the dread that one of the Mai Mai would assault Béatrice.

There was also the pain between his toes. Both feet. More than an itch. Someone had told him about insects that burrowed into your feet, crippling you. You could lose your feet. Every step he took was a question: was it burrowing bugs causing his feet to burn? He limped.

They followed a track through the forest. On his own, Smith could not have identified it as a track. He lacked not just familiarity with the territory but also the visual intuition. Monkeys were constantly disappearing from trees overhead into trees more distant. They sounded more happy than alarmed. He wished it was all a movie. He didn't need to be the hero in it.

When a man with a cartridge belt slung across his shoulder appeared in the path in front of the file of Mai Mai, Smith thought for a moment that it was an ambush. These men must have enemies of their own. But the man had evidently been waiting for them. They stopped, they saluted. Everyone talked at once, and most of them laughed. Sergeant Abelino stepped off the trail and spoke alone to the man who had appeared out of the woods. After a few minutes, the man came over to inspect Smith.

He carried a rifle. There was a knife in a scabbard in his belt. From the belt there also hung a holster for his radio, which was silent, and one for his cell phone. He had a bullet head, a broad face, two weeks' growth of beard. When he spoke, his mouth contorted as if every word caused him its own little spasm of pain. It was obvious that the man outranked Abelino.

"American," he said.

Smith nodded. His nationality seemed to be a matter of considerable interest to his captors. Maybe they wanted to hold him for ransom. If that was the idea, he would not survive long. He was no longer Dauphin Petroleum's problem, and as soon as the Mai Mai discovered that the American government was not going to fork over any cash to get him back, he would be deadweight, slowing them down.

He felt Béatrice's eyes on him. Was this a test? If it was, he had no idea how to pass it.

The man with the cartridge belt told him in French, "The Colonel says your coming to us here in the forest may be a sign from God."

"I guess that means you are not the Colonel."

The idea was preposterous. The broad face wrinkled again, as if smiling hurt.

"I am Major Lokole. Colonel Sikatenda is the man you know as Foxtrot Five."

It took Smith a moment to realize "Foxtrot Five" was meant to be English. When the words registered on his stressed-out brain he said, "I don't know anybody by that name."

His response puzzled the major, but he told the American, "You have done the correct thing."

"What correct thing is that?"

"You must tell the Colonel, and only the Colonel, where the gold is hidden."

"I don't know anything about any gold," Smith told the man.

It came out strong; headstrong. Good.

The man blinked impassively. "Of course not."

Smith wanted to convince him of the truth. But Major Lokole had heard as much as he wanted to hear. The Mai Mai were already moving off the track into the forest.

They were good at moving through the underbrush without getting tangled in it. Smith was not. Every time he tripped in the shrubbery, it was good for a laugh, as though it were the first time. The laughter was hearty and strangely wholesome. Smith's presence anywhere had never before been considered a sign from God.

His first year on the rig, Dauphin Petroleum sent Smith to a personal security workshop. For a mandatory gig it was sweet: three days at a Pointe Noire hotel where the food was good and the wine kept up with it. The afternoon sessions broke early enough to get in some pool time while the sun was still cooperative. An Israeli firm with an English name ran the workshop in French. For the most part Smith did not take to the trainers of Secure Solutions. Ex-military, paramilitary, intelligence types, to a man and one woman they were swashbuckling fatalists. Every moment of every day they kept their eyes peeled for what they called the threat. The threat was out there. It was never not out there. The certainty of incoming was their article of faith, linking them in a league of watchers.

Smith had no interest in joining their club. But after the last session on the third afternoon, he had a drink at the poolside cabana, which featured a thatched roof and a bartender in a bikini who never quit smiling. There must have been days, it occurred to Smith, when that was a hard thing to keep doing. He wound up talking with one of the trainers, an English Jew named Eitan Jones. They got some predictable mileage out of their surnames, which sounded like disguises, and Smith asked Jones why he was working for Secure Solutions.

"It's a job."

"Doesn't strike me as the kind of work you do just to have a job," Smith said.

He was self-lubricating with gin, which brought out his sense of play, which was another name for his sense of the absurd.

Jones's face was scarred as from smallpox. He was a small man who looked as though he belonged to a different historical epoch; the music he heard was not on the current broadcast schedule. Instead of a security trainer he might be a minor government official in an old-fashioned republic, the kind of person for whom his job was a duty. He tapped his cigarette pack on the edge of the bar and pulled one out. The bartender was there in a flash to light it for him, but he shook his head and lit his own smoke.

"My family emigrated to Israel when I was a teenager," he told Smith. "We hadn't been there six months when I got myself in trouble. Went exploring in a neighborhood where I had no business being. Teenage boys are tossers by definition, are they not? Predictably, I was abducted. I don't believe they were an organized faction of any group, they were just a handful of young Palestinian men going about looking for excitement, hating the Jews and wishing they could fuck beautiful women. Capturing me was an unexpected bonus."

"Yet here you are."

"Yes, here I am. Because my people had been students of the Talmud for I don't know how many generations."

"I get it," Smith said. "Zen and the art of thinking upside down."

"I was your classic rebellious teen. Refused to go into the family business. To prove I was my own man I learned Arabic. But I could not escape my heritage entirely. We were scholars, weren't we? I read Arabic literature."

"And the Palestinians fell at your feet when you recited the Q'uran."

Jones shook his head, a reflex of irritation, and Smith wished his first instinct were not always to be a wiseass. He signaled to the bartender. He wanted to ask her how much it bothered her to have strange men ogling her breasts for the length of her shift, but there was no way into that conversation. He settled for requesting another gin and tonic, which she delivered without looking at him.

Jones told him, "The bloke who led the group was a student of literature. We talked about Averroes."

"That's some sort of cheese, I'm guessing."

Jones grinned through cigarette smoke. "Averroes was an Arab writer. A philosopher and theorist of the law. The young Palestinian man who captured me could not get past the idea that a Jew had something useful to say about Averroes."

"You were lucky."

"That's one way of putting it. When the Palestinians let me go, our government interviewed me for two weeks. Worse than being taken prisoner by testosterone-fueled tossers, really. They made a case study from what happened to me. It's classified, I've never seen it. But I'm told the study has a nickname. The Averroes File."

"So your advice is, before you get yourself kidnapped, read an Arab philosopher."

"My advice is look for the human connection. It's there. There's no guarantee, of course, that it will do you any good. How many politically active Palestinians ever heard of Averroes? How many would have the courage to release a captive Jew in the face of overwhelming social pressure? But something will be there. You'll have some time on your hands. Look for it."

At the camp of the Army of the Revival of the Word of God, Smith was looking for it. If there was anything promising to be found, it would be in the vicinity of Crispin Sikatenda, who remembered the American because—as he had told Smith at the club back in Goma—he stood out.

The sergeant, directed by the major, had delivered the prisoners to Sikatenda in a space of beaten-down grass in front of what appeared to be their headquarters, alongside which a mud-splashed Land Cruiser was parked at a canting angle. It had reached the camp on a rutted single-lane dirt road and looked like a war horse at rest. The commander's ride.

The headquarters was the second-largest structure at the camp. At the opposite end of the clearing, the church was larger by design. On the cross that marked the church as a place of worship, a hand-carved four-foot black Jesus in a bloody loincloth hung at an angle meant to suggest resignation. In Smith's opinion the bitter expression on the statue's face had nothing to do with resignation. It was rage, pure and simple.

"Untie them," Sikatenda ordered Abelino, who pretended not to be surprised.

What was the point of depriving a person of his liberty if you weren't going to take advantage of his helplessness? Hiking through the forest with a bum leg had taken its toll. He looked haggard.

Sikatenda pointed at Smith, and two boys untied his hands and those of Gideon. Gideon rubbed his wrists in relief but knew better than to celebrate anything. Béatrice's hands had not been bound. She inched slowly as far from the men as she could get without drawing anybody's attention. It was not far enough. Anyway where would she run? She was street smart, not forest smart.

Crispin Sikatenda had promoted himself to the rank of colonel and gave every indication of excelling at the business of war, which had been his job since he was a teenager and the Democratic Republic of Congo exploded in conflict. His fatigues were of the design manufactured for jungle fighters, unlike those of the men under his command, who wore a combination of desert gear and civilian castoffs.

He ignored Gideon. Gideon the unlucky Munyamulenge was a sideshow, a classic case of being in the wrong place at the wrong time. And the girl? Despite the curiosity he had shown at the Mirage, the girl was insignificant. The American was the person of interest, and Sikatenda got in Smith's face with a mixture of courtesy and formal intimidation. He spoke in English as though trying to remember what the language sounded like when you pronounced the words out loud rather than just thinking them in the privacy of your mind.

"You told me, I seem to remember, that you were passing through the country. Clearly that was a lie. Hearing a lie from an American citizen disappoints me."

He was chewing on a clove. When he opened his mouth, Smith could see the wet black nail of the thing between his tongue and his teeth, and the smell wafted to him on the words. It made him homesick even though he had never chewed a clove in his Louisiana life. Fear was messing up the circuits of his motherboard.

Smith was not sure how to respond to what Sikatenda said. His usual instinct, which was to make a game of the situation and see what happened, might get all three of them killed. He told the man the simple truth.

"There is nothing that I would like more than to get out of the Congo. Tomorrow. Today."

Sikatenda looked skeptical. He had an actor's face, capable of displaying a range of emotions that left no doubt in the mind of anyone watching what he felt, or what he intended others to feel. Inside five minutes it was clear to Smith that the commander of the irregular army that had captured them was moody. One moment he was sunk in sullen reserve, burrowed so deep inside himself you'd have to blast your way in to have a word. The next moment he came charging out, engaged and engaging. When he was on, he had the kind of charisma that persuaded men to go into combat knowing in their secret heart of hearts that their magic was not going to turn their enemy's bullets to water.

"What is the English word I want?" he bellowed suddenly.

"Freedom," Smith could not help suggesting. "Letting people go wherever they want to go."

Sikatenda shook his head. His face showed ferocious frustration.

"Too many years are gone since I spoke English every day on the Kansas street. The word I want . . . When the foot of a person causes pain, and he walks oddly so as to spare himself."

"Limp," said Smith, playing it straight.

"Yes, that's it. You were limping when you came into our camp."

"I think there are insects in my feet."

What happened next was both humiliation and release. The Colonel spoke to the major, who spoke to Abelino. Abelino issued orders. A chair was brought, and Smith obliged to sit in it. His shoes and filthy socks were removed, his feet placed in a basin of water. Then two men with knives approached.

Smith watched the men's mouths for a smile. There was none. He studied the knives, which had ridiculously long blades. Someone handed him a bottle of White Horse Whiskey and indicated he should drink. He uncapped the bottle and drank, ashamed of his shaking hand.

The conversation going on around him was commentary. Everybody had an opinion about one or another aspect of Smith's strange moment: his pale dirty feet, the sharpness of the knives, the usefulness of whiskey in blunting foot pain. Nobody was willing to listen to the man standing next to him. It was twenty-five monologues happening at the same time. He was pretty sure he knew what the men with knives were intending to do, but there was a moment, a silver flash of inaccurate insight, when it felt like the opening gambit to human sacrifice. An American prisoner of war was being offered up in the name of a concept nobody had bothered to explain to him.

Squatting at his feet, the two men dug out the deeply burrowed bugs with a deft touch that was hard to credit, given the length of the blades. It hurt like hell. The whiskey did not help, but Smith did his best not to flinch since everybody in the army was watching. When it was over, he stood on his bleeding feet and the Mai Mai army cheered. Smith, reverting to his normal self, put his hands together, raised his arms and offered the crowd a victory wave.

Colonel Sikatenda lifted a hand for silence and got it. If he was bipolar, he had barreled along the axis of definition to a happy extreme. With enthusiasm he gave an order, and two boys rushed to bring Smith a rag to wipe the blood from his feet. Wobbling, he cleaned his feet, conscious of being observed. This was how babies felt.

Sikatenda asked him in French, "Do you speak Bembe?"

"I don't know what Bembe is."

"We are the Bembe people, and Bembe is our mother tongue. Do you speak Swahili?"

"I used to."

"Then we must speak French. In a democracy, the people have the right to understand what their leaders discuss, do they not?"

"They do."

"Good. Smith? Yes, Smith. I once knew a man with that name. This was in Kansas. He was what your people call an African American. His ears were larger than the ears of a normal person. And yet, do you know? He was quite hard of hearing."

That got a laugh.

"Are you a Christian, Monsieur Smith?"

There were few questions Smith wanted less to answer than the one about his religious belief, such as it was, such as it wasn't. He could not think of a single question he wanted less to answer in front of a crowd of strangers.

"What's the right answer?"

"The right answer is the truth. Never mind, my friend. I do not wish to put you on the spot. Very soon we will have a complete and candid conversation, just the two of us. Private, like two diplomats in the privacy of their embassy. I am certain you know the subject of our talk."

"I don't know anything about gold, if that's what you're talking about."

"Allow me to offer you a hint. In the conversation to which I refer, you will be obliged to render a truthful answer. There is no alternative. But before we reach the crossroads of decision, you must feel free to ask us whatever you care to ask."

"Okay," said Smith. "Who are you?"

The colonel nodded. Hovering at the happy end of the bipolar axis, he had full access to the positive virtues: patience, tolerance, generosity. He was able and willing to call on all of them.

"We are fighters," he said with hard pride.

He was giving a truthful answer, like the one he would demand of Smith in their private conversation to come. Pride was the wellspring of his authority.

"We are independent men," he said. "Men of reason and faith. Men who understand what a sacred commitment is. We fight to recover the land that was stolen from us by the people of that man over there."

He pointed at Gideon. That was enough to bring down the butt of another rifle on the reporter's head. This time, Smith saw blood spurt in the air. Going down, Gideon lay still in the grass. Béatrice moved an inch further away. Colonel Sikatenda did not appear to notice what had just happened to the Munyamulenge.

"We will regain our land," he told Smith, making a motivational speech out of it. "God willing, there will be justice in Kivu, and we shall live under the reign not of men but of laws."

"Amen," Smith said.

The colonel nodded. "Others, the Bembe who have gone before us, along with other dispossessed peoples, worked to achieve this goal. For their pains, they paid with their life. Why was that, you will ask."

"All right," said Smith. "Why was it?"

"Because they chose the wrong path and persisted in following it to the ruination of their cause, not less to their death. Now what, you will also ask, was this wrong path?"

He was not talking to Smith, he was reminding the men of his small army why they were in the forest.

Smith had no objection to playing a bit part in the colonel's living history play. It might help him understand what was going on.

"Tell me, please, what the wrong path was."

In his high-energy mode, Sikatenda had an artillery voice. It boomed, launching words that crashed on the ears of his listeners.

"Ever since Mulele, ever since Lumumba, back into the nineteen sixties and even before, we Bembe listened to those who only sought to lead us astray."

The lesson morphed into a political sermon. The men who heard it swayed. They nodded. They affirmed in Bembe and Swahili and a word or two of French that they knew the story, they knew the history of their history and it was true, every last word of it was true.

Smith being Smith, he got into it. "Who was it that led you astray?"

"The Russians," the colonel thundered. "The Cubans. The Chinese. In a word, the enemies of the West. The enemies, it will be obvious to you, of the United States of America. Our fathers, our grandfathers, were simple men. They were gullible. They believed the lies."

Unused to playing the straight man but finding it useful, Smith said, "I would like to know what those lies were."

Sikatenda's scorn was scalding. "Inventions of the Devil, that's what they were. The atheists tried to get us to deny our Creator. No wonder they failed. Through the grace of God, I saw the light in Kansas."

"What were you doing in Kansas?"

"The army of the USA selected me. Why? Because I showed promise. As a young officer in the armed forces of my nation I was lifted up. I was flown across the Atlantic Ocean. I saw New York. I saw Washington. I was trained. I learned important military skills. I was christened with a new name, an army name. I am Foxtrot Five. And I learned to think. I saw with my own eyes the stupendous bounty with which God has blessed the American people. It can be no coincidence."

"What can be no coincidence?"

"The people who chose the path that leads to God have been showered with such blessings, such wealth. In Kansas, even the poor man drives an automobile. He wears clothes no man would be ashamed to put on. How, then, can he be considered poor? Was it not obvious, after Kansas, that we Bembe must also elect to follow the correct path to redemption? Only then will God choose to reward us with the good things we seek, the things we are owed."

There was a tactical pause, giving his men the time they needed to absorb again the lesson that Sikatenda had been teaching them since they went into the forest and became an army.

"What do you notice about us?" the colonel asked Smith.

It was a minefield of a question. For once, Smith knew better than to step onto it. He did not say, I *notice the Jesus on your cross is seriously pissed off.* He did not say, *None of the men who beat up Gideon seems bothered by what he did to an innocent man.* He did not say, *I have a sick feeling that the girl I am traveling with will stir up the wrong kind of sex in your men.*

He shook his head, and Sikatenda told him, "What you do not see, perhaps, is that the rifles we carry are of American manufacture. What do you know about guns, Monsieur Smith?"

"Not a whole lot."

"It doesn't matter. Look around. Observe them with care. The weapons in the hands of my men are AR-15s, they are M-16s. Believe me that obtaining these weapons was not easy. We could lay our hands on all the Kalashnikovs in the world with little difficulty. It was only a question of price. But at what profit would we take on our enemies with Russian guns? A contradiction such as that we could not abide."

Smith understood, now, what the soldier had been trying to tell him back on the road to Minembwe, showing him his rifle as though sharing a secret.

"If you let the others go," Smith said to Sikatenda, "it will be easier for me to think."

He could trust Gideon to make sure Béatrice made the last leg of her journey, regardless of what she found when she got there.

The idea of ransoming an American suddenly seemed improbable, where they stood in the forest. What would they do, mail a letter to the American embassy in Kinshasa and wait for the mailman to deliver a check? If ransom was not a realistic option, the question was simple: was he worth killing?

Gideon sat up. A Mai Mai clubbed him down again. Béatrice stood stiller than Smith had ever seen her.

Sikatenda's mood was swinging in the wrong direction. He snapped an order. An emaciated-looking man in flip-flops and a Bulls T-shirt with 23 on it ran to the Land Cruiser. From the back of the vehicle the man carried back a rectangular black box, maybe a foot long. He handed the box to Sikatenda with a deference intended to deflect attention. He knew what his commanding officer was like when he needed a target and no enemy presented himself.

Colonel Crispin Sikatenda, who had created an army that would renew the word of God in the lives of the dispossessed Bembe, opened the box. He lifted out a clock. The clock was wood, with Eiffel Tower legs. He placed the empty box on the ground. Then he inserted a double A battery in the back of the clock and held it up so that everyone in the clearing could see it. Holding the clock high, he moved the minute hand around the face with his thumb. When the hand hit twelve, a door opened on the front of the clock, beneath the face.

As the door opened, the clock played "Yankee Doodle Dandy" and Uncle Sam came out grinning on a spring. He was made of plastic and had a pointy white beard. His suit had red stripes and blue stripes and white ones. The Mai Mai laughed hard and long. For Smith, it was impossible to interpret their laughter. Sikatenda laughed, too. When the tune was finished, Uncle Sam went back inside the clock, closing the door after him. People kept laughing, Béatrice among them although not Gideon. For Gideon, nothing was funny.

After a few minutes, thunder rolled in the throat of the darkening sky, and Colonel Sikatenda coldly told Smith, "You had better put your shoes back on."

That evening the rain brought cooler air, or cooler air brought the rain. It made a confidential sound falling on the dense thatch of the church roof, which did not leak. The worshipers were dry and sheltered. They were free in their isolation. They were remote, or everything was remote from them. Captivity, or the Congo, was forcing Smith to rethink his perspective.

His captors had placed him on a bench at the front of the church, contriving to make him understand that it was a place of honor. Until otherwise notified he was a person of privilege. In front of him, the chancel was a space of bare ground across which the colonel paced as he preached, moving in a way no Louisiana Catholic priest ever moved in front of his parishioners. He was not a shepherd leading his flock, he was a lion with ideas.

Smith tried to hide the shiver that went through him. It was the cool wet air, that was what caused it, or else it was the pacing lion. It was the certainty that he could not make things come out right.

Foxtrot Five had changed clothes. There was no rule in the Army of the Renoveau du Verbe de Dieu against preaching in fatigues. But he liked to imagine, and project to his men, a time when the war was won, the Bembe were secure on their own land, and excombatants quit lugging around assault rifles because they were heavy, they were a nuisance. Civilian clothes helped them all to picture peace. Crispin wore dark pants, creased and pressed. A white shirt open at the collar, long sleeves buttoned at the wrist. Black shoes with pointed toes as scrupulously shined as his boots. An index finger marked the page in the Bible he clasped in case he was moved to recite a passage.

In the afternoon he had given orders to separate the American from Béatrice and Gideon. As Banyamulenge, they were automatic enemies. They no longer represented a threat to the Bembe, but by virtue of being who they were, they had earned the punishment that would surely be brought down on them.

Smith was different. Traveling with Banyamulenge made him suspicious. There was no logical explanation for such a thing. On top of that he was strangely reluctant to be honest about Eckstein's gold, even with the people who had more of a legal right to claim it than anyone in the country. That deepened the Mai Mai's suspicion of him. But, and this was the main point, he was an American. And Crispin, the commander in whom they put their trust, had discovered America.

As best as Smith could piece together the story, the U.S. Army had somehow evaluated a young Congolese army officer named Crispin Sikatenda as a future leader and decided he was worth cultivating. They sent him to a training course at Fort Leavenworth. The course included a mix of strategy, tactics, and indoctrination in democratic values. For Smith, Leavenworth meant bread-and-water prisoners, hardcases put away for good for the good of society. But for Crispin the place, and the state of Kansas surrounding it, had been a revelation. He experienced what Jasmine would call culture shock. From the Congo's endless lack, endless violence, endless upheaval, he plunged into America's lake of perpetual plenty. When he came up for air he found that the experience had indeed changed him. Presumably that was what the U.S. Army wanted all along. It did not, however, change him in the way the American government had in mind.

Coming home, he deserted from the Congolese army. In the multiple confusions of permanent war, leaving was easier than it ought to be. In Crispin's own telling, seeing America made him realize just how messed up the country of his birth was, how far the Bembe were from having a life worthy of the name, how unlikely the government in Kinshasa was to do anything except what they had always done: intimidate, exploit, rob; they took a bad situation, an intolerable situation, and made it worse. If there was a solution—and, as a Christian, Sikatenda believed there must be a happy ending for those whom God favored—if there was a way out of the cycle of loss and depredation, it began with him.

He learned to pray and mean it, to listen for the unspoken response in the sacred silence. Catch it and reflect and do his best to understand the message, which was not vouchsafed to him in words. At first he prayed alone, at home, in his truck, on the street in Bukavu. Later, curiosity drove him into churches, where the congregants' resignation to their fate, however ecstatically expressed, put him off. He hated their acceptance of things as they were, their belief that bad could only lead to worse.

On the airplane, flying home from Kansas, Crispin had written out a plan in a notebook he bought at a Walmart. Step one of his plan was recruiting, and he found he liked it, which helped make him good at it. The men he enlisted to their own cause had nothing to their name. Empty pockets. Hopelessness was where they woke in the morning, what they saw when they got out of bed, the bulletin on the radio, the disappearing lizard on hot stones.

They did however have ears, and their ears were pricked to catch Crispin's message. Justice belonged to those who found favor with God. The secret was finding the spot on which the light shone. You had to stand in the light, soak in it, let it cleanse you. Only then could you begin to think about the land that had been taken from you. Stay in the light, live in it, and God would allow you to reclaim your heritage. They went into the woods not to hide from the light but to begin their campaign of double redemption. Save their souls and recover the earth. The plan made perfect sense to Crispin's men.

It made sense to a woman in Bukavu, too. Lilou ran a small hotel. The Cygne Noir had belonged to Belgians. They left the Congo after independence bitterly certain they would be invited back once the country went to hell. The country went to hell. They were not invited back.

The hotel's infrastructure had been neglected for years. Lilou did the best she could. She thought she might be able to restore the place to respectable service if things settled down. She had lost three sisters, and the sisters' children, in a single incident in the war.

She had a high tolerance for Crispin. His unpredictable comings and goings, his religious fervor, his responsibilities running an irregular army. She and he both were well enough worn to recognize how their own jagged angles meshed with the other's depressions. Meshed, they made a shape worth protecting.

On the bench in his place of honor Smith let the sound of the colonel's sermon wash over him. Not words. There were times when he did his best to pick out individual words in what he heard, which was always hitting him in a flood. There were times when he tried to understand foreign. Not now.

He was fried.

His feet throbbed. The men who operated on them might have missed a couple bugs, or else the flesh was tender from the knives' incisions. Same difference, Maybelline would point out. He wished he could take back his email proposal. That had been a mistake. He should have waited until he was home, gone down on bended knee the way they did it in chick flicks. Of course if he didn't make it home, now she knew he loved her.

His go bag was gone.

There was something else sawing at him, making an indentation. Premature survivor's guilt. It was clear that the gospel that Foxtrot Five preached made an exception to the rule of mercy. For the Banyamulenge there would be none. Eyes for weeping eyes, teeth for bloody broken teeth. Being separated from Béatrice, Smith was letting her down again. Under the circumstances, letting down was betrayal.

The service was long. Sometimes, without warning, the men sang. When they sang, they channeled angels. This was what Heaven sounded like, a melodious place to spend eternity. Sometimes two men toward the front of the nave in a space of their own played drums, bouncing off each other's sounds, the heels of their hands striking the head with the authority of joy. Once in a while a man in the congregation was moved to speak, and the colonel gave him the floor. The man was allowed as much time as he required and no more. Then the colonel took up his sermon again.

Smith lost it. Not so as anybody would know. It was an interior shift, a letting down and letting go. He was not sure what was happening, at first. But it came to him. He was giving up. He was quitting. For an amateur, a man who knew nothing about the Congo, a man whose skills were limited to fixing broken machines, he had maybe done okay. He bulled his way forward from one unknown place to the next. Kinshasa, Goma, Bukavu, Uvira. At every stop he had stubbornly looked around for go. And for a while it worked. He found a way past the obstacles that kept jumping up in front of them. Forget why. He would never figure that one out.

It came down to this: he drove forward with Béatrice until they fell in a hole too deep to climb out of. There was nothing he could do for her now. Why pretend? Back in Goma, the peace musician Paul Kanea had told him. *You cannot save the girl, it's not your place to try*. And Paul was right, he was totally right. Smith should have left her where she found him, back in Kinshasa. Soeur Placide said there was a hellhound on the girl's trail. It would catch up to her, sure. But a hound trailing you was better than a lion that had you in its mouth.

He sat straight on the bench, slumping internally. Sikatenda had not yet interrogated him about the gold, but that was coming. When it happened, and Foxtrot Five learned the hard way or the easy way that Smith really did have no frigging clue about it, that would be the beginning of the end. Screw it. Nothing Smith could do, nothing he could fail to do, changed the end game.

Words. The air in the church in the forest was full of them. They drowned out the sounds of the night. The trick was converting the words to pure sound, then letting the sound lull you to sleep.

No hope. The lizard that was supposed to drop it at your feet was always disappearing. You saw it, you thought you saw it, but it wasn't there.

One night, a long time ago, Baylee Smith shook his kids awake. Get up, he told them, get your shoes on. In the front yard when they went outside the engine of their father's Ford was running and their mother was sitting in the front seat, a sweater around her shoulders. She smelled like all the flowers of North America and was in a cheerful mood. Lu Ann asked where they were going. She got no answer, didn't need one, it was only in his sister's nature to ask.

They drove in the dark down old roads. The trees they went past were bearded with Spanish moss like old men roused from their beds by the car lights.

Eventually Baylee parked the car in high brush alongside the edge of the road, and they made their way through dew-damped woods to a boat Smith had never seen before, just the size for a family of four. Ava Marie got in first and helped Lu Ann. Smith went next, feeling his father as a reassuring presence just behind him.

Out on the water they floated, dropped fish lines, ate sugar cookies from a brown paper poke. Baylee and Ava Marie took turns pulling at a bottle of liquor with great poise as though they had practiced this, all of it, until they mastered it and pushed off from swampy ground to a place their forefathers, their foremothers had dreamed about, told stories about until the day they died.

Everybody had the right to one perfect memory. If you didn't have one you went crazy and died, you melted into a pool of antimatter and unbecame. Poof, you were static on somebody else's radio.

Did they catch any fish? Likely, or not likely at all. What stayed in Smith's mind was the quiet hilarity of it all, the frictionless ease, the unworded pleasure. They were sharing a secret that would last. It would feed them, and it would last. Once his mother pointed and said *Look!* Overhead, clouds split apart like a piece of fabric being ripped by God's strong hands, and there was the moon, full or just about full, spilling light down on the water and the boat and the people in the boat out of sheer generosity. *I'll be danged,* Baylee said, and whistled his appreciation.

The memory was torn from Smith by Foxtrot Five, who was urging him to stand and deliver. A little blood on the extremities never hurt anybody, American man, everybody had sore feet at one time or another. Your turn now. Come to the chancel, say something to the men of my army. Explain yourself.

What choice did Smith have? The French came out of his mouth like a borrowed hammer, handy for the job at hand but not ideal.

"I didn't want to be here. I don't want to be here. You brought me here against my will. That's against the rules. There have to be rules, and people ought to play by them. Gideon is my friend, and you beat the living shit out of him. That's not my fault, it's your fault."

There were angry murmurs. Sikatenda silenced them with a raised hand. Maybe this too was part of his plan. In a democracy you had to hear stuff you didn't like, even stuff you hated. You had to learn how to put up with it.

"I don't know the first thing about the Bembe people. Until you kidnapped me I didn't even know there were any Bembe people. That tells you something about me, doesn't it? Not a good thing. I don't speak Swahili, either. Never did, although I like to think I have an open mind.'

"There's one other thing I want you to know. I would like to be allowed to leave this place and go home. Louisiana is my home state. It has its good points and its bad points. If you've never been there, don't judge it."

He stopped. He wondered where he was going. He wondered if he had a fever. He thought he might but was self-conscious, standing in front of a churchful of Mai Mai fighters, and could not bring himself to feel his cheek with the back of his hand. That was how you checked a person's temperature in Flannery Parish, he had seen it done by experts. These Mai Mai could not take that away from him, let them try.

He was telling them his secrets. He was giving himself away. Fuck it. Fuck it. And fuck it a third time. It wasn't going to make any difference in how things went.

"The reason I want to go home," he told them, "is I need to get married. I didn't used to know that. Now I do. Let me go, and you're all invited to the wedding. Her name is Maybelline Beaudry, maybe you've heard of her? The big news is, Hank Williams is providing the music. We've been in touch.

I have his word he'll be there. Hank never breaks a promise he can't keep."

Smith was confusing his listeners. Good. Talk long enough and maybe they caught up to him where he stood, on the corner of Confusion and Dismay, hands in his pockets and whistling off key. Baylee once taught him how to whistle off key. This was after he taught him how to fall off a bicycle. Whistling off key was a useful skill to have if you planned on walking backwards past a graveyard. Good old Baylee Smith, he deserved a second look. Like the doctors said, you may want to get a second opinion. They only said that, of course, when the news was bad.

"You have said enough," Foxtrot Five told him, the soft light of a kerosene lantern glinting off his glasses. He looked, for a moment, like a wooden saint, stern and sinless. The picture did not last.

Only a fool would contradict a saint. Smith was a fool.

"I haven't gotten to the good part yet."

"Then get there."

"The girl you stole," Smith told the Mai Mai. "Her name is Béatrice. Bet you never thought to ask, did you? She's a queen. She doesn't have a country to rule, but she's a queen all right. Go back in history and you won't find a queen of such high quality as Béatrice Mutebusi. I say that even though the name alone is enough to set you against her. Nobody can see it, everybody is blind. Béatrice has the strength of ten thousand elephants. I don't mean that crummy Asian model, I'm talking about the real thing. If the lion is the king of beasts, the African elephant has got to be the emperor. A queen needs that kind of strength. But it doesn't make any difference to you, does it? You could give a shit."

If it wasn't the words, which possibly made sense only to the person who spoke them, it was the attitude. There was enough of that to swallow with a tablespoon and get some serious indigestion. The Mai Mai were riled now, men and boys both, and the colonel decided it was time to put an end to Smith's tirade. On the way back to the bench, he stumbled on his bad feet.

He was becoming retroactively clairvoyant, seeing things he had not been around to see. Eitan Jones, the Secure Solutions trainer, had been right. *You'll have some time on your hands.* Jones had used the time he was held by the Palestinians to work up talking points for a conversation about a dead philosopher. Smith, captive under different conditions and lacking the necessary background reading, saw backwards.

A classroom at Fort Leavenworth. A spring morning in Kansas. A cheerful breeze across the corn fields and sun streaming through the classroom windows. Before class begins, men in uniforms from countries across Africa and South America, along with some strategically significant island nations, stand around drinking coffee from Styrofoam cups. In the course of the day, the thought *Walmart* will occur to all of them. They have packed light, coming to this training course, planning to go home heavy. Consumer goods are cheap in America. On the way out they will stuff a second suitcase with presents for wives and children, along with secreted gifts for secret lovers.

Among the crowd of students stands the lecturer, also in uniform. He is a no-nonsense redheaded army captain from, say, Louisiana. He likes his job and knows how to talk to military men from anywhere, everywhere. It's a brotherhood, he is always telling his wife. We speak the same language.

"Gentlemen," he announces to the assembled officers. "Sharpen your pencils, this morning we are going to sharpen your minds."

The subject of the lecture is psychological warfare. Get inside your enemy's head and mess with it, part one. In an orderly bustle the students take their seats. Seated with them, Crispin Sikatenda, also a captain, has a perfectly sharp pencil, although he is self-conscious about his uniform. It looks second-rate compared to those of some of his classmates. His discomfort is doubled any time he has to introduce himself. From the Congo, yes, where war never stops breaking out. Yes, it's the country where the Ebola River, of deadly disease fame, runs. Yes, they had endured a dictator in a leopard-skin hat who pillaged the country for thirty years. No, his name was not Idi Amin. Why do we call it the Democratic Republic of Congo? That's a tough one.

It was the red-haired course instructor who gave Sikatenda his nickname. Foxtrot Five seemed to fit the man. Something about the Congolese captain marked him out. He was going to do something big. And he aced the course, grasping the material without effort and testing the concepts with shrewd questions. What the American did not see was the quiet controlled fury with which Sikatenda was working out how to put his Leavenworth lessons into practice. Halfway through the curriculum he was organizing the future.

Here, for example. Now, for example. The tactics the American army taught him turned out to be useful in the camp of the Army of the Revival of the Word of God. How else explain the location of his American prisoner?

Apart from the church and the headquarters building, where Sikatenda worked and ate and slept, there were about a dozen huts in the camp, which looked a lot like the African villages you saw on documentary television, the ones with a respectful voice-over gassing on about hallowed ancient traditions. The huts were basic: thatch and mud walls, with a hole for the door. In some of the houses a piece of fabric hung covering the doorway, whether for privacy or to keep the dust down Smith did not know. Sikatenda had ordered him placed in the hut farthest from headquarters, on the edge of the forest.

Isolation worked in the colonel's favor. So did separating Smith from Béatrice. Sikatenda had figured out that the American cared about the wellbeing of the Munyamulenge girl.

Smith's prison hut was not just far from the center, it was the smallest building in camp and in rotten shape; an afterthought on the village fringe. No cloth covered the doorway, and a hole in the thatch of the roof let rain through. The rain made a mud puddle on the floor that would not evaporate until the dry season came again. The skin of water in the puddle drew mosquitoes that might or might not be of the variety whose bite killed a person in three days. The mud walls were crumbling. If Smith stayed there long enough he would watch them fall in the human equivalent of time-lapse photography.

That was not very likely. He had a hunch that whatever happened, it would come at them fast.

The only furniture was a low table, the kind of thing you put a lamp on next to the couch and never thought about again. On the table a small American flag rose out of a black plastic base. Smith touched it. The stars and stripes were gritty.

They had not tied Smith's hands again or otherwise restricted his physical movement. That too must be part of Foxtrot Five's training. Keep your prisoner feeling free and vulnerable, and the odds of securing his cooperation go up. But a boy soldier with a rifle was posted on guard ten feet from the hut. As if Smith might make a break for it. What would he do in the forest? Look for moss on the north side of the trees, trap pythons for protein, drink water deadly with microscopic dinosaurs in it? In addition to the rifle, which Smith decided was an AR-15, the boy had a bayonet. It lacked a handle, so he had wrapped black tape around a flat stick, fixing the blade to it. If he used the knife in a fight he was as likely to cut himself as do any damage to his enemy. Toussaint, they called him.

One other thing the hut did not have was a pissoir. The Mai Mai had dug a latrine in the woods behind the camp. Even from the distance at which Smith had caught sight of it, it stank. The morning after Sikatenda preached to the men and

Smith harangued them, he had to use the latrine. Earlier, not long after daybreak, a boy had brought Smith something in a bowl. He ate it. It was tasteless and mushy. Now, the urge to excrete was strong, but he could not make himself understood.

Rain was falling slowly and steadily. The puddle in the hut was not getting smaller.

Discipline. The colonel preached it, Toussaint was practicing it. He sat in the mud under a plastic poncho holding the rifle across his lap. He had forlorn eyes and the hangdog look of an unemployed forty-year-old. He did not speak a word of French.

When Smith went to the door of the hut, the boy made a gesture of sticking a cigarette in his mouth, lighting up, inhaling, enjoying it. Oscar worthy. The category was best supporting child fighter in a Mai Mai abduction.

"You won't live long enough to die of lung cancer," Smith told him.

The boy shook his head.

Smith raised his voice. He growled. "I need to piss, goddamn it."

The boy shook his head again. Since he didn't understand a word of what Smith told him, saying no was the safest course of action. The American's animation was disturbing, and after thinking it over for a moment he stood up and loped in the morning rain toward the other huts.

In two minutes he was back with another boy. It was the kid with the cartridge necklace, although he did not have it on now. Probably he wore it only when they went into action. He did however carry the American flag tiebar in his pocket, and he pulled it out again in what Smith took to be a gesture of goodwill.

"You speak French?"

The tiebar boy did not speak any, either. Smith pantomimed for both of them, pretending to unzip his pants and take a leak. They laughed. They got it. They led him to the latrine.

Up close, the odor was obscene. It was the first time Smith ever relieved himself with two boys watching, one of them armed. They were curious. Did they think Americans shat diamonds?

You got used to what you had to. His guards marched him back in the rain to the low-rent hut Foxtrot Five had assigned him.

Boredom made him sleepy. Strange that a person could sleep, knowing what Smith knew, expecting disaster even if he didn't know the form it was going to take. There was no pallet, no sheet, and without his go bag there was nothing he could rig a makeshift bed with. He lay on the dirt floor as far as he could get from the puddle. He dozed and then slept hard until Abelino poked him awake with the muzzle of his rifle.

"Get up."

Smith got to his feet, disoriented. It took a minute to remember where he was and why he hated Abelino. Maybelline, he thought, but that was as far as he got. It was going to be important not to let the antipathy he felt for the sergeant get out of control. There were only so many boneheaded mistakes he could make. Better to ration them, save them for when they really counted.

"The colonel wants to see you."

"Fine. Tell him to drop by whenever he feels like it."

Abelino glared, but it was only a dumb comment, not serious enough to count against Smith's stock of mistakes.

"So," he said, aiming for a conversational tone of voice. "Tell me about yourself, Abelino. Are you married? Any kids? You play football? Like taking long walks on the beach? What's your wife's name?"

Abelino told him, "You're not a real American."

"What do you know about Americans?"

The Mai Mai jabbed at his belly with the rifle muzzle, probing as if to locate the most vital of Smith's vital organs.

"There's a word in English for people like you," Smith told him. "You want to learn it?"

"*Non.*"

"Asshole. Can you say it?"

The muzzle dug harder into Smith's belly. Smith decided he would not translate the insult. Instead he asked Abelino, "What's a real American?"

"Look in the mirror."

"I don't have one."

"Everything you do not see when you look in a mirror, that is an American. Come."

He withdrew the rifle from Smith's person. He led him to Sikatenda's headquarters. Inside, out of the rain, there was a lesson going on. Major Lokole was lecturing half a dozen barefoot boys who sat in a semicircle on the floor. When the American came into the room, the lesson stopped. The boys looked at him wondering if he should be cheered or beaten.

Sikatenda welcomed Smith as though he were a guest and a pleasant surprise. Abelino wanted to stay, but the colonel told him in Swahili to get lost. The sergeant gave Smith a hostile look as he left. It was the American's fault.

"Good morning, Monsieur Smith," the colonel said. "You are experiencing the rain we Congolese put up with each year. My advice is to keep moving, stay active. Stand still and the green stuff begins to grow on you. You may be mistaken for a tree."

"Does that mean you don't plan on killing me?"

The colonel's surprise seemed genuine. "Kill you? Whey would we do that? It must be plain to you by now that we hold the nation you represent in high regard."

Smith hated it when people tagged him as an American, as though being born in Flannery Parish somehow made him responsible for bad things bigger than he was. Little Boy and Fat Man, napalm and Agent Orange, hooded prisoners at Abu Ghraib: they were all being laid at his feet.

"I don't represent anything."

"Never mind. We'll talk. But first we will listen to Major Lokole for a few moments more. He is imparting a history lesson. Do you mind?"

Smith shrugged.

"Understand," Sikatenda said, "that we will never prosper as a people, we will never come together as a nation, until our young ones are properly educated. They must know how to think. That was the most valuable gift your country gave me, the ability to think clearly. The key is to apply reason to the solution of problems, not allow oneself to be mastered by passion. The Creator endows us with an intellect, no? Well, then, He intends that we use it. Allow me to thank you for your country's investment in the future of mine."

"Sure, any time."

"These history lessons with our *kadogos* are a first step. Our means are modest, of course, but our intentions are impeccable. Sit, please."

He pointed to a chair. Smith sat. Jasmine had told him about the *kadogos*, boy soldiers in the Mai Mai militias. Some of the NGOs ran reclamation projects designed to give boys rescued from combat a semblance of peace and childhood. Mostly they were too late.

The major picked up where he had left off. Sikatenda, who knew the material by heart, gave the American a running summary in schoolteacher French.

A long time ago, as far back as the nineteenth century, tall strangers from a long way off came to the mountains of Itombwe. They were Tutsis, deceitful and overbearing, driven by their desire to establish an empire. Somehow—this part was not clear to Smith— they became the Banyamulenge. Béatrice's people. They conquered the legitimate inhabitants and stole their land. The *kadogos* listening to the major were the inheritors of a tradition of resistance. It was a noble tradition but it had failed, so far, to achieve its goals. There was something called the list of seven errors, which explained why they had gone wrong. Creating his army, Colonel Sikatenda added an eighth. The resistance had fallen short because the militias had turned away from God.

When the lesson was over, the major led a short prayer. The *kadogos* had choirboy voices and the faces to go with them. They belonged at Doctor Ace's non-orphanage in Uvira, making music and something better of their chances.

"Go," said the colonel at the conclusion of the prayer.

They saluted and went.

"Where is Béatrice?" Smith asked Sikatenda.

"First we will talk."

"I need to see her."

"Why?"

"To know she's okay."

"The child is well."

"I want to talk to her."

The military man in Foxtrot Five liked issuing orders and seeing them carried out. That was natural enough. Armies needed officers. But there was more to the man than the habit of command. He had been sitting in a camp chair of camouflage canvas. He stood and went to the doorway. He watched the rain for a while. When he was ready he told Major Lokole, "Take him away."

Away meant back to the hut, and it was Abelino who took him there. The sergeant did his best to provoke him on the short trip, but Smith ignored the man. He was no good at being a prisoner. He lacked Eitan Jones's patience, not to mention the smarts that went along with it. The moment was coming when he did something reckless.

In the hut he sat on the floor in a funk for ten minutes apologizing mentally to Maybelline. The apology began with an explanation, which instantly went off the rails. He was not much of an engineer, couldn't keep the train on the track. Then Béatrice was there, escorted by one of the *kadogos*, a boy her own age or thereabouts. Some first date.

"Smith," she said.

It might be the first time she spoke first. She was muddy, she was bedraggled. Her hair was growing out and needed cleaning, brushing, some attention. The scar on her leg stood up on her skin like the map of a new place. Could stress do that? But she was surprisingly calm.

"You're okay," he said.

"Gideon is bad."

"Bad how?"

"His head got big."

"You mean it's swollen."

"Yes. Because they hit him so hard, so many times. It makes him talk strange. He falls asleep and then wakes up and says crazy things."

"What about you? Are they bothering you?"

She shook her head hard. "They leave me alone. I made a decision, Smith."

"What is the decision?"

"I must not think about my grandmother now, I must think about Gideon. Only Gideon. If I do not think about him, he will be alone."

What was it? She had a generous spirit, sure. That was remarkable. She had seen little generosity herself and could be forgiven for not knowing how it worked. But there was more to it than that. To make sense of Béatrice, to get it right, you needed vocabulary. Finding the right word was not one of Smith's strong points. She seemed, at that moment, wise. Could a kid her age be wise? He had no idea. Brave. Yes, there was no doubt about that. She was brave to the point of fierce. And now he was seeing something else. Gideon was raving in his swollen head, his body aching from beatings inflicted by men who hated him on sight. His wife was not there to comfort and care for him. And in response, Béatrice was tender. It was the tenderness that blew Smith away.

"Be strong, Béatrice."

She nodded. Then the boy soldier poked his head into the hut and ordered her out. It was a rush, ordering around an enemy girl, and it took him no time at all to get the hang of it.

Sikatenda had threatened Smith with a tête-à-tête to grill him about Eckstein's gold, but when he summoned the American back to headquarters Major Lokole was there as witness, or note taker, or maybe to get a lesson in interrogation techniques as instilled by American army captains to promising foreign military officers.

It was the beginning of the rainy season, and Smith was tired of being soggy. The rain had stopped, the sky cleared. Then within an hour it clouded up again and more rain fell, harder this time. Smith resented the greed with which the forest drank it in. If the trees weren't so goddamn thirsty, there would be no need for all that downfall, and he would stay dry.

From the moment Smith came into the room, the major said little. Smith did his best, as he was being questioned, to figure out the working relationship between the two men. The more information he amassed during captivity, the better placed he was to act when the time came. That was the theory. But he got nowhere. Sikatenda and Lokole behaved almost formally with each other. That might mean something. Maybe Lokole was new on the job. Or they'd had a falling-out. Over what? Tactics, beer, the affections of a woman? How did that help Smith? Anyway, what seemed to him like formality might mean nothing at all.

Lokole made up in facial gestures what he lacked in conversation. His jaw waggled, his eyes squinched and unsquinched like traffic lights, his head shook vehemently back and forth and nodded up and down as he listened to Sikatenda's summary of the American detainee's story.

"Tell me if I have your story right," Foxtrot Five said to Smith. "Across the river in Brazzaville, you came into the possession of what you believed to be a treasure map. The map was supposed to lead you to a sackful of diamonds in Kinshasa. Congolese diamonds, not American diamonds. The same Belgian who told you about the diamonds gave you a letter of reference—in his name, not your own—from our minister of the interior. Is all of that correct?"

Smith nodded.

"While you were in Kinshasa, an orphan girl, a Munyamulenge, got your attention. She threw a stone at you, and you agreed to accompany her out east on a pilgrimage to find her grandmother. Still correct?"

The way Sikatenda laid it out, Smith's story was more than just fishy, it was preposterous.

"In my defense, she said she knew where the diamonds were."

"Despite false starts and disappointments," the colonel went on, "you refused to give up your noble pursuit."

"It wasn't noble, I was just trying to give the kid a hand."

Lokole shook his head. His shoulders shrugged. He had the air of a dog off its feed.

"You discover," said the colonel, "that the child is as persistent as you are. Finally you decide to look for the grandmother in Minembwe, a haven of the Banyamulenge. In Uvira, you obtain the services of a guide, a man who claims to be a journalist and to know the region. Perfect?"

"Perfect," Smith agreed.

"And all goes well until you meet a unit of our army out on patrol."

Smith had to force himself not to fixate on Lokole's face, which was all drama all the time. He told Sikatenda, "Everything you just said is true."

With no warning, the colonel was at his throat, squeezing with both thumbs and choking off his air supply. An interrogation technique, and it was effective. Smith forced himself not to resist, and just as quickly, the colonel let him go. In his disgust he shoved Smith hard, and the American fell. He got up. He stood there, hands hanging at his sides, fists balling and unballing. He had no good ideas.

The colonel spoke to Major Lokole as to a person he did not know well. "This man's story is *ridicule*. Let me suggest an alternative."

The major nodded. He made a good straight man to the colonel's hard man.

"In Tel Aviv, a certain Monsieur Eckstein arranges the delivery of a shipment of Congolese gold, taken from the earth with enormous difficulty and oceans of sweat by Congolese hands, Congolese backs, Congolese bodies. You and I have seen those bodies at work, have we not? We stand witness to the bruises, the blisters, the broken bones their labor induces. Eckstein has years of experience. But this time the unusual comes to pass. The gold goes mysteriously astray. He is assured by intermediaries that it has not left the Congo. He telephones his American agent, a man who goes by the dubious name of Smith. Smith contacts a Munyamulenge who knows precisely what happened to the gold. They set off to reclaim it for the Israeli."

Saying it would not protect Gideon. Smith said it anyway, for a record nobody was keeping.

"Gideon doesn't know any more about the gold you're looking for than I do."

But the colonel ignored him. He went to the table he used as a desk. He sat down. He became a stone. The most determined ray of light would not penetrate to the man's motionless core. At the same time, working at a smaller table the height of a grade-school desk, Lokole busied himself making a map, knees high in a short-legged chair. Painstakingly he taped together pages of what looked like printouts from Google maps.

Sikatenda was out of it, so Smith said to Lokole, "What if it's a joke?"

Lokole looked up from his map project. "What if what is a joke?"

"Eckstein's gold. What if somebody started a rumor, and everybody who heard it believed the rumor was true because they wanted it to be true?"

Skepticism displayed itself on the major's mobile face. The American's comment was a clumsy ploy to turn them aside. Now, just now, when they had caught a break and were getting close. The Army of the Revival of the Word of God were not the only ones hunting the gold. But he was not the kind of person who spoke his thoughts out loud. He kept them on the inside where the words did not have to sort themselves into sentences. He told Smith to shut up.

Smith disliked standing there while the two men sat, ignoring him. It made him feel like a kid in the principal's office waiting for his punishment to be pronounced. But he did not have much time to be uncomfortable. After a few minutes Sikatenda uncurled the ball of himself and spoke.

"You claim the Munyamulenge knows nothing about the gold."

"I do."

The colonel nodded thoughtfully. "Then you will defend him."

"Come again?"

"There must be a trial, and you will represent the accused as his lawyer. Are you familiar with the Congolese system of jurisprudence?"

"No."

"That's a pity. Your lack of acquaintance with our way of doing things puts your client at a disadvantage." He turned to the major. "Set it up."

Lokole left. No salute. The colonel stood, facing Smith. His warm spirits had returned. "Shall I make a prediction?"

I don't give a shit, Smith did not say. He shrugged.

"Very well, here it is: before the sun comes up tomorrow you will have told me where the gold is. Come."

"Where are we going?"

"Forgive the truism, but a good lawyer stands with his client through thick and thin."

They waited for the rain to stop and then tried to keep Gideon upright for his trial, but they had beaten the starch out of his body. Along with his strength went his hope of survival, and every time the *kadogos* hustled him to his feet he slumped and fell. They picked him up and hit him again as though more pain would convince him to stand.

Béatrice was there. Two boys were having a great time holding her back as she struggled to get to Gideon. Their hands on her body were close to her sex. The threat was constant, but she would not give up. Smith, standing next to the reporter for the *Minembwe Trumpet* as his court-appointed lawyer, chose not to shield Gideon when the boys beat him.

Army discipline, or Sikatenda's sense of decorum, required the Mai Mai to stand in soldierly rows in the clear space in front of headquarters. They splayed out in a half circle around the spot where Gideon kept falling. The *kadogos* were their own category and had their own line. Everyone was sober, and mostly quiet. A trial was serious business.

Sikatenda, dressed in crisp camo, paced a self-defined radius holding his Bible. One of the boys had cleaned the morning's mud from his boots. He opened the proceedings with a prayer that was not in the book.

"God in Heaven who made the earth and all its sinful creatures, help us discover justice. We have sought to cleanse our hearts of hate. Send the Holy Spirit to make us cleaner still, more worthy of Your love. Scour us of our sin. Send Your only begotten Son to teach us to ask the right questions, to hear the right answers. If it is Your will that we take possession of the Israeli's gold, guide our footsteps on the path that will lead us to it. Amen."

Amen, the Mai Mai echoed him. It went around the camp like a cheer. They meant it. The trial began.

It went fast. Too fast. As presiding judge, Sikatenda read the charges. There were a lot of them, but he needed no notes. Gideon was accused of hiding Eckstein's gold. He was accused, as a stand-in for his people, of stealing land that belonged rightfully to the Bembe, to the Fulero, to other tribes and peoples Smith had never heard of. He was accused of murders and massacres, thefts and explosions and deforestation.

Gideon was invited by the court to make a statement in his own defense. He had the right, Sikatenda explained, to respond to the charges he was facing. He should talk about his crimes, and the crimes of the Banyamulenge. He should explain the inexplicable. But Gideon was past speaking.

When Sikatenda signaled Smith to assert his defense, his mind was a wet field. Crows with shimmering wings were picking at bugs in the grass. Something scattered them. Might be a rifle shot but more likely it was Colonel Sikatenda's commanding voice. Whatever wit Smith had left, the birds took with them. He was on his naked jabbering own.

"The main thing to say is we don't know anything about gold," he said, not sure whether he was addressing the colonel or the whole army. "I can say it ten times if you want. Will that help?"

He paused, got no response, began again.

"Another thing you should know is that Gideon really is a reporter. He writes about peace. That's what got him in trouble in the first place. He has a son he has never seen. Did you know that? You didn't, of course not. How great would it be to let him go so he can finally kiss his child's eyes?"

Another pause. Nobody liked what he was saying, that was clear. But a trial was a trial, and Sikatenda allowed him to proceed with the defense.

"The other thing you should know about is the girl over there. Her name is Béatrice. She's an orphan, although she doesn't like to admit it. Let her go, she'll stand where she is and listen."

Amazingly, the *kadogos* let her go. Still more amazingly, she stood between them without moving.

"Béatrice has had a lot of hard luck, way more than anybody I ever met. But there is some chance she still has a grandmother. What I would really like is to find out if that's true."

Abelino jeered him, and the boys cheered. The colonel cut them off and signaled for Smith to keep talking. Major Lokole's face was a map of the old-fashioned kind, rough and approximate, nothing to do with Google's smooth digital precision.

Smith said, "As far as all the other stuff the colonel talked about goes, it's history. Meaning it cuts both ways, right? Everybody is guilty, which maybe ought to cancel out all the bad shit. What about a fresh start? Is that possible? As for me, I can't even pretend to understand what has gone down in Kivu."

The colonel nodded. What they were doing was a performance, and he had a good feel for the timing.

"Is that all you choose to say?" he asked Smith.

"I could say more, but it would be the same thing with different words."

Sikatenda nodded and announced to the court, "The defense rests."

He went back to the crimes of the Banyamulenge. It was not fair that he got a second shot at making his case, but fairness did not really enter into what was happening at the Mai Mai camp. It was another history lesson, and the tall cattle herders with their devious ways and their dream of empire took the fall.

Hearing the charges run through a second time through was too much for Toussaint, the boy who had been guarding the American's hut. He broke ranks and rushed toward Gideon, who had been hauled to his feet yet again. The kid drove his bayonet blade on a stick into Gideon's chest, and the Manyamulenge reporter went down for good.

Just like that.

Toussaint looked around for approval. He did not get it. Sikatenda barked at Abelino, and the sergeant ran at the boy with a club. Clubbed hard, the boy screamed as he hit the mud.

His scream was nothing compared to the sound that came out of Béatrice. It scraped the ear of God and made Smith shiver. It told everything she knew. In the instant of its terrible arc, it unmanned him.

Night. Rain like silk, if silk could talk. The smell of wood smoke hung in the wet black air an hour after rain put out the cookfires. Alongside the dead fires, sticks of peeled cassava were stacked like the limbs of undersized enemies. Smith sat in the doorway of his hut. There was no air in him. The murder of Gideon had sucked it out.

When it happened, Béatrice had tried to avenge him. Abelino swung his club, the boy with the bayonet crumpled, and she went after him as he lay on his belly in the mud. She moved fast but was unable to inflict any hurt on him before half a dozen boys swarmed her. At a command from the colonel they took her away. She went furious, digging her heels into the muddy earth, but did not call Smith's name. She knew he was helpless. Helpless was useless.

In the doorway of the hut, the air he swallowed dissipated before reaching his lungs. He zoned out, losing himself in a fantasy about Maybelline. The story his imagination concocted blended sex and comfort in a single act of ongoing beauty.

It was Major Lokole who shook him out of the fantasy. The major materialized in the darkness in front of him like the power of suggestion. He surprised Smith, who had been expecting Abelino. After the farce of the trial, the knifing of the defendant, Smith had plenty of time to think about what came next. They tied his hands behind his back— what was the point of that except more humiliation?—and pushed him back to the hut. *There is a cave,* Eitan Jones had told him at the cabana bar in Pointe Noir. *Once they have you in their possession, you absolutely must go into the cave. And you absolutely must not go in too far. One step too many and you lose yourself.* He was talking about getting into the mind of your captor. In the hut, hands bound, Smith did his best to see the situation through Sikatenda's eyes.

Killing the Munyamulenge posing as a journalist had not worked. Gideon was going to die that afternoon, guaranteed. The boy with the bayonet had jumped the gun and would be punished for the infraction of discipline. But there was no doubt in anybody's mind about the outcome of the trial. In Sikatenda's original calculation, the death of the American's sidekick should have been enough to make him talk. It wasn't; he didn't. All right. There were two more weak spots to exploit.

"Stand," the major said.

Smith stood, and Lokole inspected him with a flashlight. Trussed as he was, the inspection made Smith feel like something on a shelf in the supermarket. He was consumable.

"What did you do with Gideon's body?" Smith asked him.

"It was buried."

A hole in the ground in the forest, far from Minembwe. No respect. Animals with dirty feet would cross and recross the spot where the editor of the *Minembwe Trompette* lay. Insects would burrow and shit, burrow and shit. Once in a while, a human foot, a stranger's foot, would step on Gideon's head. Cadencia, his wife, would invent a lie to tell their son about what happened to his father. The injustice of a bad death, and the disgrace. Multiply them by however many millions of Congolese had been killed in the war that would not stop, and you got a total so huge it would never add up. Smith, anyway, did not have the head for that kind of math.

"Turn around," Lokole ordered him.

Smith did as he was told, and the major untied his hands.

Two weak spots: Béatrice, and Smith himself.

It was a short conversation. At his desk, Sikatenda was cutting cuticles from his fingers with a small knife. He had large, supple hands whose backs made Smith think of the backs of violins. Lokole sat down heavily, grunting, and went back to playing with his maps. Smith stood between them as though being there were his idea, not theirs.

"I have been thinking," said the colonel, without looking up from his fingers.

"They say that's a good thing to do now and then."

Sikatenda glowered at his hands. His generosity did not extend to people poking fun at him. Dignity mattered. Nobody was going to diss this man, even if he happened to be caught in a moment of personal grooming. He mastered his reaction.

"Your being here has caused me to think hard about one of the lessons our American trainers drilled into us."

The more the Mai Mai leader talked, Smith thought, the less likely he was to kill them. "What was it they taught you?"

"To challenge our assumptions. It sounds simple, doesn't it?"

"Easy as pie," Smith said in English because the French equivalent did not come to him.

The colonel nodded; he knew about pie, though maybe not how easy it was. He cut his last cuticle and sat up straight.

"And yet in practice few things are more difficult. We acquire a belief. It takes root in us, digs down into us. We become rigid with our belief. In our heart, in our gut, we are convinced we are right. Objections are frivolous. Shall I give you an example?"

"If you want to."

"My working assumption, since you have joined us here in camp, is that your story about helping the girl find her grandmother is fiction, pure and simple. My thinking has been based on that belief, which has indeed taken root in me.

And my actions naturally proceed from my thoughts. *Voilà.* The scientific method. However, the possibility exists that my initial assumption was wrong."

"It was wrong, it is wrong."

"Ah, but my training prevents me from taking you at your word."

Screw your training, Smith did not say.

Sikatenda pointed his small knife at Smith. "All this is by way of explanation. An apology in advance, you might say. I offer it because of the unbounded respect I have for your country. I stand in awe of America's accomplishments in the world. And because there is no time to fuck around."

"What's our hurry?"

"Major Lokole here is investigating a possibility."

"What kind of possibility?"

"A piece of intelligence—let's call it a nugget—has come our way concerning Eckstein's missing shipment. If the nugget pans out, I will be forced to concede the error of my initial assumption about you."

"Look at this," Major Lokole said.

He carried one of the maps to his commander, pointed with a nervous finger. Sikatenda studied it impassively. Whatever they were focusing on, they were not about to share it with their American prisoner. The colonel looked over at Smith.

"Of course my being wrong would not absolve you of blame." He scratched the back of one hand with the sensitive fingers of the other. "Far from it." Then, after a pause the length of the history of the cosmos, he said it again. "My being wrong does not begin to absolve you of blame."

It took Smith a while to put a name to the tune. The Mai Mai were singing in the church, which was lit by lanterns. From Smith's distance, the patches of light looked unstable, like gas anxious to escape its container. But the music was solid, the voices chaste as altar boys before the age of serious sin. They were singing in Swahili, which was why it took Smith so long to identify the song. *Mine eyes have seen the glory of the coming of the Lord.* "Battle Hymn of the Republic" was coming out in sung Swahili.

Abelino was not in church with the others. The sergeant appeared at the hut soundlessly with his gun and his belligerence. He had a job to do and was eager to start, but he wanted Smith to know who it was the colonel had assigned to administer truth serum. He let the pencil-thin beam of a flash play across his own face. He grinned. That was spooky, it was weird. But the slowly moving beam forgot what it lit as soon as it went out.

"I really like the music," Smith told him.

"Keep your mouth shut. You're not going to enjoy this, I promise you that."

Smith had been beaten up two or three times when he was a kid; four at most. There was nothing serious in it except for the shame, a physical sensation like bruised nakedness, your impotence on display for whoever it was getting the better of you.

The beating that Abelino gave him now was like that but with the aggravations of age and real hurt. He was glad that Béatrice was not there to see the degradation of the man she used to call Nkoyi, the one she had elected to find her grandmother.

The main thing was not to fight back. Smith did not need advice from Eitan Jones or anybody else to know that and keep remembering it, blow by blow. Put up any kind of fight, and the sergeant had all the excuse he needed to do him permanent damage.

Abelino was systematic, in his disorganized way. He went for the legs: left then right. He went for the arms: right then left. He attacked Smith's chest, kicking him until he turned over to escape the blows. Then he went for the small of the back, where the gun butt and the toe of his boot made invisible marks that Smith's grandchildren would trace and feel with their little hands. If he and Maybelline wound up having any kids. In an irrelevant flash of insight he saw himself delivering a sack of cookies to a passel of kids jumping around on a lawn of green grass. They were Maybelline's cookies so they must have molasses in them.

Abelino pulled him to his feet, spinning him around to face him. Smith should have parried the vicious hit he took to the forehead. No. Hold it back. Blood dripped into both eyes from the cut that opened there. It blinded him, and he staggered. A traditional punch in the gut as he struggled to keep his footing took him down.

What was so great about consciousness if pain was the only thing you were aware of?

The sergeant splashed water in his face to wake him. Smith sat up smelling the man's sweat, and the woodsmoke that permeated his clothes. He smelled the filthy rat that had gotten inside the man, tunneling in tender places, inciting him to commit evil acts. Abelino and Smith were so close, it felt like intimacy. In the Itombe woods there were secrets to share.

"Are you ready to talk?"

"About what?"

It was not meant to be a punk answer. Losing consciousness had confused Smith. His brain could not get out of first gear. The singing of another beautiful hymn made everything worse. Here were two things that did not belong together: a beating at the hands of a man you had multiple reasons to hate, and the exalted clarity of altar boys making music.

Abelino thought Smith was giving him attitude. In the darkness Smith sensed him lifting the rifle to bring it down on him again. He flinched, clenched, curled. His balls shrank to nothingness, his dick disappeared into thin air, and a jolt of fear worse than anything that had come before electrified his body. But the rifle stayed where it was. If Abelino killed the American, even if it was only diligence leading him to exceed his orders, there would be hell to pay and only him to pay it. He kept it simple.

"Where is the gold?"

Every impulse in Smith was to tell the man to kiss his ass, now that they were so close. If he had been in better shape, in command of himself, he might have come up with something smarter, something more telling. But his body ached, and his mind had turned to flab. And the music. For the moment, the rain had stopped. There was nothing to compete with the singing. Steps; stairs. The Mai Mai's voices hammered out a shining staircase. The staircase went up out of the wet night in the lightless forest in the direction of Heaven. Whether anybody ever got there, that was the question. That was the big unanswerable question.

After a few moments, Abelino shook the American gently by the shoulder. Smith did not respond.

Later, when Smith was shaken awake, the night was thick. It was late. Major Lokole was squatting at his head. There was a lantern on the ground near the door. Flickering, it looked votive, the kind of thing strategically placed to draw a petition from a stranded Catholic.

"Sit up."

Smith sat up. As he moved, everything hurt. Abelino, ordered to beat the shit out of the American prisoner, had worked with a will. It wasn't every day you got the chance to do the thing you longed to do.

"Drink this," the major said.

The little bit of stretching it took to grasp the bottle made the pain in Smith's right shoulder spike. He uncapped the bottle and drank. A raw burn on the tongue, down the walls of the throat. It was some kind of whiskey. Firewater. It sent a sham sensation of relief through his body.

"Are you all right?" Lokole wanted to know.

"What do you think?"

"It had to be done. The colonel begins to believe that you tell the truth."

"Begins?"

"It was your people who taught him to be thorough. His perseverance inspires us. That is one of the reasons he is so successful, we look up to him."

"Successful? Living in the woods with a bunch of killer kids?"

Lokole would not be sidetracked.

"Understand we have little time. If our intelligence is correct we must move with dispatch."

"What are you going to do to Béatrice?"

Lokole pressed the bottle on him again. "The Colonel has made me see how difficult it is for an American to understand us."

They sat for a few moments if not like friends then companions, two men sharing space that belonged to neither of them. Smith took another swig of firewater, but he was awake enough now to focus on his throbbing head. Alcohol did not help.

When Béatrice began screaming, Smith listened for her to call his name even though there was zero chance she would. She knew better than to expect him to rescue her. Helpless was useless. The sound of her pain, her terror, was almost more than he could bear and stay conscious.

He grabbed Lokole by the arm and told him, "Stop it. Stop it now."

It was obvious that the Mai Mai major was nothing like Abelino. He derived no pleasure from another person's pain.

He belonged somewhere else, someplace where militiamen did not torture girls, someplace where citizens said please and thank you and meant it.

"I'm sorry. This is, you must see, the ultimate test of your truthfulness."

Smith got to his feet, bracing himself with a hand on the major's shoulder. A gesture of trust, or that was what it felt like to Lokole. Taken by surprise, he hesitated a moment before going after the American as he stumbled toward the door hole. He dragged Smith down; Smith toppled like blocks.

Lokole knelt by him. He slapped his face. In a fog, Smith dimly sensed that Béatrice's sharp screams were slicing up the major, too.

"Say it," said Lokole.

There was nothing to say.

"Tell me," Lokole insisted.

Smith said, "Please make them stop."

It was frustration, along with a complicated sense of fellow feeling, that powered the major's fist into Smith's face. It was better not to be forced to listen to the torture of a young girl. Lokole was right, he was wrong. He was ruthless, he was humane. He belonged in Hell but might be put out to greener pastures. Smith struggled for an instant to stay awake and make sense of the contradictions. Then he went out again.

It was not a dream but had all the features of a dream. In the first place nothing made sense. Also, everything had a fuzzy outline, like the idea of a thing not fully thought through. Worst, he was unable to make anything happen. He was not a victim, exactly, but he was more than a witness. There was no need to justify the dread he felt from start to finish. It was there in the walls, a bad smell that had wormed its way in.

Sikatenda was there, riled up and pacing like an animal in a cage. The cage was Smith's hut.

"Can you hear me?" he bellowed.

That was what the words sounded like, at any rate. Somebody had poured molasses into the part of Smith's brain that caused the driveshaft to turn, and it was all he could do to grab the words as they blew by and reassemble them in a sentence. Very likely he was getting certain elements wrong, maybe crucial elements, because he misheard important words. Short words, for some reason, were harder to catch than long ones.

"It's the medicine," the colonel said, speaking more like a human but with the same telltale menace in his voice.

His impatience scared the hell out of Smith. He could not recall why, he had lost track of what happened, but it was obviously his fault. Even if he had wanted to say he was sorry—a cowardly impulse not to be contemplated by a person in possession of himself—his mouth was all mumble, his lips were walls keeping it in.

"Abelino hurt you. Major Lokole gave you medicine to allay the pain."

Medicine, Smith understood with a slow flush of intuition, was the code word for drugs. He was in on that much of the secret. A drug was something they put in your body to fuck you up. It worked.

"As you were resting," the colonel told him, "you perhaps did not note the arrival of a vehicle. The occupants of that vehicle brought . . . some welcome news. As a result of this news, we are leaving."

His excitement was palpable now. That was the different thing going on. How could Smith have missed it? Sikatenda had the air of a man who had found a lottery ticket on the sidewalk and cashed in big.

"I accept the truth of your assertion," the colonel told him, magnanimity dripping from his lips like syrup.

Foxtrot Five, that was what the American army called him. *Look at what you've done,* Smith wished he could tell them.

Sikatenda was talking again. Smith missed some of it. For a moment, really just a millisecond, he envied the man his ability to speak. It was the kind of semi-thought that might descend on a dog, listening to its owner yak on the phone with somebody, thinking Hey, I'd kind of like to do that. Smith knew better. Speaking was for those who had something to say.

He got to his feet, not the easiest thing to do just then. He wobbled, went down, came back up again. Béatrice's scream track was playing in his head, so real it confused him.

Sikatenda took him by the arm to steady him.

"I wish you to know that I stopped them. I stopped them before things went too far. I did this out of respect for her American friend, and because that was not the goal of the exercise. The goal was to discover whether you were lying to us."

Smith spaced out, went somewhere else. Then Sikatenda was saying, "I neglected to tell you . . . "

Evidently he had been talking. Smith had missed most of it. As best he could make out, the colonel was talking about a trip to Louisiana. Fort Polk. The army flew him and his classmates there from Leavenworth in a C-130. It was a training junket designed to capture the hearts and minds of military men from around the world.

"Louisiana is the state of your birth, is it not?"

That was classified information, restricted to those who needed to know, a small group that did not include Foxtrot Five. Smith felt momentarily clever. He had avoided an easy trap. That did not mean there weren't others waiting for him in the road ahead. Conclusion: there was a road ahead.

"I enjoyed your state. I felt at home there, I felt I belonged."

That was a damn lie, but Smith let it pass. One more trap sidestepped. He was learning. Not bad for a man with molasses on the brain.

"At Fort Polk I wrestled an alligator. I won. It was Army Rangers who taught us how. Afterward I skinned the beast and made myself a handsome pair of shoes. The finest footwear I've ever had the pleasure to put on. And durable. I wept the day I finally had to throw them away."

Smith had been to Fort Polk once. He drove there with Guy Foulard, the mechanic he had worked for in high school. Guy had a cousin billeted there. The cousin had a name, but for the life of him it wouldn't come to Smith. An army guy, but was he a Ranger? The reason for the visit was weed. An errand of mercy, Guy called it, hand-delivering a quarter kilo to his cousin in town on leave from the base. Smith remembered the slow way the cousin had of answering questions and, looking back, felt some sympathy for the guy. Hooah.

When Sikatenda finished speaking he expected a response from Smith, but Smith did not know how to react since he was unable to arrive at the point of the anecdote.

"Come," the man growled.

He laughed. It was a pure sound, the sound of light ascending to a place where angels giggled.

Smith followed him across the camp to a Land Cruiser whose back gate was up. Lokole was there. So was the whole army, standing in reverent awe, not exactly in ranks but still in some sort of order. Lokole shone a flash into the back of the vehicle for Smith's benefit.

The Colonel's intelligence had turned out to be solid. Gold. A massive amount of the stuff. It was piled in crates that filled the back end of the Land Cruiser. In the untrustworthy light of the flash it looked like beans, like the high-value beans Jack stole from the giant when he climbed the beanstalk. The crates were heaped to overflowing with beans and nuggets and pebbles and twisted lumps of gold. There was every shape imaginable, created by a playful god with a flair for design. The glint in the forest night was dull and terrible.

"Jesus," said Smith.

"Touch it," Sikatenda urged him, laughing again. "Go ahead and touch it."

Still in a daze, Smith heard the murmur of a river. It was the river of wonder, flowing from the mouths of the soldiers in Sikatenda's ragged army. They were rich, if their leader so decreed. Their world was about to change. Hell, it already had. All the bounty about which the Colonel had preached to them was piled in the back of the Japanese four-wheel-drive. Land and ease, justice and peace, security and meat in the belly. If there had been any doubters in the army, now they saw, they knew, they felt the truth of Crispin Sikatenda's gospel.

Smith, in his woozy way, was part of the river, ready to raise his voice in praise. He reached out a hand. The soldiers, the *kadogos*, looked on with envy, not being permitted to touch the treasure. He caressed the gold in the first box his hand identified. It was cool to the touch and had the hard, definite shape of sin. For the first time in a long time he felt himself Catholic, and capable of awe.

"So," said Sikatenda, "you were telling us the truth."

A lot of good that did Béatrice. Smith wondered where she was.

"Unfortunately," Sikatenda said, "we cannot take you with us. We must move fast. Any number of people will be wanting to steal this gold of ours. You would slow us down."

It sounded like a death sentence. Smith realized with slow astonishment that he was clutching a gold nugget. Major Lokole must have realized it, too. He grabbed the American's wrist, peeled open his fingers, removed the lump, tossed it back into the crate from which Smith had taken it. Then, at a signal from the Colonel remarkable for how clearly it was communicated in the black complicit night, he knocked Smith down. Crumpled—there was a word he had not needed until now.

Béatrice was there in the hut when Smith woke. She sat in a corner huddled into herself, chin on her knees, which she hugged with both arms, one hand clamping the other wrist.

"Béatrice."

She lifted her head and stared at him without curiosity. Her face was bruised, and one eye was swollen shut. The one he could see did not appear to take him in.

"Are you okay?"

It was a stupid question, and he did not expect an answer. But it seemed important to ask anyway. Keep her connected. What the girl needed right now was a woman she could talk to, listen to, a woman who would take the care that needed taking. Jasmine, or Soeur Placide, or Aristide's brave wife, who had protected Béatrice from her brute of a husband. Any of them would do. None of them was around.

He got up from the ground hating Abelino for making him hurt this much, and Lokole for that final smash. He felt his face with the tips of his fingers. It was bruised, like Béatrice's, but Abelino had stayed away from his eyes. On his feet, glancing around the hut, he was aware of an absence. The American flag in its black plastic base was gone.

Sunlight was spilling into the door hole, and he stepped outside. Fog hung over the camp and the trees around the camp in silent streamers, like a party with the sound turned down, but the sun instantly made itself felt on Smith's tender skin. The first thing he noticed was nothing. The Mai Mai had cleared out. Overnight, while Smith slept under the influence of Abelino's beating and Lokole's drugs, they had evaporated. Already the camp was an artifact.

For a moment, he imagined walking away, him and Béatrice. That easy. Then he saw Abelino.

The sergeant was smoking a cigarette, enjoying a moment of luxury in the free space of a quiet morning in the wild place where he was now in charge. In addition to smoking he was also taking a leak. He sensed the American behind him and turned around slowly. He aimed his penis in Smith's direction and squirted.

"You call that a dick?" Smith hollered in English.

No response.

He repeated it in French. Still no response. Abelino was not going to let Smith ruin his smoke break. Cigarettes were scarce out here; they had to be rationed. It might well be his only one of the day.

Smith went back to the hut. Béatrice had not moved.

"I'm going to talk to you for a little while," he warned her.

Her one good eye blinked. Maybe it saw him, maybe it didn't.

"They're gone. They left Abelino—he's the mean one with the little cross in his earlobe—to keep an eye on us. They want to keep us here."

He hoped she would respond to that, show a little fight. Nothing. He went on talking.

"We're not going to do what they want us to, are we? We're going to get out of here. I don't know how, yet, but we'll get out of here."

And then? She didn't ask. Good.

He said, "Why don't you go see if you can find some water? Wash up. It will help, a little. Feeling clean, I mean."

She didn't move.

"Béatrice?"

He wanted to promise her a grandmother, but he could not bring her back with a lie.

"When the time comes, I'm going to need your help."

She looked at him as if he were speaking a language she had not yet learned. All those wagging tongues she had picked up, living hard and sleeping rough in Kinshasa, and here was one that had not come to her attention.

He did not know what to say next and was glad when the boy with the flag tiebar appeared with a few sticks of boiled cassava and some bananas. He set them on the ground. He lingered. The prisoners were a novelty, in a place with few of them. And there seemed to be a certain amount of kid left in him. War did not make a man of him, it made him a boy who had seen war.

"Do you speak French?" Smith asked him.

He shook his head but answered when Smith asked him his name.

"Parnell."

"Thank you for bringing us food, Parnell. Would you show me that little flag of yours?"

The kid pulled the tiebar from his pocket. He let Smith pick it up, handle it, appreciate it.

"Where did you get this?"

Parnell shrugged, and Smith told him, "My father had one just like this."

It was a lie. Smith could not remember Baylee Smith ever putting on a tie. The few occasions he went to Mass, he wore the same black blazer over a white shirt open at the throat, the same blue pants that always looked stiff, the same black wingtips, which he polished on the kitchen table, protecting the surface with a sheet of newsprint. He must have tied a tie around his neck now and then. But he was not a man to wave a flag, or wear one.

Smith handed the tiebar back to the boy. He pointed to Béatrice. "Your friends hurt my friend Béatrice."

Parnell nodded, managing to convey sympathy with a minimal gesture.

Both of them pretended that the boy had not been involved in the assault.

"Béatrice should wash off the blood and the dirt," Smith explained. Let the boy hear her name, let him hear it a hundred times. Let him see and feel and witness her Béatrice-ness. "Will you go bring her some water?"

Parnell looked at her, studying. Béatrice did not look back. He kept looking until he made up his mind. Then he went away and came back with a basin of brackish water.

"Put it there," Smith told him, pointing to a spot on the ground near Béatrice but not too near.

He led the boy outside to give her some privacy. Parnell seemed to want to hang around. He was bored, or else the colonel had not yet fully indoctrinated him; the *kadogo* had not fully grasped the theory of enemies, the history of hate. Smith tried to engage him, get him talking.

His attempt to be a diplomat did not last. Inside five minutes Abelino came limp-trotting across the open space at the center of the camp holding his rifle at the ready the way soldiers did in the movies. Behind him came Toussaint. He was holding a rifle-length stick, aping the sergeant's moves down to the way he swung his leg as though he, like Abelino, had some sort of problem that required compensation. They had taken his gun from him. That was part of his punishment for having killed the Munyamulenge reporter before the order to do so was given. The other part was visible in his face, which was mashed like Smith's, like Béatrice's. From the looks of the kid, the lesson was going to take. Next time he would wait to kill until he was told to.

Abelino figured out in thirty seconds what Parnell was up to. Like a certain kind of non-commissioned officer, he believed that privates learned best by doing a task while being berated, threatened, intimidated. He had Parnell dump the basin of water on Béatrice's head. Then he had him laugh. The second command was more of a challenge, but Abelino was the boss, and after a dangerous moment of hesitation Parnell laughed convincingly.

She took it. She did not flinch when the water soaked her, she did not even react. She was a statue. Her passivity saddened Smith. In a way it was worse than her puffy face, her swollen eye. But right now her submissiveness was protecting her. The normal Béatrice, the girl who had tracked him across Kinshasa and would not take no for an answer, would be a perfect target for Abelino's aggression. There must be a certain amount of frustration in being left to guard prisoners instead of going with the gold.

To complete the lesson, Abelino cuffed Parnell on the head with the heel of his hand. He had great strength, and the force of the blow made the boy stagger. He recovered his footing and stood waiting for more. Abelino said something to him that meant, *No water for the prisoners unless I say so.*

"You know," Smith told Abelino, remembering at the last second to make it come out in English, "you're a miserable limp-dick piece a shit."

The sergeant caught his drift. He aimed his rifle at the American's belly. Toussaint aimed his stick. Parnell had nothing to aim. Smith wanted to believe that was a relief to the boy.

"*Ça va,*" he said. "So this is the way it's going to go."

It did. The boredom drove Smith nuts. Over the next two days only the cruelties, large and small, that Abelino inflicted on them broke the monotony. The woods were loud with birdsong, bugsong, and once in a while the shriek of an animal Smith could not identify or be bothered to guess. Apart from the monkeys. There seemed to be plenty of them, all compulsive gossipers. They couldn't keep their mouths shut. After a while the chatter of birds and beasts became the soundtrack to a movie he could not switch off.

He spent far too much time in the boat of his imagination drifting down a congenial river with Maybelline. The great thing about making love, he finally realized now that there was no chance of any, was how good it made you feel to make the other person feel good. You kissed, and there it was. Kissing locked you into a virtuous circle of touch. The circle spun, faster but not too fast, lighting you up. At a certain point, there was no difference between touching and being touched. You climaxed, hopefully together, and then it started again. That was the secret Adam and Eve had tumbled to in the garden.

Every time he exited fantasy mode, there was Béatrice. The men and boys under the command of Foxtrot Five had broken her spirit. The hurt they had done her on the outside had nowhere to go except inside. It was a poison, and Smith could only watch it drip. He tried to bring her out of it and got nowhere. All he could do was talk, and try to get her to talk. She needed a lot more than words, none of it in his power to provide.

Once, after he took a walk around the camp, Parnell trailing him on orders from Abelino, he came back to find that she had cleaned herself up. The swelling around her eye was going down.

"You look good," he told her, trying to sound positive. Upbeat in captivity, hungry and dirty and scared? A new low in sinking low. "You look better."

She looked at him without expression, without expectation. He tried again to get her to say something. He had learned over time in her company that she was a person with plenty of words, and her words had zing. Now she was keeping them to herself again, the way she had done when they started out in Kinshasa. The orphanage, the rampaging *shegues*, Soeur Placide with her great cloaking soul. It was almost as if they were somebody else's memories.

Every hour or two Abelino came by the hut. He brought Parnell and Toussaint with him. The sergeant made it a training exercise. This was how you tortured prisoners without actually killing them. *Pay attention, you two whippersnappers. What I'm teaching you will come in handy the next time you're the ones responsible for humiliating a person. The trick, you see, is to make him fear you, fear the very thought and sight of you. You do that by taking away his self-respect. Once that goes, you can breathe easy, relax, have a beer, because you've earned it.*

He called Smith and Béatrice out of the hut. Aftershock made her docile, and she did what she was ordered to do. They stood side by side, facing their captors. The *kadogos* were in position on either side of their sergeant, two steps behind. Impassively they watched him bring the muzzle of his rifle so close to Smith's mouth that it brushed his lips.

The sky, Smith noticed, was clouding up again. More rain on the way. The weather report from where you wished you weren't, where you'd give anything not to be, the location formerly known as the middle of nowhere.

"Suck it."

Abelino hated hearing English. Never mind the colonel's fascination with America. Forget the official doctrine of the Army of the Revival of the Word of God. English bugged the shit out of him. Smith told him to fuck off in the language of Flannery Parish.

"Suck it," the sergeant told him, jabbing the rifle muzzle so close that it tapped Smith's teeth. "Suck it or you'll eat it."

"Your boss," said Smith.

Abelino looked puzzled, and Smith clarified.

"Colonel Sikatenda."

"What about him?"

"He told you not to hurt us. Did you forget already? How do you figure he'll take it if you hurt us?"

"You have no idea what my orders are."

As if to prove that Smith was wrong, he moved the rifle muzzle to Béatrice's mouth. It traced the shape of her lips. But he said nothing, and after a lingering moment he lowered the gun. He snapped something at the boys, and the two of them set off on an errand meant to divert them from the loss of face he had just suffered.

"Wait," he said to Smith.

Smith waited. Abelino shook his head. He went after the boys, walking slowly.

But being right about the sergeant's orders from Sikatenda did not protect them from being hassled. Sometimes it was Abelino himself, sometimes he sent one or both of the boys. They frog-marched the prisoners around the camp, prodding them with sticks to make them trot, using the same sticks to trip them. They got pleasure from seeing them fall, sprawling in the mud.

They smeared mud in Béatrice's hair, which was growing out noticeably.

They stood her and Smith up outside the hut and screamed at them. Smith had no idea whether the viciousness that came out of their mouths was words or only ugly sound.

They made Béatrice kneel in the mud, then went through the motions of bringing out their penis. Once or twice, they did bring them out, but when she turned her face away they zipped up and went away laughing.

For his part, Parnell was not into degradation. He did not mind trotting along behind the prisoners when they were force-marched around the camp, and he could holler invective on command. But he did not trip them with a stick when he could, and when the sergeant's stipulated abuse turned heavy-duty nasty, he hung back. Sometimes he got away with it. Other times, Abelino noticed and took offense. Enforcing discipline by his own lights, he knocked the kid around.

Toussaint, on the other hand, seemed to want to make up for his infraction by carrying out his boss's commands with enthusiasm. At some point, he hoped, upper management would decide he had earned back the right to carry an automatic rifle.

When it rained, their tormentors showed up under sheets of plastic. Smith and Béatrice could hear their feet slapping the mud as they got close to the hut, and they grew to dread the hard rustle of plastic that came with them.

Rain. It was a torture all its own. Thunder, low in the sky's throat, the slow growl reminding you the earth was in charge, you were there on sufferance.

Hunger. There was almost no food. Cassava filled the belly but did nothing to nourish the brain. Protein, that was what they craved.

Once, Smith told Béatrice, "You know what I'd really like right now? A hot monkey sandwich."

Not funny enough to make her laugh.

Mud. Rain. Humiliations, big and small. The anticipation of being humiliated. Just as bad. In some ways, worse.

He found himself wondering what Béatrice was thinking. She gave nothing away.

The second night he woke in a panic, sure the Mai Mai were back, someone had stolen their gold and they blamed the American. He listened, but all he heard was rain. It was falling softly, dropping from a windless sky onto the trees around the camp, ten billion little wet plops. It took him a long time to get back to sleep.

On the morning of the third day, the sky had cleared and Abelino sent the *kadogos* to bring Béatrice. He wanted her to cook cassava for them. She refused to get up from the ground. Not acceptable, not with Abelino waiting. Between them the boys dragged her, hauling her by the arms. Smith followed after wishing she would scream, make some kind of sound. She did not.

In front of the headquarters building, which Abelino had taken over, he was standing by a fire. A pot sat on the ground next to it. Next to the pot was a pile of cassava, still in its bark.

"Cook it," he told Béatrice, pointing to the piled tubers, and then the fire, which Toussaint was feeding with sticks.

Abelino must be speaking Swahili to the girl. Somehow people always figured out which language to speak to someone they didn't know. Béatrice knew she had to respond. She shrugged. Smith guessed that she had never cooked the stuff before, did not know how to go about it. The sergeant got in her face and hollered.

He turned to Smith. "The bark is poisonous. If she does not peel the plant correctly, we can eat it and die." His voice rising in indignation, he said, "Is that what you want? Do you want to die?"

He spoke again to Béatrice. She shook her head. There was some of the old disdain in the way she held herself, staring back at him. She looked something like the way she had looked in the street behind the orphanage when the boys stoned her. Not a good attitude to take, under the circumstances, but Smith was glad to see it.

Abelino saw it, too. He said something to Toussaint, who ran into the headquarters and came back out with a small flowered towel. He waved it at Abelino, who pointed at Béatrice. The boy folded the towel making a blindfold of it. He bound Béatrice's eyes.

A one-man firing squad.

The two boys positioned Béatrice ten yards from the sergeant. He raised his rifle and pointed it at her thin chest.

It did not seem possible to Smith that he would shoot her for not knowing how to cook a root. Killing the girl might bring down all kinds of hell on his head. Look what happened to Toussaint. But the sergeant had a habit of putting himself in situations he could not maneuver out of. He was no good at backing down. Behind the blindfold, Béatrice was frozen in fear. Her silence screamed in Smith's ears.

"The penalty for disobeying an order is death," Abelino announced in French for the American's benefit.

He released the safety on his rifle, brought it up, aimed. It might be a bluff. No way to know.

Smith went for the rifle. The only reason he got it was Abelino's lather. He was seriously worked up, hating Béatrice and loving to torment her. A firing squad, real or pretend, was better than sex. Who knew? He was so wrapped up in the anticipation of pleasure to come that he forgot to think about the other prisoner.

Smith wrenched the rifle from him and stabbed the butt into his gut with all the force he could muster. His strength had deteriorated, living on cassava and bananas. But Abelino fell. Watching, Parnell and Toussaint expected him to get up quickly. In thirty seconds he'd be back in charge. They kept their distance, and they were right. The sergeant quickly rolled over in the mud and came up like a wrestler who just missed getting pinned. He went for Smith.

The safety was off. If it hadn't been, Smith might not have figured out the mechanism in time. As it was, he pulled the trigger. The force of the bullets made a puppet of the Mai Mai sergeant. He flailed, he was driven back, he died.

Smith, having killed him, turned the gun on the two boys.

Overhead, the sky could not make up its mind. More rain, or how about some sunshine for a while?

Abelino had a story. It died with him. Smith felt no regret at not hearing it. He was sick in his gut. If there had been anything in his stomach, he would have heaved.

He watched Béatrice walk over to where Abelino lay. There was blood in the mud, and the body had a casual look. In death he had found his style, he was jaunty. She looked down. She leaned down. She spat in his face. Then she straightened up, turning her back on him. She looked at Smith.

One thing, maybe only one thing, was over.

The sound of gunfire had scared off the monkeys, but they were already making their way back through the treetops, jabbering in the animal equivalent of excitement, swinging from branch to branch, tree to tree, like the showoffs they were. Maybe monkeys got bored, too, and here was a spectacle.

They came to a creek. Six feet across, maybe a foot deep, moving fast over mostly flat stones. The trees it ran through were hardwood with straight boles. The undergrowth was thinner than it had been when they left the camp. They washed their face, their hands, their forearms in the creek, watching, in their daze, the mud that came off their skin dissolve in the rush of clear water. When the mud was gone they scooped water with their hands and drank.

It was a good place to take their first break. They sat on the creek bank, weak for all sorts of reasons. Béatrice was not talking yet. Smith had to pretend it was a conversation, not a monologue.

"See that monkey up there?"

She turned to look, shook her head meaning she had nothing to say about it.

"I'm thinking if I can knock it down with a rock, we'll figure out how to make a fire, then fix ourselves a hot monkey sandwich. There's one little problem, though."

He would give a lot for her to ask what the little problem was. She did not.

"You want a sandwich," he said, making one with his clean hands, "you need bread. And wouldn't you know it, bread is the one thing we don't have."

"The one thing," she said, might have wanted to say more, decided not to.

"We'll get ourselves something to eat soon enough," he told her. "Can you hold out?"

She shrugged. Keep it going, he told himself.

"I'm not worried about them coming after us. Are you?"

Another shrug.

"I felt kind of bad, tying Parnell up to the other boy. There were times that he could have done us a lot worse than he did."

In fact the look on Parnell's face when Smith lashed him to Toussaint with rope was going to stay with him. I *was kind to you,* the look said, *and now you betray me.* It was true. Also true that it could not be helped. Smith made sure that the knots were tight, and that the boys could not work their hands free to untie them. While he worked on that, Béatrice held the gun on the *kadogos.* There was no question in anybody's mind whether she would shoot.

He was able to think connectedly about Parnell. Abelino was a different story. Every time he came into Smith's mind there was the same image of a puppet flailing, and Béatrice spitting in the sergeant's dead face. Smith had carried the rifle with him when they left the camp. He wanted the *kadogos* to think he would be looking back, armed, on the off chance they got loose and came after them. A quarter mile into the forest, he threw the gun into the trees, far enough off the path that it would rust to uselessness before anybody ever tripped over it.

"I never expected to kill anybody," he told her. "Not in this life."

He said it to rouse her a little, spark some curiosity. And it did. She had a lot to say about the death of Abelino. Said none of it.

"I'm really hungry," he told her.

She nodded.

He pointed to the path they had been following. In order to get away from the Mai Mai camp they had climbed. They were still climbing.

"The thing about a path," he said.

"What?"

"It goes somewhere."

"Always?"

"If it didn't go somewhere, it wouldn't be a path."

She nodded. She wanted to believe him but was not sure she could. He had let her down before. Her skepticism irked him. *I made myself a killer to protect you,* he almost said. But it wasn't true. Something else had let him kill, made him want to. At some point in his life he had swallowed a stone. It was still inside him. Sometimes he could feel it there, pressing against an organ.

After resting they walked again, following the trail. Now was not the time for Smith to tell her what Gideon had said to him. I *have a confession to make.* Of course he waited until they were too far out of Uvira for Smith to change his mind and turn them around. On a break, the two men sat by the side of the road sharing a warm can of tomato juice and watching Béatrice prowl under some trees, playing like a regular kid. I *ran into a friend last night,* Gideon said. I *told him what we are doing, where we are going. He recognized the Mutebusi woman's name. Joséphine, eh? He thinks he heard that she is dead. He could not be sure. It is impossible to be sure. One hears things, that's all.*

Now, walking with Béatrice, Smith was not going to bring up her grandmother. Neither did she. What mattered was finding where the path led.

They passed trees with red fruit hanging low enough to snag.

"Do you know what they are?" he asked Béatrice.

"No."

"They might be bad for you, they might make us sick."

She reached for one of the fruits. It was half the size of an apple. She bit into it, chewed for a moment. Swallowed; gulped. Did not die. They filled their bellies. Still no protein.

They came to another creek. This one was broader than the first, and deeper. They took off their shoes and crossed it. The cold water iced their feet.

Once, ahead of them on the path, a large animal passed. It moved so quickly they did not see what it was before it was gone into the screen of green growth. It made the skin on Smith's arms prickle.

It was evening when the path came out from under the woods and died on the edge of a field. They were high up. Brilliant green fields rolled around them, intersecting at odd angles, as if a million years ago they had collided with one another and gotten stuck. Way off, in one of them, they saw an animal that might be a cow.

Above the fields the sky was the size of the known universe. Lean clouds were racing like piloted airships. They were moving west, toward the sun, which was going down red and rich and satisfied their eyes.

They stood there for a moment, getting used to being in the open, on the abrupt edge, after all the time they had spent in the woods. Smith's mind was tired. His body was tired. Any pretense of staying alert was gone. The woman was halfway across the field before he focused on her. She was carrying something in one hand. When she saw that she had their attention she lifted it so they could see.

Milk. A jug of it, and Béatrice drank half in one go. The woman's name was Melisande. Her French was bad but from the beginning she chose to speak it. A courtesy. The first thing she did was pat Béatrice's head. The first thing she said was "This is the one."

They followed her across the field to her house, which had two rooms. She fed them beans and peanuts and *fufu*. She killed a red chicken, breaking its neck with one dexterous twist. She told Béatrice to pluck it, then showed her how when the girl refused to do the job. When the bird was ready she cooked it, then watched them eat in the cool dark of the high plains night. She laughed at their hunger, not to be appeased by a single skinny chicken.

Smith guessed she was forty. She was wiry, not tall, with muscular arms. The skin on her face was smooth, like a carefully worked mask. To Smith's amateur eye, she did not look like a Munyamulenge. He was relieved that it did not appear to matter.

Melisande lived alone and wanted to talk. Smith did his best to listen. In his exhaustion all he got was fragments. War stories, family stories, stories of loss. When Béatrice fell asleep, the woman carried her to her own bed. Smith took the floor in the second room.

In the morning the strangeness of laughter woke him. Melisande was showing Béatrice how to milk a dun-colored cow she had led by a halter in from the field. Béatrice was demonstrating no aptitude. The bad job she was making of it angered her, and she slapped the cow's flank with her hand. Hard, Béatrice style. The cow took offense. It lowed and stepped sideways away from the fractious child. Melisande could not stop laughing.

The air was cool even as the sun climbed the sky. This was the *hauts plateaux*. The words had a mysterious taste when Smith mouthed them. He was as tired as he had been when he lay down the night before.

Two days became three. Béatrice and Smith could not stop being tired. On the morning of the fourth day, Melisande's brother showed up. He was an older man with burnished skin who carried a knobbed walking stick that gave him a pastoral look. Unlike his sister, he was not much of a talker, although he seemed to follow the French. Smith was unable to remember the man's name. He had taken in all the Congo he could take.

Béatrice was out in the field watching Melisande's four cows. The adults sat in the dirt yard in front of the house sharing a single can of beer the brother had brought with him.

In a voice like water just below the boiling point, Melisande told Smith, "Thank you for bringing the child to me. I did not expect God would send me such a gift."

"She won't stay with you."

"Why not?"

"She will not give up the hope of her grandmother."

Smith had already told Melisande the story. Now, she told it to her brother. In the morning he left for Minembwe, walking with a swinging gait that defied distance, ate miles, conquered space and skepticism.

He was gone two days. In his absence Melisande did her best to feed and fatten Béatrice and Smith. Her nutrition options were limited, but by the time they lay down to sleep at night their bellies felt full. The feeling of being hunted that had taken them over in the forest, escaping Sikatenda's camp, did not go away. But it attenuated, and Smith was able to picture a time when it would not inhabit him. His mind was a cushion, memories good and bad bouncing off, floating away, coming back at random. The extent of his ambition was breathing.

Béatrice was more patient than Smith would have believed she could be, waiting for Melisande's brother. She knew he had gone looking for her grandmother. She had no doubt he would come back from Minembwe with news. With luck, he might even bring Nyogokuru herself back with him. Of course she was an old woman. If she was coming she would surely walk slowly and would be obliged to borrow the man's walking stick. Béatrice could wait. She was exhausted in body, spirit and idea.

As bad luck would have it, the kid was hanging around the house the evening of the second day of the brother's absence when he came walking across the field with that steady rollicking gait of his, which identified the man as much as his name would. He carried the sky on his back, a trick Smith envied knowing he could never manage it himself. There was a spooky green cast to the light, very pale, which gave it the appearance of shimmering water.

Béatrice ran to meet him. He put her off, shaking his head emphatically, until he reached the house and Melisande and Smith stood facing him knowing from the lack of expression on his face there was no good news.

It would have been good to confer. Decide how to say it, who should do the saying. Smith had a hunch Melisande would have said it fell to him, never mind his lack of qualifications. But there was no way they could come up with a communication strategy, not with the girl standing there demanding with Béatrice-like intensity to know the truth. The brother said what he had to say.

"Your grandmother has died, little one."

Béatrice shook her head.

"Her heart gave out on her. Last year. She died in bed in the home of a friend, a woman who was taking care of her. How lucky she was!"

Béatrice crossed her arms. She threw back her head in a gesture Smith was familiar with. She glared.

"In a time of war," the brother said in a voice in which reason had its place but not the only place, "to die in bed in the home of a friend, it is a blessing."

"He is right, *ma chère*," said Melisande. "God smiled on your grandmother."

The attack took Smith by surprise. It shouldn't have. The girl came at him windmilling hard fists and screaming. She was too angry to cry. Again and again she connected with her fists, pounding at his chest, doing her best to knock him down.

"*Menteur*," she called him. "Liar liar liar liar liar liar."

She knew how to throw a punch. He was not so good at taking one from a child. He stood there absorbing everything she had to give.

"You told me you would take me to her. You told me you would find her. You lied, Smith. You did nothing. You did nothing, and she died."

She pulled back for a moment. Her body shuddered, the way he imagined she might do if she ingested poison. Then she pronounced judgment.

"You are not Nkyoi, you are a worthless American man."

Her contempt was bigger than she was. She took a deep breath and came back at him, fists flailing. For a moment, because he was still weak, he thought he might lose consciousness. He saw a little preview of himself toppling over into the dirt, a heap of shame. But he stayed on his feet.

He was crying the tears Béatrice was too angry to shed.

He tried to embrace her, get her to stop beating him. She screamed and cursed him in beautiful French and pulled away from his encircling arms. Then she came back at him a third time. When the fit was spent—it took a long time—she turned away. Before he could reach to embrace her she was running. She ran out of the yard and across the field in the direction of the woods. They watched the trees capture her the way the forest in fairy tales captured children at risk.

"Do I go after her?" Smith asked Melisande.

"*Non*. She will come back."

Smith was not convinced the woman was right. When it came to Béatrice, the rules did not matter, the expectations were her own. She was one of a kind.

Among the abandoned adults, nobody wanted to talk. The Congolese were embarrassed on the American's behalf. They sat awkwardly to eat. There were no more chickens, no eggs. There was milk, of course. And the brother had carried in a tin of corned beef, which Melisande fried with cassava sticks. She had no cooking oil, and shreds of meat stuck to the bottom of the pan. They scraped off the shreds and ate them. Melisande made sure Smith got a little more than his share of the shreds.

The water Smith drank was going to make him sick again, but he drained the plastic container the brother passed him.

They went to sleep early, all of them gloomy in their own way and in a common way they shared, the way people shared a secret. Melisande and her brother snored in striking syncopation. This was not the first night they had spent under the same roof. Smith lay awake on the floor unable to sleep in his exhaustion. The snoring of brother and sister drowned out the sound of the insects of the Congolese night, which he longed never to hear again in fact or memory.

In the morning, he woke aching. It was the beating Béatrice had administered the day before. In his weakened condition, her angry fists had done him in. He had slept late. Melisande and her brother were outside, talking quietly in a language Smith did not recognize. The multiple griefs and numberless sadnesses, all the losses and horrors of the wars that had come down on them and the people they loved, somehow coalesced into a single feeling of pain associated with the orphan girl who had run into the woods upon learning that her grandmother was dead. For a moment, Smith resented Maybelline, who would never have to see what he was seeing. He shrugged off the feeling—it was on him to explain it all, although he doubted his ability—and took a seat in the dirt next to Melisande.

"My heart," she said carefully, doing her damnedest to make it come out in such French as a man like Smith could understand. "I thought, after everything, that my heart had died in my chest. Now I find it is alive. It beats for the child."

The brother spat in the dirt by way of agreement.

Béatrice did not come back that morning. Or that afternoon. They thought she must relent by evening, but there was no sign of her.

"What will you do?" Melisande asked Smith.

"I don't know."

"Will you leave?"

The truth was, he could neither stay nor go. The truth was, the kid had ruined him for ordinary life, the life he used to live and was more or less okay with. As though it followed, as though it were part of the same conundrum of thought, he pictured Eckstein's gold in the back of Sikatenda's Land Cruiser. He saw Abelino flailing like a puppet, taking bullets from his own gun. He heard the sonorous voice of the one-armed waiter at the Hotel Oiseau charging Smith, on America's behalf, with sinning against the Congo.

When he slept that night he went deeper than he had gone in a long time. That increased the distance he had to climb when screaming from the woods jolted him awake. Béatrice. It had to be. He pulled on his pants and raced out into the yard. The screaming had stopped. The night was suspect in its quiet. He hollered her name.

There was no response. He hollered it again. Béatrice Béatrice Béatrice, each time louder and more frantic so that the noise finally brought Melisande and her brother out into the yard.

"What is it?" she demanded to know.

Having known genuine terror, she knew it could return at any moment. If she had to, she could run.

"It's Béatrice," Smith told them. "I heard her, out there."

All three of them listened intently. Smith, for his part, listened harder than he had ever listened for anything, heard or unheard. There was nothing. After a few moments, the insects began where they had left off.

"I am sorry, Monsieur Smith."

"I will leave tomorrow."

"That is best," she told him. "Clément will take you. Otherwise you will certainly get lost."

Clément. Smith thought he could remember the name now.

They went back to sleep. Smith woke in the morning early knowing he would not leave. Not today, not yet.

When the sun was at its brief zenith Béatrice came out of the woods, emerging from the same spot at which she had gone in, as if she had only been hiding there, just over the edge, in the secret wild. But she was bedraggled. She was haggard. She was filthy. Her face was screwed into an expression of permanent pain. Her hair, getting longer, was still in the fight.

Melisande tried to scoop her up. She wanted to bathe her, gentle her, soothe her to the extent that soothing was a possible thing. But Béatrice squirmed. She escaped the woman's ministering clutches. She made a beeline to Smith.

"Go," she told him.

Her voice was cold, her mind made up.

"Go where?"

"To America."

"Béatrice, I'm sorry."

"*Ma grand-mère est morte.*"

"Yes," he repeated. "Your grandmother has died."

"I can no longer look for her."

"No."

"My grandmother died in the home of a friend."

"Yes," said Smith. "Her heart gave out."

"God smiled on her."

Smith nodded. If there was a God, and if he felt as bad as he ought to feel for all the hurt in Creation, all the harm done and still doing, the least he could do was smile on Joséfine Mutebusi as she lay on a pallet in the home of a friend feeling her heart give out, her mind go elsewhere, her memory take the perfect smooth shape of blankness.

"What will you do, Béatrice?"

The question offended her. He knew it would. But it had to be asked. It had to be answered.

She looked out across the field to where the dun cow grazed with the others, head down. She pointed.

"I will milk the cow."

Smith heard Melisande's sharp intake of breath. Clément whistled through his teeth, making an unconvincing sound of a man who didn't give a damn. Smith forcibly stopped himself from asking any more questions.

"Come, child," Melisande said. "You want to be clean."

Here was the moment. It arrived without ceremony. Béatrice allowed Melisande to lead her away for a bath.

Clément spat in the dirt again.

Smith was hurt that evening when the girl avoided him. That was stupid, and he knew it, but of course he was an expert in all things stupid, he was the uncrowned king of the famous land of fools. When she saw what was going on, Melisande tried to make the American feel better.

"She cares for you."

"Sure she does."

But for as long as the evening's light lasted Béatrice refused to make eye contact with him. She defined a radius around him and stayed on its far side. When she spoke, it was to Melisande. Once or twice she said a trivial something to Clément, absently answering a question. Smith might as well not have been there.

She was gone in the morning when Smith woke. He went looking, finding her on the edge of Melisande's field observing the cows. She had the air of a person conducting a scientific experiment that involved close observation. What would these interesting animals do next?

"I came to say goodbye, Béatrice."

She nodded but did not remove her gaze from the cattle.

"Yes," she agreed. "You must go."

"You'll be okay here, with Melisande."

"Gideon," she said, half turning her head.

There was something she needed to say about the murdered reporter who had been her friend and done his futile best to be her protector. But it could not be said. The words for such a conversation did not yet exist.

"We will remember him," said Smith.

No response.

He wanted more from her. He wanted an acknowledgement not so much of him as of what they had been through together. He could say words, say names, and those words and names would have a meaning that only the two of them got: Crispin Sikatenda, Abelino, Eckstein and his gold. Rémy the Twa boatman, and night pirates on Lake Kivu. Phone-stealing *shegues* on a Kinshasa street. But she would not give him the acknowledgement he wanted. He accepted, standing there watching her watch the cows, that it was too much to ask.

"Goodbye, beautiful Béatrice," he said quietly.

She nodded. She waved as if to brush him off. He went back to the house.

He had nothing to take with him. There arrived a moment when he looked up to see Clément halfway across the field, heading for a trail he liked better than the one Smith and Béatrice had come in on. Smith had to jog to catch up to him. His feet hurt in the places between the toes where Sikatenda's men had dug out insects.

A long hike but not a killer trek. They walked without talking, Smith doing his best to keep up with the older man, who had staying power. As the day progressed, once in a while they came across people on the trail. Sometimes they were lapped by people moving with swift purpose. Clément handled the explanation of why he was traveling with a disheveled *mzungu*. Smith had had enough. Of everything. He could not bring himself to smile as his curious appearance was inspected.

He did not allow himself to feel any relief until they came out of a patch of woods and saw Lake Tanganyika below them in the distance. It was raining, so it was difficult to make out where the lake ended and the sky began. He didn't care. It looked like Louisiana.

"I can make it on my own from here," he said.

Clément was glad to hear it. He had no good reason to walk all the way into Uvira. Smith had some money in his pocket and tried to give him some. Clément put up his hand and said something that might mean Melisande would give him a hard time if he accepted it, and he couldn't very well show up cash in hand without her knowing where it came from.

"*Nous sommes ensemble, non?*" he said.

Smith agreed with him. "Yes. We understand each other."

"I forgot," Melisande's brother said.

"Forgot what?"

"The girl said to give you this."

He took a rolled up snakeskin from a leather pouch he carried on his belt. He handed it to Smith. Smith unrolled the skin from around the marble it protected. It was blue, yes. He rerolled the skin around the marble. He put Béatrice's magic in his pocket.

A former foreign service officer, MARK JACOBS has published more than 200 stories in magazines including *The Atlantic*, *Playboy*, *The Baffler*, *The Kenyon Review*, and *The Southern Review*. His story "How Birds Communicate" won *The Iowa Review* fiction prize. His story "Dream State" won the Dr. T. J. Eckleburg Kafka Prize. His five books include *A Handful of Kings* (Simon & Schuster) and *Stone Cowboy* (Soho Press), which won the Maria Thomas Award. His website can be found at www.markjacobsauthor.com.

Printed in the USA
CPSIA information can be obtained
at www.ICGtesting.com
JSHW021831290924
70697JS00003B/3

9 781682 194430